An
Amish Country
Christmas

Books by Suzanne Woods Fisher

Amish Peace: Simple Wisdom for a Complicated World
Amish Proverbs: Words of Wisdom from the Simple Life
Amish Values for Your Family:
What We Can Learn from the Simple Life
The Heart of the Amish

Lancaster County Secrets

The Choice • *The Waiting*
The Search

Seasons of Stoney Ridge

The Keeper • *The Haven*
The Lesson

The Inn at Eagle Hill

The Letters • *The Calling*
The Revealing

The Bishop's Family

The Imposter • *The Quieting*
The Devoted

Amish Beginnings

Anna's Crossing • *The Newcomer*
The Return

An
AMISH COUNTRY
CHRISTMAS

2-IN-I COLLECTION
A LANCASTER COUNTY CHRISTMAS
CHRISTMAS AT ROSE HILL FARM

SUZANNE
WOODS
FISHER

Revell

a division of Baker Publishing Group
Grand Rapids, Michigan

© 2013, 2014 by Suzanne Woods Fisher

Published by Revell
a division of Baker Publishing Group
P.O. Box 6287, Grand Rapids, MI 49516-6287
www.revellbooks.com

Combined edition published 2017
ISBN 978-0-8007-2987-5

Previously published in two separate volumes:
A Lancaster County Christmas © 2013
Christmas at Rose Hill Farm © 2014

Printed in the United States of America

Scripture used in this book, whether quoted or paraphrased by the characters, is taken from:

King James Version of the Bible

Holy Bible, New International Version®. NIV®. Copyright © 1973, 1978, 1984, 2011 by Biblica, Inc.™ Used by permission of Zondervan. All rights reserved worldwide. www.zondervan.com

Published in association with Joyce Hart of the Hartline Literary Agency, LLC.

This book is a work of fiction. Names, characters, places, and incidents are the product of the author's imagination or are used fictitiously. Any resemblance to actual events, locales, or persons, living or dead, is coincidental.

17   18   19   20   21   22   23   7   6   5   4   3   2   1

LANCASTER COUNTY
CHRISTMAS

To a very special woman,
a friend extraordinaire for nearly thirty years,
Nyna Dolby.

The first thin flakes of snow had begun to swirl. Mattie Riehl glanced out the buggy windshield and up at the troubling clouds during the trip into town for a doctor's appointment. When they reached the parking lot, she hesitated before climbing out of the buggy. "The sky is more ferocious looking than when we left home."

Solomon, her husband, reached his hands around her waist to help her down. "We'll be home in plenty of time before it hits."

"Bet we'll get fresh snow for Christmas!" Danny nosedived over the front bench of the buggy and slipped out behind his mother. He lifted his small face to the sky, scanning it for snowflakes.

"Looks like we might," Mattie said. She straightened her son's glasses and turned to her husband. "I still don't think this appointment is necessary."

Sol paid her no mind. "Well, we're already here. The doctor thought it would be wise, Mattie. Just to be safe."

When she lifted her head, her eyes caught her husband's gaze. A look of joy and suffering, woven together. *That's*

*what these last few weeks have been like. Love and pain,
joy and suffering.* Sol bent down and tugged the felt brim
hat on his son's forehead, then gently steered Mattie into
the doctor's office.

Mattie and Danny sat down in the empty waiting room
while Sol spoke to the receptionist. Mattie glanced around the
room, amused. It was covered with English-style Christmas
decorations. Gold garland draped the walls, Christmas cards
were thumbtacked onto a bulging bulletin board, an artificial
spruce tree sat in the corner, blinking its colored lights. The
door opened and a young English girl swept in, nearly knocking
down the wreath made of shiny gold and silver metal sleigh
bells that practically engulfed the door. The girl steadied the
wreath before she walked up to the desk to check in.

After Sol finished talking to the receptionist, he sat down
next to Mattie. "It'll be a few minutes. The doctor's running
behind."

Danny walked around the room, examining the walls.
"Dad, where is that music coming from?"

Sol pointed out the speakers in the ceiling. Mattie hadn't
even noticed the music until Danny mentioned it. Then she
heard strange lyrics pour out: "Grandma Got Run Over by
a Reindeer." She and Sol exchanged a startled look.

"*Englische Schpieles,*" Sol murmured and shrugged his
shoulders. *English music.*

The English girl, still talking to the receptionist, pulled off
her hat and scarf. Hair the color of ripened peaches spilled
around her shoulders.

"Is that a Burberry scarf?" the receptionist asked the girl.

"What kind of a berry is a burr-berry?" Danny asked
Mattie, but she hushed him before he could ask another

question. Once her son got going, nothing stopped him. He had more questions than there were answers.

Mattie overheard the English girl ask the receptionist if she could just pick something up and go.

"No, no," the receptionist said. "The doctor always likes to talk to his patients before he renews a prescription."

"Why?" the girl asked, her voice a little louder, exasperated. "I just saw him six months ago."

The telephone rang and the receptionist turned her attention to it, grabbing the receiver as she pointed to a chair for the girl to sit in. "Take a seat," she mouthed. "He'll be with you as soon as he can." She pointed to a basket of candy canes. "Help yourself."

The girl picked out a candy cane, turned slowly around, and found an empty seat.

Mattie had it wrong. The English girl wasn't a girl at all, but a woman. A woman with a very odd haircut. It was longer on one side than the other. Peculiar! Other than the cockeyed haircut, the woman was quite lovely, Mattie realized, with blue eyes that tilted at the corners and a soft, round face. But there was turmoil behind those eyes—as if the world were all at sea. Danny whispered a question to Sol and the woman startled, as if she had forgotten anyone else was in the room. She looked curiously at Mattie and Sol and Danny as she took in their Plain clothes—a look of puzzlement Mattie was long accustomed to. Then Danny left his father's side to cross the room to the English woman. Mattie reached out to stop him, but Sol put a hand on her knee. Danny was known for wandering off, talking to strangers. Sol always said to let him be, that it was in his nature to be curious. Mattie used to be more agreeable, allowing Danny room to be adventurous, but over the last year or so, she could feel herself changing in a way she didn't like and couldn't help.

Danny sat down next to the woman and showed her a wooden whistle. The woman looked at the whistle politely, but seemed a little uncomfortable around a child, especially a Plain one. Danny didn't seem to notice her discomfort, but then, that was Danny. He assumed everyone liked to talk to him. "My dad made this for me. For my birthday." He looked up at her. "Want to hear what it sounds like? It's an owl whistle."

"Danny," Sol said in a warning voice. "You're in a doctor's office."

As soon as Danny mentioned the word "owl," the English woman visibly relaxed. "He won't bother anyone," she said, her eyes glued to Danny's whistle. "It's just us in the waiting room. I'd like to hear it."

Danny's cheeks puffed with air as he blew out three short hoots. "It's a screech owl. Everybody thinks a screech owl should sound screechy, but it's really a hoot sound. It's the barn owl that sounds so screechy." He then imitated the ear-piercing sound of a barn owl. "I found a baby barn owl with a broken wing. I feed it mice every day."

The woman fingered the wooden whistle. "Must be nice to have an owl for a pet."

"Oh, it's not a pet," Danny said solemnly. "Wild animals should never be pets. My dad helped me set the wing, and after it's healed, we're going to release it."

"I've always admired owls," she said. "I think I read somewhere that owls are the only birds that fly without making any sound."

"That's true!" Danny said. "And they're not waterproof

like other birds. They get soaking wet and weighed down by their soggy feathers so that they can't fly. If an owl can't dry off quickly, it can shiver with cold and die." He wrapped his arms around himself and started to shake, to show her how a wet, cold owl acted.

The woman burst out with a laugh. "How old are you?"

"Six-and-a-half," Danny said, as if it were one word. He poked his spectacles higher up on his nose. "How old are you?"

"Danny!" Mattie said sharply.

A slow smile softened the woman's features. "It's only fair. I asked him. He's asking me." She turned to Danny. "I'm twenty-five. And my name is Jaime. Jaime Fitzpatrick." She held out her hand to Danny.

He reached over and shook her hand. "Danny Riehl."

"Are birds your favorite animals?" she asked.

He wrinkled his nose, a sign he was deep in thought. "I haven't decided yet."

"I used to take pictures of rare birds," Jaime said to Danny. "And once I photographed the migration flyway during the Audubon Christmas Count."

"I know about that!" Danny said. "My cousin lives in Ohio and rides bicycles to count the birds. My cousin and his friends set records on how many birds they counted." He sat down next to her. "What do you take pictures of now?"

Jaime hesitated. "I take pictures of people, mostly. I've been working at Sears Portrait Studio. Just down the street from here."

"You don't take pictures of birds anymore?"

"Not like I used to. But it's my favorite thing—to take pictures of nature and wildlife. It's not easy to do. Movement is a photographer's greatest challenge, and birds are always on the move. But then you've got a trade-off—because natural light is so much better than artificial lighting."

Danny's face scrunched up. "If you like to be outside so much, then why would you work inside?"

A strange expression crossed Jaime's face. "Well, the backdrops for the portraits can make it look like a person is outside." She glanced at her watch.

"Danny, du hast genug sach Fraugt," Mattie said. *Danny, you've asked enough questions.*

The nurse opened the door and asked sternly, "Did somebody let a wild bird loose in the waiting room?" Her face broke into a mischievous grin as Danny's eyes went round. "Why, lo and behold, it's not a wild bird at all. It's just a wild *boy!*" She winked at Danny and he giggled. "We're ready for you now, Mrs. Riehl." She turned to Sol. "Shouldn't be a long appointment."

"Danny and I will go outside," Sol told Mattie, giving her a look of reassurance.

"We can play catch with snowballs!" Danny said.

He ran to the door and opened it, letting in a blast of cold air. Then he turned and waved goodbye to the English woman. She tossed him the candy cane and he caught it in his mittened hands. He turned to Mattie, a silent request to eat it. She nodded, and he gave the English woman what Sol called his jack-o'-lantern grin. Four front teeth were missing.

As soon as the Amish woman disappeared into an exam room, the nurse returned to the waiting room and motioned to Jaime to follow her into the doctor's office and step on the scale. She moved the weight until it finally balanced, whistling two notes: up, down. "You're sure inching your way up that scale!"

Jaime studied her feet. "Must be these shoes." Along with her new hobby of grief snacking.

"I don't think so, hon."

Jaime frowned at her, but the nurse was oblivious as she scribbled down the weight. "Five pounds is really not all *that* much."

The nurse snorted. "No, but ten sure is, sugar."

Jaime winced. The funk she'd been in since her mother's death last summer was taking its toll in more ways than just increasingly uncomfortable clothes.

As the nurse wrapped the blood pressure cuff around Jaime's arm, she turned to face the instrument on the wall. Long blond hair swung around the perfect oval of the nurse's face. Jaime poked an errant curl behind her ear and wondered how the nurse's hair fell like that—sleek and smooth—unlike her own hair, which continued to defy the new straightening product she'd paid way too much for.

"Born that way," she said, reading Jaime's mind.

"I figured," Jaime sighed. Her own hair was the curse of her existence, especially on a windy winter day when even industrial-strength styling gel couldn't keep her hair settled down.

The nurse rolled up the cuff and stuffed it into the holder on the wall. "Your hair is . . . unusual."

Okay. Now the nurse had sailed past mildly irritating and was flirting in the annoying zone.

"You don't see that color every day . . . unless it's out of a bottle."

This nurse had a knack for poking Jaime's raw spots: her blossoming weight, her unruly hair. What was next, her ever-so-absent father? Or better still, what about her fragile marriage? "Well, it's not," Jaime said, sounding a tad more defensive than she intended. At least her hair color added some flash to the rest of what she considered her very ordinary features. She'd always liked her eyes, though, and she liked to believe their slight tilt gave her a mysterious look. As a child she used to wear a scarf over the bottom half of her face as a veil and pretend she was a Moroccan spy.

"So, doll, are you ready for Christmas?"

Jaime never understood why people used diminutives in place of names. Hon, doll, sugar. Why didn't the nurse just admit she couldn't remember Jaime's name? "This year will be a little different. We're not really celebrating. We're going away for Christmas."

The nurse turned to leave. "Christmas has a way of coming, wherever you might be." She snapped Jaime's chart shut. "Dr. Engel will be seeing you today. He's on-call for the regular doctor."

Jaime's head snapped up. "What happened to Dr. Cramer?"

"Dr. Cramer is at his daughter's preschool recital. Dr. Engel agreed to take over his office visits today, as a favor." She tilted her head. "Dr. Engel will just be a moment. Or two."

The nurse hummed along with the tinny music piped in through the ceiling speaker: "I Saw Mommy Kissing Santa Claus." She smiled distractedly at Jaime as she reached for the door. The door was decorated as a giant gift—covered with shiny foil wrapping paper and taped with a big red bow. The bow came loose and fluttered to the floor. "Blasted bow," she muttered as she picked it up and pressed the sticky side against the door. "These decorations have been up since before Thanksgiving. I'll be glad when Christmas is over and this place can go back to looking like a doctor's office."

As the door closed behind the nurse, Jaime glanced at her wristwatch and weighed her options. She was frustrated with herself for leaving this errand to the last minute. She heard a gust of wind blow a tree limb against the building and walked over to the window to look at the ominous clouds.

She saw two black hats outside—the Amish father and his son gathering snow that had dusted the ground, packing it into balls, and pelting each other. The Amish boy's snowballs weren't packed hard enough and they splayed apart after release. Soon there was as much snow being flung through the air as rested on the ground. The sight made her laugh out loud. That little boy was so cute! Strawberry blond hair, thick blond lashes framing saucer-sized brown eyes, and freckles across his nose, like someone had sprinkled it with cinnamon. The nosepiece of his eyeglasses was wrapped with adhesive tape. And such round cheeks! He didn't walk so much as he bounced; he didn't talk so much as he bubbled over like a shaken-up can of soda. She wasn't really one to notice children. C.J., her husband, was the one who noticed kids, in restaurants or at parks. But then, he was a teacher.

The little boy nailed his father square in the face with a snowball. Jaime's gaze shifted to the father. She felt a pang of worry for the boy, fully expecting the father to start bellowing. Instead, she saw the father wipe snow dramatically off his face and laugh. Then he chased his son and grabbed him in a bear hug. That sight . . . it was so unexpected, so charming, she framed it in her mind like a photograph. If her mother were still here, she would've turned it into a Currier & Ives type of Christmas card, with such a caption as "The best things to give your children aren't things!"

Tears pricked Jaime's eyes. She had to stop doing that. Stop cobbling together imaginary conversations with her mother as if she were still alive. She wasn't.

Jaime's mother had worked as a writer for an inspirational greeting card company. She spent all day thinking up verses and phrases: An Easter card that read, "No bunny loves you like Jesus!" Or a pick-me-up card: "Exercise daily! Walk with Jesus!" These platitudes—always with exclamation points!—infused her mother's everyday speech in a way that used to embarrass Jaime, especially around her friends.

No longer.

She leaned her forehead against the cold windowpane. A moment ago she had been laughing. Now she felt an aching sadness that she couldn't understand.

Jaime heard the slightly accented voice of the Amish woman talking to the nurse as she walked down the hall to leave.

Then the door to the examining room where Jaime was waiting opened slowly. The doctor shuffled in and gave her a warm smile. He had penetrating blue eyes and a shock of white hair. But he was old, so old that Jaime's heart sank. *This won't be quick.* Jaime extended her hand to shake his. "Dr. Engel, I'm Jaime Fitzpatrick. And I won't take but a moment of your time."

The doctor reached out and clasped her hands with both of his as if he were greeting a long-lost friend. Or maybe it was the way he looked at her straight on, in a manner that was so frank and plain it might have been mistaken for rudeness if his blue eyes had not been so kind.

"Nonsense! I've got all the time in the world." Dr. Engel pulled up a chair and eased himself into it, facing Jaime. "So, Jaime Fitzpatrick. How are you today?"

Something in his greeting, his solicitous tone as he asked how she was feeling, made a sick anticipation rise from the center of her stomach. It felt as if time was slipping into slow motion, matching Dr. Engel's leisurely pace. Even the song now playing on the radio was an instrumental version of "Silent Night."

Jaime lowered herself to her chair. "I really just stopped by to get a prescription refilled. Dr. Cramer prescribed it for me awhile ago." She enunciated each word carefully in case he was possibly deaf on top of being slow.

Dr. Engel opened Jaime's chart, scanned it, humming as he read, then let it drop on his lap. He leaned back in his chair. "You didn't answer my question. How are you today?"

"Fine. I'm just fine." *Hurry, hurry, hurry!*

"A note here said that Dr. Cramer suggested getting some counseling along with the sleeping pills. Have you done that?"

Jaime folded her hands in her lap. "No. I've solved my problem."

"Is that right?" Dr. Engel lifted his bushy eyebrows and tapped the chart. "So that's why you're here today, because you're sleeping so well?"

She sighed and tucked a loose curl behind her ear. "Not exactly 'well,' but . . ." *Not exactly at all.* "Look, I don't use the pills every night. Just when I really need them. I've had a lot on my mind and I've needed a clear head to make good decisions."

Dr. Engel picked up her chart, peering at it through his bifocals. "So your mother passed away recently?"

19

Jaime shifted in her seat and crossed one leg over the other. "Last summer."

"So this will be your first Christmas without her."

She stiffened. *Oh pull-eez.* Did he think she wasn't aware of that?

"Grief takes awhile to work through. It can't be rushed."

"I'm fine. Really." She froze when she noticed that Dr. Engel's gaze was on her foot, wiggling back and forth in the air.

"I know I'm old school, but I believe that pain can be the most important tool in a person's life. It forces a person to pay attention to something that needs to be changed. I worry that drugs like sleeping pills mask pain just enough that the real root of the problem gets buried, deeper and deeper. A problem—even something like grief—just doesn't go away until it's dealt with."

Jaime glanced out the window and saw large snowflakes, drifting in the wind. "I'm making a change. A big one." Starting today. One hour ago, to be exact, when she told her manager at Sears Portrait Studio she was quitting.

"Change isn't the same thing as addressing grief, Jaime. It'll just keep resurfacing. Avoidance is not a way to cope. There are better coping methods."

"Such as?" Jaime said coldly. She didn't mean to sound so rude. Why was she acting so prickly with everyone? She always had a tendency to speak before thinking, but today, it seemed as if she had no filter at all.

This doctor meant well, she had no doubt, but he had no right to be poking into her private business. Dr. Cramer never asked these kinds of probing questions. But she needed those pills! This morning, while photographing a fussy elderly woman and her cat, she felt a wave of dizziness from lack of sleep. Her entire body ached with fatigue. She simply could not get a good night's rest. She would lie in bed and watch the glowing digital numbers on the alarm clock flip over and over, her mind bubbling with anxieties.

"Some folks find solace and guidance in faith, for one."

Oh no! Talking about religion was like walking toward a bee swarm, just waiting to get stung. Same thing. She was determined to avoid *that* particular topic and all the unsolvable turmoil that came with it. Jaime rose to her feet. "I really need to be on my way. If you wouldn't mind giving me the prescription slip, I'd like to get going before the storm hits."

Dr. Engel held her eyes for a long moment. Then he handed her the writ. "Dr. Cramer had already filled it out for you when you called in this morning." He eased himself to a stand, creaking as he went. "Jaime, you just have to ask for help when you need it."

Isn't that why I'm here? Jaime gave him a stiff smile, took the writ, and stuffed it—along with his surfeit of advice—in her purse.

The snow was falling steadily, damp and clinging. The wind had whipped up, finding every crack and crevice in the buggy to slip through. At moments like these, Sol thought back to that time in his life when he was in his Rumspringa and hid a car from his folks. He didn't object to living the Plain life, but on bitter winter days he did think back fondly to that car. He could blast on the heat, roll up the windows, cut off the wind, and crank up the radio.

He glanced over at Mattie as she spread the buggy blanket over her lap. What would she think of his thoughts? She was so pure, his Mattie. He doubted she ever had a taste for the worldly life, not like he did. Not like Zach did. Mattie's seventeen-year-old cousin had been living with them since summer. Zach ran with a wild group of friends, a choice that had caused growing tension between him and his parents. All spring, his parents were at their wits' end. Finally, after one major mishap, his father had given him an ultimatum: get baptized or get out. So Zach got out. With no place to go and no money in his pocket, Mattie scooped him up like a stray puppy and insisted he live with them. It wasn't that Sol was entirely unsympathetic to Zach's plight—he was no stranger to teenage shenanigans. When he was not much older than Zach, he had gone so far as to leave the community and abandon the girl he adored because he had a once-in-a-lifetime opportunity to pitch for the Lancaster Barnstormers. It was a wonderful, awful time. He knew firsthand the dangers and temptations of the outside world. He knew the pain and heartache he had inflicted on those he loved.

When Mattie told Sol she wanted Zach to stay with them, he thought it over and finally agreed. Sol hoped he could help Zach avoid the regrets he had—but it was starting to trouble him to see the influence he had on their Danny. Danny adored Zach. To him, Zach was the older brother he never had. He talked like him, he walked like him. He was even starting to wait to dress in the morning until he saw what color shirt Zach was wearing. It shamed Sol to admit this, but he felt as if Zach had displaced him in his own son's life. Danny used to imitate Sol the way he was imitating Zach.

And behind it was the nagging worry that Zach was bringing the outside world into their home.

Sol could already see Danny would have a difficult time

of it when he reached Rumspringa. Danny's mind was eager for new things, new information. Could the Plain life satisfy a mind like that? So much of their life was routine. There was great comfort in routine, he knew, and he had grown to love his life. But he understood the longing a young man might have for the excitement of the world.

Mattie shivered and snuggled closer to him.

"So what did the doctor say?"

She kept her gaze on the swishing tail of the horse. "He said not to lose hope. Miracles can happen, he said." Mattie's voice was sweet but thin. She spoke with forced cheer, like those narcissus bulbs she put in little paper cups every January and lined up on the kitchen windowsill.

"That's exactly right," he said reassuringly. His spirits lightened slightly. He put his arm around her and drew her close. She was still weak from her miscarriage, just four weeks ago. "I don't think we should be giving up, Mattie," he whispered. "You always said we should expect miracles in this life."

"The Lord God had already given us a miracle," she said quietly. "Danny is our miracle."

Hearing his name, Danny popped up and hung over the backseat of the buggy. Mattie tapped the tip of his nose.

"He is indeed," Sol said, "but that doesn't mean the Lord won't grant us another miracle."

They had such high hopes for this pregnancy. Mattie hadn't conceived since Danny was born, and then one day this fall, she told Sol she was going to have a child. Their prayers had been answered! Until the day after Thanksgiving, when the bleeding and cramping started. And their hope was extinguished.

Mattie tucked her arm through Sol's and leaned her chin on his shoulder. He turned the horse into the driveway that led to their farmhouse. The horse picked up his pace, knowing that a hay dinner and a warm stall would be waiting for him. Sol pulled the buggy as close to the kitchen door as he could and helped Mattie inside, hoping she might lie down for a few minutes before dinner. He sent Danny directly to the barn to help Zach feed the animals. He unhooked the horse from the buggy traces, led it inside the barn to its stall, and pushed the buggy into the barn to keep it sheltered. Snow crunched under his feet as he crossed the yard to the house.

In the kitchen, Sol pushed the coals around in the woodstove and added logs to warm up the downstairs. Mattie was checking on Buster, Danny's baby barn owl. Mattie babied Buster and kept it in the kitchen, even though Sol assured her the owl would be fine in the barn. Mattie didn't agree. So Buster stayed in a cozy box by the stove.

He smiled as he watched her crouch by the box, talking softly to Buster. Then his smile faded. He knew she had given up hope for another baby. He could see it in her eyes, even the way she nurtured that silly barn owl.

Mattie hadn't just lost her hope. She had lost her joy.

Jaime stood by the front door of the doctor's office and put on her hat and scarf, bracing herself for a shock of cold. She buttoned her top coat button. It looked bitter outside, with dark clouds racing across the sky. Just as she stuffed one hand into a glove, Dr. Engel opened the waiting room door and called her name.

"Would you mind doing me a favor? That Amish boy left

his toy. They live on a farm right on the edge of town . . . not far from the highway."

She hesitated. The snow was sticking to the road, and she was anxious to get to the drugstore to pick up her prescription before her husband expected her at his school. She didn't want C.J. to know she had been to the doctor. He worried she might become dependent on sleeping pills. "Maybe they can just come back and get it."

The nurse with the perfect hair popped her head out of the reception window. "That Amish mama miscarried just a few weeks ago. She's been trying and trying to have a baby." She clucked her tongue.

Oh. The extra ten pounds that had crept up on Jaime's small-boned frame since her mother's death no longer seemed like such a big problem.

Dr. Engel gave the nurse a look, and she quietly closed the window. He walked up to Jaime. "After today, I won't be seeing the Amish woman for a while. She's going to be just fine." He put the whistle into her gloveless hand and curled her fingers around it. "Amish kids don't have a lot of toys. This one must have been pretty special for him if he brought it into town."

"Not so special that he couldn't have remembered it," Jaime said.

"Boys are boys. And no boy should be parted with his whistle. You don't mind, do you?"

Do I really have a choice? "Fine. I'll take it."

Dr. Engel gave her vague directions about how to reach the farmhouse. "When you see an old roadside cemetery—with small plain markers behind low stone walls—then you're getting close. Turn left into the driveway when you see a long white fence that wraps along the road. The Riehl farm is hard to miss—big unpainted barn. Green shutters. White clapboard. Big wraparound porch out front." He held the door open for her. "Not to worry. You'll know it when you see it."

Jaime ran to her car and turned on the ignition, setting the heat to full blast. She sat there for a while, waiting for the car's engine to warm up. It was a habit ingrained by her husband. C.J. was deliberate about taking good care of cars—changing the oil regularly, getting tune-ups, giving the engine time to get warm. He was deliberate about everything.

As she waited, she looked more closely at the whistle. There was something about the way that Dr. Engel asked her to deliver it—the way he looked at her—that made her think this whistle had some kind of special significance.

Though she'd lived in Lancaster County all of her life, she had never really known any Amish. Other than a brief chat here and there at an Amish roadside fruit stand, today's conversation with the little boy was the longest one she'd ever had with an Amish person. It seemed there was an invisible wall between the two cultures. They felt it. She felt it.

She held the whistle up to her lips and blew on it, gently at first, then louder. The funny squeaks made her laugh out loud. It felt good, easing the tight feeling in her chest that had been her constant companion lately.

She turned on the wipers to knock some snow off the windshield. The entire parking lot was covered with a thick, one-inch layer of snow, just in the time she had been in the doctor's office. She listened to the weather report on the radio and cringed when she heard the weatherman warn people to prepare for power outages and get supplies to last for a few days. She and C.J. absolutely, positively had to get to her father's tonight. Her father had told her he had a huge surprise waiting for her, and she had a pretty good idea what it was going to be.

Mattie covered the casserole with tinfoil and slipped it into the oven. The air was redolent with Danny's favorite meal: roast pork and oven potatoes. Danny would be happy when he caught a whiff of this, she thought. She made a double portion so that there would be plenty for tomorrow's lunch. She really should start cooking in smaller batches, but she just didn't seem to be able to. A casserole as big as the one she just made would have filled up four of her six brothers. The bulk of her mother's time, like most every woman, was spent preparing meals. Not so for Mattie. She should be finding the good in that, she knew, but instead she looked at the big kitchen table and thought about the children she had hoped would fill it. She took out forks, knives, and spoons and set four places at the table—the pine harvest table that Sol had built for her when they were newly married.

Dear Sol. He was trying so hard to make things a little better. How she loved him—his steadiness, his honesty, his humor, and his kind, kind heart. The buggy ride home from the doctor's office today nearly undid her. Sol's eyes, so sad, searching her face, trying to see into her heart, hoping there would be good news. He liked problems he could fell like trees, problems he could solve. Mattie's barrenness left him confounded.

She ran a hand along the tablecloth and brushed off some

crumbs from Danny's spot. Maybe they should think about getting a smaller table. Maybe, then, it wouldn't seem like someone was always missing.

A single tear seeped from the corner of her eye and spilled down her cheek. She rubbed her face and took a deep breath. She had to stay strong for Sol, for Danny, but it was hard, so hard, to accept the will of God.

C.J. Fitzpatrick wiped down the dry erase board and scanned his classroom. "Looks like a wrap for the year, Tucker." His yellow Labrador retriever stared up at him with large dark eyes. C.J. stooped down and unhooked Tucker's service jacket. "You're off-duty, buddy. School's out." He patted Tucker's large head. He adored that dog. Tucker had been bred to be a guide dog for the blind, but was career changed because he was considered "too much dog"—a euphemism for a dog that was hard to handle. C.J. had been volunteering for Search and Rescue when the organization called him and said they thought they had a prospect for an SAR dog. They were right. Tucker was the best SAR dog C.J. had ever worked with—this dog was wired to work. He would go to any lengths for a Find.

C.J. and Tucker had rescued many lost people over the past two years. Most were Live Finds, but not all. He knew that would come with the territory of SAR, but it was still a terrible blow when he and Tucker found twin five-year-old boys last fall, too late, after a twenty-four hour search. The boys had wandered off while their parents were setting up camp. One boy was found first, early into the search. He had fallen down a steep ridge and hit his head. It took another nineteen hours to find the other boy. C.J. shuddered. The boy must have wandered in circles because his trail—his scent path—was scattered in all directions. C.J. finally found him quite a distance away, badly dehydrated and in severe shock. The boy was airlifted to a hospital, but pneumonia had set in and he died a day later. C.J. couldn't shake that experience off.

Tucker licked his hand, as if sharing the thought.

"Come on, Tuck, we need to get over that. We win some and we lose some. We *know* that." He walked over to the window to see if Jaime had arrived yet.

His thoughts drifted to the argument they'd had this morning. They'd started the day off on the wrong foot. But what had triggered it? He had just asked her if she was packed for the trip and she snapped at him. He had stepped in mud and he hadn't even seen it. Where was safe ground anymore? All that he was wondering was if she needed him to take her suitcase out to the car, but she assumed he was nagging her to get ready. Jaime was so tense about this trip. He sighed. Lately, Jaime was tense about everything. The past few months, things seemed to be unraveling between them. He couldn't remember the last conversation they'd had that didn't end with Jaime upset with him, or worse still, silent. He could feel them drifting, drifting, and he didn't know what to do about it.

"C.J.? Yoohoo, are you there?"

C.J. spun around to find Eve, the principal's receptionist, standing by his desk with an envelope in her hand. He gave her a warm smile. "I'm sorry, Eve. I was just daydreaming."

"Here's your paycheck, darlin'. I already locked up the office and thought you might have forgotten about it." She put the envelope on his desk and turned to go, then came over to give him a hug. "Have a very merry Christmas, C.J. You deserve it. Especially after being nominated for the district's Teacher of the Year award. What a Christmas this is going to be!"

Sol told Zach to finish up in the barn while he and Danny went up the hill behind the farm to check the trap he had set yesterday for a pesky bobcat. He wanted to check on it before the storm hit. He told Mattie he thought there would be a good chance of outsmarting a hungry cat in a winter storm. Mattie watched her husband and son climb the hill until they were swallowed by the falling snow. The air was raw and piercing, and dozens of chores awaited her inside, yet she lingered still. She drew in a deep breath, smelling the cold that pinched her nose and the acrid smoke from the chimney that rose into the sky. She lifted her face to the snow, tasting it on her lips, letting its coldness sting her flushed face. Shivering, she gathered her shawl closer to her and went up the porch steps that led to the kitchen.

Mattie walked through the silent house. She always found it unsettling to rattle around in a house meant for ten. Five empty bedrooms. Too quiet. Too empty. Maybe, she thought, they should move. Far away from here. Into town.

Upstairs in her bedroom, a dimming afternoon light slanted through the window. She sat helplessly on the edge of the bed, a shirt of Sol's that she should iron for Sunday church hanging limp in her hands. She had so much to do, she really shouldn't give in to taking a rest, but she felt a bone-deep weariness and didn't have the energy to fight it.

What was more and more distressing, she didn't seem to care. She felt tears coming on. What was *wrong* with her? The doctor said she should be feeling better after a month or so, but she didn't. She felt just the same. Worse, maybe. What was happening to her sense of peace, her happiness? What was happening to her?

Her head itched as it often did after a day of wearing her starchy prayer cap. She pulled out the pins that held the cap in place and set them on the nightstand. The pins released her hair and she thrust her fingers through it, rubbing her scalp. She picked up her brush from the nightstand and took a moment to indulge herself, crossing the room to sit in the rocker by the window. She brushed her hair slowly, a hundred strokes, the way her mother taught her. How many times had she sat in this rocker? She had rocked Danny as a baby to sleep in this rocker. When she woke in the night, she often sat in it, listening to the evening songs of nature—the throaty song of bullfrogs, the violin scrape of crickets' wings, the clap of a thundercloud. Sol thought she was crazy to get up out of bed in the night—sleep was precious to him. But what she really loved was having time alone with the Lord—time that passed sweet and slow. It was her time for praying. And there were times when she felt God talking to her. Not like a person might talk, but a sense, a prodding. An idea would pop into her head—an insight or a solution to a problem. And then a sweet peace would flood her soul. She knew it was the presence of God.

But no longer. Since she had miscarried, God had gone silent, so silent. And in her soul, there had been only emptiness left behind, an emptiness that felt hard and cold as stone. She moved through the days as best as she could, but she could summon only a pale shadow of the faith that had always steadied and comforted her.

Her brush was full when she finished, a thick nest of pale silk, all the luxuriance of pregnancy slipping away as her hormone levels readjusted. Looking at all that hair in the brush made her want to weep. The world had become so very fragile. She slammed the brush on the arm of the rocker. *That's enough,* she said sternly to herself, blinking away the tears. She'd been paralyzed with grief, too full of sorrow even to weep. *That's enough, Mathilda Zook Riehl.*

She should go downstairs and iron Sol's shirt. Sol and Danny would be home soon, wondering where she was. She should go. In a moment. The breath eased out of her in a soft sigh. Her head fell back and she drifted off to sleep.

"A marriage unwraps slowly." Jaime said the words aloud as she left the pharmacy and drove toward C.J.'s school. She had heard that phrase uttered on *Oprah* recently, and it seemed to be meant for her. That's just what had been happening with her and C.J.—their marriage was slowly unwrapping. "It's time for a radical change," she said to the rearview mirror. "It's as simple as that." She had practiced this speech dozens of times over the last week, after finally deciding she was going to accept her father's suggestion to move to New York City and sign with a photography agent friend of his. By the time she reached C.J.'s school, she was so tightly coiled, she ached.

She pulled into the parking lot of the junior high where her husband worked as a math teacher, and parked next to his yellow jeep. She glanced at her wristwatch: half past four. *Perfect.* For once she wasn't late! They were going to drive straight to her father's house in the city. The plan was to fly to Miami early Christmas morning to embark on a weeklong Caribbean cruise with her father. It was just what they needed.

A knock on her window made her jump. It was C.J. She quickly turned on the ignition to lower the window.

"I was starting to worry about you, driving in this snow," he said.

An expression of genuine concern filled his dark brown eyes. That way he had of looking at her, as if she was the most beautiful woman in the world when she knew she wasn't—it always made her knees go weak. Today, it made her feel like an emotional nutcase. How could he be thinking of having an affair with another woman and yet be so warm and loving to his wife? She couldn't process it. She turned back to face the steering wheel. "We'd better get going. If we hurry we can stay ahead of the storm."

"I thought we'd take the jeep."

She shook her head. "I want to have the GPS system so we don't get lost."

He hesitated. "Jaime, I have Tucker."

Jaime leaned over the open window to face the large coffee-colored eyes of the gigantic yellow lab. He was peering at her, standing by C.J.'s knees. "You said you were going to leave him with the principal."

"Al couldn't take him. They're going to his sister's house for the weekend and she's allergic to dogs. But he did say it was okay to leave your car here for the week. He said the lot would be locked up."

Jaime frowned. "There's got to be somebody else. What

about that Eve woman?" *That she-wolf who is preying on another woman's husband?* She sneaked a sideways glance at C.J. to catch his reaction.

"She's got company staying with her for the holiday. I called and made a reservation at a kennel near your dad's house. It shouldn't be any problem. Your dad doesn't even have to know."

"My new car is the problem! Hair on the seat and drool on the windows and—"

"Then we'll take my jeep."

Jaime looked at the yellow jeep. She hated that jeep. She used to love it, used to imagine that this was what it felt like to be on an African safari. But now, it embarrassed her. The shocks were shot, you couldn't hear one another, the heater didn't always work, and Tucker would have to sit between them on the front seat. Plus, she would miss her beloved GPS system. "No. Just put a blanket down." She flipped up the trunk of her car so that C.J. could get a blanket. While C.J. settled Tucker into the backseat, Jaime set the GPS system for the street name the doctor had given her for the Amish family.

"Want me to drive?" C.J. asked.

"No thanks. I . . . I have a quick errand to make as we head out of town."

He climbed into the passenger seat beside her and touched her arm briefly. She tensed, lifting her chin to look straight ahead, and put the car in gear. C.J. withdrew his hand as if he had touched a hot stove. They fell silent as Jaime drove through Main Street, under white holiday banners that stretched from side to side of the street with cheerful greetings: "Seasons Greetings!" "Happy Hanukkah!" and "Happy Kwanzaa!"

As she turned onto a side street, C.J. said quietly, "When did wishing someone a Merry Christmas become politically incorrect?"

She shrugged, and turned her attention to the homes that lined the street. It wasn't quite dusk yet, but many houses had turned on their outdoor Christmas lights. The neighborhood looked like they must be having a contest to out-decorate each other: one had an enormous plastic Santa Claus in a plastic sleigh, pulled by eight plastic reindeer. Another was practically covered with blinking lights. She thought she might wind up with epilepsy if she lived across the street from that house.

C.J. shifted in his seat and turned to her. "A kid said the funniest thing to me a minute ago. I had an envelope sticking out of my shirt pocket and the kid asked what it was. I told him it was my paycheck and he said, 'Yeah? Where do you work?'" He chuckled to himself. "I love middle school humor."

"Did you deposit the check?"

C.J. rolled his eyes. "No, Jaime. I didn't have time."

Jaime groaned. "That means it won't get deposited until next week, and then the money won't be available for a few days past that. C.J., this time of year, we have so many bills to pay. We have Christmas gifts and—"

"Your credit card debt. Your cell phone payment." He reached over and picked up the edge of her scarf. "And let's not forget Burberry scarves."

"Don't. Start." She frowned. "I work just as hard as you do."

"At this rate, we're never going to be able to save enough for a house."

"You could have accepted my father's offer to provide the down payment."

"Let's not go there." He turned toward the window and was quiet for a while.

She glanced over at him and wondered what was running through his mind. He was usually pretty talkative. Had they already exhausted all neutral territory?

"I'm thinking I might start tutoring after school and weekends. Eve said some parents have been asking her about it."

Eve. *That* Eve. "You're trying to make me feel guilty." How incredibly trite that C.J. would be tempted to cheat on his wife with a woman named Eve. The original temptress! She glanced at him. She wondered if C.J. was in love with Eve. She wondered whether he would ask for a divorce soon. *That's what men do. They leave when they have someone new to go to.* She knew that from watching *Oprah*. From watching her dad.

"No, I'm not trying to make you feel guilty. But we need to face facts."

Which facts? Jaime wondered. *Yours or mine?* Should she confront him? No. Not now. Not today. Not on Christmas weekend. And maybe . . . if things worked out the way she hoped, if she could persuade him that they needed a radical change . . . maybe she wouldn't even have to.

C.J. was waiting for a response from her, but before she could get her words set into order, the GPS system told her to make a right.

"This doesn't seem like the way it was described to me," she said, under her breath.

"Did you set it correctly?"

"Of course I set it correctly," she snapped, turning right.

C.J. peered at the map on the GPS screen and looked skeptical. "If it doesn't feel right, why would you trust a piece of technical equipment over your gut instinct?" His placating tone was rimmed with an edge of exasperation.

She clenched her jaw. She knew that question wasn't just about directions. That question was a perfect metaphor for the differences between them—C.J. followed hunches, especially in his Search and Rescue volunteer work with Tucker. Jaime relied on reality. Equipment. State-of-the-art digital photography.

It was odd—they met three years ago. He was taking a class to become qualified as a volunteer in Search and Rescue and she was doing a freelance assignment to take pictures of the training sessions for the SAR website. They started in the same place. How had they drifted so far apart?

The persistent voice on the GPS system interrupted her thoughts to tell her to turn left, so she quickly veered left. They were heading away from town and into a much less populated area.

"Jaime, what kind of errand did you say you needed to make?"

Tucker popped his big head over the front seat and C.J. gently pushed it back.

"I just have to drop something off at a person's house."

"Whose house?"

"It's . . . a long story. Please be patient for a few minutes."

Then they were silent. Stilted. C.J., who usually never ran out of things to say, seemed reserved, distracted. Finally, he closed his eyes and yawned. As his breathing settled into a rhythm, Jaime felt relieved, knowing he had drifted off to sleep. She wished she hadn't promised that ancient Dr.

Engel to deliver this silly whistle. He made it sound like it would be easy to find, but he didn't realize Jaime had no sense of direction. In spite of the urgency she felt, she slowed down—partly because the snow was falling even harder. Partly because, despite everything, she was enjoying the scenery. She lived so resolutely in town that she had forgotten all this was out here—all this *country*. She used to drive out this way with her mother on sunny weekend afternoons. She recognized this area, despite the whirling snow. Blue Lake Pond spread out silvery blue to her left, and just a mile down the road was the most beautiful Amish farm she had ever seen, Beacon Hollow. She and her mother had always wanted to turn up that driveway and meet the family who lived there.

Five minutes passed. Then ten. It was taking all of her concentration to focus on driving. Jaime thought she knew where they were, but felt a slight panic when the GPS system told her to turn off a main road onto a one-lane road.

C.J. jerked awake. He blinked and looked around. "Where the heck are we?"

"Almost there."

"What? Something just isn't making sense, Jaime. You're driving west, into the countryside."

"I have complete confidence in this car and its Global Positioning Satellite system." At least, she usually did. She felt a twinge of unease as she turned onto a one-lane road that had more than a few inches of fresh, untouched snow on the ground.

Jaime glanced at C.J.'s hands—the way he had them clenched in his lap was a dead giveaway that he was trying hard not to tell her "I told you so." She was just about ready to turn the car around when the GPS system told her to turn right to reach her destination. She turned her windshield wipers up as fast as they could go, knocking fat flakes off the windshield, and practically let out a whoop of joy when she saw the numbers on the black mailbox. Voilà!

She smiled victoriously. Her GPS had not failed her. "See? I told you we were nearly there."

He stared at her like she had spoken in Chinese. She ignored him.

Jaime drove up a long lane, using the fence rails to guide her along the snow-covered road. When she reached the top of the lane, the sight nearly took her breath away. Before her was a farmhouse glowing with buttery lights, smoke from the chimney rising to the sky. A cozy, welcoming beacon in the storm.

"Where *are* we?" C.J. asked.

She pointed to the whistle that was on the car seat between them. "I just need to drop this off at the house."

His eyebrows arched in surprise. "Are you kidding me? We've lost an hour of driving time because you needed to drop off a toy? What could be so important about this toy?"

"What's so important?" Jaime repeated, anger lifting through her like a wave. Those words incensed her.

How was it that anything Tucker-related never seemed to be unimportant to C.J.? Slobbering all over her car, taking extra time to find Tucker's kennel—those inconveniences were just fine for C.J. But stopping by a farmhouse to drop off a forgotten whistle to a little boy—that didn't rank as important? "What do you mean by that?"

"I didn't mean anything by that, other than wondering why this toy seemed so important," he said, exasperated.

"Oh honestly, Jaime. What's wrong with you lately?" He was obviously at the end of his patience.

She wanted to shout, *You're what's wrong. I'm what's wrong. This whole thing is wrong!* But she didn't say a word.

The blue of early evening had settled over the room by the time Mattie awoke.

She regathered her bun so that it stuck off the back of her head like a knob and pinned her prayer cap in place. Downstairs, she glanced over her shoulder at the grandfather clock that stood beside Sol's desk—after five o'clock. Soon it would be dark. Sol and Danny were late coming home. She knew Sol was careful with their boy, but she never quite trusted him to watch Danny as closely as she did. So much danger lurked in the wilderness: rabid wolves and black bears and coyotes. And now the bobcat was prowling around, stealing her chickens! Danny could so easily become lost in the woods or fall into those streams with their steep, slippery banks that meandered through their property. Water was her greatest fear. The Schrocks' youngest child had died last spring in just that way. These dangers were a constant thing, yet he was her baby no longer, and as Sol was always telling her, she couldn't coddle him forever.

Just this very morning, they sat at the kitchen table, sipping coffee, and watched Danny run outside to meet up with Zach. Danny pointed toward the house and said something that made Zach's head fall back in laughter. Zach bent over and swung his cousin up in the air. The morning sun glinted off their two strawberry blond heads and something broke inside of Mattie in a terrible gush of pain.

"He's growing up so fast on us," Sol had said quietly.

His words, an echo of her own thoughts, pulled her gaze away from the window. She shared the sorrow in his voice.

Already she felt she was losing Danny. To the world outside of her safe home, to the land he was growing up to love as naturally as he breathed the air and ran through the wheat fields and laughed beneath the azure sky. And she was losing him to Sol and to Zach, into that male world where mothers felt unnecessary, a nuisance.

Mattie added a fresh stick of wood to the fire, punching the coals to stir them up. She dropped the lid back on the stove with a loud clatter, then went to the window to see if she could find some sign of Sol and Danny. She let her forehead fall to rest against the chilled pane. Where were they? The worry seeped into her like cold from the glass.

She heard the sound of a car through the wind. Probably someone lost, needing directions. For a moment longer, Mattie stayed where she was, feeling drained of energy, hoping Zach would see them first and send them on their way.

Jaime threw the car into park and grabbed the owl whistle. "This won't take long." The wind whipped into the car as she opened the door, ripping the car door from her hand.

Heavy snow bit at her as she hurried up the porch steps. She had just reached the porch when she thought she heard C.J. yelling. Before she could turn around, Tucker bounded past her and jumped up on the front door, barking. Jaime grabbed Tucker's collar to pull him back as the door opened. She was relieved to find the Amish mother from the doctor's office. She had the right house!

"Here," Jaime said, teeth chattering, as she thrust the whistle in the Amish mother's hands. "Your son left it at the doctor's office."

She spun around, hurried down the porch steps, and stopped in her tracks, stunned. Her car had disappeared.

As Zachary Zook hung a horse harness on a peg in the barn, he could have sworn he heard a car pull into the driveway. A gust of wind swirled past him as he slid open the barn door, knocking off his black felt hat. There *was* a car! A fancy-looking red sports car with a black convertible top. As he bent down to pick up his hat, a blur in a red coat emerged out of the driver's side and dashed up the stone path to the farmhouse. In the next instant, a big yellow dog bounded out of the car, chasing the red coat. And then a man jumped out of the passenger side of the car and ran behind the dog, hollering for it to come back.

Zach looked back at the car and saw it start to move—in reverse—and pick up speed until it crashed through the fence and rolled down the hill, finally coming to a stop as its back tires slid into the pond that Sol kept stocked with trout. It happened so fast that Zach didn't even have time to think—he felt as if he were dreaming. The woman in the red coat started to scream and ran toward the car. Zach ran after her, yelling as loud as he could, his words ringing through the bitter air, his mouth exhaling a frozen cloud, but she didn't stop. The snow, in parts, was at least four or five inches deep. He finally tackled her right before she reached the pond. The dog caught up to them and barked at Zach.

"Let me go!" the woman called out in a muffled voice, facedown in the snow. "My car! My beautiful car!"

She struggled to try to get up, but Zach wasn't letting her go. He was pretty sure she was crazy and would end up drowning if he let her get near that half-sunk car.

"At least let me get my camera!"

"Where is it?" he asked, keeping her pinned to the ground.

"Front seat. Black bag! I have to get it before it gets wet! I need it!" She stilled for a moment and Zach released his grasp, slightly. By now the man had caught up to them. He stood staring at the car in the pond, stunned.

"If you promise to stay put," Zach told the woman, "I'll try and get it. But you have to promise me you'll stay away from that pond. One step in and you'll sink like a stone and I have no intention of rescuing you." He relaxed his hold but waited to make sure she wasn't struggling before he finally released her.

She scrambled to her feet and glared at him. "I promise, I promise! I'll stay put! Now go, quick! Before it's too late!" She pointed to the car.

"Jaime! You can't expect this poor boy to risk his life in a freezing cold pond just to get your camera!" the man said in a firm voice.

She looked Zach up and down. "He's no boy! He's a grown man." She glanced at the man. "And I didn't ask him to. He offered."

Despite these bizarre circumstances, Zach felt a warm glow of pleasure at being called a grown man.

"Somebody needs to get my camera! Or I will go in there and get it!" She took a few steps closer to the pond.

The warm glow Zach felt instantly vanished. She shocked

him, this English woman. The way she was pointing at the pond, she seemed like a queen directing her faithful manservant. Queen Bee, Zach named her. He rose to his feet, found his hat, and put it back on, all the while watching her suspiciously. "You stay there. Right there."

The man started coming toward Zach, but he waved him off. At least Zach had boots on. The man was wearing loafers. "Just keep her away from the pond's bank. It's steeper than it looks."

The woman frowned but didn't budge. Zach walked carefully to the edge of the pond, grateful that the car door was above the waterline. He turned to look back at her to object, but she only pointed again to the car.

"I have to have that bag!" She walked a few steps closer to the pond until the man grabbed her arm.

"You stay put!" Zach yelled.

The wind was howling around them, but she actually listened to him and took a step back.

"Please! I have to have my camera."

It figured, Zach thought. Something stupid like a camera. He waded into the icy water, stepping gingerly so he didn't slip in the muck, and tried to yank open the car door. It wouldn't budge, so he grabbed the handle with both hands and pulled with all of his might.

As it flew open, he slipped backward, seat first, into the murky water. The shock of the cold hit him and his chest felt pinched for air.

Can't breathe. Can't feel anything. I'm paralyzed. I'm dying.

But then—a gasp! His breath came out in short, frozen bursts, and his chest rose and fell heavily as relief flooded through him.

I'm alive!

He pushed himself up onto his elbows, then slipped again as he tried to regain his footing.

The big yellow dog jumped into the water like it was a hot summer day, swam over to him, and planted himself, giving Zach the boost he needed to pull himself to his feet.

Zach tried to act fast before he turned into a frozen ice block. He grabbed the black bag, turned off the ignition, and practically leaped onto the shore. He threw the bag at the English man's outstretched arms and made a dash to the farmhouse.

Sol and Danny had just emerged from the woods that ran along the top ridge of the farm and stopped for a moment to look over the valley as it filled with snow. It was Sol's favorite spot on earth. From that vista, he could see from one end of his farm to the other. It gave him a deep-down satisfaction, that one speck on the planet. Even today, with the wind biting and the snow falling hard.

Danny tugged at his pant leg. "Mom will be upset."

Sol nodded. "You're right. She's probably ready to send Zach out on a search party for us."

They had gotten distracted by a gory sight at the bob-cat trap. It took awhile to find the trap in the new-fallen snow, but when they reached it, Sol found that the trap had been tripped. The animal had gotten away, leaving behind its bloody stump of a paw. The bobcat had chewed his paw off to save himself.

Sol had crouched down to examine the paw, to identify it as definitely belonging to a bobcat. This particular bobcat was the craftiest one he had ever tangled with. It found its way into Mattie's henhouse on a regular basis, helping itself to plump hens. With the kind of winter storms they were due to have, he knew this cat would be looking for a meal. He set that trap just yesterday, thinking it would tempt a hungry cat.

He let out a soft sough.

"Dad, that's not good, is it? An injured bobcat?"

Sol looked up at Danny. "Nope. Not good at all." He was sure the jaws of the trap must have cut the bobcat bone-deep. It would be crippled and bleeding, struggling hard to survive. And vicious.

"I feel a little sorry for it." Danny looked to Sol to see if that was all right.

Sol nodded that it certainly was. Anyone who grew up around farm animals couldn't side with a bobcat in the long clash of species. But it was another thing entirely to know a creature was suffering.

"Should we tell Mom?"

Sol sighed. "I sure don't want to but I probably should."

Danny tugged on Sol's pant leg again, snapping him back to the moment at hand. Sol straightened up and started down the hill, bracing himself against the wind with Danny following close behind him. They took a moment to stop at the next ridge to look over the valley. Then, as they started down the hill again, Sol saw the headlights of a car drive up the lane and come to a stop by the house. They picked up their pace after they saw some people get out of the car.

Then Danny suddenly let out a yelp. "Die Kaer!" *The car!* He pointed down the hill, a horrified look on his face. The car was heading backward, fast, right toward the pond.

By the time they reached the pond, Zach was bottom first in the water, somebody's big dog was swimming toward him, an English woman in a red coat stood at the pond's edge yelling directions, and an English man was beside her, looking mortified. Sol hunted for any kind of branch or stick that he could hold out to Zach. By the time he found something that could suffice, Zach was up and slogging through the snow and ice to reach the edge, then running up toward the farmhouse.

Sol's bewildered gaze shifted from the dog, shaking itself and getting everyone splattered with cold water, to the man, who had a very apologetic look on his face, to the back of the woman in the red coat. She remained facing her car in the pond, sadly shaking her head. Sol was flummoxed, unsure of what to say or do next.

It was Danny who knew what to do. Danny went up to the woman and patted her back, like a parent consoling a child. "Es ist nur eine Kaer. Es ist nur eine Kaer." *It's only a car. It's only a car.*

As Zach hurried to the farmhouse before he froze like a popsicle, he rushed past Mattie, who held the door open for him.

"Get by the stove!" she ordered. She shut the door behind him, and blocked the blast of frigid air. She guided him to a chair by the stove and pushed him into it, yanking off his shoes and socks. His teeth started chattering as he felt the heat from the stove; it seemed like pinpricks on his hands and feet.

Sol came through the kitchen door next.

Over her shoulder, Mattie said, "Sol! Go get some dry clothes. Quick!"

Sol bolted up the stairs, two at a time.

Mattie started to unbutton Zach's shirt, but he shook his head and jutted his chin in the direction of the kitchen door. Danny had come into the kitchen with the English couple and their dog; they all stood staring at Zach. Even the dog.

Mattie turned to the Queen Bee. "Would you get that afghan from the couch in the other room?"

The Queen Bee disappeared for a moment and returned with the afghan.

Mattie took it from her, then asked, "Would you mind turning around so we can get my cousin's wet clothes off?"

The woman flushed a deep red and spun around to face the wall, still hanging on tightly to her black bag.

Zach's hands felt like they were burning hot, they were so cold. Strange, he thought, how hot and cold felt like such similar pain.

"Come on, lift up," Mattie said. He raised his arms and she tugged his shirt up over his head. "There," she said triumphantly, as she tossed the shirt on the floor. She wrapped an afghan around his bare chest and he leaned closer to the stove to try to capture its warmth. "You've got to get those wet pants off, Zach."

"You t-turn a-around t-too," he chattered.

Mattie rolled her eyes and turned around. With uncoordinated, shaking fingers, Zach unhooked his pants and tried to yank them off, but he couldn't bend very easily, he was still so stiff and cold. Sol came down, just in time, and helped by pulling. Zach stepped gingerly into the dry pants Sol held at his feet.

Mattie piled more blankets on top of Zach and told him to stay by the stove until his teeth stopped chattering. With the wet clothes off of him, he was getting feeling back into his hands and feet. Warmth had started to creep over his body.

"Seems like a funny time of year for a swim," Sol said, toweling off Zach's hair. "Even for you." He left the towel hanging over Zach's head.

Zach snatched the towel off and managed a grin. A good sign! His face was thawing. "You'll think it's even funnier," he tried to say though his mouth felt stiff, "when you throw out a line next summer, hoping for trout, and you end up reeling in a car."

He stole a glance at the Queen Bee—this woman who nearly caused him to freeze to death tonight. He did a double take when he saw what she was doing. She was holding the baby barn owl, rocking it gently, as calm and soothing as a seasoned Amish mother. Mattie and Sol and Danny were watching the girl too, plus the man who was with her. All five of them seemed surprised to see the tender look on her face as she gazed at the owl.

Suddenly, she looked up, her large blue eyes round with wonder. "Isn't it beautiful?" Her eyes shifted from Zach to Sol to Danny to Mattie before resting on the English man's. "It's just the most beautiful thing in the world."

C.J. was, as usual, the one who thought to start proper introductions, taking a bit of the discomfort out of the air. For that, Jaime was thankful. C.J. made noises about trying to call for a cab and Mattie dismissed his words with a wave.

"No one is going anywhere in this storm," she told him,

setting two more places at the table. "Dinner will be ready in a few minutes."

The storm had hit with a vengeance in the last half hour. Whiteout conditions. The snow was blowing sideways and drifts were already piling up on the driveway.

Jaime handed the baby owl back to Danny. She fought back a growing desire to pull out her camera and start snapping pictures, but she knew that the Amish eschewed being photographed. She had always been fascinated by these people—an interest she had shared with her mother. She looked around the house, trying to memorize every feature. It was low-ceilinged with small rooms. Everything had a secondhand look—the faded linoleum, the crooked blue cover on the couch. The only item of value in the room seemed to be a distinguished grandfather clock that chimed every fifteen minutes. The kitchen, like the rest of the house, was unremarkable. A harvest table with ten painted wooden chairs. Simple pine cupboards that lined the walls. Pale green formica countertops, outdated by decades. It was really old-fashioned, complete with stacked firewood on the porch. But the house was orderly and clean and comfortable and quite nice in every detail. It reminded Jaime of the summer cottage that her mother had rented for a week each summer for the two of them. Life pared down, scaled way back. There was no TV, no microwave, no computer. Were the Amish happier, living with so much less?

An awareness bounced into her mind. There were no Christmas decorations. None! No Christmas tree in the corner of the living room, no cheerful presents, no gaudy lights hanging outside, no stockings on the chimney. It was two days before Christmas and there was not a single sign of it anywhere. She knew the Amish celebrated Christmas. But how? These were Jaime's thoughts as she looked around the room.

Mattie finished setting the table and turned toward them, a satisfied look on her face. "It's nice for us to have company."

"But we're intruding," Jaime said. "If we could just get to a phone, we could call for a tow truck."

"The phone shanty lost power this afternoon when a tree branch went down on it," Mattie said.

"Phone shanty?" C.J. asked.

"The only phones we're allowed to have are kept outdoors, shared by neighbors, in a shanty," Mattie's husband said, pointing a thumb at the window. "About a half mile down the road."

Jaime banged her palm against her forehead. "My cell phone! If I could just get to it, I could call."

Zach gave her a suspicious look. "And where would *that* be?"

"In my purse," Jaime said. "In the car. Front seat!"

"No," Zach said, shaking his head firmly. "No way. Not happening. N.O." He spelled the letters in the air as if he were writing on a chalkboard.

C.J. ducked his head, trying unsuccessfully to hide a smile. It annoyed Jaime to see how amused C.J. was by Zach's boldness. That boy wasn't just bold, he was downright rude. So much for the stereotype of quiet Amish children! And he looked at her with undisguised interest, as though she were some kind of curious wildlife. How old was he? Sixteen? Seventeen? It was hard to tell with his Beatle hairdo, floppy bangs hanging down his forehead.

By the way that boy was glaring at her now, it was as if

he was daring her to ask him to go back into that pond and fetch her purse for her. What was his problem, anyway? She was more than capable of retrieving it herself. She'd done crazier things than dipping in an icy pond while trying to snap photographs of wildlife. Besides, she *had* offered to go in to the pond herself! *He* was the one who insisted that she stay on the shore.

Sol snorted. "By now, it's either sunk or frozen until April."

Jaime regarded Sol, not appreciating that sentiment. Earlier this afternoon, at the doctor's office, she admired what a gentle and loving father he was, but now, in his home, with these unexpected visitors, she wasn't sure what she thought of him. She could tell he viewed them with minimal tolerance, or at the very best, as an inconvenience. He had hardly said more than a word to them, and she caught him frowning at Mattie as she set two extra place settings. She was starting to think he had the personality of a prison warden. Stiff, grim, unsmiling. But she had to admit he was exceptionally good looking.

"You remind me of someone I photographed once," she told Sol. "A calendar model. Mr. September."

As soon as she said the words, she wished them back. She was afraid Sol was going to choke. His lips crimped together while his Adam's apple bobbed. C.J. pinched his lips together in a line, as if trying not to laugh.

Then came a burst out of Zach, a guffaw that would have put Santa Claus to shame. "Mr. September!" he cackled out. Finally, his fit of laughter broke off into helpless snorts.

Jaime's face felt beet red. She should have kept her mouth shut. Saying "Mr. September" out loud did sound ridiculous. From now on, she was just going to answer questions.

But Sol did remind her of Mr. September! Her best-paying freelance job to date had been to photograph college fraternity boys for a calendar used to raise funds for a charity. Shave off Sol's silly horseshoe beard, give him a styled haircut, and he was a dead ringer for that photo of Mr. September—a handsome young man with a head of thick dark hair, in jeans, leaning against a split-rail fence.

Mattie, Sol's wife, was shockingly plain. She couldn't be more than five feet tall, with pale skin and large gray eyes that seemed too big for her small face. Jaime doubted she weighed one hundred pounds with a pocket full of change. She wore her wheat-colored hair in a bun so tight it made Jaime's head ache just to look at it. Mattie was unremarkable, easy to overlook, yet something about her was compelling, like the hub of a wheel. Yes, that was it. She was the center of this family wheel.

Jaime looked out the window. It was so dark it was impossible to even see the barn anymore.

"I might be able to help," Zach said, more kindly. "I might have"—he glanced down at the table—"a way to get to the main road."

Danny blinked at Zach through his round eyeglasses. A fleeting look of panic passed over him. "Ich hab dei Kaer gelast springa!"

"Was?" Zach roared, as though something hot had been spilled on him. "Ich hab dich gsagt fa weg bleiva!"

"Kaer?" Sol asked, in a tight, clipped voice. "Was fa Kaer?"

Everyone in the room was quiet—extra quiet?—and all that could be heard was the sound of the wind gusting outside.

Zach glared at Danny and pushed himself away from the

table, grabbed his coat, hat, gloves, and a flashlight, and rushed outside.

Danny's face lit up. "Waarde, Zach! Woch will ich kumme!"

Before Danny could scramble off his chair to join Zach, Mattie and Sol shouted, in unison, "Nee!"

Crestfallen, Danny slipped back onto his chair.

Zach had left in such a hurry that the door didn't shut tight, and winter came into the kitchen on a blast of arctic air. Sol hurried to close it. As he sat down at the table, he said something else to Mattie in Pennsylvania Dutch. All that Jaime could pick out was something about a car. Zach's car. Zach had a car someplace—and Jaime knew enough about the Amish to know that he wasn't supposed to have a car.

And Sol was *not* happy. Mattie looked extremely uncomfortable, caught between loyalty to her cousin and her husband.

Oh. My. Gosh. Mattie knew about the car! Jaime could see it in her eyes. *She knows!* Mattie suddenly became elevated to a person of intrigue to Jaime.

In a calming voice, Mattie said something to Sol in Dutch. Jaime guessed it was probably something close to, "Not now. We have company. We'll talk about this later." Then she turned to Jaime. "Is there someone who's expecting you tonight? Is someone worrying about you?"

Jaime exchanged a look with C.J.

"We were headed to Jaime's father's home," C.J. offered. "We're supposed to fly out on Sunday to go on a cruise over Christmas with her father." He put a reassuring hand on Jaime's forearm. "I think he'll be able to figure out that the storm is creating problems for us."

Jaime's stomach did a flip-flop. They *had* to get there in

time to make the cruise. They just had to! This was the very first time her father had invited Jaime to spend a holiday with him. She had such hopes for this Christmas together, that it would be the first of many.

Danny cocked his head and whispered loudly to his mother, "Why would anyone not want to be home for Christmas?"

Mattie rested a hand on his head, trying to still him for a moment.

Jaime wasn't positive, but she thought she heard Sol say, under his breath, "Only the English."

Sol took his time at the kitchen sink, washing up before dinner. His mind was far away, mulling over what to do with Mattie's cousin Zach. Lately, he was starting to feel some empathy for Eli, Zach's father. Eli Zook was a stern man who saw everything in black and white. No gray. Zach always had a knack for aggravating his father with multiple shades of gray. And Zach's friends were part of a wild gang—wilder than any Sol had joined during his late teen years. True fence jumpers.

In her quiet, persistent way, Mattie talked Sol into offering a home to Zach. She believed that doing so could keep Zach close to the fold. "Remember a saying my grandfather Caleb used to tell us, Sol?" she would ask him with her big gray eyes. "'Better to stop one paddle short than one too far.' If we let him go now, if we're all against him, it's like going one paddle too far. It's too much. He might never find his way back."

In the end, Sol buckled. How could he refuse her? Mattie always saw the best in others. *She saw the best in me, when I*

was just like Zach. A foolish young man. Mattie even talked
Sol into meeting with the judge who oversaw Zach's court
case. He was facing Minor In Possession charges for alcohol
use. Since it was Zach's first offense, and Sol and Mattie were
supporting him, the judge was willing to give Zach a steep
fine coupled with a generous amount of community service
hours to work off the misdemeanor charges.

Sol understood Zach's leaning toward the English world,
no different than his own. And now, just like Sol had once
done, Zach hid a car from his family. *How can I judge him
when I did the same?* Besides, he had always been fond of
Mattie's cousin. Zach's continual rebellious antics had been
funny and irritating, but harmless, in a salt-in-the-sugar-bowl
kind of way. If Sol would have ever had a brother, he imagined
him to be like Zach. The feckless little brother, the talented
one, the handsome one, the one no one could stay mad at.

Sol had plenty of conversations with Zach out in the barn
about what it was really like out there, in that big world.
He did his best to convince Zach that what he would gain
wouldn't equal all that he would lose. Zach pretended to
listen, but Sol could tell he didn't believe him.

Mattie scolded Sol once when he told her about their
talks. She didn't feel he should be trying to influence Zach
one way or the other. "It's his life to live, Sol," she said. "You
just keep being an example of a fine man to him and leave
the rest to God." That was his Mattie for you. She trusted
God on everything, right down to the dollars in the bank.

The hot food had been served up on the table while Sol's
mind was still out in the barn. He grabbed a dishcloth and
dried his hands. As soon as everyone sat down at the table,
Sol signaled for a prayer and bowed his head.

Lord God, he silently prayed, *I don't know why you would want us to have English houseguests on this weekend—Christmas weekend—but please give me the grace to tolerate them.* No, that wasn't quite right. The English fellow seemed to be a good sort. He really needed grace to tolerate her—the English woman. His thoughts wandered to other English girls he had met during his Rumspringa. They were all the same: shallow and worldly. She was a pretty one, this girl. It worried him to see the look Zach had on his face, about ten minutes ago, while he had watched the woman stare out the window at the storm.

Another dark cloud burst in on Sol's train of thoughts. He was starting to understand Eli's fear that Zach would turn his other children against the church. Sol had assumed Danny was too young to be noticing Zach's sloppy work habits—late weekend nights, falling asleep during church. Just a few days ago, he found Danny with a pack of cigarettes. Danny had unearthed Zach's stash, hidden in a barn rafter, and was fingering a cigarette, sniffing the tobacco. It made Sol furious to think Zach was smoking in the barn. The *barn*, of all places! And tonight, he discovered that Danny had known about the car and hadn't told him about it. That he had even turned it on and left it running! What else was Danny picking up from Zach? Six-year-old boys were naturally curious and Danny was particularly observant.

Mattie gently nudged him under the table and Sol, embarrassed, realized he had gone lost in his thoughts again. *Oh Lord,* he hastened to add, *thank you for the provision of this fine meal. Amen.*

He cleared his throat and tipped his head up, giving up a grin as he saw Danny try to slip that biscuit-colored dog a piece of pork. What he saw next gave him a start—the dog refused the pork. Its large brown eyes were fixed on the English fellow.

"Tucker knows not to eat unless I give him an OK," C.J. explained. "It's part of his training as a service dog."

"I didn't even think about what your dog might need for dinner," Mattie said. "I have dry dog food in the pantry. We keep some handy for strays."

"*We* don't," Sol said. "My wife does. She feeds the birds, stray cats and dogs—"

"Lost people too," Danny interrupted.

C.J. looked relieved. "That would be fine, if you don't mind. The bag of dog food I brought is in the trunk of Jaime's car." As Mattie got up, he added, "Not now. He can wait." He pointed to the floor and the dog collapsed onto the floor, burying his nose in his paws.

Sol had never seen such a well-behaved dog. He was worried the dog would go after Danny's barn owl, but other than an investigative sniff in its direction, he ignored it, as if he didn't expect to be here long so why bother making friends? "Is he always that good?"

C.J. looked down at Tucker and stroked his head. "He's a fine dog, but he's still a dog."

Sol picked up the mashed potatoes and passed the bowl to C.J. "What do you mean, a service dog?"

"Tucker and I volunteer for Search and Rescue," C.J. said, scooping some potatoes on his plate. "For the sheriff's department."

"That's your job?" Danny said. "I'd like that job."

C.J. laughed. "No. Just in my spare time. My full-time job is being a math teacher at the junior high."

"I'd rather be searching in the woods with a dog all day than stuck in a classroom," Danny said.

C.J. grinned. "I love Search and Rescue. SAR, they call it. In fact, that's how Jaime and I met. She was photographing the training exercises. Jaime works as a photographer. The best in the state of Pennsylvania."

Jaime blushed. "I'm not. Not by a long shot." She speared a piece of meat with her fork. "It's really quite interesting to see how the dogs are trained. You'd love watching it sometime, Danny." She took a spoonful of the chow-chow onto her plate. "What is this?" she asked, pushing it around on her fork.

"Chow-chow," Mattie said. "It's an Amish dish. A staple, really. I think I could count on one hand the times I've sat at supper without chow-chow."

"But what's in it?" Jaime asked.

"Pickled vegetables," Mattie said, looking up at the ceiling as if she was reading a recipe card. "Cucumbers, cauliflower, carrots, green peppers, lots and lots of vinegar. And sugar."

"How did it get a name like chow-chow?" Jaime asked.

Mattie shrugged. "Nobody knows."

"How'd you get a name like C.J. and Jaime?" Danny asked.

"Danny!" Sol warned. He gave his son the look, but Danny's attention was riveted to the English guests. Danny couldn't help asking questions. It was just the way his mind worked. He had such a curiosity about most everything, much more than Sol did at that young age. And he was so unusually bright! Sol often worried what choices Danny would make as an adult. Would he remain in the church? Would a farmer's life be enough for him? But that was a worry that could wait for another day.

"C.J. are my initials," C.J. said. "Stands for Charles Joseph. Kind of a mouthful for my mother to holler out when I got into trouble so it was shortened to C.J."

Danny snorted. "My dad was named Solomon because his father wanted him to be as wise as King Solomon."

Sol tousled his hair. "And that's why I prefer being called Sol. Lowers expectations." He exchanged a fond smile with Mattie. She often told him that Solomon suited him and he knew it didn't.

Danny's eyes were turned to Jaime, waiting for an answer to his question. He didn't give up, that boy of his.

"I was named Jaime after my father, James, because I was a girl. My father told my mother that one child was his limit . . . and he wanted a boy." Jaime spread butter delicately on the roll before taking a bite.

An awkward silence covered the kitchen. Only the English, Sol thought, would put a limit on a family. They didn't understand what he knew to be true—that every child was a blessing from the Lord. Why would anyone want to limit blessings?

When they were nearly done eating, Zach blew into the house and took his seat at the table, sullen and mad. He scowled at Danny and didn't offer to drive the English folks anywhere. No matter where he had hidden that car, it would be tire-deep in snow by now. Sol had to stifle a smile at the thought of the car left running by Danny. It was wrong of his boy to mess with the car, but Sol couldn't help but find pleasure at the thought of the car's engine freezing up in this storm. *Too bad! Ha!*

After watching Zach wolf down his meal, Sol offered a silent prayer to give thanks back to God for daily bread. He stood and plucked his coat from the wall peg. "Danny and Zach and I will go check on the stock."

"Sol, let me help you." C.J. grabbed his coat and hat from the wall peg. "Let the boys stay in the warm kitchen. Heaven knows Zach earned a reprieve."

Zach frowned and Sol knew why. It bothered him to be referred to as a boy. He was itching to be considered a man.

Zach pushed back his chair and stood. "I'm fine." He rubbed the top of Danny's head. "Let him stay."

"But I need mice!" Danny looked at his father with panic. "To feed the owl!"

Sol nodded. "I'll bring your mice. When I get back, we'll finish up that puzzle."

"Stay out of the pond," Mattie told Zach, lifting her eyebrows with an innocent look. "That's your only dry coat."

"I'll do my best," Zach said. He cast a glance in Sol's direction with just a wisp of mischief coming through. "If I forget, I'm sure Mr. September will remind me."

Sol tried to doff Zach's hat, but Zach expected it and stepped closer to the door. He braced himself before heading out the door, pausing for a moment with his hand on the door handle. He took a deep breath and rushed outside. Sol and C.J. followed behind and Tucker dashed through the door before it closed.

As Mattie collected the plates, she basked in a feeling of sweet relief. How kind of that English fellow to offer help so that Danny could stay inside! It was much too cold outside for a little boy. But her relief went deeper than that. She could hardly bear having Danny away from her. She knew it wasn't right to feel so anxious about a child. She couldn't seem to help it and the thought troubled her. So many things troubled her. Things she couldn't tell anyone about. Not her mother or her sisters-in-law or her best friend, Carrie. Not Sol, either. Everyone expected Mattie Riehl to be the strong one and she wouldn't disappoint them. But oh, she longed to spill all the troubling thoughts that had plagued her lately.

Who could possibly comprehend, though? Who could understand that she was turning into someone she hardly recognized? Going to baby showers for her friends and sisters-in-law and feeling so terribly envious that they were popping babies out right and left, while her arms remained empty. Everyone was kind, but she knew they pitied her. She knew that she was now defined by her faulty womb. *Mattie's the one having difficulty. Something's wrong, poor thing.*

This time, conceiving after so many years, she was sure she would finally have another baby. When the bleeding came, it nearly undid her. She couldn't get out of bed for days. The doctor told Sol it was to be expected with so much blood loss, but she knew it was more than that.

She gathered every dirty dish and utensil from the table, as well as the English woman's plate that still held leftover chow-chow. She must not have liked it; she left it untouched on her plate. The English man ate everything.

Mattie had shooed away an offer of dishwashing help from the English woman. She could tell the woman didn't have much experience in a kitchen, and she could clean the dishes in half the time without someone asking her what to do or where a bowl went.

When Mattie finished with the dishes, she glanced over at Danny, sitting cross-legged on the floor with the barn owl in his lap. That was when she noticed that Jaime was crouched on the floor, just a few feet away from Danny and the owl, snapping pictures of them with that fancy camera.

Mattie reached out and pulled the camera out of Jaime's hands. "While you're in our home, I expect you to respect our ways," Mattie said in a sharp tone. As soon as the words left her mouth, she wished them back. The shocked look on her son's face shamed her. What was the matter with her? What made her snap at a stranger like that?

Jaime rose to her feet. "I'm sorry. I thought . . . they made such a sweet sight."

Mattie took a deep breath. She laid the camera on the table and sat down. "We Amish, we don't want our pictures taken."

"I thought it was different with children," Jaime said. "Before they were baptized. I thought it was just adults who were off-limits."

"Ask, first," Mattie said, more gently.

Jaime tucked a stray curl behind her ear. "Of course, you're right. I'm sorry. I'm a photographer. That's what I do. It's who I am. I just . . . I looked over at them and in my mind, I saw the picture. I just . . . I did what I do."

Mattie softened. "So this piece of metal is why you sent my poor cousin into that frigid pond?"

Jaime's eyes went wide, then she burst into a laugh when she saw that Mattie was teasing. She reached over and picked up the camera. "I would've dived in after it myself, if he'd only let me. I've only had this camera for a few months. It takes amazing pictures." She let out a sigh. "C.J. thinks I take better pictures with my old camera. He thinks I rely too much on the bells and whistles of this digital camera and not enough on my instincts."

Mattie leaned forward in her chair and clasped her hands together. "That's the first time tonight you've stopped looking so worried!" She pulled a chair out for Jaime. She found herself fascinated by her, this English woman. She wasn't like the Amish women Mattie knew, who were so careful about what they said and how they said it. This woman just blurted out whatever was on her mind. She had a way of looking right at you as if she was searching for something, hoping you had the answer for her. Jaime had held the camera carefully, as gently as if it were a robin's blue egg. It was precious to her, Mattie could see that. "Your husband must have a lot of confidence in you, thinking your way of seeing is better than a camera's."

An odd, uncomfortable look came over Jaime's face. What was it? Guilt? No. No . . . it was misery. Whatever did this English woman have to feel miserable about? Mattie thought the woman was going to share what troubled her, but then Danny coughed and the woman looked startled, as if she had forgotten he was there. And the moment passed.

Mattie went over to Danny and put a hand on his forehead. "Maybe you should put on a sweater."

"Mom, I'm fine."

"A sweater is something a boy wears when his mother is chilly," Jaime said.

Mattie looked at Jaime strangely.

"It's a saying. Something my mother used to say."

Mattie turned back to Danny and pointed to the sweater lying on the bench by the door.

Danny sighed, deeply aggrieved, but got up and put it on. "Can't I go out and help Dad?"

"No," Mattie said. "Not in this storm. I'll whip up hot chocolate and popcorn."

Satisfied, Danny went into the other room to start working on the puzzle.

Mattie watched him for a moment, then asked Jaime, "You said you were going on a trip with your father for Christmas. Where's your mother?"

Jaime winced, as if that was the last question she had anticipated. "She passed away."

Mattie reached out and covered Jaime's hand. "You must miss her very much."

Jaime closed her eyes for a split second. "Oh, I do. I would give anything to have another day with her. Just one day."

The strange note of weariness in her voice touched Mattie's heart with pity. She gave Jaime's hand a slight squeeze. Then she turned her attention to filling a pot with milk from the refrigerator before setting it on the burner. She poured vegetable oil in the bottom of a large kettle, added popcorn kernels, and swished them all around so they would be covered in oil before covering the kettle with a heavy lid. She stayed by the stove to shake the kettle as the kernels popped. She could feel Jaime's eyes on her, watching, taking it all in. Was her kitchen so very different from an English person's kitchen?

"So, Jaime, tell me about taking pictures." She glanced back at her.

Jaime looked at Mattie curiously. "What do you want to know?"

"I want to know why you like to take pictures." She heard the oil start to sizzle and gave the kettle a shake. She glanced over her shoulder at Jaime. "What was the first picture you ever took?"

A sweet look came over Jaime's face. "My mother gave

me an inexpensive throw-away camera when I was seven. I snapped shots of everything a seven-year-old thinks is fascinating: spiderwebs, a cat's nose, a flower." She smiled. "My mom had the pictures developed at one of those one-hour places. I wouldn't leave the store so we waited by the counter until the pictures were done." She shook her head. "Those pictures were terrible, just terrible, but I was hooked from that moment on."

"Why?" Mattie asked. "Why were you hooked?" It was plain to see how much this meant to Jaime. Her entire face lit up as she talked about taking pictures.

"There is nothing more satisfying than capturing that one, perfect image," Jaime said. "I enjoy the trial and error of it all, tinkering with various positions and lighting and composition until I get it right. I love the variety of the work. And I guess the photographs make me feel like I matter. As if I had something to say, and I can use photographs to say it." She shook her head. "Probably sounds silly to an Amish farmwife."

Mattie was quiet for a long moment. A few kernels of popcorn started to pop so she held on to the kettle's edges with two potholders and gave it a hard shake. "What kinds of pictures do you most like to take?"

"Outdoor photographs—of nature, of wildlife. I enjoy the unpredictability of photographing the outdoors. So many things are out of your control—lighting or posing—but there are times when I capture something that just takes my breath away."

"Sounds challenging."

Jaime sighed. "It can be. Even indoors, in Sears Portrait Studio." She clicked something on her camera and the lens folded up. "Photography is a very competitive field. It's hard to stand out. I don't want to be just another two-bit photographer. I don't want to be ordinary, you know?"

Mattie pinched her lips together in a line, trying not to laugh.

"What?" Jaime asked, confused. "What did I say that was so funny?"

"Now *that* . . . that does sound silly to an Amish farmwife. Wanting to not be ordinary. We do everything we can to avoid standing out. You English . . . you do everything you can to draw attention to yourself."

"But . . . that's not what I mean. That's not what I'm like."

"No?" Mattie asked. She looked over at the wall pegs, filled with black coats and black hats and her own black bonnet. Jaime's red coat hung on the end peg. "You wear a bright red coat, for one. If that's not someone who wants to stand out in a crowd, I don't know what you'd call it."

Jaime frowned. "I guess what I meant is that I want to do something with my photography that makes a difference. I want to feel like this is what I was meant for, the reason I'm on this earth." She looked up at Mattie. "Haven't you ever felt that way about anything?"

Mattie was quiet as she took the kettle of popcorn off the burner and dumped the steaming popcorn into a large bowl. She drizzled melted butter on top and shook salt over it before setting it on the table. Danny came into the kitchen and sat on a chair to stir the popcorn with a large wooden spoon. Mattie stroked his hair. Motherhood was firmly ensconced in Mattie, anchored deeply in her body. "Yes," she told Jaime. "Oh, yes. I have felt that way."

Jaime followed the beam of flashlight that Danny held in front of her as they went up to the second story of the farmhouse. She had a new appreciation for central heating! The kitchen was warm and cozy and well-lit, but the rest of the house was pitch black, cold as a refrigerator. Danny opened up a door and shined the beam of the flashlight around it. Like the rest of the house, the furnishings were spare: a full-sized bed, a bureau, and a night table.

Danny went to the night table and picked up the lantern. "Mom won't let me use matches, but you can light this yourself."

Jaime went over to him. "Show me what to do."

He pulled off the glass hurricane and turned the wick up on the base of the kerosene lantern. "Here's where you light it."

Jaime tried to light a match, but her fingers were clumsy with cold. After watching her try three tries, Danny took the matchbox from her and lit a match, held it to the wick, then put the hurricane back on the lantern base.

"Mom said to show you where the bathroom was." He picked up the flashlight and went back out to the hall.

She followed behind him. "Do you use a lantern in your room?"

"No. Just a flashlight. She worries I'll read too late and a lantern would catch fire."

"Most moms tend to worry a lot."

Danny nodded solemnly before opening another door. He beamed the light around a small bathroom with a big porcelain tub, a sink, and a toilet.

Indoor plumbing! Jaime didn't really know what to expect

inside an Amish farmhouse, but she wasn't sure she should expect indoor plumbing. Hallelujah!

"There are towels on the hooks. Mom said she put a nightgown for you on your bed and a new toothbrush in the bathroom." He turned and walked down the hallway back to her bedroom. At the door, he scrunched up his small face, peering at her intently through his glasses. "Maybe my mom doesn't need to know that I lit the match."

"We'll keep that our secret. After all, you were just helping me, Danny. Thank you."

He gave her a shy smile. "Thanks for bringing my whistle back. My dad made it for me after we found a snowy owl's nest. They migrate here for the winter. They can find their prey by listening for it, even under the snow."

"No kidding? I would love to photograph a snowy owl."

"Sometime, I'll take you to see a bald eagles' nest. It's made of sticks, with clumps of grass inside to line it like velvet. It's as big as—" He looked toward the door to see if anyone was coming. "It's as big as a 1983 Toyota Corolla. The eagles moved in and built the nest last spring and no one knows they're here. I'm not telling anyone."

"Why not?"

An uncomfortable look passed over Danny's face. "If the game warden knows, he'll post no trespassing signs up on our property but those are like an advertisement for folks. They'll come with their binoculars and telescopes and cameras and set up camp." He pushed his glasses up on his nose. "Eagles are the most amazing birds you ever could believe. They have a wingspan," he stretched his arms as wide as he could, "as big as this. Eight or nine feet." He sat on the bed. "But if you come with me you'll have to wear glasses. Did you know that predators go after the eyes of their prey? Even spitting cobras. They have perfect shots that spit poison right at an animal's eyes—"

"Danny!" Mattie's voice floated up the stairs.

He jumped off the bed at the sound of his mother's voice and gave Jaime a wave as he slipped out the door. Mattie did keep a close watch on her son, Jaime noticed. Almost as if she didn't want him out of her sight for more than a moment or two. Jaime closed the door as Danny's light footsteps jumped down the stairs. That boy was intriguing. He was small for his age but talked like a docent at a natural history museum. She found herself unexpectedly drawn to him. He reminded her of . . . a little of herself as a child. Serious, studious, more comfortable with adults than with other children. But unlike Danny, she was always trying, trying, trying to fit in, like a square peg in a round hole. She always felt she was missing something essential, something everyone else in the world seemed to have.

A father.

She thought of all of the lies she had told when she was Danny's age to excuse the inexcusable absence of her father: He's a spy for the CIA. He's a scientist who studies melting glaciers. He works six months at Antarctica, six months at the Arctic Pole. And her favorite: he's in the Federal Witness Protection Program. Her ruses worked for a few years, but soon, the kids grew wise to her. And far less tolerant of someone who didn't fit their mold. Her mother dragged her to a counselor once, concerned that Jaime had no friends. The counselor asked Jaime why she didn't just tell kids the truth.

The truth was simpler, but far less intriguing—and it was

too painful. Her father didn't want to be a father. Or maybe he just didn't want to be *her* father.

She wondered if other children picked on Danny the way she had been picked on. She was always happier out in nature, among wildlife, where no one made fun of her, especially about her hair: Woody Woodpecker. Medusa. Cardinal head. Her mother told her to pay no mind to others, that one day she would love her hair. Well, she was now at the advanced age of twenty-five and she still hated it.

C.J. loved her hair. He said it was the first thing he noticed about her—that day when she was assigned to photograph the Search and Rescue training. He had made her feel beautiful for the first time ever in her life. He would tangle his hands in her wild mop of hair and implore her to promise that she would never cut it. She would laugh and tell him he was crazy, but she would never promise that she wouldn't cut it. Someday, she knew she would find the right haircut for her mess of hair.

And that's just what happened. Her father appeared one day, not long after her mother had died, treated her to a haircut at a very expensive salon, and voilà! Her hair looked the way she had always wanted it to. Short, straight, asymmetrical. It looked amazing! At least, for the rest of that day. She had never been able to style it the way the hair salon had. And the new short style made it surprisingly high maintenance, requiring frequent haircuts. Trying to make curly hair straight required expensive bottles of mysterious potions and sprays. Plus a vicious-looking hair iron.

The look on C.J.'s face when she came home from the hair salon that first time still irked her. He looked betrayed. As hurt as if she had brought home a lover. But she had never promised not to cut it. After all, it was her hair!

And it wasn't long after that she noticed how often he brought up the name of Eve. *That* Eve. That home-wrecker.

A month or so later, he started staying late to work on a project with her. A project. What kind of project would a junior high math teacher and a school receptionist have in common? The thought would not recede: C.J. was having an affair.

Once, she almost asked him how he felt about Eve, but the words clogged in her throat like a dammed-up river. It was just as well. What if C.J. said he cared for Eve, what would happen then? It was better not knowing, she decided. It was better to hope somehow she was wrong than to know she was right.

It's sad, Jaime pondered, how the feeling of falling in love doesn't last forever. She thought back to how wonderful things had been with C.J. when they were first dating, over three years ago now. He had courted her with a slow, persistent patience, showing up at Sears Portrait Studio, solid and steady, week after week, offering a fistful of flowers or some other corny gift, the pleasure on his face so real that she could not bear to turn him away.

She'd never met anyone like C.J. He was funny, charming, self-deprecating. As they zipped around streets in Stoney Ridge—a town she had grown up in and he was new to—he pointed out things she never would have noticed on her own. Well, that wasn't entirely true—she did notice things. But they were *things*. The unusual architecture of an old, neglected house. C.J. would look at the same house and ask her what she thought the couple was like who first built the house. Were they young or old? Did they build it large to accommodate a growing family? "Can't you just hear the quiet echoes of their voices, Jaime? Children, now grown, playing in the backyard? A mother and father on the front porch, sipping lemonade on a hot summer night?" And the funny thing was—she started to see what he saw. How an object related to a person. C.J. was all about relationships. At that point, Jaime's photography jumped a level in subtlety and sophistication; even she could see the difference.

She was driving to a freelance assignment on a winter morning, just after a snowfall, and came across three Amish quilts hanging on a clothesline. Nothing else was around, just those vibrant, brilliantly colored quilts against a white backdrop. She pulled over, put a roll of fresh film into her camera, and used up the entire roll. She took them back to develop in the makeshift darkroom in her apartment—a seldom-used bathroom. She adjusted the lighting so the vibrant patterns of quilts would pop against the crystalline detail of the snow.

Later, C.J. studied the picture. That was when he said to her, "The composition of this photograph is pure genius, Jaime. You should send this in."

"To what?"

He handed her an entry form for a national photography contest sponsored by *National Geographic*. "To this."

"That's crazy!" It was something she had never considered, although she wasn't sure why not. Failure, she supposed. She couldn't bear the thought of failing at something she cared so much about. But he convinced her to send it in.

She wondered if C.J. ever regretted it, knowing that contest would become the point in their relationship when the ground shifted. As real as if they had been tectonic plates that lined up against each other until an earthquake split them into a yawning crevasse. That's what winning the contest felt like—an earthquake.

Because that was the moment her father first began to notice her. That was the point when he started to call her, to invite her to New York, to provide guidance to help build her career, to surprise her with thoughtful gifts. To act like a father.

Jaime picked up Mattie's nightgown but decided she was so cold she didn't want to get out of her clothes. She piled quilts on top of the bed and shivered as she climbed between the chilly sheets. The sheets were white and crisp, the pillows so soft it was like sinking her head into whipped cream. Even still, she lay in bed, stiff and cold. How did the Amish live like this year-round? Didn't they know what they were missing? Electric blankets. Central heating. She would never get to sleep. It would be another night where she tossed and turned, waking exhausted and cranky.

She heard C.J. and Sol and Zach come inside, stomp the snow off their feet, and laugh over something. They seemed to hit it off. Not that it surprised her—everyone liked C.J.

As her eyes adjusted to the dark, she noticed the pattern of the quilt on the bed. It was an enormous white star with rays spread out across a field of midnight blue. In the murky light, the star looked jagged and broken as if it had fallen from the sky and shattered. She turned over on her side and punched up the pillow under her head. The wind whistled like a pipe, blowing shrill. The walls moaned in deep bass, resonating in her bones.

Sol's voice, laughing as he and Danny worked on a puzzle together, floated up the stairs. Mr. September. As she listened to him laugh and tease his son, she adjusted her assessment of him once again. There was more to him than she had thought there was at dinner, when she assumed he was a fellow all tied up in his own righteousness. There was more to all of them than she had first thought. These Amish weren't at all what she expected. A little odd, but oddly appealing.

Take Mattie. She seemed to genuinely want to know why Jaime was so interested in photography. Of all things for an Amish woman to ask about! She never would have thought she and Mattie would have such an instant rapport as they did tonight, after the men left to go to the barn. As they talked in that little kitchen—a homey, comforting place, accompanied with the soft gurgling of the oil in the lamp as background music—Jaime felt the freedom to open up about her life in a way she didn't with anyone else. It wasn't long before the two women were talking to each other about all kinds of things. It felt good to talk to another woman. Mattie listened, really listened to her, and didn't try to fix everything. She just empathized. At one point, Jaime couldn't believe she was here, talking so intimately with a stranger. It was odd but thrilling too, like confiding in a person you met on a train or a bus.

Jaime even told Mattie about her father's offer to set her up with an agent in New York City. "It's amazing, really, to think my father would help me at all," she confided in Mattie. "He used to say that photography is a hobby, not a career. And that a woman needs to be able to support herself."

The puzzled look on Mattie's face surprised Jaime. For a moment, Jaime had forgotten how different their worlds were.

When Mattie asked how C.J. felt about giving up his teaching job and his Search and Rescue work to move to New York

City, Jaime said they hadn't worked everything out yet. That wasn't technically true. They hadn't worked anything out yet, because C.J. didn't know about it.

"You see, I didn't really think I wanted to move until this week. Then, suddenly I did. I really want to live in New York. I want to sign with this agent and do some big-time photography." She knew she couldn't stand another year being stuck in Sears Portrait Studio, photographing unhappy babies. Or crying toddlers in ballerina tutus. Or little girls dressed up in so many ruffles they looked like Victorian valentines. Or cats. So many people wanted their cat in their annual Christmas picture! This morning's cat with Mrs. Peterson did her in. Jaime had scratches all over her hands from that hostile cat. After the shoot, she went straight to the manager's office and told her she wouldn't be coming back after Christmas. She quit!

Jaime expected to see judgment in Mattie's eyes. Instead, she saw understanding. Mattie covered Jaime's scratched-up hand with her own and said, "It can be hard to say important things to the person in our life who matters the most."

Jaime flipped onto her back and looked up at the ceiling. It was so dark outside that no moonlight shone through the clouds, but she could see the ceiling was painted the same glossy color as the walls. Pale blue.

Mattie had made an odd, poignant remark that struck at Jaime's heart—it penetrated so deeply that she excused herself and went to bed.

"Poor communication doesn't disconnect souls," Mattie said. "It's the disconnected souls who poorly communicate." Then she added, "But love is so much more than words."

What did *that* mean? *Does she think I'm disconnected with my soul?* Suddenly, Mattie's words became clear to Jaime. *She thinks I'm disconnected from C.J.*

Me? It's C.J. who is disconnected from me. He's the one who's cheating! If it hadn't happened yet, it wouldn't be long before it was an actual affair. Twice during dinner tonight, C.J. mentioned that Eve woman. Twice! Once when they were talking about Tucker, and he said how Eve loved Tucker so much that she took him out for walks at lunch. And then, later, he thought Eve might enjoy Mattie's recipe for chow-chow. When Mattie asked him who Eve was, he said she was just a co-worker. *Just a co-worker.*

Mattie might be insightful—surprisingly astute—but she obviously wasn't clairvoyant. *You missed that one, Mattie. It sailed right past you.*

Just a few hours ago, Jaime had thought of Mattie as a plain woman. The plainest of Plain women. Yet tonight, in the soft lantern light in the kitchen, Jaime reframed that opinion. Mattie was intriguing. She was not a beautiful woman, but yet she *was*, because she was completely herself. She was slender; she carried herself with a dancer's grace and reserve. But there was something else she carried, as obvious as her plum-colored dress and white prayer cap: a mark of strength and wisdom, of motherhood.

Jaime knew she ought to feel sorry for Mattie; her father certainly would. Mattie lived in a drafty old farmhouse and had a husband who worked as a farmer. They would never make much money. She had never been on an airplane in her life. Or a cruise! But the three of them—Mattie, Sol, Danny—they were a happy family. Unlike Jaime's father, Sol was home. And when he wasn't, they always knew where to find him. Mattie's home was filled with peace, comfort, and constant, safe companionship. Jaime felt a growing tickle of admiration for these Plain people.

Whenever Jaime had thought of her father—there had been no one to picture. It had always been just Jaime and her mother, Connie, and random checks from her father that would arrive without any note included. There was never anyone to help them out, no man in Jaime's childhood. She grew up with an empty spot inside, a part of her missing. A hole. A *black* hole.

C.J. had come from a completely different kind of home. Simple but loving. Like the Riehls'. C.J.'s solidness was one of the qualities that drew Jaime to him. He was a rock. He had a genuine interest in the lives of people. He remembered their names, their children's names, their situations—if they were thinking of buying a new car, or if they were caring for an elderly parent, or if their dog had just died. This was stuff he cataloged in his brain. It was unusual how much he remembered, how much he truly cared. People lapped it up. Everyone adored C.J.

She was the opposite—happier to be out in the woods, behind the lens of a camera, observing, alone with her interior life. When people asked her too many questions, she felt like she was being pecked at by chickens.

Downstairs, a peal of laughter burst out of Danny. Jaime wondered what had made him laugh. There was something about that little boy that touched her. The way he looked, so small and thin and solemn. The way he talked and asked big questions and the brightness of his laughter that was like a glow on his face. She felt as if . . . well, if she ever had a child, she would want him to be like Danny.

What was she thinking?! She didn't even *like* children! And worse—they didn't like her! Babies and children always cried when they were in the studio, no matter what tricks she used to get them to smile in their picture.

She had come to bed early to try to get much-needed rest. She wished she had thought to put those stupid sleeping pills in her coat pocket instead of her purse—which was in the car. She was sure it was going to be one of *those* nights, when her mind spun and her brain pleaded for the relief of sleep but her body would not oblige.

Jaime punched the pillow again and rolled over, watching the snow whirl through the undraped window. She felt an aching sadness that she couldn't understand. A hollow emptiness. What would fill it?

She didn't know.

The house was quiet. That was perhaps the most noticeable difference, C.J. thought, between living in town and living in the country. The absence of noise. He slipped into the full-size bed next to Jaime, careful not to waken her. Tucker jumped up on the bed right behind him and C.J. pushed him down toward the footboard before the dog bounced on Jaime. He rubbed Tucker's head and whispered to him to lie down. Tucker peered at him solemnly before curling into a ball and releasing a big sigh. Then C.J. stretched out. He never would have believed he would end this day—the day before Christmas Eve—needing refuge at an Amish farmhouse. In the dark, he smiled. He had a new appreciation for Mary and Joseph, seeking shelter and finding it in an unlikely place, before the very first Christmas.

When Jaime's car went into the pond, he felt horrified— both at her carelessness but also at what it meant. It wasn't that he minded missing a day with Jaime's father—just the opposite. The thought relieved him. And it wasn't his fault! Surely, James MacComber couldn't blame a storm on C.J. that was walloping the entire Eastern seaboard.

James was convinced Jaime had married beneath her, which was ironic because he had just become interested in getting to know his daughter. James made no secret of how he felt about C.J. A junior high teacher barely scratching out a living in a small town in southeastern Pennsylvania—who had turned down a promotion to become an assistant principal. He'd never forget the afternoon when James called and Jaime told him C.J. had turned down the opportunity. There was dead silence. C.J. counted down in his mind: *5, 4, 3, 2, 1.* And then the grenade blew up! "He did *WHAT?*" C.J. heard James's voice echo across the room. He knew James could never understand that C.J. loved being a teacher and had no desire to get into administration. No indeed, it didn't bother C.J. to have a bona fide reason to spend one day less this Christmas with his father-in-law.

But how could they impose on this Amish family? Mattie, in particular, couldn't have been kinder about the intrusion. She could sense C.J.'s discomfort. As she handed him a pair of her husband's pajamas to wear, she told him, "God doesn't make mistakes. He has a reason for bringing you here."

He thought it must be wonderful to have that kind of solid faith. This year, he had started attending church and tried talking Jaime into going with him. So far, no luck.

"Are you asleep?" Jaime whispered.

He turned onto his back. "I thought you were. I was trying to be quiet."

"How could anyone possibly sleep with a dog the size of a humpback whale taking over the bed?"

C.J. grinned and lifted his head. "Did you hear that, Tuck? She called you a whale." Tucker let out a soft snore at the foot of the bed. "He forgives you. He's not easily offended."

"Hmmph," Jaime murmured.

C.J. folded his hands behind his head. He stretched out in the bed, careful not to disturb Tucker, and wriggled closer to her. "Maybe this is how the Amish have so many children. Small beds and cold winters."

"Not this family."

"No. When we were in the barn, Sol told me that Mattie had just miscarried."

Jaime stilled.

C.J. looked over at her. "He said that was why they were at the doctor's today. That they had met you there."

"Danny left the whistle at the doctor's office."

"Mind telling me why you were at the doctor's?"

She blew out a deep breath. "Just a prescription I needed."

"For . . ."

Jaime turned to face the window. "For some sleeping pills. In case I needed them for the trip."

C.J. sat up and leaned on his hands, peering over her at the window. "Looks like Mother Nature might have a say in that. I'm not sure we'll be able to get a tow truck out here tomorrow."

"What? It can't take long to get those roads plowed."

"Sol says another storm is right behind this one. A storm from the north is blowing through. It's supposed to bring twice as much snow." He stretched back on the bed. "Funny thing is, I don't really mind. I kind of like this. It feels like a chance to slow down and think about things. Important things." He leaned up on one elbow to face her. "We've needed time like this. We've needed it for a long while. There's a lot we need to talk over."

They lay in silence for a time, listening to the wind, to the crack of a frozen tree branch that snapped off in a gust.

It was easier in the dark like this, to talk. "It seems as if we're growing apart, Jaime, and it worries me. I know the last year has been difficult, with your mother passing. And suddenly your father is in your life. I still feel badly about that weekend when your father was visiting and I had my first . . . unsuccessful search." He couldn't say it aloud. Deceased Finds. "The timing was just bad." It had taken him a long time to get over that event. He had felt like such a failure. He couldn't even talk about it with Jaime. He raised his hand to stroke her cheek, but then thought better of it. He let it fall without touching her.

"It's not your fault. It's not anybody's fault."

Were they talking about the same thing? These days they were like two planets, orbiting without colliding, but not drawing any closer either. "What isn't?"

"Drifting apart. Sometimes, it just happens."

Why did her voice sound so settled, so defeated? "Jaime, this is no way to have a marriage."

She was quiet. "No. It isn't."

"We can do better."

"I suppose you're right." Her voice was flat and the answer was quick, like she didn't even have to think about it. What was the undercurrent he heard in those words? Disappointment? Resignation?

The comfort of the darkness gave way to a deeper unease and a chill went through C.J. He didn't want to hear any more. "We'd better get some sleep." He rolled onto his side, away from Jaime. "I love you, Jaime."

"Me too, you, but sometimes love is just not enough."

C.J. lay awake, unable to sleep, running over their conversation in his mind. He'd wanted to connect with Jaime, to have a moment when they understood each other, but his good intentions had spiraled into distance.

The wind smacked against the house, startling Mattie awake. She was disoriented for a moment, aware only of the cold that lay thick and deep around her. Then a fresh gust slammed against the wall, making it moan. Or was that Danny?

She slipped out of bed to go check on him in his room. She touched a hand to his forehead; his skin was warm and damp. He had Sol's thick eyelashes, which curled against his cheek when he slept. There was no more beautiful sight than her child asleep. She loved Danny so profoundly, his perfect little body and all the complexity it contained. *My child,* she thought. *My son.*

He stirred and mumbled a few words that she couldn't make out before he settled back into his dreams. What did a six-year-old boy dream about? A scooter? A pony? A cart to go with it? Those were the things he wanted most, and he made Mattie set timelines. Can I have a scooter when I'm seven? Can I have a pony when I'm eight? Danny was charging through his childhood, eager to be as old as Zach.

"Slow down, sweet boy," Mattie whispered, and covered him.

He was so capable, so independent, so smart. He had

taught himself to read when he was three, he knew his addition and subtraction tables up to ten by age four, he kept a list of rare animals that he and Sol spotted—bog turtle, piping plover, Indiana bat.

Slow down, sweet boy.

As soon as he learned to talk, a day with Danny was one long conversation, filled with unanswerable questions. Why is the sky blue? How far away is the moon? Did you know a blue whale's heart is as big as a small car?

Slow down, sweet boy.

She stood for a minute in the wind-echoing room with her hand on the doorknob, moved by Danny's smallness, by all the ways she would not be able to protect her son in the world. She closed the door softly and stopped by Zach's room when she noticed the light under the door.

She knocked gently and poked her head in the door. "Can't sleep?"

Zach lifted his book. "In the middle of a good chapter." He yawned.

She took a few steps inside and leaned against the wall, crossing her arms against the cold. She and Zach were more than ten years apart in age, but they'd always had a special closeness. He was right on the precipice of leaving the church. She sensed the restlessness within him. The knowledge didn't trouble her, not like it did her uncle Eli. The way it bothered Sol. She felt about Zach the way she used to feel about Sol— she saw the man he could be. She knew Zach would make the right decision . . . in the end, if he could have a little room right now to think it all through for himself. But instead of giving him some margin, Zach's parents had cut him off. In their minds, he had two choices. Settle down and become baptized, or leave now. All that his parents had succeeded in doing was to drive Zach further away.

"How bad off is your car?"

He closed the book. "Bad. Couldn't even start it. The ignition was frozen. The key broke off."

"I'm sorry," she said, meaning it. Danny should not have been fooling around in that car. When did he get into it, anyway? She watched him like a hawk. "I can't remember a storm like this one." Every hour, the temperature dropped a few more degrees and the windchill stirred the air to make it even colder.

"Bet those English folks are feeling the cold," Zach said with a devilish grin. He didn't look at all sorry for them.

"They seem very grateful to be here."

Zach shrugged.

"I had a good talk with the English woman while you were all out in the barn. She's not what she seems."

Zach put his book down. "What's that supposed to mean?"

"I suppose that she might have seemed a little selfish, at first, letting you go into that cold pond. But there's turmoil in her life. She reminds me of a lost little lamb. I think she's trying to decide something important."

"And what would that be? Which new shoes to buy?"

Mattie smiled. "I'm just saying . . . that maybe God brought them here for a reason. Maybe we can help them."

"Mattie, she's not one of those stray puppies that follow you home. You can't fix everybody."

"Just . . . give her a chance. We should be pitying her for her lostness. Maybe . . . you could be a little . . . nicer."

He rolled his eyes at her and she smiled, then she left. As she walked down the hallway to her bedroom, she caught a reflection of herself in the night-blackened glass window, illuminated by the glow from her flashlight. The woman who stared back at her was not herself at all, but a stranger who looked so thin and so sad. She put her hands up to her face and squeezed. *Stop! Stop feeling so sad!*

Behind her, Sol slipped his arms around her waist. She felt the tickle of his beard as his lips grazed her neck. "Were you watching our son sleep again?"

She leaned her back against him and covered his hands with hers. "I thought I heard him call out."

Sol's hands were warm, large, and comforting. He had been so patient all these years, so reassuring. Always optimistic that they would have more children. She raised his hand and kissed his palm, strong, rough with calluses, marked with lines. She placed his hand on her heart, held it there.

"You worry too much about the wrong things, Mattie." He kissed the top of her head. "He's nearly seven years old. You hardly let him out of your sight. He needs to be doing much more around the farm with me. Like other boys his age. Most eight-year-olds can do the work of a man."

She stiffened. "Danny's *not* like other children his age."

"That's why we need to give him more practical experiences. More chances for him to learn skills."

"That's not what I meant. He's small for his age. He can't do the kind of work you and Zach do. It isn't fair to expect so much."

"That's not what I'm saying. It's time that we give him more responsibility. More independence."

This wasn't a new conversation between them. It went round and round, like a loop. It was the same discussion that they'd been having for two years now. Sol said their boy was trying hard to grow up and she shamed him with her fussing. She felt he didn't understand the way Danny was. The way she felt.

Sol turned her around to face him and pulled her close. She felt the press of his beard against her neck.

"I know you're hurting, Mattie. I know how much you want to fill this house with children. But we still need to raise the boy we have into a man."

Mattie was still for a long time, listening to the wind, her head resting on Sol's chest. She knew, deep down, that he was right. He was a good husband to her, a good father to Danny. But her desire to be a mother was a physical, painful hunger. She could think of nothing else. Tears pricked her eyes, and her throat ached. A deep sense of loss rose up in her, so forceful, woven from month after month of spoiled dreams for a baby. Tears were slipping down her cheeks. "It's not fair," she whispered.

"It's not fair," Sol agreed.

He kissed her then, full on the lips, and pulled her close. She pressed her cheek against his, taking in his scent and warmth.

"Come to bed," he invited.

She nodded and put her hand in his.

CHRISTMAS EVE

Zach woke with a start and jumped out of bed. He had promised Sol he would check on that laboring ewe before dawn. He threw on his clothes, shivering as the cold fabric touched his body. He tried to creep quietly down the stairs so he wouldn't wake Sol. Mattie's husband liked to think that they were cut from the same cloth, but Zach knew better. Sol acted more like a father to him than a cousin. He didn't want to risk a disapproving look from Sol if he forgot that ewe. He got plenty of those dark looks from his own dad.

When he reached the bottom step, he was surprised to find Queen Bee sitting at the kitchen table, fully dressed, with the yellow dog sitting beside her. The lantern on the table created a glowing circle around her. Queen Bee's hair, which had been loose yesterday, was now held in a stubby ponytail, and little ringlets fell around her neck. Wide blue eyes the color of a summer sky. He had definitely admired her looks—as soon as he recovered from the dip in the pond—but this morning, she looked different. Cheerful and sweet and pretty. And pretty old, he guessed. Maybe twenty-five or thirty.

"Uh, we won't be having breakfast for a while," he told her.

She shrugged. "I couldn't sleep. Thought I'd just come downstairs and read for a while. It's warmer down here."

Zach glanced at the grandfather clock. "I need to go out to the barn and check on the animals." He headed to the door, then turned back. "There's a ewe that might be lambing soon." He noticed Jaime's camera, left on the table. "If you want to take a picture of something special, a lamb born on Christmas Eve . . . I wouldn't object." He reached for her red coat, plucked it off the wall peg, and held it out for her. He wasn't really sure why he thought she might like to see the newborn lamb. He supposed it was Mattie's comment that Queen Bee seemed like a lost little sheep herself.

The delighted look on Jaime's face warmed him. Ah—he was a sucker for attractive women. It was one of the complaints he had about being Amish—the women were just so bland looking. His thoughts drifted to Susie Blank, his particular friend, and he felt a twinge of guilt. Susie wasn't bland. She was pretty, with thick chestnut hair and emerald green eyes. And she had an effect on him that could make his thoughts travel down dangerous and wicked paths. He stole a glance in Jaime's direction as she put on her coat and hat and gloves, then tucked her camera inside her jacket.

She looked up at him and gave him a dazzling smile. "Ready?"

Nope. Cute as she was, even Susie Blank did *not* hold a candle to this English woman.

A blast of cold air shocked Jaime when Zach opened the door. The cold stung like needles on her face. She debated if she really wanted to bother venturing out in that bitter, black cold only to end up in a bitter, black, and cold barn.

When she started to complain, Zach turned to her and said, "Are you always this whiny?"

Pretty much, she thought. At least this past year. But that was going to change, starting now.

Tucker didn't seem to mind the cold at all. He bolted out of the door and disappeared into the dark to find a private place to relieve himself. Zach paid no mind to either of them. Suddenly remembering Jaime, he pointed out the holes he made with his boots so she could follow in his tracks. The flashlight he held in front of him cast a bright circle onto the snow.

Just trying to walk across the yard to the barn felt like climbing a mountain, the wind was pushing that hard against them. Finally, Zach pulled open the barn door, yanked Jaime in, and shut it tightly just as Tucker slipped around his feet and into the barn.

At the sound of someone coming, the animals stirred in their stalls, murmuring and huffing. It was pitch black inside, as dark as if they were in a box. Zach pulled off a glove and lit a match against the wall. He shielded the flame with his other hand and took a few steps to where a lantern hung on the wall. The match blew out before he had time to light the wick, so he set the lantern down, crouched next to it, and lit another match. The wick sputtered, then caught, splaying light into the shadows.

Jaime's eyes watered at the sour stink of sheep and cows and horses and pigs and hay and manure. She nearly gagged but fought it back; she was eager to photograph the birth of a lamb. Zach laughed when he saw her pinch her nostrils together. His smile, she thought, was like the sun coming from behind clouds. It was a dazzling smile. She watched Tucker, delighted by rich layers of earthy smells, make his way around the barn by sniffing the perimeters. A dog's paradise!

Zach walked over to the ewe's pen and motioned to Jaime to follow him. The two of them stood side by side, watching the ewe. Their breath came out in puffs of cloud, though Jaime felt better without the wind slicing through her coat.

"There," Zach said, pointing his chin toward the ewe. "See the shudder that runs through her belly? That's a labor pain."

The ewe's water had broken some time ago; the straw was littered with blood and birth mucus. The ewe dropped down on her front knees and lifted her bottom in the air. Her lips slipped back over her teeth, grimacing in pain.

"Can't you help her?" Jaime asked.

Zach picked up a piece of timothy hay. He dangled it from his lower lip and leaned against the rough boards of the lambing shed, crossing one foot over the other. "Nope. She's no amateur. She knows what she's doing."

The ewe raised her head to look at them with such a serene, gentle look despite her suffering that the sight took Jaime's breath away. She snapped a few shots of the ewe, hoping to capture the deep look in her eyes. It was haunting! She felt tears sting her eyes but fought them back. Lately her moods teetered precariously. They felt like a basket of fruit balancing on her head.

Zach plucked the hay out of his mouth and pushed himself off the shed wall. He took another flashlight and headed down the aisle of the barn, checking on each animal. Jaime remained transfixed by the ewe's stall, watching her body still as she prepared for each contraction that rippled through her body.

The ewe let out a deep moan and Jaime said, "Can't you do *something* to ease her pain?"

Zach emerged out of the shadows and looked at the ewe. "Pain isn't always a bad thing."

Oh, you're so wrong about that. Pain is a terrible thing. It chews up your insides and tears you apart.

He glanced at Jaime. "This kind of pain—this birthing pain—this is right and natural. It may hurt for a while, but soon, you'll see—she won't even remember it." His attention riveted back to the ewe. "Better get your camera."

Almost as if on cue, the ewe knelt down again and started to push. Jaime took picture after picture as the birthing sac pushed through the opening. Each time the ewe labored, a little black nose appeared—only an inch or two—and then disappeared. Finally, she gave a mighty heave and the lamb slid, bloody and sticky, into the straw. Zach jumped over the small railing and was right there to cradle the lamb. His fingers tore away the membrane from the tiny black nose. Jaime snapped frame after frame.

He picked up some hay to tickle the lamb's nose. The lamb sneezed, then gasped, then let out a loud, indignant *baa*! The ewe came around to sniff it, to make sure it was hers, Zach explained. Laughing, he collapsed into the straw, cuddling the bawling lamb in his lap. His mouth broke into a smile that blazed across his face like the explosion of light from a photographer's flash. He motioned to Jaime to come inside the stall, so she did as she continued to take pictures. She only stopped for a second when he asked if she was going to run out of film.

"It's digital," she said. "I have a huge card."

She was just about to show him how to view the pictures when the ewe decided the lamb must be hers and she let out some pleased-sounding bleats, nuzzling with her baby, nose to nose.

Lost in the moment, Jaime took more pictures. Finally, as the lamb settled in to nurse, she put her camera away. "Amazing, how white the lamb is and how dark the ewe is."

"That's dirt on the old ewe. Sheep don't clean themselves off like other animals do. A cat can clean itself. So can a dog. A bird gets into a birdbath. But sheep? They get dirty and stay that way. They don't mind being filthy. They're not the brightest creatures." He gave a short laugh. "Probably why the Bible often refers to us feeble-minded humans as sheep." He leaned his back against the stall. "The Lord is my shepherd, I shall not want. He leadeth me beside still waters, he maketh me lie down in green pastures, he restoreth my soul." He gave her a shy grin. "Do more beloved words exist?"

Jaime didn't know how to respond. She was startled—floored—to hear words of Scripture spill from this teenager's mouth as easily and naturally as if he was talking about the weather. She had heard those words all of her life, yet they seemed so alive, so real, here in an Amish barn.

Zach didn't seem to be expecting a response, which was good because she didn't have one. She wasn't on speaking terms with God at the moment. For over six months now. She hadn't been, ever since her mother's random, senseless death.

Sol woke at dawn when he heard someone thundering down the stairs. He recognized Zach's loud footsteps—the boy would have insisted he was being quiet. Sol thought about getting up to go into the barn with him, but then thought better of it. Zach was up and would check on the ewe and the other stock, his own bed was warm, his wife was sleeping next to him. Why get up? He had woken often during the night, restless, hearing the wind that battered the house and shook the windows. He couldn't remember a blizzard like this one. Every hour, the temperature dropped a few more degrees and the windchill stirred the air to make it even colder.

But then he heard a loud bang. It would be just like Zach to leave a barn door unlatched. Just last week, he left the sliding door to the barn wide open and two horses wandered out and down the driveway. Mattie stirred as he swung his feet out of bed onto the cold wooden floor.

"Go back to sleep. I just want to check that a barn door didn't fly open." He leaned back to bundle her up in the covers and kissed her on the forehead. He grabbed his shirt and pants, threw them over his shoulder, and quietly left the room. He looked through the hallway window at the barn and saw light from a lantern shining through a small window. No door seemed to be open. Still, he was wide awake now, and it was chore time.

He went into Danny's room and shook him gently on the shoulder to wake up. "We've got choring to do, son." Danny groaned and Sol smiled. That boy of his could sleep through a tornado. "Up. I mean it." He waited until he saw Danny's feet slip out of bed and onto the floor.

Danny followed Sol into the bathroom and sat on the edge of the tub, rubbing his eyes and yawning, while Sol shaved. It was their morning routine. Then, like always, one question spilled out of Danny: "What makes soap start to bubble?" It was followed by another unanswerable question, then another and another. Sol craned his head around to look at him. Danny and his questions! Soon, Danny was talking in that excited way of his and kicking his heels against the tub. Sol lathered his cheeks with soap from the soft brush, taking pleasure in listening to his son. The razor blade slid in smooth, clean strokes against his cheeks.

For a moment the whole world seemed to be held, suspended: the start of a new day, the sharp scent of laurel soap, and the animated voice of his son.

Zach and Jaime stood there for a while, gazing at the ewe and the lamb. Tucker trotted up to investigate, sniff, and get a pat on the head from Jaime. Satisfied all was well, he disappeared into the recesses of the barn for more sniffing.

It was Zach who broke the silence. "What do you want to name the lamb?"

"Can I?" Jaime said. "Hmmm . . . let's name her Noel. It's French for Christmas."

"Noel it is." He pronounced it as a man's name. "She's a he." Grinning, he rose to his feet.

She flipped the switch on her camera. "Here, look at these." She showed him the pictures through the screen. He was fascinated by it and stood right behind her shoulder. There was one picture where he was holding the lamb and laughing. She looked up at him, wondering if he would object. "I can delete it if you'd prefer."

Zach only grinned. "What a good looker that fellow is." He wiggled his eyebrows. "Just don't go showing that one around at church on Sunday."

"Oh, we won't be here on Sunday," she said. "Later this morning, we'll be on our way."

"Think so?" Zach asked, in a tone that implied she was kidding herself.

She spun to face him. "Absolutely. This storm can't last forever."

"Maybe not, but the *Almanac* says another one is right on its heels." He puffed out a big white cloud of breath to illustrate his point.

"What's the *Almanac*?"

Zach cocked his head. "*The Farmer's Almanac*. A book. Comes out every year. Something we rely on to tell us the weather."

"You're kidding, right?" She started to laugh, but then her face grew serious. "There are satellites out there, taking pictures of moving jet streams."

Zach shrugged. "I know about satellites. Amish aren't stupid, you know."

Jaime looked embarrassed. "I didn't mean—I just . . . I just can't believe that a book printed long ago could be more accurate than a satellite."

"Do they always get it right? Your weathermen."

A smile spread over Jaime's face. "No. They're right about half the time."

"Well, then, I guess the *Farmer's Almanac* isn't such a bad risk."

"So you really think another storm is on its way?" Her eyebrows knit together. "My father is expecting us. He planned this trip to the Caribbean for Christmas to help me through that first holiday without my mother."

"Where's your mother?"

"She died in a car accident about six months ago." She frowned. "My folks divorced when I was a baby. My father has been married and divorced . . . uh, let's see," she looked to the rafters, "four times now."

Zach's eyebrows arched, his mouth formed a silent O. She had shocked him and he didn't shock easily. It's not that all Plain marriages were perfect. Most were pretty happy, but he knew of a few couples who had troubles. Money troubles, usually. But they didn't just give up. Every couple knew what kind of commitment they faced when they wanted to marry. They married for life.

The ewe lay down on her side and the lamb cuddled in close beside her, practically disappearing under her woolly fleece.

"I don't know why I'm telling you all this."

Zach filled with warmth. He liked that she was confiding in him. "Maybe my cousin was right. Mattie usually is."

"Right about what?"

"Maybe the Lord brought you here this weekend for a reason."

"You make me smile—the way you talk."

"Good. You need to smile more."

She laughed and linked her arm through his. This, Zach decided, would forever be the moment in his life when he first felt like a man. Standing with a beautiful girl, with her arm entwined through his. Zach felt a sort of thrill when she touched him, and on the heels of that thrill was a worry. What was he thinking? She was married!

This was also when Jaime asked, "Zach, why aren't you living at home?" in a grave way, as though she knew there was more to the story than met the eye. And instead of giving his usual brush-off: "Just working for Sol," Zach expelled what felt like all the air from his lungs. "It's a long, boring story about a father and son."

She smiled gently. "I've got just enough time for a long and boring story."

It was the sincere and interested look in Jaime's face that opened the floodgates for him. He told Jaime things about the last year that he would never think of sharing with anyone else. About feeling so invisible to his father, so insignificant. She seemed fascinated by what he was telling her. He had grown up as the middle boy in a family of eight children; no one had paid close attention to him, ever. He told her thoughts he had never shared with another, not even with his friends. They had all been raised to not stand out—how could anyone understand his need to be noticed?

Zach explained how he and his friends had been caught by the police with alcohol, and his father blew up. "He didn't even ask me if I had been drinking. He just told me to get out. Told me I would sour my younger siblings like a bad apple. Soft and rotted."

"Had you? Been drinking?"

Zach scowled. "Well, yeah, but that's not the point. One little mistake! And he tosses me out like I'm a piece of junk." He kicked at the ground with his boot.

Jaime's eyes went wide. "Really? One little mistake?"

Zach gave her a sneaky sideways glance. "Maybe two or three." Or a dozen. Getting into trouble with the law was the last straw for his father. After he had been charged with an M.I.P., his father had told him that he washed his hands of him and that the Lord God would see fit to deal with him now. It was well known that Eli Zook and the Lord God held similar convictions on nearly every subject.

"Your father sounds like an intimidating man."

Zach kept his eyes on the ewe. "He gives me the same sort of feeling I get in church, and not a little fear in it." He smiled ruefully. "I'm my father's middle son. Most of my life, I spent working beside him. I was born to work. That's all I'm good for, in his eyes. And now, no matter where I go, I'm surrounded by my father's family. It's been a burden."

Jaime shrugged. "Or a treasure."

Maybe both, Zach thought. A burden and a treasure. When he had exhausted himself of all the frustration and anger and discouragement of the last year, she didn't say a word. "Now it's my turn to say that I don't know why I'm telling you this," he said.

"Maybe because I like to hear."

Jaime was a good listener. She did not automatically take his father's side, as Zach had expected. She was understanding his side; she was—still!—holding on to his arm. They just stood there in the peace of the morning, watching the ewe and her baby.

Finally, Jaime broke the silence. "Have you thought about leaving?"

"I've thought of nothing *but* leaving. The thing is . . . I love cars. Everything about them."

"Oh, me too! The smell of a new car is heaven."

He cocked his head at her. "I guess . . . I meant what's under the hood. The mechanics. The horsepower. The sound of a purring engine." They looked at each other. Her blue eyes matched his shirt. She was ridiculously, absurdly beautiful, and Zach looked into her blue eyes until he knew looking one more second wouldn't be good for him. It would be like eating too much chocolate.

He shifted his gaze and noticed her hand, resting on his arm. She had taken off her glove when she took pictures of the ewe. Her hand was so small! And so white. Impossibly soft and white. Her fingernails were painted dark pink; they looked like raspberries. *Enough!* he thought, and he may have actually spoken the word because when he glanced up at Jaime, she tilted her head and looked at him strangely, as if to say, *Enough what?*

He cleared his throat and looked away.

"Then, maybe a better question is, why do you stay?"

"Why?" Zach shrugged and kicked at a dirt clod on the ground. "It's hard to explain."

Despite the uncomfortable circumstances that brought him to Mattie and Sol's home, Zach felt himself growing attached to Danny. Danny followed him around the farm whenever he could slip away from his mother, wore his black felt hat tipped back on his forehead the way Zach did, saved cookies for Zach, he even started walking the way Zach walked—hands jammed deep in his pockets with a long gait. Last week, Danny told him, "I wish you were my brother." And Zach felt his heart grow three sizes.

To be adored? He loved it. A little kid affecting him this way? No one would have believed it.

In the kitchen, Sol fed the fire in the woodstove. He shook down the ashes and threw in some kindling before tossing in a log. The new wood settled into the fire with a pop and a hiss. It pleased him that Mattie was still sleeping. She needed her rest.

Danny came down the stairs and went straight to sit on the backdoor bench. He pulled on his boots and coat, waiting for Sol. Together, they made their way through the snow to the barn. When they got inside, the big yellow dog greeted them as if he was the welcoming committee to a barn frolic. Danny ran to the lambing pen where Zach and the English girl were standing together.

"You've got yourself a Christmas lamb!" Zach said when he saw them, grinning from ear to ear. "Mom and baby, happy and healthy."

Danny climbed through the slats to reach the lamb. First, though, he patted the ewe and congratulated her.

Sol watched the lamb nuzzle against Danny. "I'm sorry I missed it." He was too. There was nothing so wonderful as the birth of an animal. Something he never tired of.

"Would you like to see pictures of the lamb being born?" Jaime asked.

Sol surprised even himself with a quick nod. Jaime unzipped her camera bag and flicked on a switch, then brought the camera over to Sol to look through the viewing screen. Mesmerized, Sol looked at the pictures, frame after frame.

"It's as if you're just inches away," he said.

Jaime continued scrolling through images. When Sol saw the pictures of Danny, sitting in the kitchen, holding the barn owl, he inhaled sharply.

"I'm sorry!" Jaime said. "I didn't know it was wrong, not until Mattie told me. I'll delete them."

"No," Sol said firmly. The answer came up deep inside of him. "No. Leave them." He looked up at the ceiling rafters. "Maybe . . . you could send those pictures to us sometime."

Jaime clicked off the camera and tucked it back in the padded bag. An awkward silence was finally broken by Danny.

"The owl! I need to see if there's a mouse in the trap." He

leaped over the lambing pen, grabbed a flashlight, and ran toward the feed room. The sound of his footsteps echoed through the barn.

Jaime watched him disappear into the feed room. "I'll go help him." She hurried down the center of the barn. Tucker trotted behind her, tail up.

Sol's gaze was fixed on Zach. He saw Zach's eyes follow Jaime as she walked into the darkness. "Zachary," he said firmly. "No."

Zach shrugged and lifted his palms in the air, his eyes round with innocence. "What?"

"No." Sol shook his head. "For so many reasons, no."

Mattie rubbed a circle of frost on the kitchen window to peer outside toward the barn. She could see the lantern light streaming through cracks in the siding. She turned toward C.J., sitting at the table with a cup of coffee in his hand.

"Looks like they're still out there. Probably the ewe had her lamb." She wondered if Danny had dressed warmly enough. She thought she had heard him coughing, earlier this morning when Sol was shaving. But then, she hadn't slept well, and with the racket the wind was making, who knew if what she heard was a cough? Still, a sound woke her and then began the circle of endless worries. She blew air out of her mouth. *Stop. Stop, Mattie!*

C.J. stood. "I'll go out and help. I used to milk cows. I could squirt a stream of milk straight into the cat's mouth."

Mattie glanced at C.J., surprised by that comment. He wasn't nearly as tall as Sol, but he didn't look short either. A square-faced man with a cap of close-clipped blond hair and dark brown eyes and smooth-shaven cheeks. He wore jeans, a T-shirt, with a thick gray sweatshirt that said "Slippery Rock State University." He had a clean, friendly look about him. Not so much handsome as wholesome looking. And he had a way of smiling, she thought, that was just with his eyes. But what she found most appealing of all about him was his way with Danny.

Last night after dinner, C.J. started telling silly knock-knock jokes. Danny laughed so hard that he nearly fell off his chair. She loved watching Danny laugh with abandon. "Don't go. They should be back in just a few minutes. Those boys like their time together in the barn."

"Well, this morning, they've got Jaime out there too."

Mattie was surprised. "I figured she was still sleeping."

"Not Jaime. She's usually up at dawn." C.J. poured himself another cup of coffee. "She likes to take pictures early in the morning. She says the light is best then."

Mattie cracked an egg on the side of a bowl, then another and another. She tried to figure how many more scrambled eggs she should include to feed C.J. and Jaime. It gave her a moment of happiness, a feeling that had been dormant for too long, to have extra mouths to feed. She found she was enjoying having these English guests for Christmas.

"Do you mind if I ask you something personal, Mattie?" C.J. leaned against the counter.

She took out the whisk and started stirring the eggs. "Ask away."

"Have you ever thought about fostering a child?"

The question shocked Mattie. She lost her grip on the bowl and it tilted on its side, so that slippery yolks and whites splattered all over her clean linoleum floor.

C.J. quickly reached for some rags and started to wipe it up. "I'm sorry. Yesterday, in the barn, your husband told me about your miscarriage. I hope . . . I didn't mean to cross a line."

Mattie didn't know what to say. It was sad information, handed to this man within hours of making his acquaintance. But C.J. looked so sorrowful she couldn't help but smile. "Don't apologize. Sounds like Sol told you quite a bit out in the barn." She squeezed out a rag. "More talking goes on in that barn than I would ever imagine."

C.J. leaned back on his heels. "It's just that . . . there's a family at my school who have foster kids. Really great couple. They couldn't have children of their own, but that didn't stop them. They've fostered . . . hmm, I've lost count . . . at least five or six kids. They even adopted two—a brother and a sister. This couple, well, they wanted to be parents and found a way to make it work. And what a difference they've made in the lives of these kids! But if you tell them that, they'd only say that they've been more blessed than the kids. The wife, you kind of remind me of her." Two spots on his cheeks started to flame. "But what do I know? Maybe the Amish don't sponsor foster children?"

"Some do." Mattie took more eggs out of the refrigerator. She wasn't sure what to say, so she didn't say anything.

The truth was, she had brought the topic of adoption up to Sol last summer and was surprised by his strong opposition to the idea. It was the only time they had ever argued. He said he didn't want an outsider's influence in their home.

"But it's a child!" she said. "Hardly an outsider."

Sol didn't see it that way. To him, an invisible wall separated the Amish and the English. He knew the turmoil that came when someone tried to live in both worlds. The wall, Sol insisted, served as protection. It had always been there and it should always remain.

"Seems like fostering is what you're doing with Zach." C.J. stood. "I just meant that it doesn't seem nearly as important to bear a child as it might be to parent a child." He tossed the rags into the sink. "How about if you sit down and let me do the cooking? I know my way around a kitchen."

Mattie was shocked! Every once in a while, Sol would cook something, but only if she wasn't home. C.J. brought her a cup of coffee and pulled out a chair for her. At first, she felt awkward. Imagine sitting in a chair while a man made your breakfast. An English man! Whom she had only known since yesterday! Yet he was very at ease, which made her feel at ease. He was comfortable with himself, with who he was as a man. Unlike his wife, Jaime, who seemed so unsure of herself. Mattie started to relax. It felt rather nice to be waited on.

She listened to him chatter on, this English man in her kitchen, as he cracked eggs with one hand and used the other to slide a slab of butter into a heated cast-iron pan. As the eggs slipped onto the pan, they sizzled. She watched him carefully, worried he would ruin the eggs, but he knew how to cook. Not to cook tidy, though. He was making a big mess and she tried not to cringe as eggshells flew on the floor and dishes piled up in the sink.

He talked as he cooked, telling her that he always wanted to have a big family and he was just waiting for Jaime to feel ready. As he worked, he talked and she listened. He reminded her of her brothers. When they were in the mood, especially when they had a question about girls that perplexed them, they would find Mattie somewhere in the house or the yard, chore alongside her, and just talk and talk. People liked to talk to Mattie about their troubles, she was aware, but she never knew why. She didn't think she had much to offer them other than a listening ear. But she didn't mind listening.

As the sky began to lighten outside, C.J. admitted that he was worried about Jaime. "One of her pictures won a category in a *National Geographic* contest and *boom!*, she hit the radar for her dad—suddenly, he was paying all kinds of attention to her. One weekend, he breezed in like he had just been down to the corner store for a carton of milk. Jaime was thrilled to have him visit. I'd only met him once before—during the wedding—and the wedding was a whole other story—" He rolled his eyes. "That weekend was terrible, just terrible. I was gone on a Search and Rescue. Tucker and I found the victims . . . but it was too late. I was feeling pretty bad about that, and when I finally got home, Jaime and her dad had a surprise for me. They had found a house for us to buy—her dad said he was going to put a down payment on it."

"Why was that such a bad thing?" Mattie asked.

"For one, I'm not really sure he would have ponied up the down payment. He talks big. But even more than that, it seemed his way of undermining me. He doesn't think teaching is a real job."

Mattie's eyebrows went up. "Our elders are trying to pay our teachers more, so that men can raise a family and keep teaching. They think it's that important."

C.J. gave up a wry smile. "Jaime's dad thinks there's only one real job—selling. He's pretty well-to-do—so he says—and he uses his money to impress people." He covered the scrambled eggs with a lid and put the pan into the oven to keep it warm. He flipped over the sizzling bacon in the second frying pan.

"He had also bought a new camera for Jaime that weekend—that very one she was so anxious to get out of the car yesterday. I listened to the two of them trying to convince me to buy this house . . . and I just blew up. Said things I shouldn't have said." He laid the bacon on a paper towel to drain. "I tried to apologize to James later. But he wouldn't accept my apology." He filled a pot with water and set it to boil.

Mattie took a sip of coffee. "Forgiveness works both ways. If you ask for forgiveness from someone, then a person has his own responsibility to accept it."

"Try telling that to her dad. He likes holding power over people." He poured oatmeal into the pot of boiling water. "Seems as if things haven't been the same between Jaime and me since that weekend when her father visited. It's as if she has expectations of me that I can never fulfill." As the oatmeal bubbled up, he started to stir it down. "You know what's funny? I don't think Jaime's pictures with that camera are as good as the ones she took with her old camera. She used to rely on her own eye, on her instincts. It was a film camera. This new one is state-of-the-art digital, with all kinds of bells and whistles. Now she relies on that camera to tell her what a good picture is."

A thought occurred to Mattie. "By any chance, did you give her the old camera?"

He nodded. "It was my wedding gift to her." He shook his head. "I'm sorry to be dumping all of this on you."

Mattie smiled. "My grandfather Caleb used to say, 'Things can get good again. Even things like a marriage.'"

"What if only one of us believes that?"

"Then you wait," Mattie said quietly, stirring a spoonful of sugar into her coffee. "That's what my grandfather would say that we Plain people do best. We wait."

The barn door rumbled shut. Through the window, Mattie could barely make out four bundled figures running toward the house. When they reached the porch, Mattie heard Jaime's musical giggle as she stomped off clumps of snow from her boots. She could see that the sight and sound of her hurt C.J. so much that he flinched.

He turned to Mattie. "What if I'm running out of time?"

Zach drained his juice glass, then spun it absentmindedly on the table. It was the best breakfast he had ever eaten. The English man made them all perfectly cooked scrambled eggs, soft and buttery, topped with sautéed onions and mushrooms and cheese. Zach had wanted to dislike that fellow, the man married to this beautiful creature sitting across the table from him. But he could tell C.J. was a good man. Impossible to dislike, despite his best efforts. He admired the way C.J. treated Jaime—he was kind to her, the way Sol was kind to Mattie. It was one of the things Zach liked about living with Sol and Mattie. He was able to observe, day in and day out, a different kind of marriage than his own folks'. The kind he wanted for himself one day.

It amazed him that the English fellow cooked for everybody. His wife said he cooked most of the time at home. That thought would have baffled his father. He couldn't even imagine his father in a kitchen, other than eating at the table. Nor could he imagine his father treating his mother with kindness.

He glanced over at the mountain of dirty dishes in the kitchen sink. The pale green formica countertops were buried in dishes. The stovetop was splattered with bacon grease and bits of dried-on eggs. C.J. must have used every dish in the house. Ha! That fellow may be able to cook, but he sure couldn't keep a kitchen clean.

He watched Jaime slather jam over her toast. He found himself watching her every move; she was a mystery to him. He was mesmerized by every word she uttered. He had to be careful watching her because he knew that Sol was watching him, but the complexity of her fascinated him. There were so many things he was starting to wonder about her, the loneliness and the restlessness he saw in her.

He finished his eggs and buttered one more piece of toast to go. He was so full he could hardly even sit up, much less bring himself to leave. But the worst of the storm had passed and he wanted to get out to his car to see if he could get it running. Assuming, of course, it wasn't completely buried in a snowdrift. As soon as Sol finished the prayer for breakfast, Zach jumped from the table and plucked his coat and hat off the wall pegs.

"Zach," Sol said, and Zach froze, mid-air. "Before you go fussing over that car of yours, why don't you do Mattie a favor and clean up the breakfast dishes for her?" Sol gave him a cat-in-the-cream smile. "Consider it an early Christmas gift."

The storm was finally losing its bluster. It had taken Zach two hours to clean up the kitchen, including many sighs and moans, but Sol wouldn't let C.J. or anyone else help him. He insisted that Zach wanted to do this for Mattie and ushered everyone into the living room.

C.J. felt a little badly about that—he knew he was a messy cook. At home, he cooked and Jaime cleaned up. It worked for them, though others thought it was a little odd. Jaime's mother had given him an apron for his birthday one year with the saying "I love a man with dishpan hands!"

As soon as Zach finished the last dish, he scowled at Sol and blew out the door to go rescue his car.

In the meantime, Danny peppered C.J. with questions—he wanted to know everything about Search and Rescue, about his Finds, about Tucker, until C.J. felt he had run clean out of stories. Taking pity on C.J., Sol suggested a game of checkers with his son. C.J. envied Mattie and Sol and Danny—not because of their Amish-ness but because of their family-ness: They were smug without meaning to be, smug about the simplest and yet most enduring things in life—their love for each other, their love for their child.

This was how he always sort of imagined it. His life. A cozy day by the hearth, his wife and his children (two sons and two daughters, as long as he was imagining), a big dog like Tucker curled up in front of the fire. Everyone content, just being together.

When they had finished breakfast this morning, Sol prayed aloud a prayer that was profound in its simplicity: "The days available to say a kind word to someone this year are rapidly drawing to a close. Lord God, teach us to be kind."

That's the word he would use to tell Eve what the Amish were like: kind. They have a culture of kindness. He and Eve played a game called One Word they invented during a rainy lunch in the teacher's lounge. She had asked him to describe his work, his mother, his father, his dog, his wife—each one in a single word. Eve used words like *philology* and *pedantic* without batting an eye. So he had spent time finding just the right word to impress her. In the end, he said *unpredictable* (work), *mother wit* (mother), *trustworthy* (father), *loyal* (Tucker).

"And your wife?" Eve had asked. "How would you describe her?"

He took a long time with that one. *Charming*, he considered. *Cute. Talented. Funny. Insecure. Enthralling. Independent.* Which one word best described Jaime? Then, suddenly, he knew.

"Asymmetrical."

C.J. looked across the room at his wife. Mattie was trying to teach Jaime how to sew a straight stitch. Their two heads were bowed over the frame. The sight made him smile. He doubted Jaime had ever threaded a needle in her life. She looked so relaxed, so at ease. She had showered after breakfast and her hair hung loose and curly, the way it naturally was before she started her Anti-Curl Program. Her hair was finally growing longer.

He had been horrified when she surprised him with that bizarre haircut—clipped short on one side, but jaw-length and jagged on the other. They had a terrible fight over it— their worst ever. She cried when she saw how disappointed he was in the haircut. Everyone in New York City was wearing their hair this way, she insisted. Why would *that* matter? he pointed out, when we live in Stoney Ridge? Then he asked, under his breath but a little too loudly, when was she ever going to stop reinventing herself?

"When I finally get it right!" she shouted and stomped away.

This morning, she wasn't wearing any makeup. Her shirt wasn't tucked in; it hung over her pants. She looked . . . the way she used to look before James MacComber entered the scene and took her to get an expensive makeover. Before she became Asymmetrical Haircut Jaime. That blasted haircut had become a metaphor for how she had changed this last year. Out of balance.

C.J. had always thought Jaime was a beauty—a natural outdoor beauty. No makeup, no hairspray. She smelled like a pinecone. But lately she looked like an exquisite china doll, delicate, fragile, but a little hard and stiff, just like the hairspray she lacquered on her hair to keep every strand in place. Jaime liked her new look, but he missed the old Jaime. Now she was constantly worried about money and clothes and a house and new cars and money again. He missed the Jaime who used to love his jeep, loved to hike in the woods, loved Tucker. The Jaime who loved him.

The woodstove kept the room warm and toasty, and for a moment, C.J. wished the storm would just continue raging. He glanced out the window and saw some blue behind some clouds, and he actually felt disappointed. Suddenly this Christmas weekend felt short and precious; he wanted it to last forever.

The thought of leaving this cozy room to go on a cruise with James MacComber made C.J. feel ill, as if he were being smothered. A cruise meant he would be trapped with nowhere to go but to listen to Jaime's father pontificate about his latest sales deal. Her father was mysteriously wealthy. C.J. could never quite figure how or what he did for a living—he wheeled and dealed and dabbled in all kinds of things. He loved to name-drop too—famous people he had met (the truth of which C.J. had somehow always doubted), or designer this or that, or had C.J. seen this latest technology? and he would whip out some new gadget. He did not trust James MacComber. Never had.

The first time he met Jaime's father was the day before their wedding, when he suddenly arrived and acted like he was footing the bill for the entire wedding. He told Jaime he wanted to walk her down the aisle—and Jaime let him! Then he didn't think that a buffet meal for the reception was ritzy enough, so he canceled the buffet C.J. and Jaime had chosen and substituted a sit-down dinner menu, including lobster tails for everyone. Lobster tails. In Pennsylvania, in late December. Although he had made a big show of acting like a host at the reception, he never did end up paying for anything. Jaime's mother didn't have the money to pay for a sit-down dinner, so C.J. sold his motorcycle to pay off the restaurant bill. How he had loved that motorcycle! Thus ended his first experience with James MacComber's style of fatherhood.

But C.J. had agreed to go on this cruise and he would go, for Jaime's sake. By noon, the sky was empty of clouds, bright blue, and the winter sun reflected off the snow so brightly that it hurt to gaze outside the windows too long. C.J. saw something on the road and shaded his eyes to look as the object turned into Sol and Mattie's drive. It was a horse-drawn sleigh, led by an enormous horse, carrying three Amish men.

Sol came up behind him. "Well, look at that. Our neighbors are here to help get that car out of the pond." He reached for his hat and jacket off the wall peg.

C.J. grabbed his jacket too. "But how could they possibly

have known? With a doozy of a storm like that, how could they have known?"

Sol grinned. "One farmer probably passed by and saw it, told another, then another. It's called the Amish telegraph system."

Jaime came into the kitchen. "Do you think they can get the car out of the pond without a tow truck?"

"Looks like we're going to give it a try," Sol said. "But we're sure to need another horse. I'll go get Dixie."

Danny pulled on his boots and coat and mittens as Sol spoke to Jaime.

Mattie stood against the doorjamb between the kitchen and the living room. Her arms were folded against her chest. "Sol, that's dangerous work. I don't know that Danny should be down there."

"Oh Mom!" Danny whined.

"Mattie," Sol said in a sharp voice. "The boy needs to learn how to do things like this. You can't keep him in the kitchen for the rest of his life."

C.J. saw Mattie glance from Jaime to him, then turn her head away, embarrassed. She lifted her head and drew her shoulders up proud. It was her quiet way, C.J. thought, of making her stand. Stubborn but silent. He held back a smile. It relieved him to see that even a couple like Mattie and Sol had their tense moments.

"I'll keep a close watch on him," Sol said in a softer tone. He touched Mattie's arm and they exchanged a long look, connected for a moment in a way that excluded everyone else.

C.J. watched with a rush of longing. He and Jaime used to have those kinds of looks—filled with silent communication.

Maybe Mattie's grandfather was right. Maybe things could get good again.

Mattie's light spirits from the pleasant morning had fizzled away. She watched Sol lead Dixie, their buggy horse, out of the barn and down toward the pond. Danny followed close behind, holding a coil of rope. The English visitors trailed behind both of them, following in the path cleared by Dixie's large hoofprints. That big dog, Tucker, didn't need a path. He was jumping around for joy in the snowdrifts.

She felt a pull on her heart as she watched Danny trudge down the hill. She hoped Sol would truly pay close attention to him. Even though the pond was probably frozen solid from last night's freezing temperatures, pulling the car out would break up the ice. Danny had just learned to swim last August and he wasn't very good at it. She wondered if she should go down with them, but she knew Sol would know why she was there, that she didn't trust him to watch over their son.

She wondered how long pulling the car out would take, and if the neighbors would be expecting lunch. Just the thought of making lunch for all of them made her feel tired. She was always so tired lately, worn down by worries and what-ifs. She knew it wasn't right, but she couldn't seem to keep her mind from racing. She rubbed her face.

What is happening to me? I'm turning into someone I never wanted to be. She thought of the dark feelings, foreign feelings, that filled her when she was at Carrie Miller's last weekend. She held Carrie's beautiful newborn daughter in her arms—oh, how she wished she were hers! She hugged the baby close to her, breathing in her baby smell. The baby was even named Mathilda after Mattie—and yet she felt something close to bitterness toward Carrie—*a woman who is like a sister to me.* Bitterness that felt like bile in her throat. It disgusted Mattie to admit those feelings to herself.

But why couldn't it be she who had a baby? Why was it that her sisters-in-law and friends could do something that she couldn't seem to do? Carrie and Abel had three children now; some of her friends had even more!

Mattie had grown up wanting thirteen children. A baker's dozen, her mother had called it. She remembered the early years of her marriage, remembered lying in Sol's arms and whispering dreams of all the babies they would make together. They even had names picked out. But the nights had passed into months, and the months into years. *I've got to surrender this deep longing, but I just can't seem to let it go. Dear God, when I am weak, you are strong.* Tears blurred her eyes and filled her throat. She had to swallow twice to fight them back. She would not cry!

As she turned to go upstairs, she noticed Jaime's camera on the table. She stopped and picked it up. It was a complicated piece of equipment, covered with precise dials and levers. She set it down again, fearful she would break it. Then she rolled her eyes. *I'm even afraid of a silly thing like a camera.*

Zach shifted his weight from foot to foot, trying to keep from freezing. The wind had a stiff bite to it, and even though the sky was blue and clear, there was talk that another storm was heading in. Standing next to him and Sol were three other men, discussing the best way to get the English visitors' car out of the pond. He was sure that if these neighbors knew of the stuck car, his father did too. But, of course, his father was too righteous to help anyone with car trouble.

He didn't know why this endeavor took so much discussion. Seemed to him all they needed to do was to get rope, horses, and start to pull. But the ice worried the older men. He wasn't sure why *they* were so worried. He knew they would be sending him to wade into that pond to tie the rope to the bumper. At least he was wearing his fishing boots today.

He wasn't terribly eager to have the car pulled out of the pond. That meant Jaime Fitzpatrick would be on her way, out of his life forever. It was wrong to have such thoughts about an English woman, a *married* English woman, but Jaime was different than any woman he had ever met. He looked over at her and saw how impatient she was to get her car out of the pond. She was stretching up and down on her toes, her arms folded tightly against her chest. He could practically see her biting her tongue to keep from telling the men to get going. Get that car—that sleek, stunning piece of machinery—out of the pond!

Who could blame her? What kind of a woman had a sports car like that, anyway? Owning such a vehicle was one more thing about Jaime that fascinated him. Sol elbowed him, and when Zach looked to see what he wanted, he saw the warning scowl on Sol's face.

Zach felt his cheeks start to flush. Oh, surely, nothing good could come from such wicked thoughts.

If Sol weren't standing next to the three most humorless men in his church, he would have picked up Zach by the scruff of his neck and thrown him in the pond to cool off his ardor. That ridiculous look of adoration on Zach's face as he gawked at the English woman was the last straw. What thoughts ran through that boy's head? None with any sense, that's for sure.

When Zach first came to live with them, Sol saw him as the lovable screw-up of the family. He and Mattie would shake their heads at his antics in fond disbelief. But Zach's self-absorbed behavior soon grew tiresome—late nights, careless work habits, his immature friends. The gall to hide a car on Sol's farm. And now, he'd developed a schoolboy crush on a married English woman. *Married!* Enough! Sol had *had it* with that boy. It was time for Zach to move on.

Mattie would not like his decision. He could practically hear her objections: "Is that what you're going to do with our own Danny when it's time for him to try out his wings? Cut him off? Pretend he doesn't exist? But you know as well as anybody, Solomon Riehl"—she only called him Solomon when she wanted to make a point—"God doesn't write *anybody* off."

He did know that. He was a church member today because Mattie didn't write him off. She kept seeing the potential of manhood within him, even when he wasn't sure it was there himself. But she also wasn't aware of the pressure he was getting from church members, from Zach's own father, to allow the boy to face up to his own consequences.

"He'll never learn," Eli Zook told him at church two weeks ago, pointing a long bony finger at Sol's chest, "if you and Mattie keep sheltering him. You're only hobbling the boy with kindness."

It looked like the three men were finally coming to a consensus about how to get the car out of the pond. That meant the English visitors could be on their way. He felt a tiny twinge of sorrow about that. It surprised him to have such a thought cross his mind, but these visitors had been good for Mattie. He saw the sadness leave her face this morning during breakfast, a sadness that had covered her lately like a blanket. She even laughed a few times. She used to laugh so often. It pleased him to see her enjoying herself. Life could be funny like that, Sol thought. *Here I thought we were helping those English guests out, when the truth was they were helping us.*

Sol had encouraged Mattie to believe the doctor's words, that there was plenty of time for more children, that God would bless them still. But Sol knew life wasn't turning out the way they planned. Not having more children was a source of great grief to him and it was a hard thing to accept. He scolded Mattie for overprotecting Danny, but the truth was, he was just as guilty of it. Maybe not trying to keep him from every possible physical danger, the way Mattie did, but he was terrified of losing Danny to the world.

He glanced at Zach. *That* was the real reason he wanted to send Zach on his way—back to his parents or out to the world. This weekend, his worry about Zach's sway over Danny spiked to a new level; he felt he had to do something . . . soon. Danny was far more observant of Zach than Sol had realized. He had ferreted out that car. And it was the first time Danny had kept something secret from his father.

Nip it now, Sol thought, as he followed the men down to the pond. *Nip it in the bud.*

It was fascinating, C.J. thought, to see how the Amish improvised. They got things done quite efficiently without the benefit of a motor. The harnesses of two deluxe-sized horses, with legs thicker than tree trunks, were attached to a plow, which was attached by ropes to the bumper of Jaime's car. Little by little, the horses eased the car out of the frozen pond, breaking up the ice. Jaime jumped up and down like a schoolgirl when the back wheels of the car rose out of the shards of ice and murky water. Sol kept the horses moving forward, pulling and straining, until they reached flat ground. C.J. thought he would never forget the sound of horses' hooves sucking and plopping in the banks of the pond. It was a miracle! Without any modern intervention. He had figured it might be February before that car could be budged.

Not that he cared. He hated that car. Jaime's father had given it to her for her birthday in October—it was waiting outside of their apartment with a gigantic ribbon on it and included one of those horrible vanity plates: My #1 Girl. Jaime burst into happy tears when she discovered it was from her father.

Then, one week later, came the real surprise. The first monthly leasing bill, forty-eight to follow, the contract said. He called James to ask him about it and James just laughed it off. "Oh, must be a billing mistake. I'll take care of it."

Then the bill for November came. Then December.

C.J. talked it over with Eve and she suggested returning the car to the dealer, but that would mean he would have to tell Jaime the slippery trick her father had done. He just couldn't do it. She had been so pleased with the attention her father was showing her. He knew the toll her mother's death had taken on her. Tolerating this car seemed like a small way to lessen that pain, so instead, he quietly paid the bills with money they didn't have to spare.

Sol gave C.J. the go-ahead to get inside the car and set the emergency brake before he unhooked the horses. At first, the car's door handle was frozen, but one of the Amish neighbors gently pushed C.J. aside and cupped his mouth around the lock. He blew and blew on it, then pulled it again.

"Bingo!" the Amish man said, revealing missing molars in his large grin.

C.J. jumped into the driver's seat, turned over the ignition once, then twice, and the engine caught! He looked at Jaime and gave her a thumbs-up, grinning when he saw the delighted look on her face.

As Jaime saw her car emerge out of the water—her beautiful new car—she felt almost giddy with happiness. She hoped that the sleigh might pack down the snow hard enough that they could follow behind it until they reached the main road. Surely, the roads would be cleared by snowplows soon. She felt a bloom of optimism from the thought and let out a deep, relieved sigh. They would be able to meet her father today in time to leave for the trip. Everything was back on track.

She saw C.J. talking to the Amish farmers, then he went back to the car and reached in to get her purse. He brought it to her.

"They're debating what to do next." He looked back at the group of bearded men, huddling together in a circle, listening carefully to each other. "They seem to feel a consensus is important before they take the next step."

Jaime laughed. "Aren't they wonderful to us, C.J.? One way or another, we're going to make it on the cruise ship tomorrow. It's a miracle!"

C.J. rolled his eyes. "Oh sure. I can't think of anything more pressing on God's agenda on this Christmas Eve than making sure we get on that cruise."

While he kept his gaze on the group of farmers, Jaime took a step back. Then another. She stopped and scooped up a handful of snow, packing it into a ball. She heaved the snowball at C.J.'s head but missed and hit his back instead. He turned toward her with a startled look on his face. She bent over to gather more snow, straightened up, and fired a snowball that hit him on his chin. He looked at her, stunned, then broke into a smile. Slowly, he bent down and picked up some snow, then packed it into a hard ball.

He took a step toward her; she whirled to run, but the snow made her clumsy and she fell. C.J.'s snowball landed gently on the top of her head, making her shudder as the snow went down inside the open collar of her coat. She spat snow out of her mouth, shook it off her eyelashes and her hair. He came over to help her get up and she put her hands up to grab his, then released him so he fell down too. They looked at each other, and Jaime started to smile, then to laugh at the sight of C.J., toppled over. He started laughing too, and the two of them sat there, ridiculously, in the snow like a couple of kids, laughing so hard that tears rolled down their cheeks.

When had they last laughed like that? She couldn't remember. But it felt so good.

C.J. reached over and gently brushed snow off Jaime's face. His gaze fastened on her mouth. His hand stole up to frame her cheek, his thumb stroking the line of her jaw. Their breath entwined like white wedding ribbons in the air. As he lowered his head to kiss her, he caught sight of five Amish farmers and Danny, staring at the two of them sitting in the snow like a couple of kids.

He froze.

In the silence of that moment, he heard a strange ringing sound. The Amish men, including Danny, turned their heads in the direction of the sound. Could that possibly be . . . a cell phone? How could a cell phone have a signal out here in the middle of nowhere? It was coming from Jaime's purse.

C.J. scrambled to his feet and grabbed her purse to toss to her. "I think your cell is ringing."

He brushed the snow off his jacket and pants, shivering as he felt some snow slip down his back. He thought about trying to get into the car's trunk to see if water had seeped in. He felt a tap on his shoulder and turned toward Jaime. She handed him the cell phone with a strange, hard look on her face.

"It's for you," Jaime said coldly. "It's Eve."

Eve? How did she get Jaime's cell phone number? "Hello?" he said warily.

"C.J.!" Eve said. "I'm so glad I caught you before you left on the cruise! Guess what?"

C.J. watched Jaime watching him. She looked steamed. "Um, Eve, I'm in a little bit of a predicament here. How did you get this number?"

"It's your emergency number, for work. And this is an emergency!"

"What's wrong?" He turned away from Jaime's stare and lowered his voice. "Are you all right? Has something happened?"

"Yes, something has happened! You've been chosen as the district's Teacher of the Year! You won, C.J! That means that now you're a finalist for regionals, then state! Al found out yesterday and he would have called you himself, but he had that big family get-together, so he asked me to call you, and you don't carry a cell phone so I had to find another way to reach you." She finally took a breath. "You don't mind, do you? Am I interrupting anything important?"

C.J. was stunned. He had been pleased his principal, Al, had wanted to nominate him for the award—Eve had spent hours helping to fill out the application this fall. He never dreamed he would win. Never! He was so sure he wouldn't win that he didn't even tell Jaime about it. He didn't want her telling her father about it, only to have to face him if he lost. To C.J., getting nominated was enough.

Before he could even react, a click came through on call waiting. "Eve, that's great news. Really great! Thanks for letting me know. I'll get back to you. Merry Christmas!" He pressed the call waiting button. "Hello?"

Oh. Jaime's father. He said a brief hello to James and handed the phone to Jaime. He turned back to see if the Amish farmers had decided if they were going to tow the car to the road or not. For a moment, though, he stood right where he was, letting Eve's news sink in. *Teacher of the Year! Me?!*

Danny came up to him and pulled on his jacket sleeve to get his attention. He pointed a small finger toward Jaime, so C.J. spun around to face her.

Jaime had the receiver pressed against her ear. "Dad, the snowstorm kind of derailed us—it's a long story, but I'll fill you in later. We can still make it. There's even time to meet the agent." As she listened to her father, C.J. saw the enthusiasm drain from her face. "What does that mean? What do you mean, 'some other time'? Why?" Her face went from

looking worried to shocked. Then, horrified. "You're getting *married*? Married? *That's* the big surprise you had for
me?" An expression of panic crossed over her as she listened.
"Dad, why can't you just wait? The car just got pulled—"
She looked at C.J., dazed. "He hung up."

C.J. forgot about the car and the Amish men and the
Teacher of the Year recognition. He took a few steps closer
to her. Her gaze was fixed on the phone she held in her hands.

"He's at the airport," she said quietly. "He and . . . Sheila,
I think he said her name was. They're leaving now, to beat
the next storm. They're getting married on the cruise. That's
his big surprise. Getting married. He's leaving without me."

She covered her face with her hands. Then she started
to cry in a way that he had only seen her cry once or twice
before—slowly at first, then louder and louder, shaking and
sobbing. C.J. wrapped her up in his arms and held her, patting her back to console her.

At first, the bewildered look on the Amish men's faces as
they observed Jaime's meltdown almost made C.J. laugh. It
shouldn't have struck him as funny, but it did. The somber
worry on their kind, bearded faces, trying to help pry a car
out of a frozen pond—when the Amish didn't even drive cars.

C.J. saw Sol lift his shoulders helplessly and C.J. gave
him the OK signal with his fingers. Sol turned and spoke to
the others. It looked like they had come to a decision. They
were going to drag the car down to the end of the lane, so
it would be ready to go when the snowplows came through,
he assumed. They seemed relieved to be doing something,
talking to each other in their language. They must think that
he and Jaime were . . . crazy. Crazy English people. Here she
was, crying as if her heart was breaking. He didn't blame

them for being confused by Jaime's weeping. How could he explain Jaime's father to these gentle people? He hardly understood James MacComber himself.

What kind of father ignores his daughter most of her life? Then suddenly decides she's worth paying attention to, after all. The kind of attention James paid usually left Jaime feeling conflicted and upset . . . about herself, about her work, about him.

And now James is getting married. It figured! What was this, wife number five?

It was good that his thoughts were hidden, C.J. realized. They were running along the lines of being delighted that the cruise was off. Overjoyed! And behind that was a deep-down lingering happiness that started when Jaime threw a snowball at him. They hadn't had fun together in such a long time. He couldn't even remember the last time they shared a laugh, the way they used to. How he missed her! He had lost her six months ago, when he wasn't watching, and although it wasn't his fault entirely, he didn't want to lose her again.

Danny came up beside C.J. and whispered, "I have an idea to help. Can I take Tucker with me?"

C.J. nodded and Danny turned and ran up toward the house, with Tucker following close behind.

After the car was towed to the end of the long driveway, Sol helped his neighbors hook the sleigh traces back to the horse's harness and waved goodbye as they disappeared down the street. He led Dixie into her stall and gave her a few handfuls of oats as a thank-you for helping pull that car out of the pond. Dixie mouthed Sol's hands with her big lips, scattering oats over the ground. He made sure the water bucket was full, then checked the rest of the stock in the barn, as he always did. His last stop was with the ewe and lamb. He paused for a moment. A ray of sun beamed through the upper barn window and shone down on the pair, sleeping in a corner. It felt holy, that moment.

He lingered awhile longer, hoping the English woman was done with her wailing. At first, he thought someone had died, she was *that* overcome. But then he heard she was upset because her father left on that boat trip. It seemed odd to him that the father wouldn't wait. He knew if his own father were in that spot, he would rather give up a trip than give up time with his family. He didn't know if that was what set her off, but he was happy to get away from it.

Sol felt a little sorry for the English husband. He and Mattie were no strangers to sorrow, but he could never imagine her carrying on the way that English woman did.

Mattie! Suddenly he realized that he didn't know where Danny was.

He picked up his hat and fit it snug. Just as he reached out to slide open the barn door, Zach beat him to it, carrying a large bundle of rope over his shoulder. Zach nodded at him and walked past him to hang the rope on the wall.

Sol kept a hand on the open door, looked back at Zach, let out a sigh, and closed the door shut. "Zach, let's talk for a moment."

A dull ache had spread through Jaime's chest as her father's intent became clear on the phone. She felt as if she had been hit by a tidal wave of grief, of longing.

Why did her father have that effect on her? More important, why did she let him? She pulled back from C.J. and wiped her face with her gloves. "I'm sorry, C.J. I wish I knew what was wrong with me. I'm such a mess."

"Maybe it would be good to talk to someone."

"Oh great. You mean, a shrink? You think I'm a mess too." She crossed her arms against her chest.

"No, I don't think you're a mess. And I didn't mean a shrink. Maybe, like a pastor. Or better still, God."

She stepped back from him. Lately, things always circled back to church for C.J. They belonged to the Presbyterian church in Lancaster that they had been married in, but they had never been strict about attending. Jaime was certain God existed, but she wasn't quite as certain that God knew she existed. She had never had much use for faith—not the way her mother relied on her faith, or C.J. was starting to rely on his—and the day her mother was killed, Jaime found her spiritual reserve empty. There was nothing to draw on.

"On the phone to your dad, you said something about meeting an agent." C.J. looked at her suspiciously. "What was that about? What has your father promised you now?"

There was a pause. One beat. Then two. She was cornered. She had planned to tell C.J. about the photography agent friend of her father's while they were driving to her father's. Not now. Not like this.

C.J. took a step closer to Jaime. "Listen to me. Your father is all talk. No action."

"My father has been incredibly generous to us!" She pointed to the car. "He bought me that car! He bought me the camera. He sends me flowers! He takes me shopping!"

"You're defending him? Today? Just as he's getting married to wife number twelve—"

"Four!"

"Five! And he's leaving without you on a cruise that he had promised to take you on, to help you get through this first Christmas without your mother—"

"It's not his fault that the storm has interfered! At least he's trying! He wanted me there for his wedding to Shelley."

"Sheila."

"Whatever! The point is, he wants us to join him. He said he would buy our plane tickets if we were able to join them."

"What?" C.J. roared. "I thought he had offered to pay for our trip! Do you mean that we were going to have to pay for it ourselves?" He was livid. "Money! It always boils down to your dad and his money."

"That's his way of making up for all those years of being absent! He's showing his love!"

"Love? This is his way of throwing his weight around! And he always waits until he has an audience, then he pulls out his wallet and gives you his Visa. Or hundred dollar bills."

"You're just jealous of his success!" She knew she sounded childish, but she was upset and angry and . . . so *very* disappointed. Her father had given her the impression that her Christmas surprise was going to be setting her up with a New York photography agent. He had practically promised! This was going to be the way she would finally connect to him, to finally have him in her life. She was willing to completely uproot her life to be near him. And this cruise was going to patch up her marriage! It was going to be the answer they needed. Time away from Stoney Ridge, from sad memories, from that harridan, Eve. She was sure she could convince

C.J. that they needed to make this move. It would launch her photography career. She would finally start making some money. Big money, real money, her dad had said. And C.J. could find a teaching job anywhere!

Instead, her father was getting married, to some Sherry-bimbo that he probably met last month. All of Jaime's plans, her hopes—they were all disappearing, like wisps of steam from a cup of tea.

C.J. threw his hands in the air. "What are you talking about? I have never wanted that kind of success. Success for me is having a job with meaning. It's having relationships that endure!"

Like the enduring relationship with Eve?! she wanted to shout, but she refused to say it out loud. She wasn't going to make this easy for him. He was the one who was dallying with someone else. Not her. "And that job means we'll be living in an apartment for the rest of our life."

"It might mean we don't have the kind of house your father thinks you should have, but we'll have a house, in due time."

She threw up her hands. "When, C.J.? And how are we ever going to be able to buy a house on a teacher's salary?"

He crossed his arms against his chest. "You knew what my life was like when you married me."

But did I? Did anybody really know what married life would be like? "You don't understand—"

"What? What *don't* I understand? That you seem to feel entitled to things, because that's how your father shows you affection? That's not love, Jaime. He might be your father, but he's never been your dad. Dads stick around. Dads don't disappear and only show up when their child wins a contest."

His face was flushed, and his voice was strong, filling the air around them, demanding an answer.

They stared at each other for a long time, until an odd grinding sound floated across the hillside. It was a snow-plow, slowly making its way along the road in front of the farmhouse.

Jaime turned to C.J. with a delighted look on her face. "The trip! Maybe we could still make it!"

She saw Sol and Zach cross from the barn to the house and ran to meet them, to tell them that they would be leaving. It wasn't until she almost reached the farmhouse that she looked back and saw C.J. was still standing there, by the pond's edge, where she had left him.

Mattie woke from a nap, startled by the rumble of voices below her bedroom window. It took her a moment to gather her thoughts, and as soon as she did, she jumped out of bed and hurried to the window. She saw that Jaime's red car was no longer in the pond, but now it was down at the edge of the driveway. The hood was up and she could see Zach, bent over, examining the engine. There was no sign of their neighbors. Land sakes, how long had she slept? She just meant to lie down on the bed for a moment. As she smoothed her hair under her prayer cap, she realized it was Sol's deep voice that woke her. He was below their bedroom window, talking to Jaime on the porch.

She pinned her black apron back over her teal-colored dress and tied her sneaker laces. Before she reached the bottom of the stairs, Jaime and Sol came through the kitchen door. When Jaime saw her, she rushed to meet her.

"Mattie! It's a miracle! The car is down by the lane and the snowplow just came through. We're able to get back on schedule!" As Jaime gave Mattie a blow-by-blow account of the last hour, C.J. opened the door to join them in the kitchen.

Mattie took in Jaime's excitement; she noticed C.J. didn't look quite as excited. Then she turned to Sol. "Where's Danny?"

An unnatural silence fell over the room as Sol, C.J., and Jaime exchanged puzzled looks.

"I thought he went up to the house with Tucker," C.J. said. "Awhile ago."

Mattie felt as if the strange quiet were expanding from someplace in the center of her, rippling through the kitchen.

The first thing C.J. did, as Sol went out to the barn to look for Danny, was to quietly slip out and run down to the pond. He was methodical in all things, and so in this endeavor he moved through standard operating procedure for Search and Rescue. He didn't want to alarm Mattie or Sol, but in the confusion of the moment, he knew that the pond had to be ruled out first.

It relieved him that Tucker was with Danny. He whistled for Tucker, scanning the pond for any sign of the boy or the dog. He started to try to catalog details about Danny: the clothes he was wearing, what kind of boots he had on, whether the weight of his clothes would cause him to sink. He knew Tucker wouldn't leave Danny, but it crossed his mind that they both could have drowned in the frigid temperatures, quickly and quietly.

How long ago had he seen Danny? He thought of Danny coming up to him, telling him that he wanted to borrow Tucker, right after Jaime got off the phone with her father. How long ago was that? He guessed it was twenty minutes, at least. Maybe longer.

He walked along the edge of the pond until he was satisfied that there was no sign of them. No tracks. No disturbance of the ice other than where the car was ripped out. He took a large stick and pushed the ice around where the car had been, until he was thoroughly satisfied. He threw the stick down and started looking around the yard to see if there were any fresh tracks. Every few minutes, he whistled for Tucker, then listened carefully for a bark in return.

Nothing.

If Tucker heard his whistle, he wouldn't ignore it. He saw Sol cross from the barn to the house, no sign of Danny and Tucker. Concern started to spike inside of C.J. He looked up at the sky. The clear blue of an hour ago was beginning to change. Some gray clouds were starting to gather in the north—a portent of that second storm.

Jaime met him halfway down the lane. "Mattie and I have looked all through the house. Where could he be?"

C.J. blew air out of his mouth. "He's a bright boy. He knows this farm."

She glanced at the pond. "Did you think he was down there?"

"I just wanted to make sure. There was so much going on. He could have slipped and fallen in without anyone seeing."

"Tucker would have barked."

C.J. nodded.

"Mattie's terribly worried."

C.J. started back up to the house. "Little boys wander off all the time. I'm sure he'll be back soon."

She hurried to catch up to him. "So then, maybe . . . do you think . . . maybe we could leave pretty soon?"

C.J. stopped in his tracks. "With Danny missing? With Tucker gone?"

She studied her feet. "If you feel they're not in any trouble, don't you think it would be okay to leave? We could come back and get Tucker when we get back. I'm sure they wouldn't mind watching him for the week. We could pay them, instead of the kennel." She lifted her head, a pleading look on her face. "I wouldn't ask if it weren't so important."

C.J. looked at his wife, stunned. When C.J. first met Jaime, he knew this was the girl he'd been waiting for. He'd always thought love at first sight was a tired cliché, but that's what happened to him. It was like getting hit in the gut, a right cross to the chin. She was funny, fascinating, quirky, ridiculously insecure. Beautiful—and completely indifferent to it. He knew she was young, a little immature, with some lingering issues from her father's abandonment. Even more issues since James had shown back up—and what was the deal with James promising to set her up with a big-time agent? He'd overheard enough of their conversation to know he'd eventually have to clean up that mess too. Why couldn't her father behave like a father instead of a manager?

But not a day had gone by that C.J. hadn't looked at Jaime with love in his heart. Right now, though—at this very moment—he didn't like this person who stood before him. "You go ahead and go, if it's that important to you. But I'm not leaving. Not until I know Danny is safe." He started back up to the house.

"C.J., I'm not meaning to sound heartless," she called out. "You said yourself that Danny will be back soon."

C.J. didn't stop walking, even as Jaime caught up with him. "I'm not going to leave until Danny and Tucker are home, safe and sound." With a grand sweep of his hand, he added, "But *you* are free to go."

Mattie rushed upstairs from the basement when she heard Sol's footsteps in the kitchen. When Danny was four, he had gone missing and she had found him down in the basement. He had gone down to sample the deer jerky that had just come out of the smoker and fell sound asleep.

"Was he in the barn?"

Sol shook his head.

"Did you look everywhere? The hayloft? You know how he likes to play up there. Could he have fallen?"

"I looked every place in the barn that I could think of."

Mattie held on to the counter to steady herself. She felt as if the world had become very fragile. At any given moment, anything at all could happen. "I have a terrible feeling inside, Sol. I can't explain it. Something is wrong."

Sol put his hands on her shoulders. "Mattie, you think something terrible is going to happen every blessed day. You've been thinking that way for a long time now."

She buried her face in his shoulder. "I know. But this feels different."

Sol squeezed her tightly against him. "You have to get ahold of yourself and let him be a normal boy, Mattie. Knowing Danny, he probably wandered off for a hike in the woods with the dog. It's good he has that dog with him too."

She pulled back. "Why? Why is that good?"

"Because he's not alone. That English dog won't leave him."

Mattie felt her fear lighten a little, but she couldn't let go of a foreboding. Was it just her mind playing tricks on her? "Didn't you say another storm was coming in? Right on the heels of this one, you said so yourself, at breakfast." She looked over at the windows in the living room at the sky. A few gray clouds were sailing across the blue.

"He's fine. He'll be back long before then."

"You don't know that, Sol. Just by saying something doesn't make it so. You can't fix everything! People are not machines, like a table saw that just needs a new part. You can't give out new parts!"

Sol looked confused. "Are we talking about Danny?"

"Yes! No! I don't know." She sniffed and wiped her cheeks with her hands.

"He'll be back soon, safe and sound." He put his arms around her and pulled her close to his body. "I don't want you to fret about this."

But both of them knew she would.

Jaime watched C.J. walk into the farmhouse kitchen. She couldn't believe he told her she could leave without him! Those words pierced her. Jaime was sure he would insist on going with her. Didn't he want to go with her? Did he mean it? Would he really let her leave without him?

She glanced back at the car. The snowplow was coming the other way now, clearing off the side of the road that led to Mattie and Sol's driveway. She *could* leave now. She could make it to the airport and catch an afternoon flight to Miami. Maybe she should call C.J.'s bluff. He was always so hard on her father. He never tried to see things from her father's viewpoint. Maybe her father was just trying to hide his disappointment that they weren't able to make the trip. Maybe the tickets were nonrefundable and her father was just too thoughtful to say so. It might be easier to take that trip without C.J. Maybe they both needed time apart, to think. But what would it mean to them if she left now? She rubbed her face with her gloves. Why did it feel as if he had left her?

She felt the sting of C.J.'s words, that she thought she was entitled to things. He wasn't wrong. She did want more. Was it so wrong to want a house and a car and nice things to go along with it? Or what about wanting a husband who didn't get phone calls from a woman named Eve? She looked up at the farmhouse. It was so simple and plain. There was nothing fancy about this Amish home, cheerful and bustling with activity. They may not have much, but they had love. What would her father say about a house like this? Not long ago, he told Jaime he had the Italian marble torn out of a bathroom because he didn't quite like the color. What would Mattie and Sol think of that?

Then an odd thought crossed her mind. Her father's home was empty. And lonely. And now he was going on his fifth marriage.

She noticed Mattie looking out the kitchen window as Sol came up behind her, putting an arm protectively around her shoulders. C.J. stood nearby. Could Danny really be in trouble? Boys wandered off all the time, C.J. had said so himself.

Stop me! she wanted to shout to C.J. *Come and get me!*

Don't let me leave! As it was, she was going to have to take this step of her own free will. The decision was hers.

Jaime turned and walked down to her car. Zach had the hood up and was hovering over the engine like a surgeon puzzling over his patient in an operating room. "Zach, have you seen Danny? Or Tucker?"

Zach shook his hands at his sides, loosely, as if to release leftover energy. "Not for a little while."

"Think it's true that another storm is coming in?" She scanned the clear blue sky for clouds but didn't see any.

Zach shrugged. "Maybe."

"Mattie thinks he's gone missing."

Zach scratched his head. "Mattie . . . she tends to be a little . . ." He made a clockwise motion with his hand. "She tends to worry a lot. But then, I might worry about a boy like Danny too."

"Does he go missing very much?"

"Danny's always getting into something or other. He's six . . . and he's just . . . Danny."

Jaime's gaze shifted up toward the house, then back to her car.

"You leaving soon?" he asked.

She let out a soughing sound. "I think so."

"Would you mind dropping me off in town on your way out?"

"Where are you headed on Christmas Eve?"

Zach looked away. "I'm leaving. Sol told me that it's time I make it on my own. The car was the last straw. He wants me to leave." He thrust his hands to the bottoms of his pockets and hunched up as if he were in a hailstorm. "Says he thinks I'm a bad influence on Danny."

"Are you?"

He wiggled his eyebrows in that way that made her laugh. "Sometimes." He took a step closer to her and lowered his voice. "Have you ever seen an ocean?"

She nodded. "Sure. A bunch of times. My mom and I used to go to the Jersey shore for a week each summer."

"What's it like?"

"The ocean?" She smiled. "The biggest thing you ever could imagine. Water that stretches as far as your eye can see, until it slips off the horizon. And every day is different. The water changes color! Sometimes, the ocean is a glassy sea, a shimmering blue, one shade lighter than the sky. Other times, it's gray-green, all churned up, with whitecaps and heavy surf. But the best part of the ocean is the air. It has a salty tinge to it. It feels as if you can't breathe it in enough. As if you're flushing your whole system with that oxygen-rich air."

"What does it feel like to have the sea mist on your face?"

"Not unlike spitting rain."

A satisfied look covered Zach's face, a matter decided. "I'm going. Today. I'm headed to the ocean. I'm done here."

Sol answered C.J.'s questions about Danny's habits and favorite places to go as patiently as he could, but he knew that time was passing. He tried to be calm, for Mattie's sake, but he was starting to worry himself. Mattie was right—something felt ominous. That sweet blue sky didn't fool him—he knew a brewing storm was due in. He knew how fickle weather could be.

Mattie was barely holding herself in one piece. He could

feel her worry vibrate through the air. Finally, he held up a hand. "C.J., I know you mean well, but time's a-wasting. I need to just go on out and start looking for my boy."

"Look here, Sol," C.J. began slowly, the steadiness of his voice some kind of anchor. "You're right that time is of the essence. But we're not wasting time right now. We need to go about looking for him in a logical way. Do you have a map of the area?"

Sol realized C.J. was being deliberately calm, deliberately soothing, and it felt condescending.

"Sol! Answer him!" Mattie said firmly.

Sol frowned. "No map. Never needed one."

"Then can you draw one for me?" C.J. asked. "Pretend you're a bird in the sky, looking down at your farm. I want to divide it into grids." He scanned the kitchen counters and Mattie quickly went to a desk and pulled out a paper and pen for Sol. "Give me an idea of how long it would take to get from the house to the edge of the property. Take into consideration the snow."

Sol leaned over the kitchen table and started to sketch out the farm, the fields, the hillsides that surrounded the level land, and the ridges beyond that. He paused for a moment. Where could his boy be? Danny did wander off without telling them what he had planned. Sol hadn't even told Mattie half the times Danny had wandered off. But why now, through this heavy snow? It just didn't make sense. He was half furious with his son for causing his mother such worry, half terrified that something had happened to him.

"Finish, Sol," Mattie urged.

"Mattie, while Sol is drawing the map, describe to me what Danny was wearing."

"He had on a black coat, a black felt hat, a gray sweater," she said.

"How warm were those things?" C.J. asked.

Sol saw panic rise in Mattie's eyes. "What do you mean?" she asked. "Are you worried he'll get frostbite?"

C.J.'s voice stayed low and steady. "I just wondered what he had on his hands. If he had a scarf on. Anything colorful, something easy to spot."

She closed her eyes tightly. "Red mittens."

"Red. That's good!" C.J. said. "That color is easy to spot. What else? Anything missing on the coat rack?"

Mattie walked over to it and looked through some of the coats. She looked over at Sol. "He's wearing his boots."

"That's good too," C.J. said. "They're bigger than shoes and they're sturdy. His tracks will be easier to follow. No chance of confusing boot tracks with animal tracks, in this deep snow."

Mattie's hands flew to her heart. "Animals! I didn't even think of that. There's a wounded bobcat prowling around the area." Her calm broken, she began to tremble.

"Now, Mattie," Sol said. "Bobcats don't go after people."

She spun toward him, her face contorting with anger. "Don't 'now Mattie' me! You know how dangerous an injured animal can be!"

Sol blew out a puff of air. Mattie's maternal instincts whistled like a tea kettle. He looked at C.J. "She's right."

When Jaime looked up at Zach, something had changed. He looked . . . weird. Nervous. He bounced on the balls of his feet and rubbed his hands together. Then he reached out and picked up Jaime's hand and kissed her palm.

141

"You could come with me. To the ocean! Right now. Today! Let's take your sports car and head straight to the beautiful Jersey shore!"

Jaime barely resisted laughing out loud at this ridiculous teenager and his silly fantasies but knew she would hurt him deeply if she laughed. She gently reclaimed her hand and worked to keep her face solemn. "Leaving is a big deal to your people, isn't it?"

Zach shoved his hands in his pockets. "I don't have much of a choice, do I? First my father told me to leave. Now Sol."

"From the way I see it, it's all about choices. Your choices. You want it all. You want your family but you want to keep your car." She tilted her head. "Would you actually leave your family? The place you belong? You'd throw it all away because of . . . *a car*?"

"Yes! No! It's not . . . that simple." Gone was Zach's usual peppermint breeze of self-confidence. Suddenly, he looked like a child.

Jaime's voice softened. "But it is, Zach. What you have here—a family that cares about you—most people would give anything to have what you have. And you're tossing it away like it's worthless. You can't have it both ways. You have to make some choices."

His mouth twitched, and for a moment she could see him struggling within himself, trying to fight off the bitterness and resentment. "My father is the one who thinks I'm worthless! He's the one who tossed me away!" His words grew louder and louder until he was shouting at her.

At first, Jaime felt bewildered by Zach's strong reaction, as if she had struck a match and tossed it onto gasoline. She resisted the urge to back away from the blast of his anger.

In the barn this morning, Zach had seemed so together for a boy his age, so mature and wise, but now she saw him for what he was: a hurt and lost child, desperately seeking his father's attention. As he ran out of words, his eyes filled with boyish disappointment.

What was worse, she felt as if she were listening to herself. She saw herself in him!

Dear Lord, she sounded like she was seventeen again, as childish as Zach. She may be going about it in a different way, but she was doing everything she could to win her father's approval and attention.

She took a step closer to him. "Zach, I understand."

"No! I don't think you do."

"Listen to me. Tell me if this is what it feels like to you. It feels like having a space, you see, right here—" she tapped her breastbone—"and that space needs to be filled." She let out a deep sigh. She didn't want to chase her father's love anymore. She didn't want to pursue a futile dream. *Just admit it, Jaime!* It was time to call an end to her lifelong quest to be her father's daughter. It was as if someone was rapping the gavel. *Time to move on!*

She looked down at her shoes in the snow. Her feet were getting cold. Maybe her father loved her in his own peculiar way—but it wasn't the comforting kind of dad love she wanted. A love that didn't have any strings attached to it. A love she didn't have to work so hard to deserve.

You want something from your father that he can't give you. No one can. Only God gives perfect love.

Jaime's chin lifted. "What did you say?"

Zach turned to face her. "I didn't say anything."

She looked around her. "Did you hear something? A voice?"

Zach's forehead wrinkled. "Uh, no."

She heard it again. *You want something from your father that he can't give you. No one can. Only God gives perfect love.* She could hear it as plain as day. Where had that voice come from?

A thought came to Jaime then—a thought so luminous it made her feel flushed. It made her heart move in her chest as though it were trying to escape. Something clicked inside of her. Or unclicked.

She needed to talk to someone about The Voice. She needed to think long and hard about it, to examine it and ponder it.

But there wasn't time! Zach stood in front of her, strawberry haired, ruddy faced, handsome, sad. She felt drawn to Zach—she felt *paired* with him—they were so similar. She couldn't wait; she had to tell him what The Voice said. Part of it anyway.

"That dream—of getting your father's love—it isn't going to come true. Not today, maybe not ever. Sometimes, we want more from people than they can give us. They simply don't have it to give."

It made so much sense! But she didn't add what The Voice said about God's perfect love. *That* . . . she did not understand.

Zach was listening so earnestly, concentrating so carefully on what she said, that she wanted to throw her arms around him and give him a big smacker right on his cute little mouth. But she knew he would misinterpret that so she leaned over and kissed him on the cheek. The lightest kiss.

"Thank you," she said.

"You're welcome," he said. "For what?"

"For the offer to go with you today. For everything." Jaime

took the keys out of her pocket and handed them to him. "If you want to leave, go ahead and take my car. But only to meet up with your friends. Take them for a ride. Not to the ocean, mind you! You know that Friendly's Ice Cream Parlour at the edge of town, right before the highway entrance? Leave the car in the parking lot, put the keys under the mat."

He couldn't have looked more surprised if she had handed him an airplane ticket to the moon.

She walked past him and stopped. "Just know that you will never find anything out there"—she pointed to the road—"that comes close to what you're giving up here." She swung her arm to point to the farmhouse, like a weathervane turning in the wind. She started up the hill toward the house.

"Wait a minute!" Zach caught up to her. "Where are you going? I thought you needed to be someplace."

"I do," she said. She pointed to the kitchen. "In there."

Zach had never imagined himself behind the wheel of a car like this. Old beaters, yes, like the one he had hidden away on a seldom-considered corner of Sol and Mattie's wooded property. He bought the 1983 yellow Toyota Corolla from a man as old as Noah, and this guy wheezed when he talked, the way Zach imagined Noah might wheeze after climbing a deck or two on the Ark. He paid the old guy $500 plus cleaned out his garage. The car didn't even run, but Zach fixed it up by buying used parts from a dealer. The car had no turn signals, and even in December when it was ten below zero, he had to crank down his window and stick his arm out so that oncoming traffic would know he was turning. There was something wrong with the ignition—sometimes it started, sometimes it didn't. Many a time he had to run alongside that car to get it started, and Susie Blank—bless her—was right there with him, running, pushing, hopping into the passenger side.

It wasn't much of a car and it smelled like a polecat had expired in the trunk, but at least it got him places faster than a buggy. And it gave him time alone for . . . well, time alone with Susie Blank. At least, it *could* provide a little privacy and transportation until his little cousin got into it. When he went to check on it, he had to shovel snow out of it because Danny left the windows open. And then when he tried to turn the key to get the engine started, the key snapped off in his hand. Frozen solid.

As a kid, Zach used to love winter. Sledding, skating, bonfires, snowball fights.

Now? He hated snow. Hated it! It was nothing but a nuisance.

A loud, rumbling noise startled him and pulled his thoughts back to the present. He watched the snowplow head down the road. The driver tipped his head at Zach as he went past, and even turned the plow forward so it wouldn't leave a drift in front of the car. Zach was sure he detected a hint of admiration in the man's eyes. He probably thought Zach owned this car. Such an assumption made Zach grin from ear to ear.

He thought he might drive by Susie Blank's farmhouse and see if she happened to be outside now that the storm had passed by. He wondered if she was still mad at him. He had climbed up on the Blanks' roof last weekend, to rap on Susie's window, like they had planned. She was going to sneak out with him for a midnight drive. He had no trouble climbing up the rose trellis onto the porch. He had no trouble finding a window. Unfortunately, he rapped on the wrong window, and next thing he knew, the sash slid up with a loud screech and Zach was suddenly nose to nose with someone who had salt-and-pepper bushy hair and a weak chin.

"Why, Susie!" Zach said, blinking his eyes in surprise. "You've gone and gotten ugly on me!"

The bushy hair and weak chin belonged to Susie's father.

Susie was no longer allowed to run around with Zach. The next day, after a singing, she told Zach he was an idiot.

"I told you which window to go to!" she told him with eyes narrowed. "I even drew a picture for you!"

"I lost the drawing!" he tried to object.

"Du ware gsoffe!" *You were drunk!*

That, he couldn't deny. And it was at that moment that she called him a Dummkopp! *An idiot!* "My father thinks you will always be a reckless fool. In your heart and in your head. I'm starting to think he's right!"

Whatever happened to mercy? To Christian grace? What about love covering up all sins and not being steamed at a fellow forever, and forgiving that same fellow for a few measly trespasses? *What about that, Susie Blank? Huh?* But he didn't say it out loud. Even he wasn't that big a fool.

She ended up going home from the singing in Raymond Troyer's buggy, a pimply faced boy who would never risk the wrath of Susie's father.

Maybe Susie was right. Maybe he would always be a reckless fool. He himself couldn't grasp what it was inside of him, where it came from, this terrible urge that drove him to have things he shouldn't have, to want things he shouldn't want. Like this longing to sit behind the driver's wheel in such a car as this red convertible.

Ah, well, why worry about that little spat with Susie on a day like today? He fiddled with a few buttons and switches on the dashboard. The windshield wipers worked like a charm, and suddenly, he had a clear view of the open road.

What if he just took it for a quick spin? Just down to Susie Blank's house and back. It was the chance of a lifetime, the chance for pure happiness. He knew he was standing on a precipice here, that he should think this over very carefully, very thoroughly. Should he drive off in this wonder car? No, never.

But he might.

C.J. picked up the map Sol had left on the table and mentally split it into sections. "Show me the most likely areas that Danny would head to."

"I doubt he'd be in the fields. He must be heading uphill." Sol pointed to the ridge behind the farm.

"Okay, then we're going to take this grid first." C.J. circled that area.

"Let's go," Sol said.

As he started for the door, C.J. stopped him. "Sol, bear with my questions for a few more minutes. Help me reconstruct the last time we saw Danny. Do you remember anything he said? Whom he spoke to last?"

Sol shook his head. "I left him with you when I took Dixie into the barn. What did he say to you?"

C.J. scratched his head. "He wanted Tucker to go with him someplace. He said . . . he said, 'I know what could help.'" C.J. saw Jaime slip behind the men into the kitchen. He tried not to look as shocked as he felt to see her. He assumed she had left.

Jaime looked around the kitchen. "Where's my camera?" She looked at C.J. "Maybe Danny took it."

"Danny would never just take your camera," Mattie said. "Besides, he doesn't even know how to use it."

Jaime winced. "He does," she said. "I showed him. This morning, in the barn. He took some pictures of the baby lamb."

"What would he be trying to photograph?" C.J. asked. "What would 'make it better'?" He looked at Jaime. "He was talking about you. He wanted to find something to make you feel better after you talked to your father." He walked up to her. "Think, Jaime. Did you have any conversation with him that could be a clue?"

Jaime looked baffled. "We talked about all kinds of things. Danny talked . . . a lot." She frowned, then her eyes lit up. "He showed me his box of arrowheads and tomahawks. Indian artifacts. He said that the amazing thing is when you find an arrowhead, the last person who had touched it was possibly an Indian."

C.J. turned to Sol. "Any idea where he would go to find arrowheads?"

Sol grabbed his hat. "There are a few places that we've found them." He pointed to a top section of the map. "It's this northern area."

C.J. held up the map and pointed to sections. "We'll split into three. Cover more territory." He looked around the room. "Where's Zach?"

"Um," Jaime said, "he had something he had to do."

"Is he coming back?" C.J. asked.

Sol narrowed his eyes. "Don't count on him."

Something was going on with Zach that seemed to involve

Jaime and Sol, but C.J. didn't have time to wonder what. There was so much drama going on in this little farmhouse! He turned to Sol. "Never mind. We'll split the farm into two, with four quarter sections. Remember to call out Tucker's name too, as well as Danny's. Whistle for him, call his name, then listen for a bark. Call, then listen. Call, then listen. It's important to be quiet long enough to be able to hear a response. The snow muffles sounds." He held the map out to Sol. "If you feel confident that you've searched an area completely, then take this next quarter section. I'll take the lower areas and go north." He glanced at his wristwatch. "We'll meet back at the house in two hours. No matter what. Meet me back here at four thirty."

"What do you mean, no matter what?" Mattie asked. "What then?"

He turned to Mattie. He saw the dread in her eyes. "We'll need to regroup and cover another area. But chances are we'll find him long before then."

Mattie grabbed a coat. "I'm coming with you."

"No, Mattie," C.J. said, his voice kind and indulgent. "It's important that someone remains here. If Danny comes home on his own, he needs to find someone here waiting for him. Otherwise, he'll just go out again."

She stopped putting on her coat. "Bring my boy back. Please." Her mouth was a line.

"That dog won't leave him alone, Mattie," C.J. said. "Tucker is the best chance Danny has to stay warm and get back to you before the storm hits."

Sol and C.J. moved toward the door. Jaime stopped C.J. on the porch. "Do you want me to come too?"

He didn't look at her. "I thought you had a plane to catch."

"No, I don't," she said. "I'm not leaving, C.J. I'll go searching with you."

Sol interrupted. "Stay with Mattie. Keep her mind from worrying."

Mattie joined them on the porch. "What if Danny is truly lost? It can happen to the best of woodsmen, you said. You said it just this morning when you were talking to Danny about your work. You said that even experienced woodsmen get disoriented."

"I also told Danny other things about Search and Rescue—about how to survive in the woods if you get lost," C.J. said. "Remember? Hug-a-tree. Sit-and-stay. He heard those things just this morning."

"It's true, Mattie," Sol said. "God was watching over him, even then."

"Mattie, it's not time to worry yet," C.J. said. "He hasn't been gone that long."

"How often have you found children alive?" Mattie's voice was eerily calm. She was looking deep into C.J.'s eyes.

He tried to think of something to say to her, something that was truthful, and hopeful, and positive. "All the time, Mattie. Clever kids—ones like Danny—are smart and resourceful."

But Mattie kept looking at him, as if she was reading his thoughts. She had that way about her, of reading a person's soul. Then she pressed her eyes closed for a long second, like she was praying.

For C.J., the silence that followed was studded with guilt. He couldn't tell her about the twins who died last fall, who might have been saved if he had been better skilled at his job. He couldn't tell her the truth, that he felt a spike of worry himself. He had expected Danny and Tucker to have come flying through the kitchen door while he and Sol were dividing up the farm to search for them.

Jaime stepped between them. "C.J. is good at what he does, Mattie. The best, best, best. He's had dozens of successful searches. He doesn't give up."

Relief crossed Mattie's face like a ray of light.

Jaime put her arm around Mattie. "We need to let these guys get started."

As she steered her inside, into the warmth of the kitchen, she looked over her shoulder at C.J. She mouthed the words, "Go find him."

It was all Mattie could do to keep herself from running after the men. How was it possible that Danny would be out in that dangerous and unpredictable world? She stood for several minutes, staring out after them. She pressed her hand flat against the window and shook her head to clear it. Outside, there were now more clouds than sky.

She stepped onto the porch, where she lifted her face to the sky. Where was Danny? she wondered, sudden tears in her eyes. Where could he be?

Jaime brought out her coat and wrapped it around Mattie's shoulders. "C.J. will find him, Mattie."

Mattie was almost shivering with frantic energy. She was holding herself together with a thin layer of skin and teeth-gritting determination. She had to think about something else, or she'd simply explode. "Where's Zach? You said he had something he had to do. Where did he go?"

As she saw Jaime's hesitation, she was suddenly furious.

Why were people keeping things from her? Why did everyone assume she would shatter like a teacup at the first sign of trouble? She wasn't made of spun sugar. "Tell me what you know." She stopped, interrupted by the sudden tightness in her throat.

Jaime's gaze shifted down the driveway. Mattie hadn't noticed before, but that car of hers was gone. "When is he coming back?"

Jaime's eyes darted nervously. "Let's go inside and get warm."

They sat at the kitchen table and Jaime told her what she did know—that Sol had asked Zach to leave, and that Zach had taken her car to meet some friends. Mattie tried not to show it but she was livid with Sol. How dare he do such a thing without talking to her first! It troubled her to see how rigid and unbending Sol could be with Zach. She never imagined Sol would become this kind of man, but he was acting more like Zach's own father every day. Stiff and rule-bound. And she knew it was because Sol didn't want Danny exposed to Zach's errant ways. Sol accused her of babying their son—well, he was trying to create a cocoon of his own making for their boy.

She felt so badly for Zach—she was sure he must have left their home hurt, feeling abandoned. And because of Sol's ridiculous declaration, they had one less person on the farm to help look for Danny.

Mattie rubbed her forehead. How had this happened? She wanted to start this day all over again, to rewrite the way this day had gone. One moment they were all safe, the next moment not.

Mattie blamed herself for Danny's disappearance. She

had not been watching him. She had been absorbed in her own thoughts, her own sadness. She had been sleeping . . . while her son wandered into danger. She felt preoccupied, muddled, distracted. She put her hand to her forehead. It was hot and damp, like she had a fever. The tears started up again, out of her control.

Jaime reached out and covered her hand with hers. "It's okay, Mattie," she said soothingly.

But, of course, it wasn't okay.

A cloud smothered the sun, and the kitchen darkened.

Sol tried to think the way Danny's mind worked and went up a trail they'd traveled many times over the years. If Danny wanted to find arrowheads, this would be the path he would have taken. Sol looked carefully for tracks, for any sign of Danny's footprints, or of a dog's pawprints. Every fifty feet or so, he would stop and call out Danny's name. Then Tucker's. Then he would wait for an answer. And pray.

It was not reasonable, at this point, to panic, because there might be a simple answer to his boy's whereabouts. Since Danny learned to walk, he had been one to wander. He would get absorbed in following something—a bird, a squirrel, and he would follow its trail. Sol used to say he wanted to put a cowbell around that boy just to know where he had gone to.

He passed a place where he and Mattie and Danny had once had a picnic, when Danny was just a toddler. Mattie had led them off the main path and through the trees, following a creek, until they emerged in a sunstruck place she remembered for its wild blackberries. Wind moved lightly in the long grass and the dark green leaves of the blackberry canes shimmered against the earth. The air was full of sweetness and the hum of insects. It was a perfect summer day.

They had spread out their picnic: sandwiches and lemonade and homemade cookies and clusters of Concord grapes from their garden. Sol sat down on the blanket and held Danny in his lap, holding his hands—those plump, dimpled hands—to keep him from pulling off his knitted socks. He remembered thinking idly of his own father's hands, stocky and strong, with skilled, blunt fingers that covered Sol's hands as he taught him to heft an ax or milk the cow or pound a nail. Was that how Danny would remember Sol's hands?

Danny was never one to sit still for long. He succeeded in pulling off one sock, then dropped it and crawled off toward the grassy world beyond the blanket. Even then, he was intent on exploring the world.

Sol watched him pick up a rock and put it in his mouth, a look of surprise flashing across his small face at the strange texture and taste.

"Awful, isn't it?" he said softly, wiping dirt and drool from Danny's chin.

Mattie moved beside him, quietly, efficiently, taking out things from the basket.

"Should he have that in his mouth?" Mattie asked, settling down beside him, so close he was aware of her sweet scent, filling the air.

"Probably not," he said, unclenching the rock from Danny's fist and replacing it with a torn off piece of bread instead.

They ate lazily, then picked ripe blackberries for dessert, sun-washed and tender. Danny ate them by fistfuls, juice running down his cheeks onto his bib. He lifted a chubby arm to point to two golden eagles, circling in the deep blue sky.

Later, when he fell asleep, Mattie moved him on a blanket in the shade.

"This is nice," Mattie observed, settling against Sol, who leaned with his back against a tree. "We should do this more often."

Sol looked at Danny, sleeping so deeply with his head turned to the side, his long hair curling against his damp neck. He kissed the top of his wife's head, warmed by the sun. It *was* nice. It was more than nice. It was a hint of heaven. Mattie looked up at him, expecting him to say something, but he kept his face turned away; he didn't want her to see him so stirred by emotion.

No sooner did the memory of that perfect day seep into his head than it began to snow. Great wet clots of flakes as big as fists. He looked back over his shoulder, blinking hard to get the ice crystals off his lashes. He snapped his head around and peered through the lace curtain of falling snow ahead of him. It was a silent cold, like having your ears stuffed with cotton. The snow and the still, heavy air muffled all sound, except occasionally the sound of a raven calling out as it flew overhead, although he couldn't see it.

He pulled out his pocket watch. Nearly two o'clock. He planned to give this clock to Danny on his sixteenth birthday, the age when his father had given it to him. Sol had never begged anything of God before, but he was begging now. He was, in his heart at least, on his knees with his hands clasped in an agony of pleading. *Please God,* he prayed over and over, like a litany, with every step up the hill. *Please help me find my son. Please keep Danny safe. Please, please, please.*

The grandfather clock in the living room ding-donged out the three strokes of the hour. Certainly, Jaime thought, C.J. or Sol had found Danny by now. She glanced down at Buster, sleeping quietly on his perch. Lucky Buster. He didn't know that his surrogate father was missing, and he wouldn't care until it was time for the next mouse. He'd be fine as long as a mouse was delivered, on schedule. It wasn't so easy for people.

She tried to think of ways to get Mattie's mind off the search for Danny and on to other things. She asked Mattie if she wanted to quilt. No. Would she teach her how to bake bread? Seemed as if Amish housewives were always baking bread. But Mattie said no and went into the living room to look out the windows. Jaime decided to try to get Mattie to eat or drink something. She opened the cupboard and found a half-used jar of instant coffee. It was the kind her mother used to make every morning. Jaime unscrewed the cap and inhaled deeply. She suddenly felt overcome with a wave of grief. It really was the little things, like instant coffee, that made Jaime miss her mother the most.

Jaime took out two mugs and reached for the hot water kettle that sat on top of the woodstove so the steam would humidify the room. In the silence that was not quite silence—the sink faucet dripping, the grandfather clock ticking softly, the wind whistling through the trees—her thoughts traveled to memories of her mother.

She stirred in two heaping teaspoons into the mugs, watching the brown crystals dissolve. The smell of the coffee faded, much the way her mother's vivid, everyday presence in her mind was fading. She couldn't remember the whole of her anymore, only bits and pieces: the way she would slip off her shoes as soon as she walked into anyone's home, even if she had a hole in her sock. Or the way her face would light up when Jaime and C.J. stopped by for a visit. Her mother adored C.J. "He's a keeper, that one," she liked to say. Jaime felt so concerned about Danny that her worry over her marriage receded into the background, but it did not disappear.

What kind of card would her mother send her now, if she knew how thin was the string that was holding her and C.J. together? Jaime could imagine it: a big dog like Tucker on the front of the card, and inside it would read "DOG! Depend On God!"

Jaime's hair fell over her cheek as she bent to put a cup of coffee next to Mattie. She settled onto the couch, tucking her legs beneath her. Mattie had her Bible open on her lap and her head was bent over it. Jaime could see the white part of Mattie's scalp where her hair was parted.

Jaime picked up her spoon and stirred the milk into the coffee. *Ching!*

Mattie flinched, as if she hadn't realized Jaime was there.

"Does it help? Reading from the Bible?" she asked Mattie.

Gently, as if it were something very precious, Mattie closed the Bible. "It helps tremendously." She noticed the coffee and reached over to pick it up. "Don't you find that Scripture helps you in times of need?"

Jaime shrugged. "I don't read the Bible. C.J. does, now and then. Over the last six months or so, he's been going to church." Eve's church. Eve had the gall to invite him to join her one Sunday and he went. Happily. "I guess you could say he's got more of a religious bent than I do. Since my mother died, God and I parted ways."

Mattie looked at her, confused. "What does that mean, exactly?"

"C.J. is just more open than I am to the idea of believing in things you can't see. I tend to accept only things I can see." Or hear? Like, The Voice?

She thought about bringing up The Voice—especially because Mattie seemed to be a little less distracted with worry about Danny. Jaime still wasn't sure how or why The Voice had suddenly bounced into her head. Could it have been that God put it there? And if so, did that mean she was . . . praying? Had Jaime turned into a praying person? Did that mean she would have to start going to church? She wouldn't! She was still mad at God.

The last time she set foot in a church was on the afternoon of her mother's funeral. As she followed the casket out of the church, she left the church behind. The church where her mother had died.

Last June, on a typical Sunday morning, Connie Mac-Comber walked out of church and crossed the street to reach her parked car. She was coming over to Jaime and C.J.'s for brunch. It was their weekly get-together and C.J. always came up with a complicated new recipe to try that required every dish in the kitchen. That morning he was whipping up Belgian waffles with blueberries and pecans. Jaime vividly remembered every detail of that morning. The phone rang, and C.J. reached for it, still whisking egg whites for the waffle batter, the receiver tucked under his chin. As he listened, he stopped stirring the eggs and got a strange look on his face. It was so quiet she heard a wasp buzzing against the window screen. C.J. hung up and came over to sit with her at the table.

"That was the police," he said, in a voice that didn't sound like his. Tight, clogged with tears. "Your mother was hit by a car." He took a deep breath as if he was struggling for air. "The officer said . . . he said . . . she was killed instantly."

Ever since, Jaime felt as if her life was divided into two halves. Before that phone call. And after.

Connie MacComber, a woman who had survived all kinds of hard things—who was deserted by her husband, who had raised a child all on her own—her life was over in a matter of seconds. Killed. Boom, just like that.

The drunk driver who hit Connie MacComber was eventually sent to jail, but that didn't matter to Jaime. It didn't change the fact that her mother was dead. Better to watch your parent die of cancer, Jaime felt, than to have it happen without any warning. So sudden, so premature. Her mother was only forty-nine years old. No time for goodbyes. No time for one last "I love you." So unfair!

How could there possibly be a loving God who would allow a good person like her mother to die in such a needless, senseless way? Jaime concluded there were only two options: either there was no God—and that option didn't work because she knew there were too many mysteries in the universe to think it was all by chance—or, God didn't care.

Now *that* made sense to her. So that's what she settled on. The clockmaker theory. God set things into motion and let things go. Off to meddle in another galaxy!

She knew her mother would object to her theology. She often cobbled together imaginary conversations with her mother: "Listen here, Jaime. Don't go blaming that accident on God. He wasn't behind the wheel of that other car. All things happen for a reason."

But Jaime was never satisfied with pat answers. Her mother used to say that she was forever picking at the Bible and questioning it.

"I'm just trying to understand," Jaime would tell her.

"What's there to understand?" her mother replied confidently. "God said it. I believe it. End of story."

And then Jaime would roll her eyes and call her mother a happy, sappy Christian. She used to make fun of her for believing God spoke to her.

Until thirty minutes ago, when something—Someone?—spoke to Jaime. Today of all days!

A blast of wind hit the house and made the windows rattle, jolting Jaime out of her theological muse. She looked over at Mattie, surprised to see her leaning forward on the couch, peering intently at her. Clearly, Mattie wanted to continue this conversation.

"So, then, for example, you don't believe in the wind?" Mattie asked.

"I believe in the wind. You can feel it and sense it and observe its effects."

"But you can't touch it or see it." She picked up a book on the coffee table and dropped it on the floor with a *thunk*. "Gravity is all around us, from the heavens to the ground under us." She plucked a feather from a couch pillow and raised her arm as high as she could, then released the feather. She watched it flutter to the ground. "Isn't *that* believing in something you can't see?"

One thing that always nagged at Jaime about such declarations of belief: wasn't there such a thing as just having faith in faith? "Believing in a law of nature like gravity isn't really the same as believing in a God who is involved in our everyday life." She might have sounded a little more defensive than she intended.

Mattie looked out the window and released a sigh. "To me, it is. Powerful, invisible, majestic, mysterious. And faithful. Gravity is a force utterly consistent in its steadiness on all items—great and small. God is faithful even when we are not."

For a moment, Jaime forgot that she was in an Amish farmhouse on Christmas Eve, that the hosts' child had disappeared, that her plans for Christmas had fallen apart. For a moment, she was having a debate about the existence of God, just like she used to with her mother. She felt like a teenager again, trying to figure things out for the first time.

"Oh Mattie, do you honestly believe that God who created the universe and put laws of gravity into place—do you honestly believe he cares about our little, tiny planet in this small Milky Way galaxy, among billions of galaxies! Do you really think we're of any significance to him? And you really, truly believe that God actually cares about your thoughts and your choices and your concerns?"

Mattie locked on to her eyes. "I do." She leaned forward on the couch. "I believe God reveals his loving nature in all kinds of wondrous ways. Every single day. From sunrises and sunsets, to the families he's given to us to share this life, to—" Buster gave a loud squawk from his box in the kitchen and Mattie smiled—"to birds and animals. To the greatest miracle of all—the birth of the Christ child, a holy God entering into his creation to redeem it. God's perfect love is all around us, Jaime. But if you shut your eyes to all the light he has given to you, you can't see the evidence of his love."

God's perfect love? There it was again! What did that

mean?! Okay. *Fine!* If Mattie wanted to push her on this topic, Jaime was going to push right back. "Mattie, if you believe that God is really out there, truly watching over everyone, that he's a good and loving God like the Bible says . . . then why are you so anxious about everything? Why do you seem to live as if you're expecting a catastrophe at every turn? So if you pray, why worry? And if you worry, why pray?"

Mattie looked at her for a long while with an inscrutable expression on her face. Quietly, she stood and left the room.

Jaime heard Mattie's bedroom door shut gently but firmly. *Bad, bad idea.*

In the silence that remained, all Jaime could hear was the ticking of the old clock and Buster in his box, hissing and spitting like he was angry.

Why does my mouth seem to run ahead of my brain? She had said all the wrong things. She had only made things worse for Mattie. She was trying to distract her from worry, only to bring it right up again. She rubbed her face and leaned her head back against the couch.

She let out a loud sigh. She had blown her chance to ask Mattie about The Voice.

Not long after C.J. set out, there came the first shrieking, biting gust of wind. It sent the falling flakes spinning and whirling crazily and whipped at the loose snow on the ground. The knife slash of the wind cut through his clothes and felt as if it were shredding his lungs. He glanced at his wristwatch: twenty minutes after three. He pulled his collar up around his neck and pushed on.

C.J. had encouraged Sol to head up to the ridge that lined

the farm's property, hoping he would be able to catch sight of Danny and Tucker from a high vantage point. He wanted to stay on the low ground—to follow the stream that fed the pond. All kinds of streams crisscrossed these Amish farms, carving crevices through pastures, and he knew those banks were extremely unstable. He carefully followed the stream, calling for Tucker and Danny, listening for a response, scanning the area for signs of a boy and a dog. The stream was smothered under a blanket of fresh snow, the willows that lined the banks were all fringed with it. He tried to look as far as he could see for any sign of movement, but the whole world looked frozen dead.

He was trying not to panic. As an experienced SAR volunteer, he knew of countless stories just like this—a family was enjoying themselves, got busy and distracted, a child wandered off—and the day ended in tragedy.

But not today. Not this Christmas Eve. He wouldn't let a tragedy happen again, not like it did last summer. He had to be able to find Danny. Even without Tucker and his nose, C.J. had enough experience now to find Danny. Didn't he?

Enough. Funny how that word seemed to keep hitting him in the face lately.

His mind drifted to Jaime's comment last night, that sometimes love just wasn't enough. A few weeks ago they'd had a terrible argument. It was a Sunday morning and he had planned to meet Eve for church. He asked her if she wanted to come along—like he always did—and Jaime acted as if he had insulted her. "Why should I come?" she said. "I would just get in the way."

"What's that supposed to mean?" he had said.

"What do you think it means?" she asked.

"Jaime, what's going on? Why are you overreacting?"

"You don't love me," she said. "You've never loved me."

"I do love you." He tried to keep his voice steady. He could see she was steaming like a tea kettle and he wasn't sure why.

"Not enough! You don't love me enough."

"I do love you enough," he said. But it worried him that it would never be enough.

Before he could say anything more, she darted into the bedroom, slamming the door behind her and locking it.

C.J. knocked on the door. "Jaime? Please open up. Jaime, I don't know what's made you so upset."

He heard nothing from the other side of the door but her muffled crying. Even with his best intentions, the best he could give, he'd somehow failed. He had listened for a minute, and then he picked up his car keys and left to meet Eve.

How could he love Jaime enough when she always wanted more?

A blast of cold wind slapped him in the face. The wind shifted from southwest to due west and the sky was low and gunmetal gray. Something caught his eye in the open field he was walking through—an area of discoloration against the snow. He picked up his pace until he reached it. It was discolored, all right—a stain of fresh blood on the snow. C.J. sank down on his knees in the snow and searched around to see if he could find any clues—any fur or tracks or indication of what this was. Fresh kill? He leaned forward to examine the blood and caught sight of something slightly buried—a stick? A rope? Carefully he dug it out. His heart started thumping wildly. It was a dog collar. A small tuft of yellow fur was still attached from where the collar had been torn off. Bitten off.

C.J. had found Tucker's collar.

He cupped his hands around his mouth and called out, "Danny! Tucker!" Then he listened for a response. Nothing. He called again and again. Nothing.

He glanced at his wristwatch: ten minutes to four. He *had* to keep going.

When Jaime's cell phone started to vibrate, she dove for it and moved into the farthest reaches of the living room before she answered. Mattie was still upstairs and she wasn't sure if she was mad at her or not. The last thing she needed was to add to Mattie's aggravation by having a cell phone in the house.

"Hello?" she answered in a whisper.

"Jaime! This is Marilyn. Marilyn Steffey. From Sears Portrait Studio. Listen, I spoke to my boss who spoke to her boss who spoke to the store manager, and we're willing to offer you a promotion if you'll come back. You can be the studio manager."

"But . . . *you're* the studio manager," Jaime whispered.

"I've been promoted too! I'm going to be the district manager."

"Oh," Jaime whispered.

"Aren't you thrilled? This is highly unusual in a dismal economy. You should be thrilled!"

"I am. So, so thrilled," Jaime whispered.

"Then why don't you sound thrilled? It's a boost in salary, Jaime, from being an associate. You're on a *career* track."

"Sorry. Laryngitis," Jaime fibbed. "Could I call you back? On Monday?"

Marilyn was disappointed. "I suppose."

"I'll talk to you Monday. Merry Christmas, Marilyn. And thank you." Jaime hung up. So, she had her job back. She leaned back and rested her head on the top of the couch, staring at the ceiling.

The grandfather clock eked out another hour. This announcement was mercifully short: three o'clock. When Mattie heard it, she knew she should get downstairs in case the men came back soon. She wiped away her tears, splashed cold water on her face, and smoothed her hair. Down in the kitchen, she was pulled to the window, as if Sol and C.J. might already be turning into the yard with Danny. A layer of ice coated the glass.

Jaime joined her by the window. "Maybe we should go feed the animals. So when the men come back with Danny, they don't have to go back out."

Mattie nodded, grateful for something to do. Grateful for Jaime's brave optimism. They put on their coats and Jaime wrapped up Mattie's face with a scarf as if she was the mother and Mattie was the child. Jaime walked ahead of Mattie, shielding her from the wind the way Sol would do. In the last twenty-four hours, she and Jaime had switched roles. Jaime was the strong one now. Mattie was the weak one.

Mattie had lived in Stoney Ridge all her life, but she hadn't known it could snow this hard or be this cold. It seemed the wind blew the stinging, biting flakes right through her, as if she were invisible. The horses stood in their stalls, hunched and sad against the wind that slashed through the cracks in the barn walls. Mattie's hands were as clumsy as clubs, her arms and legs stiff, as she pitched hay to the horses and broke the ice in their water buckets. But every time she drew a breath of the icy air, it felt as if a knife were sliding into her chest. She was *that* cold, inside a barn. What was this wind doing to a small boy in a thin coat?

Mattie was measuring out grain for the horses when Jaime came into the feed room.

"I'm sorry, Mattie. I didn't mean to offend you earlier. I feel terrible that something I said made you cry."

Mattie was genuinely surprised by that comment. She finished filling the bucket, closed the wooden lid, clipped it to keep out mice, and sat down on it, facing Jaime. "You didn't offend me. Just the opposite. You were right. I went up to my room and asked the Lord to forgive me for being so fearful. For ever doubting him."

It was more than just that. Back in her room, as Mattie prayed, confessing everything to God, withholding nothing, telling him all of the thoughts—even the ugliest ones that kept swimming through her head—something broke inside of her. She felt peace within her swell and grow, connecting her back to the world. She grew calm, became again that wide tranquil river, accepting the world and carrying it easily on her currents. Danny belonged to God, not to her. If she truly believed that, why was she living as if she could control all the circumstances that surrounded him? She couldn't. She never could. She exhaled a stream of breath she had been unconsciously holding on to . . . for how long now? Four years? Five? She felt lighter. She felt centered. She felt like her best self.

The mystery of prayer! The ability to commune with the Lord God! It never ceased to astound Mattie that God would want to know her every thought. To think she had tried to hide her dark thoughts from God, to stuff them down, to pretend they didn't exist. It shamed her to think she could. She had never considered herself to be an overly prideful person, but pride was sneaky; it had so many twists and variations to tangle a person. Listening to Jaime talk about her mother's death, seeing the anger she harbored toward God for not preventing it—why, Mattie recognized herself in Jaime! She was angry with God for denying her a child. She assumed God had turned his face from her—without cause or explanation. Without love.

She remembered a sermon her grandfather Caleb Zook had given once from the book of Job, how he pointed out that Job and his friends assumed the trials of his life meant he had lost favor with God.

"Not true!" her grandfather had said. "God's favor doesn't suddenly disappear. He is kind and trustworthy from generation to generation. But our faith in God should never be fastened to circumstances. God promises to never leave us, nor forsake us—*whatever* our circumstances."

That reminder was just what she needed this very afternoon. She hadn't lost God's favor. He had never abandoned her. He was right in the midst of their lives—of Danny's disappearance, of her grieving over her miscarriage, of her barrenness. He was there yesterday, today, and tomorrow—with all its unknowns. *Emmanuel. God is with us.*

Jaime's head was down. She slowly lifted her eyes to meet Mattie's. "What if Danny isn't found soon?" she whispered. "What then?"

Mattie's breath caught. *Not found?* Jaime had voiced aloud a fear that had nagged at Mattie all through the long afternoon.

Jaime went over to sit next to her. "Bad things happen. Even to good people like you and Sol."

"Bad things do happen, but not randomly. Not without purpose."

Holding her elbows, Jaime leaned forward. "But they do, Mattie. My mother was walking across the street after leaving church and she was killed by a drunk driver! You can't tell me *that's* not random and purposeless!"

"That accident passed through the hands of God. Good hands. It wasn't random and it wasn't purposeless. It was your mother's time."

Jaime stood up and walked a few paces. "What kind of God is that? This world is so dangerous! So unpredictable! If he can't—or won't— protect people who love him . . . what's the point of having faith in him? What kind of perfect love is that?"

"God never promised us a life without pain or suffering, Jaime. He's promised to never leave us in the midst of that pain. He promised to bring purpose out of that pain. Emmanuel, God is with us. That was the name given to Jesus. Emmanuel." She patted the feed bin so that Jaime would sit down again. "*That's* perfect love, Jaime. God will never leave you nor forsake you. Not on earth. Not in heaven."

Jaime sat down next to Mattie and leaned her elbows on her knees, rubbing her forehead as if she had a headache.

Maybe she does have an aching head, Mattie thought. *She's been trying to make sense of her mother's death without any help at all from God. That would give anyone a headache.* She rubbed Jaime's back in a soothing, circling motion.

How strange, Mattie thought. Minutes ago, she was thinking that Jaime was the strong one. Now they had flip-flopped again. She was feeling brave. It felt so good! She hadn't felt brave in a very, very long time.

Mattie let out the breath she had been holding. She looked around the barn, satisfied that everything was taken care of. She picked up the bucket of grain with her clumsy, mittened hand. What had she forgotten? The laundry. She needed to get started on the laundry. If she missed a day of laundry, it spiraled out of control.

Zach thought he might love this car. The word *car* seemed too humble, too ordinary, for this engineering marvel. It should be called . . . The Dream Machine. Sleek, curvy, red like a race car, a V-6 engine with 220 horses under the hood. The thought of all that power in his hands astounded him.

When Jaime first offered to let him take the car, he sat in it for the longest while before he turned on the ignition. He figured she was just kidding, or would change her mind. But as he watched her in the rearview mirror as she walked up to the farmhouse, she never looked back. When she stepped inside the kitchen, he turned the key. The engine sprang to life. The dashboard was lit up with red numbers and symbols like the instrument panel of an airplane he'd seen in a magazine. Even after this car had spent a night partially submerged in the pond! Thankfully, it was the back end that was submerged. Zach stepped on the gas a few times and revved the engine, to make sure the exhaust pipe spewed out any leftover pond water. He fiddled with the radio and switched stations fifteen times—ah, to finally be in control of something. *Anything!*

He flipped a few more switches. All of a sudden, he heard

some strange noises. The black roof started to lift! Zach panicked and flipped more switches. Too late! The top was folding up like an accordion. He whipped his head around to see if Jaime had seen the top go up. No sign of her. He shifted the car into first gear and inched toward the street. Then, he turned left onto the road. Slowly at first, as if he were driving something made of delicate bone china. As his confidence grew, he pressed the pedal a little harder. No one was on the freshly plowed roads. He pressed another button and suddenly felt his chair grow warm. Seat warmers! What more could a man ask for in life, than a red sports car with seat warmers? *Just one more thing.* A woman like Jaime Fitzpatrick sitting in the passenger seat.

Still, for Zach, today would always be his best day. Life just could not get any better than this! He was driving a convertible—fire engine red!—and he had just been kissed by a beautiful English woman—practically on the lips. He relived the kiss for a moment. It was, quite possibly, the most exquisite kiss he had ever been given. Apologies to Susie Blank, the only other person he had kissed—and Susie was a first-rate kisser. But this Jaime Fitzpatrick! It was like your first cup of Starbucks coffee when all you'd ever tasted was Folgers. Not that he was much of a coffee drinker, but he did take Susie to Starbucks once in his Toyota Corolla, just to see what everybody was talking about. Then he went home and tried Mattie's coffee. No comparison. *None!*

If only that kiss with Jaime had lasted longer than two seconds. What could it have meant? Was it possible she was attracted to him? Was it her way of letting him know she was interested? That she might be available? Okay, this was bad—a bad thought, a bad series of thoughts, a bad, bad path he was going down. Unspeakably bad.

For over an hour, he'd driven the car slowly up and down every plowed road he could find, not straying too far from the house. Snow was starting to pile up on the seat next to him. He scooped up handfuls of it and tossed it over the side before it melted on Jaime's leather upholstery. He pressed the button to close the top, admiring the convenience of this mechanical task. He couldn't wait to show the car off to his friends—and yet . . . he was in no hurry to find them. He felt a prick of conscience, like a small pebble in his shoe that he could ignore if he wiggled his toes. Maybe he should turn this car around, go back to Sol and Mattie's, find Jaime, and try to act like a normal person. Set things straight.

He definitely should turn back. It was time he grew up. Turning around would be the wise, mature thing to do. The right thing to do. It would be the first step in the long direction of mending his ways.

But before Zach was quite ready for that, he pressed on the gas just a little more, then a little more. Something caught his eye out the window—a golden eagle soaring in the sky. He wondered if he could clock how fast that eagle was flying. The long stretch of road ahead looked clear, with just a dusting of snow. He pressed on the pedal a little harder. 25 miles per hour. 35 miles per hour. 45. Amazing! This was as fast as his 1983 Toyota Corolla could ever go—that old beater started to shake at 44 miles per hour as if it might splay apart.

As Zach zipped along at speeds he'd never traveled—faster than the snow dropping from the sky—his thoughts were filled with the wonders of the automobile. 50 miles per hour.

55, 60. Had any invention changed the world more than the car? The miracle of modern machinery! 70 miles per hour, 80. The car was driving as smooth as velvet. *Astonishing!*

Up ahead, he saw a bend in the road. He pushed on the brakes, tightening his grip around the leather steering wheel to anticipate the turn. He was halfway around the bend when suddenly, inexplicably, illogically, he knew where Danny might be.

He pushed harder on the brakes to turn around. Instead, the car started to slide toward the snowbank.

Down in the basement of the farmhouse, Jaime helped Mattie wash the clothes in the washing machine. It was such a simple machine—an agitator fed by gasoline. It got the job done nicely. She thought of the washing machine she had picked out from Sears last year—all kinds of bells and whistles. Literally. The sounds drove her crazy. Dozens of choices—wash with warm, rinse with cold, hot with hot, cold with cold. Were her clothes any cleaner than Mattie's? She doubted it.

Mattie and Jaime hung the clothes on the indoor line that Sol had rigged up, quiet for a few minutes, their elbows occasionally knocking together as they worked, until Mattie said out of the blue, "What's on your mind?"

The sadness Jaime had been trying so hard to suppress oozed to the surface. "I envy you."

"Me? Whatever for?"

Where to begin? After Mattie had come back downstairs, Jaime could see she had been crying. Her eyes were swollen, her skin was blotchy. But she radiated a calmness that was almost palpable. "So many things, Mattie. For your home, your family, your faith."

"You can have all of those things. You *have* all those things."

Jaime shook her head. "My father says that nearly every marriage is tainted in some way. Either one or both parties settled, or someone is dissatisfied, or someone is cheating or at least considering it. And he should know. He's been married a number of times."

Mattie rolled her eyes. "Rubbish."

"It's true! Maybe not for you and Sol, but for the rest of us."

"You and C.J. have a good marriage."

Jaime shook her head. "He's involved with another woman."

Mattie lifted her eyebrows in disbelief.

"A woman he works with. Eve. They have a connection that we just don't have anymore. I can tell. He's slipped away from me." She bit her lip, and her eyes stung. "Everyone I've loved has disappointed me. My father never even wanted a child—that's why he left my mother. I was six months old and he walked out the door. Then my mother died! And now C.J. is giving up." She bit her lip to hold back tears that stung her eyes.

Mattie didn't say a word. Her face didn't change expression in the slightest way. She finished hanging a small blue shirt that must have belonged to Danny, and let her hand graze it gently. She put the bucket that held the clothespins back on the shelf, then went upstairs to the warm kitchen.

Didn't she hear me? Jaime thought as she trotted behind Mattie. *I just spilled my deepest, most gut-wrenching secret, and she acted like it was no big deal!* Like she knew it all along! It suddenly occurred to Jaime . . . maybe she had already known. Had C.J. told her, this very morning?

Mattie took out a large bowl and placed it on the counter. Then she gathered flour, Crisco, salt, and measuring cups. Business as usual.

"Mattie? Don't you have anything to say?"

Mattie poured a cup of flour she had measured into the bowl. She turned to face Jaime. "I see your husband's determination to find my son. He's not going to give up. I doubt he would give up on his marriage either." She went back to measuring out more cups of flour. "But you. You seem to give up pretty easily. Just because life can be hard, it doesn't mean you give up. Maybe you've been influenced by the way your father gives up on things. Like your marriage—you're giving up on that without a fight." Mattie spoke slowly, out of the beautiful calm she seemed to wear like a coat. "Maybe you've even given up on God."

Jaime sat at the table, watching Mattie fold the Crisco and flour together with a large fork. She moved with lightning speed, yet she never hurried. It amazed Jaime. Coming from anyone else, Mattie's pointed comments would have sounded like an admonishment, a scolding, but from Mattie, it just sounded like the truth, gently spoken. Was it the truth? About Mattie's insight to C.J.'s nature, Jaime had to agree. She'd never seen him give up on anything.

"What about Eve?"

"Have you ever asked him about Eve?" Mattie stopped folding the ingredients and looked at Jaime. "Have you ever talked to him about all that worries you? Really talked?"

Jaime closed her eyes. No. She had been too afraid of the answer.

Was Mattie right? *Do I give up too easily? Even worse . . .
am I like my father?* She covered her face with her hands. She
was. She was just like him! Starting things and never finish-
ing them. Jobs. School. People. Jumping from one thing to
the next. She folded her arms on the table and clunked her
head on it.

Mattie put her fork down and sat at the table next to
Jaime. "Jesus told a story about a good shepherd who
had ninety-nine sheep in his fold, but one was missing.
He left everything to go look for that one lost sheep." She
paused to let it sink in. "What if you're that lost sheep,
Jaime? What if God brought you here this weekend, and
let your precious car slide into the pond, and permitted a
snowstorm to change your plans? All of your plans! And
what if Danny's disappearance is part of God's plan to
bring you into his fold?" She placed a hand on Jaime's
arm. "And what if God brought you to me this weekend
to help remind me that the Bible is true? That God's Word
will stand forever."

Jaime lifted her head. She hated to ask this question, but
she had to. "Even . . . if things don't work out the way you
hope they will?"

"You mean, if Danny isn't found?"

Jaime gave a quick nod.

Mattie squeezed her eyes shut. "I will deal with that if and
when I have to. For now, I have a pie crust to finish." Then
she rose to her full five-foot self. "Two kinds of pies, I think
I'll make. Apple and pumpkin."

Jaime lifted her palms. "Why pie?"

Mattie looked at her as if it was the most obvious thing in
the world. "Because pie is Danny's favorite dessert."

The clock struck the hour, the quarter hour, the half hour.

Just then, Sol burst through the kitchen door. "Is he here?" His eyes met Mattie's and his face fell.

Not a minute later, C.J. arrived. He looked at Sol and shook his head. "Did you see any sign of him?"

"No," Sol said. "No sign at all."

Mattie opened up the stove to let the two men warm their hands. She took their scarves and gloves and laid them on top of the stove to dry them. The two men stood in front of the stove, faces red and wind chapped, rubbing their hands in a heavy silence.

Jaime mixed up some cups of instant coffee and handed each man a mug. She wished the pies were ready for them, but Mattie had just slipped them into the oven.

C.J. took a sip of coffee, then turned to Sol. "Show me the map you made. Show me what area you've searched."

Sol spread the map on the kitchen table. He pointed to the areas he had covered.

As the two men worked up another plan, Jaime could sense the change. This was getting serious. It was like a bad dream. Danny had been gone over three hours now. The chance of hypothermia was real.

Sol's voice stayed low and calm, like C.J.'s. Mattie—she was silent. She made some sandwiches for the men and wrapped them carefully in wax paper to be taken out on the next search. What was going through her mind? Jaime had no idea.

Jaime thought this was probably the most frightening thing that had ever happened to Mattie and Sol. They weren't used to accidents, to bad luck, to tragedy. They hadn't lived with it, maybe, the way she had.

C.J. put on his scarf and his gloves to prepare to go out again. As Sol stood to join him, C.J. shook his head. "No, Sol. You're not going out this time."

"Why not?" Sol asked.

"Yes, why not?" Mattie echoed.

C.J. exchanged a glance with Jaime. She would know exactly why not and he was hoping she wouldn't say.

This was standard operating procedure. If there was reasonable chance of a Deceased Find, family members must not be there. *Must not.* A parent's reaction at discovering his child was deceased could create yet another dangerous situation. The worst story C.J. had ever heard had happened to Tom Flint, one of his SAR buddies. A sixteen-year-old boy had gone missing during a river rafting trip. The father insisted on joining the search. The father found his son first, drowned, caught between rocks. The father panicked and jumped into the water to get his son. The father drowned too. Then Tom nearly drowned, trying to retrieve both bodies.

Mattie and Sol were waiting for C.J. to answer them. Right now, with the storm kicking up and the temperature dropping like it was, the chance of finding Danny alive was growing dim. How could C.J. tell them that? The thought was hideous to him.

"I'll go with you," Jaime said. "You shouldn't be alone out there."

"He won't be," Sol said. "I'm going with him."

C.J. cleared his throat. "I'm sorry, Sol. Not this time."

Sol took a few steps up to C.J. "Why not?" He grabbed C.J.'s jacket lapels. "Why not? What do you know that you're not telling me?" His voice was barely a whisper.

"I don't know anything." C.J. spoke calmly and slowly. Inside, though, he felt his heart going crazy. He had to get hold of himself; he did search and rescues like this all the time. But he didn't know the victims, not like he knew Danny. He had seen anguish on parents' faces before, he empathized, but he hadn't felt the anguish, not like this.

"Then why don't you want me going with you?" Sol asked, eyes narrowed. "I will not trust my son's welfare . . . to an outsider!"

"Sol!" Mattie was horrified. "This man"—she pointed to C.J. and her voice quivered—"this man is doing everything he can do *for* our son's welfare!"

C.J. looked at Mattie. The look in her eyes shook him to the core. So trusting, so hopeful. An idea took shape. "Sol, I think it's best if you can get to a neighbor's farm and see if you can collect some men to join in the search."

Sol brightened. He loosened his hold on C.J.'s coat lapels. "We should have thought of that sooner."

C.J. turned to Jaime. "Can you call the sheriff's department to let them know we need help?"

Jaime reached into her pocket and pulled out her cellphone. "Voilà!"

Sol looked at her hopefully.

She dialed 911, listened, squinted at the face of the phone, dialed again. Then she snapped it shut. "Dead battery," she said in a flat voice.

C.J. turned back to Sol. "Have someone contact the sheriff when you round up everyone. They need to bring lanterns and flashlights and dogs. I'll be back at this house in one hour. Meet me here and we'll send out people, two at a time."

"C.J. is trained at this," Jaime told Sol. "Listen to him. He will find Danny."

C.J. looked over at her. He was grateful she didn't promise he would find Danny alive. Where could that boy be? Where was Tucker? Had they been hurt? Why couldn't he find any trace of them other than that collar?

Jaime threw two large sandwiches into a brown bag she found tucked in a kitchen cupboard. She poured the rest of the coffee into a thermos, closed the lid tight, and packed it all in a sack for C.J. She handed him the sack just as he was heading out the door. She grabbed her coat and followed him out on the porch. He stood for a moment, looking out at the falling snow, at the wind that blew it every which way. Too soon, it would be dark. She knew that could be disastrous for Danny and Tucker. Between the trees across the street, she could see where the sun lay low in the sky, hidden behind gray clouds.

"C.J., what do you know that you're not telling them?"

He shifted his gaze down toward the pond. "Something had dragged off a fresh kill. I followed it as far as I could, but then I lost the tracks."

"What kind of tracks?" She put a hand on his arm. "It could have been a fox catching a rabbit. Or a squirrel. It might have been nothing at all."

He gave a slight shake of his head. He reached into his pocket and pulled out Tucker's collar. "Bobcat tracks."

Tears sprang to Jaime's eyes. This wasn't the way things

were supposed to go. Danny should be home by now! Tucker should be staring at her with those mournful brown eyes, hungry for his dinner. "Any other clues? Fabric or . . . dog hair?"

"A few tufts of Tucker's fur. There was some kind of a tussle. If Tucker saw the bobcat going after a rabbit, I wouldn't put it past him to get in the middle of it."

Even Jaime knew that all the training in the world couldn't change an animal's natural instincts. Not Tucker's, and certainly not the bobcat's. Bobcats were solitary animals, unlikely to go after a large animal—or a little boy—but if it felt threatened . . .

"C.J.," she said softly, "what if—?"

He turned to her and put a hand in the air to stop her from saying it. "Keep Mattie's mind on other things than that." His face was pale, still, but determined. He gave her a weak smile.

"I have been." Jaime tried to find a smile of her own, but she was too ill at ease. No, *scared* was the word. She was plain scared.

He took her hand, raised it to his lips, and kissed it. She felt the press of his lips on her knuckles and his breath warm on her skin. Then he gave her Tucker's collar and vanished into the snow.

She thought about The Voice. If that was God, and if he had decided to start up a conversation, maybe she should respond. Isn't that what prayer was supposed to be? She looked up at the sky. *Are you listening, God? Do you really care? If you do, please, please, please bring that boy home safely.* She put the collar into her coat pocket so Mattie and Sol wouldn't see. *And Tucker too. I'll never ask you for anything else. But please bring them home safely.*

Jaime stood on the porch for a moment, watching the sky, until she was so cold she couldn't stand it any longer. She turned and caught sight of Sol and Mattie through the kitchen window. Jaime watched Sol move toward Mattie as if pulled by gravity. Mattie's face lifted at the sight of him. He cupped her face lightly in his hands as they kissed, and then she raised her hand and their palms touched briefly, lightly, a gesture so intimate that Jaime looked away.

It was, quite possibly, the most heartbreaking embrace she had ever seen.

Although it seemed C. J. had been walking for a long time in a perpetual dusk, he sensed the hour was truly getting late. When night fell, it would be as dark as a cave and the chances of finding Danny and Tucker would grow even slimmer. He fought down swells of panic. Where could they be?

He was about to cut through a field when he heard a shout from the road. C.J. turned and saw a figure waving at him. The man started running toward C.J. He stopped when he was fifteen feet away.

The man cupped his hands around his mouth and yelled, "Did you find Danny?"

Zach! It was *Zach!*

C.J. shook his head.

Zach waved his arm like a windmill. "Follow me! I think I know where he is!" He turned and ran back down to the road.

C.J. followed close behind, picking up speed. Zach hopped a fence and started running up the road. Puzzle pieces that were floating through C.J.'s mind started to find a place. If Danny had gone down along the road, that would explain why they couldn't find any tracks. The horses, the cars, the snowplow would have erased any sign of a small boy and a dog.

Zach didn't quit running. They'd gone half a mile up the road when he finally cut off and vaulted over another fence with easy grace. He stopped to wait for C.J. "We could keep on the road, but it'll be faster if we cut through this field. Can you keep up?"

Could he keep up? What did this kid think, that he was an old geezer? Of course he could keep up! He gave Zach the thumbs-up and climbed over the fence—he had to take it in stages and hurried to keep up with him. Zach acted like an Indian scout following a faint trail. He seemed to know exactly where he was heading. There wasn't as much snow on the ground under the thick canopy of the trees, but other than that, the conditions weren't much more favorable. The wind still had a way of hitting them hard in the face.

They came to an open field—the same field where C.J. had found Tucker's collar. Zach crossed the field, passing the traces of blood without even noticing them. As C.J. ran past the spot, he saw that the wind had covered the mess with fresh snow. If he didn't recognize the stubby cornfield, he wouldn't even be able to find that spot. Not without Tucker's nose. The wind struck in volleys, driving the corn-hard pellets of snow into his face. He stumbled, went sprawling, and got mired up to his knees in a fresh drift. Scythes of snow slashed at his eyes. He slogged on, trying to keep up with Zach.

Zach kept up a brisk pace across the field. It was the same direction C.J. had been going until he lost the trail. Through another canopy of trees, they came to a bridge. Past that was an old cobhouse. Zach stopped.

"That's it," Zach said. "I bet my life on it. They're in there."

He pointed to the back of the cobhouse, to a large object partially covered in snow. It was growing dark, but even C.J. had no doubt what it was—Zach's hidden car.

"Danny!" C.J. yelled. "Tucker!"

Zach started down the hill, but C.J. grabbed Zach and made him stop for a second, to listen for a response. Any sound.

Silence.

"Danny! Tucker!" he cried, and his voice echoed in the darkness.

A sound then, faint.

C.J. and Zach started to run down the hill toward the car. "Danny! Tucker!"

C.J. heard a muffled sound.

"Woof!" It came again. "Woof! Woof!"

Relief flooded C.J., replacing the fear that had shadowed him all afternoon. He and Zach pushed through the brushy copse and broke at last into the clearing.

"Danny! Tucker!"

They bolted toward the car, jumping through thick drifts.

Tucker's large head appeared up on the dashboard. "Woof!"

C.J. reached the car first and pulled open the door. Tucker leaped out, practically tackling him. Zach pulled the back door open and reached in headfirst to find his cousin. Danny was curled into a ball in the corner of the backseat. He didn't speak. His eyes flickered open and shut. His face was pale and his lips were blue—signs of hypothermia. But he was found. And he was alive!

"We have to get out of here, pal," Zach gently told him. "We have to get you home."

Mattie peered out the window, but she only saw darkness and the reflection of the kitchen's lamp. Winter always had an ability to make a body feel insignificant before the awesome forces of nature. It had been dark a good half hour when she heard a strange noise. With the wind blowing hard enough to peel the bark off trees, Mattie thought it had peeled something loose off the house. Then the wind stilled a moment, as it did sometimes, as if sucking in its breath to blow even harder, and she heard it again. It was a definite human sound, floating up from the driveway. Was she imagining it?

No—Jaime heard it too.

They exchanged a look and froze where they were, craning to hear it. A great whoop split the air like the clang of a fire bell, followed by a brief, sharp noise.

Jaime jumped out of her seat. "It's Tucker! That's his bark!" She ran to the kitchen door and opened it wide. "Mattie! They're back! They've got Danny!"

Lumbering up the driveway were two large figures, one of them holding a child in his arms. Tucker was running up and back, barking with excitement. Mattie ran down the porch steps and flew down the driveway, not even caring that it was snowing and bitter cold and that she didn't have a coat on.

As soon as she reached them, C.J. held Danny out to her. "He's okay, Mattie!"

She held her son close to her chest, feeling his small body against hers. He was as light as a feather to her as she ran with him back to the house. Once inside, she rushed to a chair near the woodstove, just like she had with Zach—was it only twenty-four hours ago? It felt like a lifetime.

She was barely aware of Jaime tenderly untying Danny's shoes, pulling off his socks, his gloves, looking over his hands and feet for any signs of frostbite. C.J. had filled up some bowls of tepid water for Danny's hands and feet.

"We need to warm him up slowly," he said, hovering over Danny. He kept checking Danny's eyes for dilation, he explained to Mattie. "He's getting his color back. He did a smart thing, getting in that car. It kept him and Tucker out of the wind."

"Why did he go to the car?" Jaime asked.

Zach crouched beside Danny. "My guess is because it's close to the eagles' nest. That's how he discovered my car in the first place—he was poking around there just last week, spying on the eagles."

C.J. slapped his forehead with the palm of his hand. "That's what he meant by saying he thought he could help. He was going to take a picture of the eagles." He looked at Jaime. "He wanted to make you feel better after that call from your father."

"The camera," Danny squeaked out in a raspy voice.

Everyone stopped what they were doing and looked at him.

Danny gave a slight shrug to his shoulders. "I saw the bobcat go after a cottontail and Tucker started barking." He stopped to swallow, as if it hurt his throat to talk.

Mattie stroked his hair. He was so cold! But his cheeks had lost that ghostly white look and his lips were pinking up.

"Tucker went after the bobcat and they got into a fight, so I ran to the car."

"You did the right thing, Danny," C.J. said. "You did just what Tucker wanted you to do. He was trying to protect you."

"Then Tucker jumped on the car and I let him in," Danny said slowly. "But I lost the camera."

Slowly, C.J. placed Danny's bare feet into the bowls of tepid water. "You did a smart thing. You kept yourself safe and Tucker safe. Probably kept each other warm."

Danny closed his eyes, then opened them wide. "Buster!" he squeaked out. "He needs a mouse! For dinner!"

Mattie was laughing, then crying. Danny was home and he was unharmed and everything was going to be all right.

Moments later, Sol burst through the kitchen door. Behind him was a covey of Amish men and boys, peering into the kitchen. Zach's father, Eli, pushed his way through the group to get in the kitchen. Sol stopped abruptly at the sight of Mattie crying, holding Danny in her arms by the stove.

"Is he . . . ?" Sol asked.

Danny turned his face toward his father and reached out a hand.

Mattie nodded, too moved, too relieved, to speak. She still didn't trust her voice to speak.

"Er ist okay?" Sol said. "Dank der Herr!" *He is safe? Thank God!* His eyes filled with tears. He crouched down beside Danny and stroked his head. Tears fell down his cheeks and he didn't even wipe them away.

He stood to face C.J. He grasped C.J.'s hand with both of his and shook it. "Thank you, C.J. Thank you for finding my boy."

"Don't thank me," C.J. said. He pointed to Zach. "It was Zach. He figured out where Danny had gone."

Sol walked straight to Zach and grabbed him in a powerful, wordless hug.

Later that night, after dinner, Mattie tucked Danny into bed while Sol and Zach went out to the barn to check on the livestock. C.J. and Jaime made noises about leaving, but Sol wouldn't let them. The storm was still raging, and besides, he told them, "We need to celebrate Christmas together! The best Christmas of all!" Mattie was so pleased when they agreed to stay.

She would never forget this weekend—a weekend of miracles. Danny was unharmed, protected by Zach's car despite three hours in freezing temperatures. An hour after getting inside and getting warmed up, Danny was hungry and worried about Tucker's cuts from the run-in with the bobcat. C.J. assured him Tucker was fine, that an injured, three-legged bobcat was probably in much worse shape than a big, strong dog. And that started Danny's litany of questions about dogs. Mattie smiled, still unable to say much, her heart was so full of gratitude.

Danny nearly fell asleep during dessert, and she quietly steered him upstairs for a warm bath before bed. She sat on the edge of his bed as his eyelids grew heavy in the middle of a story he was telling her about the day's adventure. She kissed him gently and tucked him in, running her hand over his soft hair. He was so big.

She closed her eyes. *Oh, Lord God,* she prayed. *Thank you for blessing me with the gift of my son. Thank you for blessing me with life and love and laughter.*

Stairs creaked, then floorboards. Her heart quickened at

Sol's footsteps on the stairs, and then he stood in the doorway, his face flushed from being outside. She reached her arms out to him and he reached for her. When she kissed him, his lips were cool against her own.

After a long hot bath, Jaime wrapped herself in a towel. It felt scratchy and stiff, dried days ago in the winter sun. She heard a knock on the door and C.J.'s voice on the other side. "Mattie wanted me to bring up some fresh towels."

She opened the door for him and he handed them to her.

"Mind if I brush my teeth while the lantern is here?"

She stepped back so he could get in the bathroom and shut the door behind him. Tucker wanted to come in too, but there wasn't enough room for the three of them. "It is so dark and so cold here. I've never realized how much I take electricity for granted."

C.J. went to the sink and brushed his teeth. "Not just electricity." He spit out a mouthful of toothpaste. "I've noticed a lot of things we've taken for granted."

He shook out the toothbrush and set it in a glass. He turned back to Jaime and cocked his head. A softness came over his face. They were silent for a moment. The faucet dripped, and steam swirled. She heard Tucker's heavy breathing, right up against the door, sounding like a bull in a ring.

"Are Tucker's cuts okay?"

"Yup. Just a few surface scratches. Not really sure if Tucker scared off the bobcat or the bobcat scared off Tucker."

Jaime felt water drip from the tips of her tousled hair strands, tucked in a towel. She turned away from him and studied the nightgown Mattie had loaned her. A rivulet of water ran down the small of her back. He took a step closer and put a hand on her bare shoulder. He kissed the water dry on the back of her neck. His stubble found the curve of her neck, then gentle lips made their way. She was paying him no mind.

"The towels smell like sunshine."

"This skin you're wearing is pretty sweet smelling." He slipped his arms around her waist. "Pretty beautiful too."

"No . . . ," she laughed, embarrassed, and tried to squirm out of his arms and reach for her nightgown. "Don't be silly . . . I'm not beautiful."

Jaime could feel him still, arms around her, tensed, steady.

"When are you ever going to believe me? That I think you're beautiful? That when I tell you I love you, I mean it." He said the words slow and low.

Jaime took a deep breath. She was glad she wasn't facing him. "And Eve? Do you love her too?"

C.J. dropped his arms. "Eve? What about Eve?"

Jaime kept her head tucked down. "Since she started working at the school last fall, she's all you talk about. Every day, you bring her up. Something she said, something she did for you. Baking brownies, taking Tucker for a walk. I know you stay late to talk to her after school. She even called you today! Earlier—right when the car came out of the pond. Remember?"

"I remember." He turned her around to face him. "So . . . you think I'm having an affair with Eve?"

"I don't know. Not yet, maybe, but it's inevitable."

"You are *jealous* of Eve." It wasn't a question. It was a statement.

"No! Of course not. How ridiculous." She sat on the edge of the tub and thought about Mattie's encouragement to be honest with each other. To really talk to each other, about everything. Thoughts, feelings, hopes, and dreams. Even fears. She took a deep breath. "Yes. Yes. I am jealous of Eve. I think she is the kind of woman you should have married. The kind you wish you had married. Someone who doesn't have issues trying to please her father. Someone who isn't a mess. Someone who would be a wonderful mother. Not like me. I'd make a terrible mother. A child would need years of therapy just to survive having me as his mother."

There. She said it all. She could feel C.J. watching her. He sat down on the floor, leaned his back on the tiled wall, his hands resting on his bent knees. "Jaime, look at me."

She lifted her eyes.

"You're right. There is something I haven't told you. It's about Eve."

Here it comes. She knew it. All along, she *knew* it.

"Jaime, Eve is seventy-three years old."

He was smiling his big, wide smile, the one that was so contagious. She looked at him in wonder.

C.J. dropped his chin to his chest, trying hard not to smile, not to laugh, but when he lifted his head and their eyes met, a short laugh rolled out of him, then another, and another, until he was doubled over. She felt so foolish. So foolish and silly. Then the laughter left his face and he stared back at her for the space of three slow, thunderous heartbeats. She was surprised he couldn't hear it, the beating of her heart.

When he saw she wasn't laughing, he stood and held his

hands out to her, pulling her close to him, wrapping her in his arms. "I love you, Jaime. Nothing can change that." He brushed her cheek with the words, with his lips.

She stood on tipped toes, hair still dripping. "Thank you, C.J."

"You mean, for this?" His eyes glinted and he kissed her, and soon they were a laughing mess.

Mattie was right, Jaime thought later, in bed, after C.J. had fallen asleep with his arms wrapped around her. Love was much more than words. It was a phrase her mother would have appreciated and used in a greeting card. Maybe tomorrow she would tell C.J. about The Voice, that she was a praying person now. Tomorrow, for sure. Right after she told him that she had quit her job at Sears Portrait Studio. She knew she couldn't go back to it, even if she was returning to a promotion.

Instead, she had an idea of what she wanted to do with her passion for photography. She wanted to get back outside, where she belonged. To photograph nature and wildlife and—dare she think it?—to become a photographer of the Amish. Not of their faces, of course, but of their lives. To chronicle the day-to-day activities of these simple, peaceloving, yet oh-so-fascinating people, for future generations to know that such a way of life could exist. Quilts hanging on a clothesline on a snowy day, like the photo that had won the *National Geographic* contest. And children at play, and well-tended barns, and buggies traveling down a country lane. Would it work? Would anyone buy her photographs? She took a deep breath. She didn't care. She would be doing something she loved.

Jaime yawned. Tomorrow, she would tell C.J. everything.

Mattie was spot-on—she and C.J. needed to talk more to each other, from-the-heart kind of talking. But right now, she felt so cozy, lying here with her back pressed against him. The simple touching of his body to hers. And with her hand still in her husband's, she fell asleep.

CHRISTMAS MORNING

On Christmas morning, Mattie rose early and made breakfast, decorating the plates of eggs, bacon, and hash browns with sprigs of parsley, grown from a little pot she kept by the sunny kitchen window.

"That sure smells good," Sol said as he came in from the barn, kissing her cheek.

At Danny's place at the table was a pile of gifts covered by a dishtowel. He lifted it and added a new whistle he had carved late last night, sitting by the fire. He looked up at Mattie, suddenly shy.

"Eagle whistle." He shrugged. "To remember." He rubbed his chin. "He could have died."

"But he didn't," Mattie said quietly but firmly.

Sol took something from his pocket and lifted the dishtowel in front of Zach's place.

"What are you up to?" Mattie asked.

Sol got a look on his face like Danny did when she caught him with his hand in the cookie jar. "It's Zach's broke-off key to his car. I got it loose this morning by using a blowtorch."

Mattie raised her eyebrows. "You're encouraging him to keep the car?"

Sol pretended to look indignant. "I'm doing nothing of the sort! I'm just . . . taking the advice of a wise woman I know and letting him chart his own path."

She smiled. "You, Solomon Riehl, are a wonderful man."

Sol's cheeks reddened. "Only because you help me be a better man." He took off his coat and hat and hung them on the wall peg.

"There's something else I need to tell you," she said.

"Sounds serious."

She nodded. "It is." She took two mugs from the cupboard and poured coffee into them. She handed one to Sol and he sat in a chair at the table. She leaned with her back against the kitchen sink. "I'd like to consider fostering children. A baby. A foster baby. I think it would be good for all of us—you, me, and Danny. And it would be good for some child out there too, who needs a home like ours. I'm not giving up—I'm still hoping we'll have another baby. But I have a great longing to be a mother, Sol, and maybe that doesn't mean I have to bear the children. Maybe God has kept me from bearing another child—for now—because he wants me to care for a motherless child. And you—you're such a fine example of a man. You could have such a strong influence for good on a child who doesn't have any men in his life."

There. She said it. She had practiced this speech last night as she was getting ready for bed. She watched him carefully to see his reaction, but he didn't seem at all surprised or resistant.

He took a long sip of coffee. Then another. He looked out the window. "Boy or girl?"

Hope filled her. "Either." She tilted her head. "Does it matter to you?"

He shook his head. "You are what matters to me. You and Danny. If you'd like us to foster a child, then we can do that."

"You mean it? You're not just saying yes because it's Christmas?"

He smiled. "I think it's a fine idea, Mattie."

Mattie put down her coffee cup and crossed the room toward Sol's open arms. She was smiling wide and laughing, really laughing.

The sun came up in a sky that was hazy with frost. The air shimmered so with the cold that it was like looking at the world through a sheet of oiled glass.

After breakfast, Danny opened his gifts and Sol read the Nativity story from the book of Luke—first in German, then in English.

And then the Riehls had church to go to, and it was time for the Fitzpatricks to be on their way. Mattie invited Jaime and C.J. to come too, but when they heard the service would last three hours, that a hymn lasted as long as twenty minutes, and that the entire service was in German . . . they quickly declined.

As Jaime went downstairs, she realized she was leaving this Amish farmhouse as a different person. How could so much happen in less than two days? On Friday night, she arrived here as a complete mess, a nutcase! Her thinking was so scrambled, so mixed up. She had such a warped sense of what love should be. No one would ever be enough to fill that empty space inside—not her father, not her mother. Not even poor, dear C.J. It wasn't a human-sized space. It was too vast, too deep. She wasn't quite sure all that it meant—about God being the only perfect love—but today, Christmas, she was starting to have a glimpse of what it meant. She was loved by a love that was *enough*!

She heard the grandfather clock ding-dong its message: half past seven. She knew they had better hurry to leave so that the Riehls could make it to their church service by eight. And she and C.J. hoped to meet Eve at her church by nine. C.J. wanted Jaime to meet Eve, face-to-face.

In the kitchen, as they said goodbyes, Jaime stooped down to envelop Danny in a bear hug. She even tried to hug Sol, though it ended up being awkward, kind of a half hug. Next Jaime turned to Mattie, taking in her pale hair and clear skin, her gray eyes, calm and penetrating. Jaime's eyes filled with tears and she tried to blink them away. Mattie took her in her arms the way a mother held a child. Jaime felt as if she was being given a hug and a prayer all wrapped up in one. Mattie made her promise to come by for dinner.

"Soon!" Mattie insisted. "I'll get you liking my chow-chow yet."

Jaime wasn't sure about chow-chow, but she knew she'd be back to this little farm. Very soon.

Zach opened the kitchen door. "Ready to go?"

Jaime sniffed and wiped her cheeks with her hands. She followed C.J. outside. In front of the kitchen step was a horse harnessed to a sled. "My car! I completely forgot about it with all the excitement going on last night. Zach, did you leave it at Friendly's Ice Cream Parlour?"

"Well. Not exactly." Zach flashed her one of his incredible smiles. "Kind of a long story. A funny story, actually. I'll tell you all about it as we head into town." He looked back at Mattie and Sol. "I'll be a little late to church. But I will be there. Tell my folks I'll be there."

He took a step toward the sled, then spun around to face Jaime. He patted down his jacket and reached inside his pocket. He pulled something out and held it up. "Hey—I almost forgot about this! After they yanked your car out of the pond, Danny was climbing around inside it when he thought no one was looking." He raised an eyebrow at Danny. "He must have left this in the car." He tossed it to Danny.

Danny caught it, gazed at it for a moment, then tossed it to Jaime, grinning his jack-o'-lantern grin. "You keep it. Dad and I can make another."

It was the owl whistle.

Mattie waved a dishcloth until she couldn't see the three figures on the sled any longer. She smiled, wondering how Jaime was going to take the news that Zach had to abandon her red car in a snowdrift after not quite making a bend in the road. She was glad not to be a witness to that particular conversation.

Sol and Danny disappeared into the barn to get the horse and buggy ready for church. Mattie knew they'd be out in a few moments, eager to leave. She should go inside to finish the dessert she had prepared for church dinner, and put on her bonnet, but not quite yet. She took in the sight of this dazzling Christmas morning, air as cold and clean as mountain ice, of the snowy fields that sparkled like crushed diamonds, of glistening icicles off roof gables, of the winter visitors at the bird feeders she and Danny kept filled with sunflower seeds. She took a deep breath. The air held the distant scent of pine, a clean scent, fresh as the snow.

Emmanuel, God is with us.

The world was immense, unpredictable, and sometimes a frightening place. But right now her son was in the barn, laughing and peppering his father with questions. And Sol was with him, buckling the buggy traces to the horse, patiently answering his son, and she didn't have to cook dinner today.

This was her life. Not quite the one she had imagined as a girl, but it was her life, built with care and attention, and it was good. She felt good.

And God was with them.

She climbed the porch steps, pulled open the kitchen door, and went inside to get ready for church.

CONVERSATION GUIDE

1. Mattie and Sol's world is very different from the world in which Jaime grew up, and probably the world you grew up in too. What attracts you to the Riehls' world?

2. The Amish do celebrate Christmas, but not the way the English do. For most Amish families, gifts are given only to the children. And a large meal will be shared among extended family. The Amish have a saying: "The best things in life are not things." Does it ever seem as if a typical American Christmas—the commercialization, the excess—has gotten out of control? What are some ways you can tone down your family's traditions so there is more time for true Christmas peace?

3. Mattie's inability to have another child consumed her. She described herself as turning into someone she didn't want to be. At a baby shower for her friend Carrie, she said she felt bitterness as real as bile in her throat. "But why couldn't it be she who had a baby? Why was it that

her sisters-in-law and friends could do something that she couldn't seem to do?" How does Mattie's experience after her miscarriage help you feel compassion for those who struggle with infertility?

4. Mattie and Jaime forged an unlikely friendship. Besides the snowstorm, what circumstances in their lives drew them together?

5. What do you think it says about Jaime that she likes to view the world through the lens of her camera? Did Jaime's insecurities frustrate you? Why? Did you ever see yourself in some of her insecurities? Did your thoughts about Jaime change at all as the story progressed?

6. In many ways, C.J. seems to be an ideal husband. He is considerate and kind. He's even a good cook! How did you feel when C.J. wondered how he could love Jaime enough when she always wanted more? Do you think we expect too much from people?

7. How did you feel about the fact that Jaime often questioned and doubted her relationship with her husband? What was the underlying, unresolved problem for Jaime that she projected onto C.J.?

8. What are your overall thoughts on Jaime's father? Have you ever known anyone like him—big ideas, poor follow-through? Discuss Jaime's revelation that she was expecting something from her father that he simply didn't have to give.

9. What was your response to The Voice? Have you ever sensed God was trying to tell you something? Was it audible? Or was it a knowing, a deep inner prompting?

10. Jaime challenged Mattie by saying that her faith didn't seem very effective in a crisis. "If you worry," she told her, "why pray? And if you pray, why worry?" Have you ever felt that your faith isn't effective? Why are circumstances and feelings the wrong focus of faith? What should be the focus of our faith?

11. In the midst of a crisis, Mattie took some time alone and prayed—*really* prayed. She poured out her soul to God. After that, "she felt peace within her swell and grow, connecting her back to the world." Even though the crisis was not resolved, Mattie was filled with the peace of God that passes all understanding (Phil. 4:7). When have you had a similar experience?

12. The theme of this story is "Emmanuel, God is with us." What does that mean to you? How does the belief that God is in the midst of your life—every up, every down—change your perspective?

Acknowledgments

My first thank-you belongs to the Lord Almighty, who entered into creation at Christmas to bring redemption to a fallen world. That's the message of this little story: Emmanuel—God is with us.

Thank you to Celeste Butrym, of Guide Dogs for the Blind, for explaining the ins and outs of Search and Rescue. Those involved in SAR work are true heroes.

Thank you to my agent, Joyce Hart, of The Hartline Literary Agency, who believed in my writing abilities before I did. To my editor, Andrea Doering, for her insight, intelligence, and patience. And to Barb Barnes, grammar-maestro, who made this a better book all the way around. To the excellent team at Revell (Twila Brothers Bennett, Michele Misiak, Janelle Mahlmann, Jennifer Nutter, Donna Hausler, Deonne Beron, Claudia Marsh, Mary Molegraaf), for their enthusiasm, professionalism, and hard work.

Finally, I'd like to thank the people in my foxhole: Lindsey

Ciraulo, Wendy How, Nyna Dolby, and Tad Fisher for the first, crucial read.

And as for my family, what can I say? You supply me with love, support, and *constant* material.

And my love and thanks to all of the readers who've come with me to Stoney Ridge this far.

CHRISTMAS AT
ROSE HILL FARM

To my very special mother-in-law,
Georgia,
who first taught me to love roses.

ONE

A pale thread of gray seeped over the windowsill, wakening Bess Riehl with its strange light. Outside, a limb tapped the eaves. Disoriented, still fuzzy from sleep, she lifted her head to peer out the window and gasped in delight. Overnight, Stoney Ridge had been blanketed with deep snow, transformed into a world of pristine white. Just in time to make the day, this Sunday, all the more special. Not just any Sunday, but the day her engagement would be announced at the end of church. Published, as they called it. And in less than two weeks, she would be married.

Married. She was going to be a married woman. This Christmas, she would be married. For the *rest* of her life. Absentmindedly, she put her hand against the frosty windowpane to feel the chill. Her insides felt as quivery as her cold fingertips.

Was it normal to feel all trembly inside, scared and excited and filled with strange feelings? She hoped so, because whenever she thought about the bishop announcing her name today in church, she felt light-headed, slightly dizzy, a little nauseous, and terribly worried about fainting. Bess was what her grandmother used to call a nervous little thing, as jumpy as a dog with fleas. Twenty now, she couldn't deny the truth of that, but she was definitely bolder than she was at fifteen when she lived for a summer with Mammi at Rose Hill Farm. Bolder, certainly, and yet Bess still preferred to be invisible in any group setting. Such as . . . church.

If she couldn't handle having her name announced in public, how would she be able to survive her wedding day? She dropped her head. She had no idea. None at all.

But she wouldn't be alone. Amos would be there too.

Amos Lapp. Her thoughts drifted off to him and a smile eased her anxiety. He was so kind, was Amos. They had met, years ago, through his cousin Billy Lapp, whom Bess refused to allow herself to think about for more than a moment or two, once or twice a week. Mostly, she wondered where Billy was and if he ever thought about her. And what he thought about her. And why he left.

Stop. Stop it, Bess!

There. She expunged Billy Lapp from her mind and went back to thinking about Amos, whom she adored. Not Billy, whom she didn't.

In a way, she envied Amos. He loved her so completely, so thoroughly. There was no doubt in his mind that Bess was the only girl for him. She didn't think she could ever feel so sure, so free of doubts about her feelings. Amos's devotion reminded her of the way she had once felt about Billy Lapp, but she was much younger then. Young and foolish. Die erscht Lieb roscht net, awwer schimmelich maag sie waerre, her grandmother used to say. *First love does not rust, but it might get moldy.*

That's what had happened to her feelings about Billy. Molded.

Amos was a fine choice for a partner in life, in work. He was older than Bess by a few years, was already managing his late father's farm at Windmill Farm, was solid and generous and accepting of Bess's timorous nature. He was trustworthy and devoted and calm natured and he wasn't wishy-washy about being Plain or loving Bess—unlike that someone else whom she tried not to think about. And then she realized what she was doing. Comparing.

Stop it, Bess. Stop it!

She covered her face with her hands. Why was she struggling to tamp down thoughts about Billy lately?

Billy Lapp had been Bess's first love. Only twelve when she had first met him after her grandfather's funeral, she remembered feeling struck dumb by his good looks. But it was on her second visit to Rose Hill Farm, when she was fifteen and had come to Stoney Ridge for a short visit only to end up staying, that she lost her heart to him.

It was the summer when her widowed father had met and married Lainey. Bess had fallen head over heels in love with Billy but was caught in something her friend Maggie Zook called a classic love triangle. Maggie knew all about these kinds of things from reading romance novels on the sly. Bess loved Billy, Billy loved Betsy Mast, Betsy loved someone else who didn't love her. Bess's love for Billy was dampened, watered down, but not extinguished. Not entirely. Then, the following year, she and Billy were slowly but surely finding their way to each other. Suddenly, Betsy Mast reappeared, out of the blue, on the same day that Billy had a terrible row with his family, and he left Stoney Ridge without a glance back.

Once again, Bess felt her heart shrink like a sponge being wrung out. It was always in the back of her mind that, given the chance, Billy might choose Betsy over her as he had once done. It had been a sore point between them, and yet she understood it too—maybe there was just something about that first love. A tiny part of her couldn't let go of Billy.

And Amos, dear Amos, had always known a part of her longed for Billy. He courted her patiently and persistently, all the while his dark brown eyes would search her face, trying to see into her heart.

Last month, when Amos asked her to marry him for the third time, he told her that he wanted an answer and he wanted it to be yes. She knew it was time to face reality. Billy was gone, Amos was here. Billy did not love her in a whole-hearted way. Amos did.

A conversation she'd once had with her grandmother floated up from the recesses of her mind. "Bess," Mammi would say, "you can't go back, not in this life. You have to go forward."

So she had said yes.

Still, a nagging thought kept poking at her, like a sliver in her finger. Why wasn't she more excited about getting married? She should be. Amos Lapp was a wonderful man. But she could never bring herself to tell him that she loved him in return. She thought she did love him, but the words clogged in her throat whenever she tried. Was it because she had imagined saying those words to Billy?

Stop it, Bess. Stop!

She turned from the window and dressed quickly, then hurried outside to be the first to make footprints in the snow, before her father woke and started choring. Childish, she knew, for someone her age, but she couldn't help herself. It was a game she and her dad had played for as long as she could remember. Lainey, her dad's wife, only smiled and rolled her eyes at their silly traditions.

Bess delighted in the seasons, each one, and took special pleasure in winter's first appearance. As she walked out the kitchen door, a cold blast of air hit her in the face, making her eyes sting. Wrapped in coat and mittens with a scarf on her head, she went out to the yard and for nearly a minute she stood utterly still, basking in the simple familiarity of such a sight, such a home. A place she loved. The world was so quiet, so muffled, under a blanket of snowfall.

She wandered through the snow to the rose fields, breathing in the crisp, clean, freezing air, cheeks numb. She stood and gazed at the roses that her grandmother loved so much, roses that were pruned down to canes for winter's rest. She turned around slowly in a circle, committing to memory every square inch of this farm she loved so dearly. The December sun was rising beyond the silhouette of the barn, pushing away the remaining clouds from last night's snowstorm. A sunbeam reflected off the glass roof of the greenhouse. On an impulse, Bess walked over to the greenhouse, trudging through the snow so she left tracks, and twisted the door handle. A blast of warm, moist, humus-scented air hit her in the face. Out of nowhere, her cat Blackie appeared and curled around her legs.

Bess bent down to scratch the cat behind its ears, then made her way down the brick walk in the dim morning light, between rows of clay pots holding shoulder-high rose canes being propagated for next spring's fields. She checked the wall thermometer and smiled, satisfied: sixty-five degrees. Only as warm as necessary.

Farther back, closer to the heat source, were bushes of

roses in bloom. When she reached them, she stopped to breathe in their scent and admire their blossoms. There was the Dainty Bess, a hybrid tea, light pink, single petals, a gift from her dad for her eighteenth birthday. Frowning, she noticed something on Lady Emily Peel and leaned over to examine it. It was beautiful, but prone to powdery mildew. The rose, of course—not Lady Emily.

The last two winters, Bess and her father had forced blooms using artificial lighting to trick the roses' internal clocks into thinking spring had come. These roses were not for sale but to keep up a steady supply of rose petals. Bess's grandmother had taught her to make soaps, teas, and jams from the petals. Among old garden roses, those with red and deep pink flowers tended to have the strongest perfume, so those varieties were the ones Bess used for rose products. Recently, she'd been studying up on another use for roses: remedies.

It had started when Eli Yoder, an older fellow from church, asked if she knew of a cure for baldness. She hunted through her grandmother's books and found a rose remedy for male baldness from a time when nature's wonder drug was a rose. Rose honey to soothe inflamed tonsils. Rose vinegar to alleviate headaches. Rose poultices to stanch wounds. Bess found a recipe for rosewater compress to allay female hysteria, though she wasn't sure there was much of a market to hysterical women. She certainly didn't know any.

Unfortunately, the remedy she found for Eli Yoder's baldness didn't have the desired effect, though he did tell her his athlete's foot had cleared up.

Warm now, Bess took off her coat and mittens and tossed them on the wooden stool. She heard the greenhouse door open and turned around to see her father cross the threshold. "You beat me to the snow!"

She grinned. "If you snooze, you lose."

Jonah Riehl walked up the path, his eyes automatically checking on rose propagations along the way. Halfway up, he stopped and put his hands on his hips, frowning at a row of slips that hadn't propagated. "This greenhouse needs a good cleaning out."

Bess nodded. Each long shelf was crowded with pots, nearly groaning with weight.

Jonah took a few more steps along the brick path, then pivoted on his heels. "Might be time to think about a new greenhouse. A bigger one."

Bess spun around and busied herself with touching the soil of a few pots with her fingertips, to see how moist they were. In most every situation, Bess was the one who pushed her father to try new things, to think more broadly, to consider new rose products for the market. But not when it came to this greenhouse. She didn't want to hear any such talk about a new greenhouse. So many cherished memories were captured under this old glass roof—of Mammi, of Bess's education about roses. Of Billy Lapp.

Even now, years later, she couldn't go into the greenhouse without being aware of Billy's influence on Rose Hill Farm. Very stirring stuff. He had been instrumental in setting Rose Hill Farm's business into action. He had taught himself to graft roses onto Mammi's strong rootstocks, ones that had been in the Riehl family for generations. The varieties were varied and unusual; grafting sped up the growing process. No longer did Mammi have to wait two years for slips to root and grow large enough to sell, or for rosehips that took even longer. Rose Hill Farm became the source for Pennsylvanians looking for heritage roses. They shipped bare root roses all winter and sold flowering rosebushes during spring and summer.

Bess loved this greenhouse more than any other place on earth. As she worked, she could almost sense her grandmother's pleasure as she peered down from heaven's curtain.

She wondered what Caleb Zook, the bishop, would say if she were to ask him such a question: Can those who have passed to Glory peer down on those who have not? She could imagine him bending over slightly, to listen carefully to what she was saying. He always did that. It was one of his nicest ways. Maybe she would ask him today after church. But maybe not.

"Tomorrow," her dad was saying, "I'll get started thinning out those dead slips to give more breathing room to the propagated ones. For now, we'd better get back to the house. Lainey will be wondering what happened to us for breakfast. Church starts in less than an hour."

"I'll be there in a moment. I'm just going to water a few dry plants."

Jonah turned and walked down the brick path, limping as he went. Years ago, when Bess was a newborn, he had been injured in a buggy accident that took the life of his first wife and left him with a bad back. She watched her father as he crossed the snowy yard to reach the house, feeling a swell of love rise in her heart. This morning, his spine seemed slightly more curved, the lines on his face etched a little deeper.

What was the matter with her today? She felt so maudlin and sentimental. But she couldn't imagine leaving Rose Hill Farm and that's exactly what was going to happen.

She watered a few plants that seemed a little dry, checked on a few others, and bent down to pick up her coat that the cat had pulled down to the ground and curled up on to nap. As she shooed Blackie away, something caught her eye. In the far corner of the greenhouse, tucked deep under the workbench, was a potted rose, fully leafed out with one lone bud, still enclosed in its green capsule. She got down on her knees and dragged the pot out into the open but it was too heavy for her to lift.

Strange. It was a rose she didn't recognize, and after so many years at Rose Hill Farm, she knew each and every rose. And why would it be about to bloom now? Yet with only one bud? She looked at it again, smelled the bud, studied the veining on the leaves. A wispy memory, fuzzy and out of focus, something she hadn't thought about in years and years, floated through her mind.

No. Not a chance. It couldn't be *that* rose. *That* rose?!

On Friday morning, Billy Lapp gave an all-over shudder as he walked into one of Penn State University's greenhouses, happy to be out of the biting wind. There was a pleasantness to the greenhouse at this time of day that could always manage to take the edge off a man's early-morning surliness, especially when the weather was bad. Even when snow, sleet, or biting cold pressed against the glass windows, inside the greenhouse, with the door sealed tightly, it was never chilly.

Billy Lapp's supervisor, Jill Koch, was waiting inside for him, examining some drought-resistant wheat seedlings he'd been experimenting with. She straightened when she saw him. "Morning. I got a call from someone who might have an unidentified rose on his property. He's spent a week trying to find someone who could identify it and was directed to us by a Rose Society. I asked if he could send a photograph, but he said he didn't own a camera."

Billy set down his thermos and brown-bag lunch on the shelf that served as a desk, yanked off his coat, and tossed it next to his lunch. "What kind of a rose?"

"He's not sure."

He rolled his eyes and groaned. "It's probably an American Beauty." The most common of all garden roses. No wonder the Rose Society shrugged it off.

"I don't think so," she said thoughtfully. "He seemed to know his roses. He said he thought it might be an old rose."

Billy stilled. He was passionate about finding old roses. It was the reason he was given the unofficial job of being the university's rose rustler. "Where did he find it? In a cemetery?" Old cemeteries were the best places to find old roses. It was an old custom to plant a mother's favorite flower beside her grave and, most often, that favorite was a rose. Unlike gardens, cemeteries weren't usually re-landscaped, so old roses survived long after they were pushed out of gardens. Many of those old heritage roses were sturdy, disease resistant, and survived complete neglect. Just wanting for someone, like Billy, to find them.

"He didn't say where he found it, but I think he said it was potted."

Billy was intrigued; nothing in the world matched the intrigue of discovering a rose's identity. Nothing. "What did he want?"

"He wanted someone to come out and identify the rose. The Rose Society told him we have a rose rustler on staff to track down unusual finds." She lifted her eyebrows and gave him a smug smile. "You."

He glanced around the greenhouse to assess how much work he needed to finish before he could take a few hours away from it. "I suppose I could check it out on Monday. Did you get the address?"

"I wrote it down the way it sounded on the answering machine. Not sure I got it all, though. I could have sworn I heard a horse passing by." Jill handed him the slip of paper but held on as he reached out for it. "Do you have plans for Christmas?"

He tugged the paper out of her hand and stuffed it in his jeans pocket. Over her shoulder he noticed that a PVC joint was coming undone in the skeleton of the greenhouse. He hated these cheap, plastic greenhouses, called hoop houses, that had sprung up in the last decade. Hoop houses with their plastic sheeting just weren't made to last. He sidled around Jill to jam the PVC joint back together with the heels of his hand, pondering how much he longed for a good old-fashioned glass greenhouse. "Is it already Christmas?"

"You're kidding, right? It's only a few weeks away." She fingered the collar of his coat, hanging over the shelf. "Are you planning to spend it with your family?"

He knew where this conversation was going and wished it were over. "To be honest, I haven't given any thought to Christmas." That was an honest comment. He scrupulously avoided any thoughts of Christmas.

Jill walked up to him, standing just a little too close. "You never talk about yourself or your family. Sometimes I wonder if you're part of the Federal Witness Protection program."

He grinned. "There's just not much to tell. I'd rather hear about you."

"You're not going to get away with that kind of talk. Someday, I'd like to find out all about you."

"Absolutely." *Not a chance.* A girl like Jill Koch would turn tail and run if she knew about his humble upbringing.

"So . . . would you like to join me for Christmas? Come for dinner?"

He stiffened. "Let me get back to you on that."

The smile on her face faded into a frown. "Why am I not surprised that you're dodging the question?"

She leaned closer to him, lingering, and he stepped back, touched his hat, and said, "Thank you for bringing the message."

"One of these days, Billy Lapp . . ." She turned and sauntered down the long narrow aisle, stopping to check a plant here and there. She stopped at the wheat seedlings and turned back to him, all stiff and starchy. "They're too dry. Get them watered."

Jill Koch was an attractive girl and had made no secret that she was interested in him, but he knew it wasn't smart to combine work and romance, especially when she happened to be his supervisor and she reported directly to the greenhouse manager—who happened to be her uncle. If it didn't work out between them, and it probably wouldn't, he'd be the one out of a job.

He needed this job. He loved it. He'd worked at Penn State Extension for almost four years now, pruning, transplanting seedlings, cultivating flowers, schlepping large bags of soil around, fertilizing, studying and implementing pest control, and gleaning as much about horticulture as he could. The work suited him perfectly.

Everything was finally going right for him.

Why, then, did something keep gnawing at him? An aching loneliness, a feeling that he was missing something. Out of habit, he tugged the end of his sweater sleeve over his left wrist. It was the holidays, he supposed. Christmas was the hardest time of all for him. Like he was always outside looking in at others.

He unrolled the hose, turned it to low, and gently sprinkled the seedlings with water as he heard a soft, rhythmic knocking, just audible over the hiss of the hose. He turned off the hose and walked to the end of the greenhouse. Swinging the door open, Billy blinked twice. A dark-skinned man stood in the dim, gray morning. Tall and lanky, a fellow down on his luck, wearing a thin overcoat that wasn't suited for a cold Pennsylvania winter.

The greenhouses were at the back of the university campus near a run-down part of town and it wasn't unusual for a stray fellow to wander in, looking for a place to warm up for a while. Hobos, tramps, vagabonds, and vagrants, Jill called them, rough customers. She warned him to chase them off, but Billy never did. To his way of thinking, everybody needed a little help now and then. Where would he be without the help a few had given him during that dark period when he first left home? "Why don't you come sit by the heater and warm yourself?"

"I don't mean to intrude," the hobo said. "I can see you're busy."

"I'm not going to let you go without a cup of coffee to warm your belly." Billy grabbed his widemouthed thermos and handed it to the hobo. Glancing at his face, he was struck by the unusual color of his eyes. Neither blue nor purple, they were a near-perfect match for the amethyst crystal interior of a geode he remembered that Dawdi Zook, his mother's father, had kept on his fireplace mantel back in Stoney Ridge. He could envision it clearly, though it had been a decade since he'd seen it up close in his grandfather's work-worn hands. Transfixed, Billy could practically hear his grandfather's deep, rumbly voice: *While the minerals on the exterior created a hard shell, the ones that seeped to the interior were transformed into beauty. An example from nature to show how God brings good out of bad.*

The hobo handed the thermos back to Billy, pulling him into the present. As Billy screwed the lid on the thermos, he was surprised to realize the man was younger than he had assumed—or maybe it was that his face was unlined. Untroubled. Without stress or strife. And he didn't act defeated like so many of the other men who wandered through College Station.

The hobo was admiring a set of orchids with their delicate blooms. "Beautiful, aren't they? So intricately designed. Fragile yet long lasting."

"Are you a flower lover?"

"Yes. Always have been. My father's a top-notch gardener."

Beyond the hobo's shoulder, Billy spotted his brown-bag lunch. "Are you hungry? I made two sandwiches." He reached for the bag, opened it, took out one sandwich, wrapped in waxed paper, and handed it to the man. "Nothing fancy— just peanut butter and jelly. Made it myself."

"I am a little hungry. Had a long way to go this morning."

"Wait here." Billy extracted a metal stool, grimy but sturdy, from under the rows of plants. Brushing it off with his hand, he set it down and beckoned the hobo to it. "Sit a spell. I'd enjoy the company on this cold morning." He pulled a crate from under a shelf and turned it over to sit on.

The hobo sat down and smiled at Billy. There was something calming about him, as if he had all the time in the world and there was no place else he'd rather be than right there, in a greenhouse with Billy.

Before the hobo unwrapped his sandwich, he bowed his head and Billy thought he heard him offer some kind of quiet prayer spoken in another language. It was mumbled so softly, he might have been mistaken. Or maybe the man was drunk, though he didn't seem to be. A few weeks ago, a drunk wandered into the greenhouse and Billy sobered him up with high-octane coffee, so thick you could cut it with a knife, before he sent him on his way.

"So you've got quite a knack for plants, from what I hear."

Billy glanced up. "Where'd you hear that?"

The man took a bite of the sandwich. "Skippy peanut butter?"

Billy nodded. "I'm Billy, by the way."

"Call me George."

George took a swig of coffee to wash down the peanut butter sandwich. He looked up at Billy. "Folger's?"

"Yup." It was on sale at the grocery store.

"Old Quaker family from Nantucket. Benjamin Franklin's mother was a Folger. Did you know that?"

"No. No I didn't." Billy took a bite of the sandwich, chewed, swallowed. "George, mind if I ask how you ended up as a hobo?"

"A hobo?" A smile flickered like a candle across George's face. He stretched his legs out in front of him and leaned back on his elbows against the shelf.

"You're obviously a bright guy. Have you had trouble finding a job?"

"Not so much. Work comes along just when it's needed." He finished the sandwich, swallowed one last swig of coffee, and rose to his feet. "Well, I'll be off then. Thanks for sharing your lunch."

Billy looked at George's threadbare overcoat. There was no way that thin coat could keep him warm. He grabbed his blue jacket from the shelf and tossed it at the hobo. "Take it. I have two."

A soft look came into George's eyes as he gripped the jacket in his hands. "Thank you, Billy." He slipped it on and slowly zipped the coat up to his chin. Then he reached out and wrapped his arms around Billy.

Billy stood there, stiffly, awkwardly. *Men don't hug!* He could never remember receiving a hug from another man. Not once. Receiving a hug from a man—a stranger! a hobo!—was awkward and uncomfortable. And yet, it felt like George was giving Billy a blessing and a benediction, wrapped up in a hug. A deep calm surrounded Billy and he felt himself relax, ever so slightly. George released him, gripping Billy's upper arms and smiling gently with that calm old-soul smile. "Until we meet again, Billy Lapp."

George turned to leave and it occurred to Billy that he wanted him to stay. The desire to remain in the company of anyone—much less a hobo—was so unfamiliar that Billy wondered if he might be coming down with something. A cold or fever, perhaps.

George stepped around Billy, then stopped and bent down to pick up a piece of paper. "I think you dropped this." He handed it to Billy and passed him to reach for the door, then glanced over his shoulder. "This has all the makings to be a wonderful Christmas, Billy Lapp. One of the best."

As the door clicked shut behind George, a disturbing thought emerged. How did this hobo know Billy's last name? That was creepy. Had George been watching him? Was he a psycho? Then Billy remembered that his nametag was pinned to his shirt pocket.

He glanced at the slip of paper in his hand. It was the information Jill had given him about the caller with the unidentified rose. He unfolded the slip of paper and swallowed. The address was Rose Hill Farm in Stoney Ridge.

Bess's home.

Billy's peaceful mood turned sour.

Two

As Amos Lapp tied the horse's reins to the hitching post in front of the hardware store on Saturday afternoon, he went through a checklist of the things he needed to buy to prep and paint the apartment above the garage. In just a few days' time, those two little rooms would be his and Bess's new home. This task should have been done weeks ago but the holdup was Bess. She couldn't decide what color to paint it—which struck him as odd, because their church didn't offer much of a choice. Pale green or pale blue.

Yesterday, Amos visited Bess at Rose Hill Farm and gently tried to press her to make a decision. She told him to just go ahead and choose, so he did, and he hoped she'd be happy with it. It was hard to tell with Bess. She was agreeable to everything he suggested, said she'd go along with either color he chose—but he didn't want her to just go along with it. He wanted her to love it.

His mind drifted back to church last Sunday, as the bishop announced they were to be published, and color drained from Bess's face. He saw it happen, right before his very eyes, the way he'd read about in books. For a moment, he thought she might faint. He knew she felt anxious about being the center of attention, but was it typical for a girl to nearly lose consciousness?

"Pssst."

Amos twitched, thinking a fly was buzzing near him, though it was too cold for flies.

"Pssst. Over here."

He spun around and found Maggie Zook standing over by the community bulletin board on the wall, under the covered porch of the hardware store. "What are you doing?"

She put a finger to her lips and shushed him, the way a teacher might. "Looking for new job postings."

He walked over to her. "Why are you whispering?"

"I didn't want to broadcast to everyone in Stoney Ridge that I'm looking for a job."

Amos squinted in confusion. "How are you going to find a job if you don't want anyone to know you're looking?"

She glanced up and down the road. "Maybe not everyone. Maybe just my father."

"Ah." Maggie's father was Caleb Zook, the bishop. "I don't want to know why." Amos wasn't sure if it might be a church issue, or a father-daughter issue—but either way, he wanted none of it. As soon as he said it, he felt a tug of regret. Her small face grew troubled. Gentling his tone, he added, "I'm sure you've got a good reason."

Maggie followed on his heels as he went in the store to look at rows of paint chips. "There's a job opening here at the hardware store. I thought you might put in a good word for me."

Oh no. Heat climbed up Amos's neck. He wasn't going to get roped into this again. The last time he helped Maggie get a job, she lasted less than a day. After she begged him, he acquiesced and recommended her to the owner of the Hay & Grain. She forgot to latch the cage filled with live mice—the owner kept a pet snake—and during the night the mice escaped. Months later, the Hay & Grain was still overrun with mice. An infestation, the owner said. Maggie claimed it was an accident, that it could have happened to anyone, but Amos had a suspicion that her humanitarian streak beat out her practical streak. Knowing her like he did, he figured that she wanted to give the mice a fighting chance to survive. She hated snakes, Maggie did.

Worse still, the owner felt Amos was partially responsible and no longer gave him a discount on bulk purchases.

And the hardware store—well, now, this was his special place. His home away from home. He enjoyed spending Saturday afternoons wandering the aisles, tinkering with gadgets. If he helped Maggie get a job here and she did something disastrous, which was very, very likely, he would be sunk.

She was gazing up at him with that riot of tangles poking out under her black bonnet, with those big liquid brown eyes of hers, like he was quite possibly the most wonderful man on earth, and his gut twisted. His firm resolve started to weaken.

Started . . . and then . . .

He had a stroke of genius. "The Sweet Tooth Bakery is hiring, at least until Christmas. Dottie Stroot told my mother that very thing just a few days ago. Dottie Stroot said she's swamped with Christmas orders and can't seem to keep good help." No surprise there. That woman might be a talented baker, but she held people, including her customers, in disdain.

Maggie brightened, the dimples in her cheeks deepening as her smile grew. "Just through Christmas?" More thoughtfully, she added, "That would be ideal. Just enough time." She turned and started for the door.

"Maggie, wait!"

She stopped and spun around.

"Which paint color should I get?"

She walked back to peer at the paint chips he held up and immediately pointed to the blue. "Oh, definitely that one. No doubt about it. That's the one."

"You're sure?"

"Absolutely. It's the color of a robin's egg."

Why, so it was.

"That awful green is the color of the inside of the schoolhouse." She shuddered. "Would make me feel like I was right back in jail. Eight long painful years of prison." School, she meant.

From the door of the hardware store, he watched her skitter across the street to the Sweet Tooth Bakery. Maggie skittered. He couldn't hold back a grin. One thing about Maggie Zook—you knew what she was thinking. If she didn't come right out and say so, her face would give it away. His attention fixed on his task and he went to get the paint mixed robin's egg blue for the apartment. To prepare a home for his bride.

Bess Riehl picked up a knife and sliced off a generous width of freshly baked bread. She lathered it with butter and closed her eyes as she chewed the first bite. The bread was still warm from the oven, soft inside with a crisp crust. Was there any taste on earth that beat fresh-baked bread?

"Oh, Lainey, it's good." She took another bite, chewed, swallowed. "It's better than good. It's the best bread you've ever made."

Lainey watched Bess as she ate. "You really think so? It's from a sourdough starter I made." She handed her a crock of strawberry jam. "Starters can be tricky."

"The best bread ever. Definitely." Bess spread the ruby-colored jam to the edge of her bread, expression thoughtful. "Did Dad hear back from Penn State yet?"

From upstairs, the sounds of little girls starting to stir—four-year-old Christy and two-year-old Lizzie—floated down to the kitchen.

Lainey cocked an ear, listening, then hurried to finish preparing a breakfast tray for Bess's father, Jonah, moving slow this morning with a stiff back. "Someone said they would send a rose rustler to come look at it."

"I wish I could remember the name of that rose. Mammi loved all her roses, but that one was special to her. I just can't remember why."

"Well, you were young. The rose rustler will probably be able to figure out what rose it is."

"Rose rustling." Bess sliced a few more pieces of bread and tucked them under the oven broiler to toast. "Sounds like something Mammi would have liked to do, especially if it was illegal." She kept one eye on the broiler and lunged for the oven with a mitt as soon as the toast was dark but not yet charcoal.

"Rustling's kind of a funny name for it, because it's not stealing anything. Just the opposite—a rose rustler tries to preserve it. He hunts for forgotten old roses that have survived for generations." Lainey took a mug off the wall hook and poured a cup of coffee to set on the tray. "Anyway, the rose rustler will be here later this morning."

The calling of the little girls for their mother could no longer be ignored. Bess lifted the tray. "I'll take it up to Dad. You go to the girls."

Lainey started toward the stairs, then pivoted at the kitchen door. "I doubt your dad's back will be able to handle the bone-rattle of a buggy ride today. Would you mind fetching the rose rustler at the bus stop?" She didn't wait for an answer but hurried upstairs to help get her little daughters dressed for the day.

Buttering the toast, Bess's knife stilled. She was being sent to fetch a rose rustler? What would she talk about with him—a stranger—on the ride home? Then she quelled her dismay and nearly smiled. Roses, of course. That's what they could discuss on the short ride to Rose Hill Farm. She wished Maggie Zook were here. Maggie could effortlessly keep up a one-sided conversation with anyone. "It's a gift," she had once told Bess, as if it was bestowed on her like the color of her eyes or hair.

A few hours later, Bess prepared to head to the bus stop in town. She put one arm into a coat sleeve, then another. Taking her black bonnet from the wall peg, she knotted the strings swift and taut, then made her way to the barn to harness Frieda to the buggy and head to town. There, she waited in the cold buggy for over thirty minutes until the bus rumbled around a bend and turned onto Main Street, coming to a jerky stop.

Forcing a confident air, Bess opened the door and climbed out of the buggy. She wondered if she should have brought a big sign that said ROSE RUSTLER, but then thought she might seem ridiculous, and if there was one thing Bess didn't want to seem, it was ridiculous. She wasn't nearly as acutely self-conscious as she used to be, the way she was when she first came to Rose Hill Farm and her grandmother said she acted scared of her own shadow and hoped nobody could tell. She was much bolder now—nowhere near as bold as her grandmother had been, though few could be *that* bold.

She studied the bus steps, waiting for the rosarian to emerge. At the top of the stairs, a young man appeared and paused, his face turned away from her as he peered down Main Street. Bess's jaw dropped open and a sharp breath gusted in; her heart hit her throat, and she felt her face heat up. She knew him immediately by the set of his sturdy shoulders and the overall familiarity of his form. Even in his big coat, she knew who he was. Speechless, she drank in every inch of him. Broader yet more angular than he used to be, a full shock of hair with long sideburns instead of the bowl cut common to her people, dressed in a dark brown coat and blue jeans over solid construction boots. She thought she might fall down and faint, right there, right on Main Street.

Bess opened her mouth as if to speak, closed it, swallowed, then opened it again. "Billy Lapp?"

Billy's head snapped around when he heard his name. His face suddenly blanched as he made a quick pass over her bonnet and dress. His eyes widened in disbelief while he stiffened as if struck by lightning. "Bess? Bess Riehl?" He quickly recovered his shock and his face closed over. "I expected your father to be coming to get me."

She moved forward with uncertain steps. "You? You're . . . the rose rustler?" She tried to hide her delight and knew it wasn't very successful. But her smile was met with a scowl that made her bristle. She tried again. Questions galloped through her mind—Where had he come from? What had he been doing?—and she found it nearly impossible to form words into a complete sentence. "So is that where you've been living? Over in College Station?"

When he spoke again, there was a hard edge to his words. "Where's your father?"

"The first snowfall of the year always causes his back injury to flare up—he can't handle the cold well. He was moving slowly this morning so I was given the job to pick up the rosarian. He'll be thrilled to see you. We never expected the rose rustler to be you."

Brows furrowed, he gave her a sharp, quelling glance. "You gonna show me this rose or what?" The question shot out like a challenge.

Bess's mouth dropped open. The nerve of Billy Lapp to treat her as if she were nothing to him but . . . a taxi driver! She squared her shoulders and turned toward Frieda, the patiently waiting buggy horse, leaving him to silently follow behind. When she reached the horse, she turned and saw his hesitation. "Are you coming?"

His eyes flicked to the buggy, then back again. "You're not supposed to be in a buggy with the likes of me."

A crack in his hard veneer. Maybe it was a sign—the old Billy was still there. "I'll risk it."

But her hope extinguished and her disillusionment continued as she snapped the reins and clucked to Frieda. Billy didn't look at her and she didn't look at him. Not too often, anyway. Only when she couldn't help herself. They drove a mile west, then turned south, and the land looked all the same: rolling fields of brown stubble lying silent under winter's chill. There wasn't much snow left from Sunday's covering, only in the shade, and though the day was sunny, the mood in the buggy was dour.

Bess wondered what thoughts were running through Billy's mind. Her head buzzed with questions. She wanted to ask where he'd been these last few years, why he hadn't tried to get in touch with her, what had happened to Betsy Mast, but she felt tongue-tied. Neither of them said a word.

She found herself remembering what he'd looked like as a young man of eighteen, just before full maturity set in, before he had whiskers and muscles and the brittle aloofness he was displaying. He had changed dramatically. He was still every bit as gloriously handsome as he always was—man-sized, broad shoulders, with curly brown hair and blue eyes rimmed with dark eyebrows. But the roguish twinkle in his eyes was gone. His face was drawn tighter than the lids of Mammi's rose petal jam jars. Those eyes were cold now. It seemed as if he could barely tolerate being here, as if she and all of Stoney Ridge were nothing but a great inconvenience to him.

Then why *was* he here?

The rose, of course, which gave her a small measure of comfort. The Billy Lapp she once knew would go to any lengths for a rose.

He turned his head to look out the window, and she noticed his long hair curling over his coat collar. She remembered the day she first laid eyes on him—she had noticed his hair, even then.

Mid-October 1969, a bright sunny day. Bess was twelve years old and had come to Stoney Ridge for her grandfather's funeral. Her grandmother had insisted Bess stay on at Rose

Hill Farm for a while afterward to help her adjust to widow-hood. That came as a surprise to Bess and her father, because most everyone, including her grandfather, had to do the adjusting for Mammi. Jonah tried to encourage his mother to come to Ohio to live with them, said they could make her very comfortable and there was plenty of room for one more, but she wouldn't hear of it. Very set in her ways, Mammi was, and wouldn't budge from her burrow.

Bess's father had to return to Ohio for work, and he relented to allow Bess to stay at Rose Hill Farm for another week. One week turned into two and there was no talk about sending Bess home. Finally, on a brisk afternoon when a cheery fire glowed in the stove, Bess broached the subject with her grandmother. "Mammi, when do you think you'll be ready for me to head back to Ohio? Dad's been asking."

"Well," Mammi said, patting her chest, "I've been having some heart trouble."

Bess eyed her grandmother suspiciously. She was as sound as a coin.

Mammi's spectacles were on her nose. "I didn't want to worry your father."

"Have you seen a doctor?"

"Doctor," she scoffed. "What do I need with a doctor?" She waved that thought away with a flick of her big wrist. She didn't trust doctors. "They'd just end up giving me pills to shorten my life."

Just as Bess opened her mouth to object, a knock interrupted her train of thought. She went to open the door and found herself staring at the most beautiful boy she had ever seen in all her twelve years. His hair was curly and thick, and it looked as if he hadn't combed it in a hundred years.

"Who is it?" Mammi bellowed from across the room. She said she was deaf, but she heard everything.

The boy looked at Bess curiously, then peered over her head at her grandmother. "It's me, Bertha. Billy. Maggie tagged along."

Mammi peered back. "Wann bischt du aaegelandt?" *What wind blew you hither?*

"Maggie said you wanted to see me."

"You're late. I was expecting you this morning." Mammi expected a lot. And she always claimed she knew when a person was coming. But then, she claimed she knew everything. "Well, come on in, Billy Lapp."

The boy stepped around Bess and crossed the room to Mammi. Behind the beautiful boy was a small girl, about ten or eleven, who looked like a pixie, with snapping dark eyes hidden behind big glasses.

"Who are you?" the girl said.

Bess's mind went blank. She couldn't get a word from her head to her mouth.

"Is she all right?" Billy whispered, pointing to his head. He spoke to Mammi, not even glancing at Bess.

"She's fine. Billy Lapp and Maggie Zook, meet Bess. She's my granddaughter from Ohio." Mammi looked at Bess. "Billy lives that way," she pointed a big thumb in one direction, "and Maggie lives the other way. Bess needs some friends."

Billy erased Mammi's comment in midair. She heard him mutter that he didn't have time to be friends with a girl, especially one who couldn't talk.

Fine. Too bad for him. She didn't want to be friends either.

Then he looked up. His eyes were blue, the clear color of

a September sky, the bluest she had ever seen. He was staring straight at her with a fierce gaze, and she felt like she was struck by lightning.

Maggie pushed her glasses up on her nose, peering at Bess. "How old are you?"

Bess was having trouble gathering her thoughts. She cleared her throat and tried to speak, but nothing came out. She was too overcome by the handsomeness of Billy Lapp.

Mammi answered for her. "She's twelve."

"Where do you live?" Billy said, enunciating carefully. He still thought Bess was slow.

"Didn't you notice her at the funeral for Samuel, Billy?" Maggie said. "I did! She came all the way from Oleo!"

"Oleo is yellow lard," Billy said.

"Ohio," Mammi corrected. "And it's not all that far, Maggie. No need to get historical."

"Hysterical," Billy said.

Maggie turned to Bess. "Don't you worry about not being able to talk. There's lots of ways to communicate. We can pass notes in school."

Wait. What? School? Bess had no intention of starting school in Stoney Ridge. She'd been more than happy to miss school these last few weeks. She couldn't wait until she finished eighth grade next year and could say goodbye to school for the rest of her life. She kept a wall calendar at home in Ohio in which she marked a red X over each passing day.

"Bess can talk. She just don't say much, unlike some other girls her age." Mammi lifted a sparse eyebrow in Maggie's direction.

"How long is she staying?" Maggie didn't realize she'd just been insulted by Mammi.

"She's staying on a bit longer to help me get through my time of sorrow," Mammi said.

Maggie slipped closer to Bess. "I've read that mutes can learn to talk with their fingers." She wiggled her fingers in front of Bess to demonstrate.

"I'm not mute," Bess whispered. "I'm just a little shy."

Maggie's coffee brown eyes went wide. "Land sakes, why didn't you say so?"

Well, Maggie Zook, besides my being struck dumb by Billy's beautiful blue eyes, you haven't given me a spare inch to fit in a word. Bess had to rummage for her response, piecing it together one word at a time like beads on a string. Before she could get the sentence out, Maggie's attention had swung to the kitchen door.

Mammi's eleven-year-old rooster had figured out how to open the kitchen door by flying up to whack the loose handle with a wing, then sticking his clawed foot in the opening. Bess would've thought Mammi would singe that rooster's tail feathers and toss him out the door, but instead she scooped him up under her arm and petted him like a cat, without missing a beat of her conversation with Billy. "I asked you here because I want you to figure something out for me." She peered at him with mortal seriousness.

"What?"

"I want you to learn how to graft roses."

"What for?"

She worked a thoughtful finger over her chins. "I'm working on a plan, that's why. I need more roses and I need them fast."

"What's the hurry?"

"I'm not going to live forever, you know." She patted her heart again.

Hours spent shadowing her grandmother these last few weeks had instructed Bess about a good many of her mannerisms and curious way of thinking. She could tell exactly what Mammi was up to. Lamenting about her imminent death was Mammi's way of stirring action out of a reluctant body. Usually Bess's.

But Billy was a fumbling fifteen-year-old, oblivious to the wiles of a clever woman and, being a boy, was slow to catch on. "Well, then, just go buy roses."

Mammi's eyes closed to a pair of dangerous slits. Bess figured her grandmother might pick up a broom and swat him home for that. Even she knew the answer to that after being at Rose Hill Farm for three weeks now. Mammi thought modern roses that were sold in nurseries were cheap imitations of the real thing. She had roses from her mother and grandmother and great-grandmother and so on and so on that she wanted to protect for generations.

Mammi must have decided to pardon Billy for his appalling ignorance. "No need to buy anything. I have everything I need. Problem is, I don't know how to graft."

"But I don't either," Billy said.

"No, but you can learn."

"But . . . how?" He appeared mystified.

"Go to the library," Mammi said wearily. Her patience, never in great supply, was running thin. "Ask around. Experiment. Figure it out. Using your brain once in a great while wouldn't be such a cats-after-me."

Maggie pushed her glasses up on the bridge of her nose. "Why is a cat after you?"

"She means catastrophe," Billy said, annoyed. "And I use my brain all the time."

And that's just what he did. Within a few years, Billy had learned how to grow roses from cuttings and graft so capably that the horse pastures of Rose Hill Farm were converted to thriving fields of roses. Mammi's heritage rose business was under way.

But that was then and this was now. Billy sat stiff on the buggy seat, eyes fastened to the road straight ahead. Bess noticed his hands grip the buggy seat as if it were holding him together. At the last second, she decided to turn Frieda down a different road than the one that passed by his father's farm and she saw Billy's hands ease up their grip.

Aha . . . *that's* what was making him act so particularly tetchy. She cast a glance at him, wondering how much of his abrupt disappearance had to do with his no-account older brothers. Billy was the youngest, dubbed Der Ruschde, the runt, and that was when they were feeling kindly.

Billy had a different way of thinking than the rest of his family. Mammi used to grumble those brothers of his were casing the joint whenever they showed up at Rose Hill Farm. She said Billy was the only one who had any spark of their mother, and she thought well of Billy's mother. Bess knew her grandmother's ulterior motive in hiring Billy was to get him away from those brothers before they ruined him. Bertha Riehl never did anything without an ulterior motive.

Billy tipped his head toward her. "Did you stop taking care of my bees?"

Just as Bess's heart was softening a little, Billy went and ruined it. "No! Of course not." She was incensed. What did he think—that just because he had left the farm, it had fallen into disrepair? Were his expectations that low? *You just wait, Billy Lapp*, she felt like saying. *Just wait until you see what my father and I have done with Rose Hill Farm. It's never looked better.*

Then her heart caught a beat. Rose Hill Farm had never looked better because there was going to be a wedding there. Her wedding. Hers and Amos's. In just a few days.

She turned onto Stone Leaf Road and past the hand-painted sign Mammi had made decades ago: *Roses for Sale, No Sunday Sales*. Up the long drive lined with cherry trees, now bare of leaves, along the fields of roses, now just sticks of canes. Billy was gazing at the rose fields.

"Jonah's expanded the fields," he said quietly, more to himself than to her.

"We've gone in a lot of different directions. I'm sure Dad will want to tell you all about it."

"I remember when your grandmother converted those pastures into rose fields." He closed his eyes, lost in a memory. "How does a bundle of prickly sticks explode into fragrant roses?"

She looked sharply at him. That sounded like something the old Billy Lapp would say. Comments like those were what made her feel dangerously drawn to him. He had taught her to find splendor and majesty in her grandmother's old-fashioned roses.

The wood-frame house at Rose Hill Farm was two stories high, absolutely unadorned, like all the other Amish farmhouses they'd passed on their way from town. As the buggy reached the top of the rise of the driveway, Lainey stepped out of the kitchen door, tucking a strand of hair into the bun at the back of her head. Four-year-old Christy was wrapped around her leg. Lainey raised one hand in greeting and stopped, halfway up in the air, as shock flittered over her. Then, joy lit her face.

"Billy Lapp!" she called, coming down two wooden steps and traversing carefully over patches of snow that covered dry grass. "Why am I not surprised to discover you are a rose rustler?"

Billy hopped out of the buggy and walked toward her. "Hello, Lainey. You're looking well."

Lainey patted her enormous belly and Bess blushed. Lainey hadn't been raised Plain and didn't understand that she should pretend her pregnancy wasn't obvious to all. "I'm feeling like a beached whale." She ruffled the hair of her daughter. "I don't think you've met Christy. She was born after you . . ." Her voice trailed off.

Billy's eyes scanned the outbuildings: the large barn, the henhouse, the greenhouse. "I'd like to see that rose."

"Have you eaten?" Lainey said. "You look as thin as a rail. Come inside and have some supper."

His face tightened, Bess thought, a gesture so minute it barely registered. The wary look came back to his eyes and his voice came reluctantly. "Can't," he answered, almost too abrupt. "I need to catch the midday bus so I can make my connection in Lancaster." Hands on hips, he studied the rose fields a long moment. At length he sighed, tugged down his hat brim, and said, "Well, let's get this over with."

And Bess's spirits sank.

THREE

From behind him, Billy Lapp heard the kitchen door open and the sound of a man's familiar gait on the porch steps. It was strange—Billy knew Jonah's walk, recognized the sound of his limp, without even seeing him. It all came rushing back to him. Bertha Riehl's mentoring, grafting roses in the greenhouse, Bess working beside him. The smell of this farm—the unique scent of rose fields, faint but present to him, even in December. He thought he had forgotten everything—put it all behind him. How many memories were locked up in a person's head? Just waiting for the right trigger to unleash them.

Slowly, he turned in a half circle to face Jonah Riehl, startled by the look of delight on his face.

"Billy Lapp."

He swallowed. "Hello, Jonah."

"How good to see you." Jonah reached out his hands and grasped Billy's hand, pumping it enthusiastically. "What brings you to Rose Hill Farm? Are you back in Stoney Ridge? Back to stay?"

"I'm from . . . I'm the . . ." Billy cleared his throat.

245

Lainey helped him out. "Penn State sent him. He's the rose rustler. Here to look at the rose."

Jonah nodded. "Ah, the rose Bess happened upon."

Bess smiled again, and Billy saw the color in her cheeks deepen, causing a sudden shakiness inside him. "I'd . . . uh . . . better get a look at it."

"Then," Jonah said, "let's go."

Billy followed behind Jonah and Bess, hoisting his heavy backpack over his shoulder. He knew that Jonah was carrying on more than his share of the conversation, aware of how uncomfortable Billy was—and he was—and kindly trying to spare him. He talked about Lainey, and their two little girls, and a little about church news, but not too much. He skirted carefully around topics, as if he knew some things might make Billy skittish.

Billy was only half listening. He had his eyes on Bess's figure as he trailed behind her on the way to the greenhouse. He still hadn't recovered from the sight of her waiting for him at the bus stop. He could feel his heart still racing though he took pains so that she wouldn't notice. Yet there she was, just the way he remembered her. Hair as pale and shiny as corn silk. Eyes so blue they seemed like a tropical ocean. He didn't know what to do or what to say, as directionless as if suddenly lost.

It wasn't supposed to be this way. Rose Hill Farm was supposed to be a pleasant memory pasted in a mental photo album, not a reminder of all Billy had lost.

He was curious about Bess, but she volunteered nothing and he wasn't about to ask. He had been sure she would have married and moved to her husband's farm by now, maybe had a child or two. He never would have come had he known she was still living at Rose Hill Farm. He would have insisted that Penn State send someone else, though there really *was* no someone else. He was the go-to guy for all things roses.

They walked along a path that led to the greenhouse, positioned a distance from the barn, out in an open area on a small rise to maximize sunlight exposure. As he saw the modest glass greenhouse, so familiar to him, so dear, Billy felt a hitch. Many hours of his youth had been spent in that post-and-rafter building, long and happy hours. His eyes swept the exterior of the greenhouse, looking for any maintenance concerns: dry rot in wood around the glass panels, impact from snow load, any cracked glass. It looked surprisingly well maintained—the way Bertha Riehl would have kept it.

As he followed Bess into the greenhouse, he gasped, stunned by the sight. Roses! Everywhere, roses . . . blooms of every shade and tint that nature had ever produced. And it was a pleasant temperature, almost warm. "A few years ago, we winterized it," Jonah explained, striding toward the center of the greenhouse.

"You winterized it?" Billy parroted. When he had worked at Rose Hill Farm, the greenhouse was cold during the winter. He was able to overwinter perennials when winter hit, avoiding frost damage, by moving everything into the center of the greenhouse, but there was no heat or lights to extend the growing season. "How are you heating it? Not through kerosene, I hope. Plants are sensitive to the gas it gives off."

Bess pointed to a row of large black horse water tubs, each covered tightly with a metal garbage can lid, also black, tucked against the south wall. "We painted them black. The black of the tub attracts the sun's heat and the water holds it, giving off heat during the night."

Billy was impressed. He felt a smile stretch his cheeks and had to work the corners of his mouth back to a line. "It really keeps the entire greenhouse warm?"

She nodded. "But we found that two tubs worked better than one. The greenhouse stays fairly warm throughout the night."

"If the temperature drops below zero for a long stretch," Jonah added, "I'll put bales of hay around the exterior. And we'll bring our most fragile plants into the barn." He crossed his arms over his chest. "Last winter, we had seven days below zero, so we added plastic jugs filled with water—painted black like those horse water tubs—let them soak up the sun during the day and set them throughout the greenhouse to balance the temperature."

"And it kept the greenhouse heated?"

"Well, not toasty, but not freezing. Water's the best for passive solar."

Billy gestured with a wing-like motion. "What about lighting?"

"That's been a little trickier," Jonah said. "Like you said, we didn't want kerosene or propane in here. A fellow in Lancaster just started a solar company and asked if he could use our greenhouse as a test site." He walked to the far end of the greenhouse, where the workbench was nestled in against the wall, and pointed to a row of solar panels on the far end of the rise, facing south. "I could never have afforded those panels had this fellow not volunteered them; they're pretty costly. They have a few glitches. Not a perfect system, but they seem to work more often than not."

Billy peered out the back end of the greenhouse to see the solar panels. Four of them stood side by side, above snow level, and at an angle to shed snow and rain. Amazing. Just amazing.

Two years ago, he had proposed a recommendation to the Extension office to consider solar panels for the greenhouses. America's developing space program had catapulted the science behind solar photovoltaic cells into viable use for homes and businesses, and he'd figured out that the panels could pay for themselves within a few years. His proposal was shot down, but that was when energy prices had dropped again and it was assumed they'd stay low. A few weeks ago, Jill told him the proposal might get a second look and could he please hurry and update it? He did, knowing it was a desperate reaction by the Extension office to combat high energy bills and the continually rising cost of gas triggered from the nation's oil embargo in 1973.

Billy was astounded by the progressive thinking on this simple Amish rose farm. He swiveled on his heel to face Jonah. "Caleb Zook had no objection with you working with a non-Amish?"

"No," Jonah said, a look on his face as if such a thought had never occurred to him. "It solved a problem of lighting, helped us extend our growing season, and didn't cost a thing. And we're not really working with this English businessman. He comes out and fixes broken pieces, makes adjustments, asks me questions. To his way of thinking, we're doing him a favor. The commercial nurseries are too large for his type of panels—he's trying to build up the home business. Or small farms, like ours." He ran a hand down the arch of his aching back, wincing slightly. "If the costs ever come down, I suspect more and more of our people will be using solar energy."

"Jonah, I'm very impressed."

Jonah's cheeks, above his beard, stained pink with embarrassment. "Sun, water, they're God's gifts. He's provided the means for man to live a sustainable life."

"You harnessed their power."

"It's worked well this fall because we've had a dry spell, nice and clear. But I didn't expect it to last." Hands on his hips, Jonah glanced around with a worried look. "Sunday's snowfall was practicing for winter's arrival."

Billy walked up and down the aisle in awe, studying varieties he hadn't seen in years. He knew them all: The shell pink Ma Perkins, named for a popular radio soap opera in 1952. Behind it was a fragrant deep pink hybrid perpetual named Helen Keller. The story behind this rose floated into his mind: The rose had been introduced in 1895 on Helen Keller's fifteenth birthday. She couldn't see a flower or hear its name, but she could smell, and she always held roses dear to her heart. Next to the Helen Keller, Billy spotted a trio of roses and glanced at Jonah. "The Peace roses?" Pax Amanda, Pax Apollo, and Pax Iola.

Billy had always appreciated the story behind those roses. A South Dakota breeder had hybridized the trio of roses in 1938, in between the two world wars, with an absence of prickles on the plants' stems. The breeder wanted everyone to know that thorns were no more necessary on roses than war was among humans.

Jonah smiled, watching him. "Probably our bestselling roses, at least in Stoney Ridge."

The beauty of these roses, the care Jonah and Bess took with them, felt like balm to Billy's soul. It was more nourishing than food for his sense of well-being and happiness, both of which had left him years ago. He felt the tension drain from him, though he held his shoulders stiff. He realized that Jonah was studying him, waiting for something from him. "Did you force blooms to sell plants through the winter?"

"It was Bess's idea to keep up income during the winter months." Jonah glanced fondly at his daughter. "She's been expanding the rose business beyond my mother's jam and soaps. To remedies." Jonah offered up a shy smile. "She's got my mother's touch."

Jonah's love for his family was evident. Billy swallowed back a deep envy that rose from his center. Why was everyone else able to find love and happiness, but not him? He tried to tamp down that ugly feeling of self-pity and looked around for the reason he was at Rose Hill Farm: the mystery rose.

Jonah saw Billy's eyes sweep the greenhouse. "Down there, in the corner. We didn't even want to move it."

There, tucked into the far left corner of the greenhouse, was a rosebush in a large clay pot. It was fully leafed out with one tight capsule of a flower bud. He walked up to it and crouched down to inspect it, noting the characteristics of the plant, trying to recognize if it was an obvious species or class. He examined the branching pattern, the veining and number of leaves, and their unique edging. He looked closely at the lone flower bud, enclosed by sepals—a cluster of leaflike structures. That one small bud wouldn't open for another week or two, longer if the weather stayed cold. "Mind if I lift it up on the workbench?"

"It's up to you," Jonah said. "We felt concerned about causing it any stress. I think it's gotten just the right amount of sunlight and moisture in that corner after we winterized the greenhouse."

"And you just noticed it?"

"I came across it over a week ago," Bess said. "My cat pulled my coat to the ground, and when I bent down to get it, I noticed the rose, tucked way under the workbench."

Billy lifted it carefully to the workbench. It was surprisingly heavy, which made him think the root ball was impacted and should be transplanted. He smelled the leaves, trying to place its scent among breeds.

"What do you think?" Jonah asked.

"I'm not sure. You have no memory of it at all? It doesn't look familiar to either of you?"

Jonah shook his head. "Bess might know a little more. She remembers my mother calling it a very precious rose."

Billy's eyes sought Bess's, but she avoided his questioning glance. She lifted a shoulder in a half shrug. "But Mammi thought all her roses were precious."

"Does it look familiar to you?" Jonah said.

"Most of the characteristics of a rose are manifest in the flower," Billy said. "Once that bud opens, it'll be easier to recognize." He glanced at Jonah, then back at the rose. "I should take the rose back with me to the university to examine it there and compare findings in the database."

"Ah." Jonah digested that for a moment before adding, "If that's what you need to do."

Inner conflict started to churn inside of Billy. This rose didn't fall under any obvious class that he could recognize. He wanted to get it to the greenhouses in College Station. He wanted to cut slips and propagate it. He wanted to dissect the one flower bud and examine it. He wondered if this might be an extinct rose—something every rosarian would give his right eye to find. An extinct "found" could be likened to a discovered comet; overnight, Billy would become a renowned, respected rosarian. His heart started to pound. He was nearly in a state of disbelief at his good fortune.

But none of that was in Jonah's best interests. Billy swallowed. These people—they used to be *his* people—they were trusting, naive. He could easily take advantage of Jonah; it would be so easy. But he just couldn't. Finally, "I can't. It wouldn't be right."

"Why not?"

"If anyone sees this rose before it's identified, before a genealogy is mapped out, before its parentage is traced, he could take a slip to reproduce it, propagate it on the sly, and sell it for mass production at a nursery. You'd be cheated out of a fortune."

"But you could do the same thing," Bess said. "I've seen you take slips and propagate cuttings. I've seen you graft dozens of roses."

"Those were roses that were known. Nothing unusual. Nothing like this."

"My mother's old-fashioneds are unusual," Jonah said.

"True, but there's still a difference. Heirloom roses or heritage roses are varieties that have been in existence for at least half a century."

Jonah reached a hand out to gently touch a leaf. "So you think this rose could be older than that?"

"If the bloom were open, I could tell more about it. But there are some distinctions about it that are rather unusual." Billy peered at the veining on a leaf. "Are either of you familiar with the term 'a found rose'?"

Jonah and Bess exchanged a look, then shook their heads.

"It's a rose with an unknown identity. It's thought to be extinct, but then one or another will turn up in an old cemetery.

Or someone's backyard. They're usually sturdy roses on old rootstock, brought over by European immigrants, who shared clips with their descendants. They're not hybrids—modern roses didn't start until the nineteenth century."

Bess listened carefully. "I read about such a rose on Alcatraz Island."

Billy tilted his head at her, not hiding his surprise. "Yes. Yes, that's exactly right. The Bardou Job. A Welsh rose." His eyes met hers and he nearly became lost in her blue, blue eyes.

Jonah seemed surprised. "Where is it? Where's this Alcatraz?"

Billy forced himself to look away from those searching eyes of Bess. "It used to be a federal prison in San Francisco Bay. On an island."

Amused, Jonah said, "What do you suppose a rose was doing at a federal prison?"

"Actually, there was more than one rose at Alcatraz. The head warden was a rosarian. After the prison was closed down, the Heritage Rose Group was inventorying the roses and discovered an heirloom Welsh rose. The Bardou Job. It had been thought to be extinct."

"And you think this rose could be a 'found'?" Bess said, taking a step closer to the rose.

She was standing so close that he caught a whiff of the rose soap she used. Even now, years later, he associated that faint scent with Bess. He backed away so there was more space between them. No whiffs of rose soap. He needed every inch of distance. "Possibly. And if so, a found rose can be extremely valuable. Both to the scientific community and also on the commercial market. You should keep this quiet until the rose can be identified."

"If it's about money . . ."

"It's not just the money, Jonah. You know how crazy people can be about roses. They're like bird-watchers on the hunt for a rare bird. Even on Alcatraz Island, the Rose Society brings out tours each year when the Bardou Job is in bloom. You'll have people climbing onto your property in the middle of the night with a pair of clippers in one hand and a plastic sandwich bag in the other to hold the slips. You'll wake up one morning and find this plant sheared down to a stump. That's if it doesn't get stolen first. Most rose rustlers are polite, but some aren't. You should lock up the greenhouse when you're not in it."

"Does a 'found' get discovered very often?" Jonah said.

Billy gave up a half laugh. "No. I'm still waiting for my first found."

Bess glanced up and smiled. "I thought the job of a rose rustler was to find extinct roses."

He made himself look away from her intoxicating smile, lifting his eyes to notice the ventilating windows of the greenhouse. "Rose rustlers go after old roses—thought to be extinct commercially, but they're rarely truly extinct. I've never come across one that can't be identified."

Bess still kept one hand lovingly on the pot. "And you really think this rose is a found?"

"I don't know. Probably not. But . . . I'd like to check it out." And as Billy voiced that thought aloud, his heart fell. This morning wasn't turning out at all like he had planned. He had known it would be difficult to be in Stoney Ridge, to see Jonah again, but he was sure Jonah wouldn't put any pressure on him to stay, or worse, to see his father. He had assumed he'd come out to Rose Hill Farm this morning, identify the rose, and get back to College Station. In, out, job done. That's the way it usually worked.

But it was Bess at the bus stop, not Jonah. And then there was *this* rose. This mysterious, unidentifiable rose.

Knowing Bertha Riehl as he did, this rose would have an interesting history. It might be a found, or it might be a variant of a known species. But if there was a chance that this rose was extinct, a true found, it would require repeated trips back and forth from College Station to Stoney Ridge to confirm it. Meticulous by nature, Billy would spend more time at Rose Hill Farm than he expected—or wanted to. "I'll need to photograph it, draw some pictures, check the database back at the university, and compare it to other known varieties. Talk to the heads of a few Rose Societies. They're a wealth of information. If it's a found, Rose Hill Farm will be in a sweet spot. It will be a highly desirable rose."

Jonah lifted his dark eyebrows, crossed his arms over his chest. "I only wanted to identify the rose so we could propagate it and add it to our inventory. That's all."

When Billy saw the hesitation on Jonah's face, he added, "A rose like this should be shared. You just need to do it the right way. Keep it quiet until I can identify it."

Jonah glanced at Bess. "Maybe I should run this by the bishop."

"Who's the bishop now?"

"Same one," Bess said quietly. "Caleb Zook."

Billy winced. Same one as when he left, she meant. His last conversation with the bishop had been a painful one. He cast a glance at Bess. "How's Maggie?"

"She's fine. Hasn't changed a bit."

Jonah added, "I'm sure she'd like to see you."

Billy stiffened up. "I've got to get back to work." He pulled his camera out of his backpack. He ripped open the foil wrapper of a new roll of film and inserted it into the camera, then rolled the film into place. He shot pictures from every angle, used up the entire roll of thirty-six pictures, took out another new roll, and took thirty-six more. As he photographed the rose, Jonah and Bess moved away to let him work uninterrupted. He set down the camera and picked up his sketch pad to scribble down some characteristics he'd noted, to study it further back at College Station. By this time Jonah had quietly excused himself and left the greenhouse. Bess remained, and he wished she would leave him alone.

He wished everyone would just leave him alone.

Bess studied Billy awhile as he stood in front of the rose. Clenched jaw, arms crossed over his chest, staring at the rose as if it were about to sprout wings and fly away. She wondered how many miles he'd drifted over the last few years, how many roses he'd rustled during his exile, how long it would take him to lose that distance he maintained so carefully. Once or twice, she saw a crack in it, but then he would roll up like a possum.

She tried to think of something to say to Billy, but couldn't. Being so close to him was making it hard to speak. She watched him photograph the rose, captivated by the sight he made as he leaned to the task. How wide his shoulders, how spare his movements, how capable his muscles. She watched him walk around the workbench to peer at the rose from different angles, noticing for the first time in her life how much narrower a man's hips were than a woman's, how powerful a man's hands could be, how beguiling. Her eyes were drawn to those hands, wider than she remembered, and certainly far stronger.

He put down his camera and took a sketch pad out of his backpack, paused to study the rose, then began to sketch it. As he concentrated, she was able to get a leisurely gander at his face. It was long and lean, like the rest of him. His mouth was straight and firm, unsmiling. With his chin tilted, his jaw had the crisp angle of a boomerang. His lips were slightly parted as he squinted skyward, his eyelashes seemed long as the corn stubble, sooty, throwing spiky shadows across his cheek.

She used to love the crinkles at the sides of his eyes, as if he couldn't help but smile, even if it were just in his eyes. So far, he kept his hat brim pulled low as if to protect any secret she might read in his eyes. He was working hard to keep expression out of those eyes. Same with his voice; it was respectful to her father and Lainey, but flat. And with her, slightly irritated.

Bess realized she'd been holding her breath as he made his way around the rose, photographing it at different angles, and so she exhaled, clasping her hands together. "A customer asked me a question awhile ago and I wasn't sure I gave her the correct answer." Her voice shook, then steadied. "She wanted to know if a China rose was an heirloom or a modern rose."

He didn't say anything, and Bess wondered if he'd heard. She sidled a little closer to him. "I told her that modern roses came *from* China roses," she said, raising her voice. "I think that was the right answer."

Billy froze. He tilted his head at her like a barn owl, then shook it as if he were very sorry for her, and she had to bite her lip to keep from grinning. How many times had he given her that same look when she was just learning about roses? More times than she could count.

"China roses were the first significant hybrids," he proceeded to inform her in his best lecturing tone. "Europeans crossbred their roses with China roses and were able to get repeat bloomers. Before that, roses bloomed only once a year. But repeat blooming wasn't the only reason they were hybridized. The Europeans hadn't seen the bright crimson color before. In nature, true red is a rare color to find in flowering plants, even among roses."

Lecture over, he turned his attention back to his work and she searched her mind for something else. Anything to keep him talking.

"So the Chinese loved roses before the Europeans did?"

"Before?" He hesitated. "Not sure about that. The world's oldest roses go back thousands and thousands of years. And loved is the wrong word. The Romans used the petals as confetti. The Chinese used the roses for cures and remedies. Rosehips are a source of Vitamin C."

Bess didn't mind hearing him tell her facts she already knew—she was that eager to hear his voice.

"The Chinese fed their children rosehip tea long before anyone else did. But they didn't have the same admiration for rose flowers as the Europeans did. European royalty used roses as legal tender."

She nearly sighed in admiration. She wondered how a man could know so much.

Then, suddenly, as if Billy realized he was slipping back into an old, comfortable role with Bess, a coldness came over him. "Look, I'm not here to give you a lesson in basic rose tending," he said brusquely. "Unless you know something about *this* rose, I need to concentrate."

Bess blinked and took a step back as if she'd been slapped. Her cheeks burned and she tried to will them to cool. She busied herself with deadheading some of the flowering roses. Billy had certainly changed in more ways than the obvious physical ones. He had hardened into manhood. Yet he was stunted somehow, Bess thought. Like a crop that had suffered an unexpected frost.

She watched his head, hat firmly in place, bent over the potted rose and its deep green leaves, its one lone rosebud. Unless you know something about *this* rose, he'd said . . . and she was suddenly transported to another time.

Mid-November 1969, a crisp autumn afternoon. Billy was peering at a leafless rosebush sitting on newspaper on the kitchen table at Rose Hill Farm. "What's so special about this rose?"

Mammi clapped her big hands together. "Now, there's a question that's finally got some sense to it." She pointed to a large book of botanical prints, resting wide open at the end of the table. "I want you to figure it out."

Billy examined the picture, then studied the rose. "How do I do that when it has no leaves and no blooms? Not to mention that I know this much—" he pinched his thumb and index finger together—"about roses."

"Study its traits."

"It's got big thorns," Bess said, trying to be helpful.

Billy gave her a look of sheer disgust. "Roses produce prickles, not thorns."

"Same thing," Bess said. Billy looked serious as a sermon.

Billy set his lips and shook his head slightly as if she were speaking gibberish. "Not hardly."

Mammi's attention was on the rosebush. "Better not be a hybrid. Dadgum hybrids have no fragrance at all. They've ruined them."

"Then why do they make them?" Bess asked in her bravest voice. They didn't hear her, so she asked again. "Why do they make hybrids?"

Billy kept his eyes on the book. "Because they're disease resistant and more cold hardy."

"Bah!" Mammi said. "The old-fashioneds are the strong ones. They've endured."

"Hybrids have a broader range of color and form," Billy said, turning pages in the book.

"Pish." Mammi dismissed that with a wave of her hand. She didn't think much of how hybrids had tinkered with Mother Nature.

Billy let out a breath and looked at Mammi. He still had barely noticed Bess existed. "Where'd you find that pathetic excuse for a rose?"

Mammi suddenly grabbed a broom and busied herself. "Here or there," she said, looking aside. She always looked aside when she wasn't telling the exact truth.

"Bertha . . . did you hear me?"

"Roses belong to everybody," Mammi said. Again she looked aside. Bess knew enough to keep her mouth closed tight.

"You could call Penn State and see what they have to say about it."

"And let them chop it apart and bisect it?"

"Dissect it," Billy corrected.

"Never!" Mammi didn't trust the government, and that included universities.

"They'll make sure it stays safe."

Mammi sat back in her chair and patted the topknot tucked under her prayer cap in a satisfied way. "It'll be safer with me. I'll make sure it has southern explosion."

"Exposure," Billy corrected. "What are you going to do with it?"

"Grow it."

Billy snorted. "First you gotta bring it back from the brink. That thing is about dead."

Mammi wasn't paying him any mind. Maggie Zook had gone unnoticed in the kitchen until she started poking at the pathetic-looking rose. "Don't touch it, Maggie Zook, or I'll have your father get after you."

Billy rolled his eyes. "As if Caleb Zook would ever scold Maggie. He's way too soft on her."

Maggie slipped across the room to whisper to Bess. "He's only saying that because his own father is a bear. Wallops him for the slightest thing."

Shocked, Bess shuddered. Her own father had never even raised his voice to her, not once.

"Billy's brothers are just like his father—big unfeeling louts—and I'm related to them so I can say so. But Billy, he's more like his mom. That's why your grandmother took Billy under her wing." Maggie patted Bess on the arm. "Your grandmother—she's one of a kind. My dad says she likes people to think she's a grizzly bear, but she's a teddy bear at heart."

Bess glanced over at Billy and Mammi, heads bent together, one brown, one salt-and-pepper, poring over the book of botanical rose prints.

With a bang, Billy closed up his books and turned to Bess, vaulting her back to the present. Should she tell him what she knew about this rose? But what did she know? Not much. She couldn't even remember what Mammi called it, or if it had a name at all; her grandmother had so many special roses. She felt the gossamer-thin memory shimmer and glint in the back of her mind, just out of reach. Something vague about a Most Special Rose. But it was there, waiting for her to bring it sharply into focus. She tried to reset her face. *Tell him. Don't tell him.*

"I'm ready to go. If you're too busy to drop me at the bus stop, I can walk. It's not far."

"You're not staying for supper?" The chickens had gone to roost, and the chill of afternoon had begun settling in. *Stay, Billy Lapp. Please stay.*

"No," he said firmly, bending over to stuff his camera into his backpack. "Dark sets in earlier these days. I want to get back."

"I'll let Dad and Lainey know that you're leaving." *Tell him? Don't tell him. Tell him?*

"No need. You can tell them goodbye for me after you get back from dropping me off." His face set stubbornly as he rose, tugged his hat brim down low, and lunged down the brick path of the greenhouse, pride stiffening his posture and adding force to his shoulders.

Definitely do not tell him. Bess closed her eyes, then opened them, as if to rewind the events of the day. But of course that was impossible. Time moved in only one direction.

The buggy ride to the bus stop was a repeat of the morning's trip. He had told her quite a bit. And he had told her nothing.

FOUR

As Billy rode the bus back to College Station, he tried to focus on the characteristics he had gleaned about the Rose Hill Farm mystery rose, but his mind kept flicking back to the events of the day. And he couldn't dispel the image of a pink-clad girl who filled his mind.

Finally, he closed his note pad, stuffed it in his backpack, and stared out the window. Over the years the vista hadn't changed at all: horses, harvest, horizon. Beyond the window the sky at twilight was awash with pink, red, and orange, but it couldn't lighten the tumble of uncertainty that rolled around inside him today: he had gone home.

Home. He thought of what he had left behind, years ago. A father, three brothers, the farm where he'd been born and raised. The town. All the familiar places and people he'd known his whole life . . . yet it wasn't home anymore. He was prepared to feel detached, cut loose, to be reminded of a vague sense of deprivation. But he had been completely unprepared for his reaction at seeing Bess again.

He felt . . . stunned, stricken. Bess, with her woman's body, hair swept and fastened in a knot, and . . . that *face.*

That breathtaking face, filled with an expression of openness glowing at him, schoolgirl's cheeks flushed pink, lips shining, azure eyes that seemed to send all the blood in his head right to his heart, causing it to pound like a jackhammer.

By the time the bus arrived in College Station, he was in a state of agitation. He forced himself to a semblance of calm before he reached the camera shop, arriving just after the manager had closed up for the night. It took cajoling, but he talked him into letting him drop off the film cartridges for development. Next stop was the Extension office at the university, where he could find resource books on lost roses. Jill had given him a key so that he could use the small library when he worked weekends. There was a rack of bookshelves and a small table under the window where he had spent many quiet Sunday afternoons, poring over dusty magazines and old books about extinct roses. He grabbed a few books and tucked them under his arm, then hurried to the place he loved best. His greenhouse. Penn State had a number of greenhouses, but one in particular felt like home to him. Even if it was a cheap hoop house, it was his.

He moved through the greenhouse to reach the shelf that doubled as his desk, breathing in the warm, moist, musty air. Here was his domain. Here he had total control. Here nobody laughed at him, like his brothers did, or found him lacking, like his father did. The greenhouse was more than a workplace to him, it was a sanctuary. During his darkest hours, when faith deserted him, his love of plants had sustained him.

This time of day, the greenhouse was clean and quiet, no work to be done. And nobody to listen to his ranting frustrations over the day's turn of events.

He went straight to his shelf, turned on the desk lamp,

and leafed through the books, trying to narrow down the parentage of the mystery rose. If only he had a better idea of what characteristics the bloom would reveal, identifying it would be much easier.

He suddenly felt a gust of warm air, looked behind him, and there was the hobo from Friday, smiling broadly as if he'd just been waiting for Billy to return so he could come in for a visit. He looked at Billy as if he was something special.

"Hello there, Billy Lapp."

Oh no. He hoped this guy wasn't going to come around to bother him every day. "George, isn't it?"

George nodded. "You're working late."

"I got something important on my mind." The hobo didn't catch his hint, so Billy added, "I'll give you a cup of coffee, but then I gotta get back to work. Not even sure the coffee's still hot, but you're welcome to it."

"What are you working on?" George glanced at Billy's sketches and the open books on the shelf.

"I'm trying to identify a rose discovered at an Amish farm." Billy had bent over to unzip his backpack and get his thermos. He opened it and sniffed. Not hot, but not cold.

"Weren't you raised Amish?"

He snapped his head up to look at George. "How do you know that?"

"Your accent, for one. I can tell English is your second language. And then there's that." He pointed to Billy's hat on the metal stool.

His old felt hat, distinctly Amish. Billy loved that hat. It had been his grandfather Zook's hat, the one thing from his old life that he couldn't get rid of. "Yeah, well, that was a lifetime ago."

George had an odd look on his face: surprised, amused, he couldn't tell. "Interesting choice of words."

Suddenly, Billy felt stupid. Here was a man who had once lived another life, was clearly well educated, and was currently just down on his luck. He could practically read the hobo's thoughts: What would Billy Lapp, at the ripe old age of twenty-three, know about other lifetimes? He probably thought Billy was a fool. Perhaps he was.

In the quiet of the evening, Billy found two fairly clean mugs and wiped their insides with a paper towel. It surprised him to discover he didn't mind the hobo's company so much; it eased the burden of his loneliness.

George walked halfway down the length of the greenhouse and stopped to sniff the orange blossoms on a potted tree. "Did you know that oranges were only eaten, not made into juice, until Albert Lasker sold packaged orange juice?" He grinned, revealing a row of bright, white teeth set against his dark face, and clasped his hands as if he held something secret in them. "I marvel at all there is to discover on earth. Just a hint of what's to come. An eternity of discoveries."

Billy gave a nod, but he had trouble parsing meaning from the hobo's curious sentences. He poured lukewarm coffee into the mugs and handed one to George. "Do you take anything in your coffee?" He looked around the shelf where he kept supplies. "Not that I have anything to offer. Maybe I could find some sugar someplace."

George took a sip. "This is fine, Billy. Just fine."

The coffee was dreadful, bitter and oily. Billy set down his mug. "George, can I ask you a question?"

"Ask me anything you like. I'll answer anything I like."

"Don't you want more for yourself than just being a drifter?"
"Well, drifting isn't all bad."
"But what have you got to show for it? You're plenty smart. Don't you want to get a real job? Find some purpose in life."
"A purpose. I like that kind of thinking, Billy Lapp. I'll give it some thought." George nodded solemnly. "Mind if I look through your sketches?"

Obviously, George wasn't leaving and Billy found he didn't mind. Not so much. He felt a tickle of admiration for the hobo's peaceful countenance, and sensed the internal churning from the day settle as he handed George the sketches. Billy moved his hat and sat on the stool and combed through the books, taking notes on different possibilities of rose species. After a while, he nearly forgot George was there.

"Maybe it's this one," Billy said aloud, looking closely at a photograph of a rose in a book.

George came up beside Billy and looked over his shoulder.

"This is the oldest known rose in the world," Billy said. "Over one thousand years old. It's from a cathedral in Hildescheim, Germany. During the Second World War, the cathedral was bombed and the rose was destroyed. Believe it or not, new canes sprouted up."

"Love those stories." George smiled. "New life coming out of something so implausible." He ran his fingers along the vein of a leaf. "Slightly different here than from your drawing."

George was right. A subtle difference that Billy didn't even notice. "But it does look close, doesn't it?" Billy bent his head over the book and tried to match any characteristics with the Hildescheim rose and with the Rose Hill Farm rose. There were marked similarities, which meant that the

Rose Hill Farm rose was probably bred in Europe. He felt encouraged. Maybe he was getting somewhere.

As the evening progressed, a comfortable companionship settled in between the two men. Now and then, George posed questions about Billy's Amish upbringing. Unguarded and relaxed, half the time with his head in a book of botanical prints, he answered them. It felt good to sort through all the emotions that were spinning through him from the day's events, and George was a good listener. He didn't pry, didn't give advice, nodded in all the right places. Billy might have said more than he intended, but what did it matter? George was a drifter who would drift away. His secrets were safe.

Billy had no idea how much time had passed when he turned a page and came awake as if someone had set off a firecracker. "That's it! That must be it. The Perle von Weissenstein! Come here, George! I found it!" He looked up, but George had already gone. When had he left? His coffee cup was on the bench, stone cold. Billy was shocked when he looked at his wristwatch: after midnight.

His attention went back to the description of the rose. This must be it. It must be. He had to get to Rose Hill Farm and question Bess. *Now.*

Bess awakened to a pink sunrise creeping over the sill and the sound of someone walking up the long driveway of Rose Hill farm, the crunch of gravel under his footsteps. Barefoot, she tiptoed to the window and peered through the frosty windowpane, watching a man approach the house with that familiar long-legged stride. Why, it was Billy Lapp! So early!

She grabbed a shawl, then rushed downstairs to open the back door and step onto the threshold, not even aware of how cold it was on her toes. "You're sure up with the chickens, Billy Lapp." She tried to hold back a smile, but she felt it tug at her mouth, then fade as she caught the grim look on his face.

"You knew what it was. You knew and you didn't tell me."

"What are you talking about?"

Billy tipped his hat brim back, hooked one boot on the bottom step, and braced a hand on the knee. It occurred to her that he had never taken his hat off yesterday. A metaphor in a way, as a covering, because he really was a different person than the boy she had known. This Billy seemed so closed up, so hardened, like a curtain was drawn over his eyes. Not the Billy she used to know, the bright, lighthearted young man she used to work alongside in her grandmother's greenhouse, who never seemed to remember his hat.

Billy was glaring at her. "Your grandmother and the rose. That October when you came out to stay with your grandmother and she had a rose she wanted me to identify, but I couldn't—all the leaves were off and I thought it was about to die." He pointed his thumb in the direction of the greenhouse. "*That* rose." He walked up to her. "You remember. You must remember." He came a few steps closer to her. "I stayed up half the night last night trying to identify that rose. You would've saved me a heap of trouble if you'd just told me about it yesterday. So why didn't you say something?"

Billy's words sounded like an accusation, and Bess felt a storm brewing in her throat.

He glanced at the farmhouse. "Maybe I should just talk to Jonah about the rose."

What? How dare he! Now he'd crossed the line. She wasn't sure if he intended that comment to sting, but a flash of indignation threatened to voice itself anyway. *Just who do you think has been tending Mammi's roses for the last few years?* she wanted to say. *Who do you think has been encouraging my father to expand the business? Certainly not* you.

She shot him what she hoped was a withering look. "And a good morning to you too, Billy Lapp."

When Billy caught sight of Bess on the kitchen stoop in a white, ankle-length nightgown, she looked so lovely that, for a moment, his heart did a stutter step and suddenly all thoughts of roses fled from his head. She had curves in places where she used to be stick thin and it definitely became her. He felt his cheeks flare and he tried not to stare as she unconsciously splayed her hand over her chest. Her hair was flying every which way, out from under her prayer cap, her feet were bare, and from this distance she looked carefree and happy.

A feeling grew inside of him, something he hadn't felt in a long, long time. Desire.

But then the door slammed and Bess disappeared.

Frustrated by her lack of response to his questions, Billy spun around to head to the greenhouse. Initially, he was annoyed to discover Jonah hadn't taken his advice to lock the greenhouse and protect the rose, but then he was grateful because it was warm in the greenhouse and he was freezing. Hungry and tired too.

After midnight, he had gone back to the Extension office to search the database for more information about the Perle von Weissenstein. There wasn't much, but he did learn that this variety was a cultivar of Daniel August Schwarzkopf, chief gardener of the castle of Weissenstein near Kassel, in Germany. Dating as far back as 1773, it was considered to be the oldest known rose of German origin. Class: Gallica. A large, strong-scented flower, dark in the center, pale at the edges.

A silky black cat showed up out of nowhere, its tail straight as a poker. The cat leaned into Billy's ankle and he paused to scratch it. "What's your name?" It stood on its hind legs, braced its forefeet on his thigh, begging. Its fur was soft and warm as it jutted against his fingers. Blackie! He'd completely forgotten about Bess's old cat.

He looked through his backpack for the Xeroxed copy he'd made of the botanical print of the Perle von Weissenstein, found it, pulled out some files he'd brought with him and some tools to measure and chart the rose. He crouched down to pull the mystery rose from its corner, inhaled, then hoisted it up on the workbench. "What's your story, little rose?" he said, wishing it could answer.

He saw Bess come out of the house, dressed now, wrapped in a warm coat and a kerchief knotted under her chin. She juggled two mugs of coffee in her hands as she traversed the yard toward the greenhouse. Once inside the greenhouse, she walked to the workbench where Billy stood and held out a mug. He reached out to take it and grazed her fingers with his. Suddenly self-conscious, he pointed to the copy he'd made of the botanical print. "I identified it. The Perle von Weissenstein. Earliest known rose of German stock."

She looked carefully at the print, then at the rose. "Nope. That's not it. Close, but not quite."

"What? Where's the variation?"

Bess pointed to the information below the print. "It says the Perle von Weissenstein has a deep purple color. It might be too soon to tell, but I think the mystery rose bud will be a lighter color. And it said the Perle von Weissenstein has a moderate to strong scent." She leaned close to the bud to inhale. "But this one's scent would be classified as bold."

Billy sniffed the bud. He looked at her suspiciously. "How do you know so much about the Perle von Weissenstein?" He'd never heard of it until last night. "I still think it's it."

"I know for sure it isn't."

"How would you know that?"

"I know because we have a Perle von Weissenstein in the greenhouse and that's not it."

"*What?* No way. I would have known if Rose Hill Farm sold such a rare rose. Your grandmother would have made sure of that."

Bess walked to the middle of the greenhouse and pointed to a large rosebush, against the back of the shelf. "See for yourself."

Billy strode a few steps to see where she was pointing. And there it was—the Perle von Weissenstein. He shook his head. "So why didn't you say something?"

"About what?"

"About the Perle von Weissenstein? If you knew that rose wasn't it?"

"You never mentioned it to me. If you had, I would have told you it was right here, under your very nose. I'm not a mind reader."

Billy fleered at Bess. "That sounds like something your grandmother would say."

Suddenly Billy realized his arm was pressed close and warm against Bess's. She must have felt it too but stayed where she was.

"So the Perle was the rose your grandmother wanted me to identify that time? The nearly dead one?"

Bess pivoted on her heels and reached for a straw broom that was leaning against a post. She started to sweep the brick walk that lined the center of the greenhouse.

"Bess?" He saw her hesitation, saw her nervous movements as she swept. "Was that the Perle? I need to know."

"No." She swept away, back and forth, left to right, eyes remaining downcast nearly all the time. Each time they flicked up they seemed drawn to something behind him. "The Perle was brought to Rose Hill Farm a year ago."

He took a few strides toward her. "How did your father locate a Perle von Weissenstein?" Incredible. He knew, better than anybody, how hard it was to find old roses.

Bess stopped sweeping and leaned the broom back against the post. "He didn't. I did."

"You?" Surprise flattened his face, though he recovered when he caught the exasperation that flickered through her eyes.

"Yes." She gave him a stern look and he backed off, worried she might start whacking the wrong end of the broom at him if he accidentally insulted her one more time. He'd seen Bertha Riehl threaten people with a broomstick for far less. It struck him for the second time that Bess was getting more and more like her grandmother. "Yes, me," she repeated, softer this time, snapping Billy back from the past to the present. "I tracked down a source from a tip someone gave me from the Lancaster Rose Society."

Billy tried not to show the shock on his face. He wondered what to make of this new Bess. The one he remembered had studiously avoided difficult things, like math, at all costs. "So why didn't you go to the Rose Society to identify the mystery rose?"

"We tried. But the man at the Rose Society slipped on ice over Thanksgiving and broke his tailbone. He wasn't able to come to the farm, so he suggested calling Penn State. He said they had a champion rose rustler." She lifted her chin in his direction. "Apparently, that was you."

Billy crossed his arms, frowning. "Well, I suppose this exercise hasn't been a complete waste of time. I'm fairly confident the mystery rose has a European rootstock. Quite possibly, a German rootstock. But I won't know more until the bud opens and reveals itself."

"You sound certain that you'll be able to identify it."

"I shouldn't sound too sure," Billy admitted. "Sometimes the trail goes cold."

"What happens then?"

"Well, usually, if a rose has an uncertain origin, then it'll be given a provisional label, like a temporary tag, until it can end up with a permanent ID. Sooner or later, after doing a lot of comparative analysis, the identity gets tracked down." He settled himself on the wooden stool. "That's what being a rose rustler is all about—tracking down clues to a rose's identity by looking through old botanicals, nursery catalogs. Once, I even traced a rose's identity through an old traveler's diary from Bermuda."

"I've read a little about the Bermuda Rose Society."

Billy straightened up like a shot. "You know of the Bermuda Rose Society?" He repeated each word clearly so that there would be no mistake. That Society was the main reason so many genealogical rose puzzles had been solved.

"Yes, of course," she said, keeping her voice steady as if she was barely holding back her annoyance with him. "I read about a survivor of a Spanish shipwreck in 1639 who described the roses in Bermuda. It's supposed to have the perfect climate for roses."

Billy nodded. "Bermuda doesn't have any native roses—they're all imported by settlers. The chain of islands sits in the middle of centuries-old trade routes. It's an incredible source for old, old vintage roses. *R. galica officinalis*—"

"The Apothecary's Rose."

"—and the *R. damascena*."

"The Damask Rose."

Again, he was startled by her knowledge. When did she get so smart?

"Someday, I'd love to see those roses," Bess said in a wistful voice. "In the springtime, when they're in full bloom."

A soft look came over her face, as if she were imagining a sea of roses, a riot of color. He had the same dream—to see Bermuda's roses in the springtime. In fact, that was why he tried to save money and live as sparingly as he could. Dreams were good. One day, he would travel to Bermuda in the spring and see those flowers in bloom. And he would see an ocean that reflected the tropical blue of Bess's eyes.

Her eyes traveled to the mystery rosebush, nestled in the corner of the greenhouse. "What should we call the rose?"

Billy shrugged. "Don't get too attached to any name. If I can find its true identity, its Latin name, that's what it'll be known by."

"But that's not always the case." She gave him a sideways glance. "Not for Louise the Unfortunate."

A slight smile tugged at the corners of Billy's mouth. Little was known about the actual Louise the Unfortunate, except that she traveled to Natchez, Mississippi, as a mail-order bride and her husband-to-be never showed up to claim her. Desperate to survive, she was forced into prostitution, then died young and penniless. A sympathetic Natchez minister raised enough money for a proper burial. Someone named a rose climber after Louise and the name stuck. "No, not poor Louise. In Bermuda, they call the Louise the Unfortunate climber the Spice Rose."

"Maybe because Louise had a spicy life."

Before he could suppress it, a laugh burst out of him. Their eyes met; he saw a blush rise in her cheeks as she realized what she had inferred, and he felt something pass between them, like a current. He looked away quickly, breaking the connection, and turned back to the rose.

"Maybe we should call it the Christmas Rose."

Billy shook his head. "Nope. Already used. It's become a legend, in fact." He hadn't thought about the story of the Christmas rose in a long time. As the fable went, a little shepherdess was saddened because she had no gift to offer baby Jesus. She wept and wept, so much that her tears soaked the ground where she stood watching her sheep.

Suddenly an angel appeared, touched the tear-softened earth, and the ground sprang alive with beautiful roses. Immediately the girl gathered a bouquet of the Christmas roses and carried them to the baby's manger. As soon as the infant caught sight of the roses, he turned away from the gifts of the Wise Men and reached his tiny hands in the direction of the flowers.

Ridiculous legend, Billy thought. *Ridiculous.*

"You're not going to try to force the bud to bloom, are you? You're not planning to use the warming lights?"

277

Billy openly stared at her. "I would *never* do that. This rose will open when it's ready and not a minute before."

"Gut Ding will Weile haben."

Billy stilled, swallowed, narrowed his eyes. "What did you just say?"

"Gut Ding will Weile haben. Good things take time. It's something my grandmother used to say."

His eyes closed, hearing Bertha's no-nonsense voice in his memory, so vivid it hurt. "I remember. I remember her saying it."

"When do you think it'll open?"

"Within a week or two, depending on the weather and amount of sunlight we get. I'm going to put it back in the corner of the greenhouse where it was growing. I don't want anyone or anything to disturb it." He glanced at Blackie, poking around the pots under the workbench. "In fact, you should keep that cat out of here."

"This cat is why I found the rose in the first place." Bess stooped down to pick up the cat and stroked its gleaming black fur. "Think I should water the rose?"

"No. Leave it just as it is. There's enough condensation in the corner to keep it moist. I'll come back every few days to check on it. I'm going to scrutinize some records and compare findings back at the university. Bess," he said, peering at her, searching her eyes, "is there anything you know about this rose? Anything at all?"

She crouched down to release the cat. "Like you said, until that bloom opens, it's hard to identify."

Something in the way she responded reminded him again of Bertha Riehl, a master at finagling her way out of a tight spot. What did Bess know about this rose that she wasn't telling him?

278

Avoiding his eyes, she straightened and bent over to examine the mystery rose. "I think the capsule is starting to expand. It looks different from yesterday."

"I'll measure and see if there's any significant difference."

Suddenly she turned and caught him studying her. Something odd happened in his chest. A brief catch, a tightening that caused him to drop his gaze to the workbench.

"Billy, why don't you just stay at Rose Hill Farm until it opens?"

He bent down to take a file out of his backpack as if she hadn't spoken. Where was that book on lost roses? He was sure he packed it.

"You could stay in the guest room. It's no bother."

"I'm going to check a few things, then get back to College Station as soon as I can this morning." He settled back down on the wooden stool and opened the file.

"If you're worried about what Caleb Zook might say, I don't think—"

He hopped to his feet as if he'd been stung by a bee. "Don't you get it?"

"Get what?" Bess's voice carried genuine confusion, but Billy paused for only a fraction of a second. Then he ceased to think at all. Suddenly, the frustration and anger he'd bottled up the last two days—the last few years—started to bubble over. "Look—I don't belong in Stoney Ridge anymore. I don't want to be here. I wouldn't even have to be here at all if that stupid rosarian hadn't slipped on ice and hurt his rear end." By the look on her face, he could tell she was getting more upset by the minute at his high-handedness and the insulting tone of his voice. He knew he should have stopped, but he couldn't help it. "So quit tryin' to get me to stay."

Bess straightened her shoulders and stared back. "Why are you so angry?"

"I'm not angry," he said, hating how blunt he sounded. "Not with you."

Bess waited. Her eyes narrowed as if she could see through him. When she spoke again, her voice was stiff, as if belonging to someone else. "I don't know what in the world's the matter with you, but you act like a bear with a thorn in his paw." Her voice became sharper. "You need to eat." She turned and walked to the greenhouse door. "Before you leave, come up to the house and have breakfast with us."

He threw her a withering glance but said nothing.

FIVE

Bess felt tears of mortification sting her eyes. As soon as the suggestion to stay at Rose Hill Farm tumbled from her mouth, she saw a hint of something hard slide across Billy's face. The ease and comfortableness they had shared briefly in the greenhouse was gone; his sharp edge had returned.

She had promised herself that she wouldn't pressure him or overwhelm him with all the questions that were threatening to explode within her. Like the rosebud, he would reveal himself when he was good and ready. But he hadn't been here thirty minutes today and look what she'd done. She swallowed back her tears as she hurried into the house.

Inside the warm kitchen, Bess threw her coat over a chair and went to the window, hugging her elbows against herself. Her heel hit the floor with an exasperated *klunk* as she glared out the window at the greenhouse. "*That* man can make me so angry!"

"I'll gander a guess that you're referring to Billy Lapp."

Bess hadn't realized that Lainey was over by the stovetop, stirring something in a pot. Lainey set the wooden spoon on the stovetop and went to the window to stand beside her.

"I just can *not* understand him. One minute, he seems like the old Billy. The next, he's as prickly as a cactus."

"Your dad got the impression that Billy didn't want to be here."

Bess snorted. "He's made that very clear. If it weren't for the fact that he can't figure out the identity to the rose, he'd be long gone."

"Seems a little strange, doesn't it? That you don't have any recollection about that particular rose?"

Bess might, just *might*, have a little recollection about it. Just a tiny one, nothing worth mentioning. Not yet, anyway. She squinted at the brightening sky, watching the clouds. "You knew Mammi. She had all kinds of roses tucked around the farm. She was full of surprises."

Lainey was silent for a long moment. "I remember something she used to say: Inside every hard person hides a softer one." She patted Bess on the shoulder and went back to the stovetop.

Bess pressed her brow against the cold glass of the windowpane, feeling her frustration slide away, replaced by a fresh resolve. It would be a difficult task to find anything soft inside of Billy, but she aimed to try.

The smoky scent of crisping bacon drifted down from the house. Billy was famished. He hadn't eaten anything since last night and his stomach was flapping against his backbone. Maybe he should eat breakfast with the Riehls, then leave.

That's all. Just one meal. He owed Bess that much. He owed Bertha Riehl much more.

The odd thing was that he loved being here. Rose Hill Farm had always been a buoy for him in an unsettled sea, but being here now churned up too many memories. Good ones, difficult ones. That inner conflict was why he snapped at Bess just now, fully knowing he was hurting her feelings but unable to stop himself. He felt ashamed of himself, even more so because he knew Bertha Riehl would be ashamed of him, and she was one person he had never wanted to disappoint.

His thoughts traveled back to the first time he realized anyone who dared to get on the bad side of Bertha Riehl was as crazy as a rat in a drainpipe.

August 1964, a hot, humid afternoon. Billy was ten years old and his brothers let him tag along to fish at Blue Lake Pond, a rare invitation. On the way home, they cut through Rose Hill Farm. During the summer, Bertha Riehl kept a roadside stand at the bottom of the driveway to sell produce from her vegetable garden. Sam helped himself to an apple and pointed to the honor jar. It was customary to leave an honor jar on the table, and folks—Amish and non-Amish—knew to put money in the jar if they took produce. Sam stuck his big paw in the honor jar and pulled out a grimy fistful of dollar bills, then Ben and Mose followed suit, as they always did. Billy was horrified. He tried to stop them, threatened to tell on them, but they only laughed.

He shouldn't have worried. Bertha Riehl saw the whole thing unfold.

As the boys stuffed the crumpled dollars into their pockets, they heard an unmistakable cock of a double-barreled shotgun behind them. They froze, every hair on Billy's head stood up, and the gun exploded. He thought for sure they were all dead, until a big black crow fell to the ground by their feet. Bertha walked over to the dead crow and picked it up by the tip of a wing to toss it over the fence. A burned-powder haze hung around her, halo-like.

"Lots of pests around this time of year," she said, pinning Billy's brothers with a stare. "Always best to take care of them before they become a nuisance."

Ben, Sam, and Mose emptied their pockets of dollars and took off running. Billy stayed behind to pick up the money, hands shaking, and stuff it all back in the honor jar. Bertha gave him a curt nod. He couldn't hear right for a week.

It was the first time, but not the last, that Billy discovered his brothers were conscienceless. He tried to make up for them. He went out of his way to help others, to do more than was required, to even the scales that his brothers had fixed.

His empty stomach rumbled, jolting him back to the present and reminding him that a good breakfast was waiting for him in the farmhouse. He grabbed his coat; the mystery rose could hold off until after breakfast.

When he reached the farmhouse, Billy raised his hand to knock on the door. Lainey's little girl—what was her name again?—came to the window, saw Billy through the glass, and ran off without opening the door. He knocked again and Bess appeared at the door.

"No need to knock. Nobody ever knocks around here." She pushed the door open and crossed the room to continue frying bacon.

She was keeping her distance from him. Fine. That suited

him just fine, but the smells in this kitchen were enough to cause his stomach to practically roll over and beg. Sweet cinnamon and sizzling bacon and percolating coffee.

From the door, Billy scanned the familiar scene. The kitchen at Rose Hill Farm was as ordinary as field straw, like any Plain home, and spotlessly clean. There was a cast-iron stove, a table as big as a hay wagon, eight spindled chairs, worn gray linoleum on the floor. A large pantry, where Bess had gone to find something. Beyond the window, cardinals were swooping around a fancy white marten birdhouse on a tall pole, hunting for forgotten seed. Out on the dry grass, Billy spotted that black cat from the greenhouse hunched up, watching the cardinals, ready to pounce.

His eyes traveled below the kitchen window to a tray of paper cups on a small table. In each cup was a narcissus bulb, paperwhites, soon to bloom. The sight stabbed him. Bertha Riehl used to give each of her neighbors a blooming narcissus bulb for Christmas. Seeing those cups, with their green stalks poking toward the sky, gave him a pain in his gut. He missed that wonderful, crotchety old woman.

Bess emerged out of the pantry with a canister of flour and set it on the counter before she returned to flip bacon on the stovetop. From behind, Billy noticed Bess's blue dress—blue as a bachelor's button—and the strings of her prayer cap fluttering on her back as she added flour, milk, and egg into a bowl and stirred vigorously. Studying the apron pinned around the shallows of her spine, Billy felt like a teenager again, awkward, a little uncertain. He remained by the door.

"Come in, Billy, and make yourself comfortable," Bess urged softly.

The little girl slipped back in from around the living room

corner and buried her nose in Bess's leg in a sudden fit of shyness. One eye stared at Billy.

"Christy, you remember meeting Billy, don't you, honey?"

Christy! That was her name. Billy was amused by her shyness. She hid her face in Bess's apron.

"She's just getting used to you," Bess said, over her shoulder. "She'll warm up to you in a minute or two." She reached a hand down to help Christy up on a chair near the stove. "Christy wanted pancakes that looked like snowmen, so that's what we're working on."

It occurred to Billy that Bess would be some mother. Always kind voiced. Always concerned about the children. Always making them feel important. His father had never made Billy feel important, only in the way.

"Dad's out in the barn. Lainey's upstairs with Lizzie. We'll be eating in a moment. Coffee's hot."

She pointed a spatula toward a blue speckled coffeepot, and Billy crossed the room to get a cup and fill it with coffee. The door swung open with a blast of cold air and in walked Jonah. The faint smell of the barn lingered on him—hay and horses—even above the aroma of boiling coffee. He smiled when he saw Billy. "Getting any closer to figuring out the rose's identity?"

"I won't know for sure until the bloom opens, but I'm narrowing it down. I'm pretty sure it's rare, if not a found." He glanced at Bess as she emerged from the pantry again, this time holding a jar of purple-looking jam. He was besieged by a startling thought.

That this was their kitchen and Bess was . . . his.

An awkward silence filled the room. "What?" Bess said. "Why are you staring at me? Do I have flour on my nose?"

"I'd better wash up before breakfast." Billy lurched for the soap at the sink, feeling his face heat. *What's the matter with you, Lapp? It's not like you haven't seen a woman before. Find somethin' else to think about.*

He lingered at the washbasin, then turned to see Lainey Riehl walk into the kitchen with a toddler on her hip—the one he'd met yesterday. What was this one's name? He hadn't spent time with children lately, if ever. He didn't notice them much.

"Come to me, Lizzie." Jonah reached out to take the little girl from her and set her in the high chair.

Lizzie! That was her name.

"Well, Billy Lapp," Lainey said with a smile. "Glad to see you've finally decided to join us. We need to put some meat on those bones of yours." It was a comment a mother might have said, and it went straight to Billy's heart.

"Yes, ma'am." Billy scrubbed his hands hard, refusing to turn and let anyone see he was blushing.

When they were seated, after a silent prayer, Lainey passed Billy a familiar white tureen; it had been Bertha Riehl's and she served her famous rabbit stew in it. He lifted the cover and found one of his favorites: baked oatmeal, thick with diced apples and cinnamon.

He openly stared at the wealth of food on his plate: three fried eggs, bacon, crispy hash browns, toast with boysenberry jam. His hands rested beside his plate while he fought the compulsion to gobble like an animal. When had he last eaten a home-cooked meal like this one? The foods he'd grown accustomed to over the last few years had as little smell as taste. As he took a scoop of baked oatmeal and dished it on his plate, Jonah asked him about the propagated roses in the greenhouse.

"How do you propagate the slips? I remember you used to dip the slips in a rooting hormone."

"A rooting hormone? No, not anymore. I've had better luck using willow water. Some professor figured out that willows have a root-promoting substance called rhizocaline. Water saturated with rhizocaline is far more effective than a store-bought rooting hormone."

"You don't say. I'll have to try it. Thank you, Billy. You're quite a resource for us."

Bess kept her eyes on her plate, but quietly added, "Mammi used to say there wasn't anything Billy Lapp didn't know, and if he didn't, he'd find the answer to it."

Embarrassed by the praise, pleased by it too, Billy concentrated on cutting his bacon. Bess had often said things like that, giving him more credit than he deserved. Calling him intelligent, inventive, resourceful. Things his father had never said to him, things that made him feel good about himself.

He looked across the table and caught Bess's eyes—eyes as blue as a summer day. How like her to try to make him feel comfortable at a moment like this, despite how rude he'd been to her in the greenhouse. He was shamed. "I wish Bertha were still here to ask about the rose. I'm confident she would have the answer to its identity."

Jonah nodded. "I don't think a day goes by when I don't wish she was still with us. But we mustn't question the Lord's will in taking her."

"Why not?" And three forks stopped in midair. Billy knew immediately he should have held his tongue. "I just . . . I wish the Lord would have considered taking someone else instead."

Jonah exchanged a look with Lainey, and Billy wondered

what they were saying to each other. But before he could ponder that, the door banged open, letting an icy blast of air swoop in, and suddenly a young woman appeared in the kitchen with a stack of cake pans in her hands. "Sorry to interrupt! Jorie said you needed to borrow her round cake pans for the wedding, so I brought them over and—" Her mouth dropped open and her eyes widened in shock. "Well, I'll be double ding donged d . . . oh, sorry, Lainey, I know you told me to watch my language around Christy. But this is quite a shock to the system!" She set the pans on the counter, put her hands on her hips, and shook her head. "Just when I think I'll never be surprised again! Billy Lapp, as I live and breathe. Whatever next? And just why am I always the last to learn anything?"

Billy rose to his feet and couldn't hold back a grin. Somehow, Maggie Zook always behaved as if the best day of her life had just gotten under way. She looked the same—snapping brown eyes beneath her glasses, dark hair, petite and fine-boned, her face as happy and hopeful as he remembered. "Hello, cousin." She had been like a little sister to him; impossible, adorable girl.

Bess jumped from her chair to set a place for Maggie.

Maggie noticed. "I can't stay, Bess. Jorie told me to drop off cake pans and come right back. She was adamant. For some reason, she's under the impression that I am easily distracted."

Bess didn't pay her any mind. "Sit. Sit and join us. Anyone who can put a smile on Billy Lapp's face deserves a good breakfast."

"Maybe just a minute or two." Maggie couldn't stop grinning. "It sure is good to see you, cousin. It sure is. I didn't think I'd ever lay eyes on you again. You just vanished, like a ghost." She snapped her fingers to emphasize Billy's abrupt disappearance. "I can't wait to tell my dad you're here. He'll want to come straight over to welcome you back to the fold."

Billy stiffened.

"Uh, Maggie," Jonah said in a diplomatic voice, "I think we should let Billy decide whom he wants to see. And when."

Maggie wasn't listening. She had reached for a big spoon to dish out the baked oatmeal. One spoonful, then another.

Same Maggie, Billy thought. *Never still, always in motion. She might not be thought of as a beauty like Bess, but sharp? So sharp, you'd think she slept in the knife drawer.* He got a kick out of watching her fill her plate. She'd always had an appetite that rivaled two growing boys. Bess, by contrast, pecked like a sparrow, hardly ate a thing. Even now, she pushed her food around on her plate.

Maggie swallowed down a large piece of bacon. "I'm sorry to be the bearer of very troubling news this morning," she said in a confidential tone. "Very, very troubling." Her gaze swept around the table, waiting to make her announcement until all eyes were on her. "The schoolteacher is leaving at Christmas. Midterm. Something about her sciatica kicking up. Personally, I think it has more to do with those frightful Glick triplets, the ones with the bright red hair and round faces covered with freckles. You know the ones. They rolled marbles down the aisle in church last month and the new minister with the watermelon belly slipped on them and fell on his backside." She grinned and quickly sent an apologetic look in Lainey's direction. "I know, I know. I shouldn't laugh, it isn't being a good example, but it *was* funny."

"Maggie," Lainey warned in a sharp tone. "So what exactly is the troubling part?"

"Troubling for every unmarried woman from the age of sixteen to ninety. Bess, you're safe, but my life is in peril. Complete peril." Maggie took a spoonful of baked oatmeal. "My dad is on the hunt for a new schoolteacher. Very worrying."

"If you say so," Jonah said, not sounding at all worried.

Maggie seemed astounded at Jonah's casual response. "It *is* worrying! If you were eighteen years old and your father was the bishop, you'd be worried sick, Jonah."

He still didn't seem too worried.

"Why am I so hard to believe? I always tell the truth." Maggie shook her head. She took a few more bites of baked oatmeal and looked up, as if something had just occurred to her. "So Billy, I always wondered, why did you leave?"

Silence fell over the table. Even Maggie noticed. "Okay then, next question. Why did you come back?"

All eyes were on Billy. "A rose," he said in a quiet voice.

Maggie's face lit up. "Ha! Of course!"

"He's a rose rustler," Bess said.

"Oh, that sounds exciting! Like cowboy cattle rustling in the Old West."

"No," Billy said, shaking his head. "Nothing like that. What I do is legal."

"What is it you do?"

"When people come across a rose they don't recognize, they find me and I try to figure out its parentage. Its identity."

"How do these people find you?"

Billy shrugged. "Rosarians know how to find each other."

"Rosarians. Sounds very official and important." Between bites, Maggie pushed her glasses up the bridge of her nose.

"But that doesn't explain why you're at Rose Hill Farm. You must know all Bertha's roses inside and outside and upside and downside and any other side." She peered at him. "Don't you?"

Jonah handed Maggie a platter of hash browns. "Bess came across one that had somehow escaped everyone's notice. We weren't sure about its identity. Right, Bess?"

Billy noticed that Bess kept her eyes down. He still had a feeling she knew something about this mystery rose that she wasn't telling him. What? And why?

Maggie chewed a piece of bacon thoughtfully. "Billy, how does a person go about finding a rose's identity?"

"I compare its characteristics on a database. If I still can't figure it out, I'll call a few Rose Societies and see if they have seen it before."

"Ever been stumped?"

"Not yet." He glanced at Jonah. "Maybe this will be the one to flummox me." But if it did, that would mean it was a very, very unique rose. He turned back to Maggie. "I have to wait until this rosebud opens to confirm its identity."

Maggie lowered her spoon and looked up. "When do you think it'll open up?"

"Maybe in a week or two. Hopefully before Christmas." Oh, *how* he hoped. He couldn't handle being near Stoney Ridge for Christmas. Near, but so far away.

Maggie clapped her hands. "Oh good! Then you'll be here for Bess's wedding."

Billy felt frozen in place, but his gaze was drawn to Bess, whose cheeks had started to flame. Her napkin slipped to the floor and she nearly overturned her juice glass when she bent down to pick up her napkin.

It took him a beat to recover and reply sensibly, "Ah, no. I'm not staying." He said it without moving a muscle. He saw Bess cast a furtive glance around the table. Lainey was wiping Lizzie's face, Jonah was stirring sugar into his coffee. Bess jumped up to rescue toast burning to a crisp in the oven.

He turned to Maggie. "And who is Bess going to marry?"

"Amos Lapp." She tapped her chin. "Let's see. Amos is your cousin on your father's side. I'm your cousin on your mother's side. So I'm not related to Amos, but we're both related to you. Sometimes it seems that everyone in Stoney Ridge is related one way or another, a twig on a tree. Bess, doesn't it sound like one of those math puzzles in school? If a train is traveling at a certain speed, when does it arrive at the station? Why are manholes round? What did we call those, Bess?"

Bess kept her eyes on the burnt toast she was scraping in the kitchen sink. "The teacher called them brainteasers. We called them conundrums."

"Yes! That's the word I was looking for! Conundrums. Because they made no sense."

An awkward silence filled the air. Bess sat back down at the table with the scraped toast and put heaping spoonfuls of boysenberry jam on top, carefully spreading it to the edges.

"When?" Billy asked, a little louder than he intended. So that's what Maggie meant when she said Bess was safe—she couldn't be the new schoolteacher because she would be married. "When will the wedding be?"

"In a few days," Bess said at last, the words coming out on a soft gust of breath. Her gaze held his for a moment, then flickered aside.

My best friend. She's marrying my best friend. Over-whelmed, Billy did the only thing he knew how to do: clamp his jaw shut and reset his features, cutting off all traces of emotion. He took a bite of baked oatmeal and chewed it, trying to look calm and thoughtful and nonchalant. The oatmeal had lost its taste. He swallowed past a large lump stuck in his throat. "I'm sure you'll both be very happy." There were a thousand more churning thoughts seething for release, but Billy kept them carefully concealed, like he was drawing the shutters in a house that was getting pelted by a rainstorm.

The grandfather clock gonged and Maggie jumped up. "Look at the time! I better get home to help Jorie. I have a job interview at the Sweet Tooth Bakery this afternoon. Wish me well!" She bolted to the door and skidded to a halt when Jonah called her back.

"Maggie," Jonah said in a solemn voice, "I'd rather you not tell your father about Billy. Or the rose."

"Got it. Top secret." She twisted her fingers on her lips as if locking a key, waved goodbye to Billy, and sailed out as gustily as she'd sailed in, leaving him feeling as if he'd just taken a ride on a tornado.

Without Maggie filling the air with chatter, the meal became strained. What little there was of conversation was stilted and came to sudden stops until finally they forsook talk altogether.

Throughout the rest of the meal, Billy ignored Bess, unable to look at her without a suffocating sense of defeat and discouragement. The family, sensing his mood, was silent. All but the toddler—what was her name again?—who hummed as she ate her scrambled eggs.

The minute the tense meal was over and Jonah offered up a silent prayer, Billy sought solace in the place he loved best. He pushed away from the table, gave a nod of thanks to Lainey, said goodbye to Jonah, and walked to the greenhouse, head bowed, footsteps automatic.

And then Bess was running to catch up, calling his name, but he didn't break his stride until she seized his elbow and yanked him to a halt.

"Please! Let me explain."

They stood a foot apart, facing each other. "Billy, I was going to tell you about my plans. I just hadn't found the right time—"

"Your plans," he echoed. The bitterness in his voice was unmistakable.

Bess wrapped her arms around herself to stay warm; her eyes watered from the cold. "Yes. My plan. Our plans. Amos's and my plans."

Billy shrugged and looked at his wristwatch. "I don't care about your plans. It doesn't matter to me who you marry."

Bess recoiled as if Billy had slapped her. "Do you mean that?"

He held her gaze. "Yes."

She took a step backward. "When . . . ," she started, a sob catching in her throat. "When did you get so hard?" She turned her back and fled to the house, leaving Billy standing in front of the greenhouse, adrift as a ship without a mast.

SIX

hen did you get so hard? Billy tried to appear calm, but a band of hurt cinched his chest when Bess spat out those words. The greenhouse door squeaked when he opened it, the first thing to register on his troubled mind. Trying to let his indignation recede, he found an oilcan in the barn workshop and returned to oil the hinges of the greenhouse door, scarcely aware of what he was doing.

Hard. Hard. Hard. The blood rushed to his face afresh as he recalled Bess's words. It was true. He *was* hard. But how dare she throw it in his face! Vehemently, he whacked the greenhouse door shut, slammed the oilcan down, marched down the aisle of the greenhouse, and tried to concentrate on this rose. This exasperating, inscrutable rose . . . that wasn't going to be hurried for anyone's sake.

Amos. Bess was marrying Amos. His best friend, his favorite cousin whom he loved, who had seen him through one of the worst times of his life.

One wouldn't guess it by watching him now, but Billy was usually slow to anger. He was uncomfortable with it—maybe because of his brothers' volatility—and tried to avoid it.

How, then, had the last two days spawned such belligerence in him? In frustration he slammed his open palms against a wooden shelf. He hadn't felt this kind of anger, this power-less, frustrating anger, since that pivotal day when he left Stoney Ridge.

But that was then and this was now. He shook his head and came back to the present. He wished he'd remembered that book on lost roses today. He stared at the rose, willing it to grow. *Open, rosebud. Open.* As soon as it did, he would be able to determine if this might be related to the Perle von Weissenstein. Maybe as old as the Perle. Possibly . . . older?

And if it were, it would be the biggest rose found of the decade. He would be credited for the identification and he could leave Stoney Ridge behind. This time, for good.

The sun disappeared behind a cloud, casting a gray pallor that matched his frame of mind. Squinting at the sky through the glass roof, he watched the cloud cover, wondering if it would thicken or diminish as the day wore on. When he heard someone say his name, he nearly jumped. "George! What are you doing here?"

George was standing in the open door of the greenhouse, studying the squeak of the hinges as he opened and shut the door. "Needs a little oil."

"I know. I thought I'd put enough on it." He scratched his neck. Why hadn't he heard it squeak when George came in?

"I noticed you forgot this. I thought you might need it." George handed him the book of lost roses, the very one he had forgotten.

"You came all this way? How'd you know where I was?"

George reached into his pocket and held out that piece of paper with the address of Rose Hill Farm on it that Jill had given to him Friday morning. "You keep dropping this." He stared at a row of jars that lined the back of the workbench. He reached out to pick up one jar of dried rose petals and held it up to the light. "Ah, roses as remedies. For the herb gardener in a medieval monastery, *R. gallica 'Officinalis'* offered the cure for many a malady."

Billy squinted at him. This erudite hobo thoroughly baffled him. "How would you know the Latin name for a rose?" He was thunderstruck. "How on earth?"

George tipped his chin in Billy's direction, though he didn't look at him directly. He set the jar of rose petals back in its place. "Have you had a chance to see your father?"

A current of indignation mixed with rage sprang up in Billy. Last night was the first time he'd spilled out his feelings to someone about his father and brothers, about the hurt they'd caused all those years ago, about how the hurt could be so intense yet, when he'd thought it mastered. But he hadn't really expected to see George again and he certainly didn't expect him to show up in Stoney Ridge where the story began. And ended.

Late summer 1973. Billy had gone to the barn to tell his brothers that supper was ready and found them adding scoops of sawdust to the bottom of empty flour sacks, then pouring freshly threshed wheat grain on top of the sawdust. "What's going on?"

His brother Ben was the first to speak. He stepped in front of Billy, hands on his hips, chin jutting. "What are you doing here?"

"Just what the die-hinker are you doing here?" echoed Mose. Some said Mose was skewed in the head, mostly because he never had a thought there that hadn't started in Sam's or Ben's head first. He followed his brothers everywhere, most often into trouble.

Billy ignored Mose. Ben glowered at him, but he always had something to be angry about, and Billy had learned long ago that the best way to handle him was to stand up to him. "Why would you put sawdust in the gunny sacks?" Billy sidestepped around Ben up to the sacks of grain as a horrible discovery dawned on him. "Are you trying to add weight to the grain?"

Ben scowled at him. "We're keeping the grain from getting mildewed. It's common practice."

That was a lie. "If they mill the grain into flour with that sawdust in there, then it'll mean folks are eating—"

His oldest brother Sam, overgrown—easily twice Billy's size—reared to his feet, his belly and thighs knocking into a barrel of oats so hard it rocked. He pulled back his hand and slapped Billy hard enough to send him flying across the aisle. He yanked Billy to his feet, swinging him around to face him. Eye level to Billy was the Adam's apple on Sam's throat, and when he saw it working strongly, he thought there was a chance Sam would let him go.

"Wait'll Dad hears this . . . ," Billy said, hoping to convince him.

A loud snort punctuated the air, coming from Mose. Billy glanced at him and saw he was holding up one of the sacks, handling it almost lovingly.

Sam gripped Billy's shoulder so tightly it left a bruise. "Not only does he know, but he's the one who told us to do it. He's been doing it for years." He released Billy with a hard jerk. "Now, get outta here."

Mose gripped the gunnysack in his fist, shaking it before Billy's face. "You heard 'im. Git."

Billy looked at the sack in Mose's hand, feeling weary and sick and scared. This was wrong.

He backed cautiously out of the barn, forgetting his hat. It all started to make sense—his father's grain delivery to Great Harvest Granary in Lancaster hadn't been reduced in the last few years since he had started no-till farming, though Billy knew the yield had dropped. His father had not only been cheating the granary but he'd added sawdust into flour destined for people's pantries.

For a long time, he stared at the barn, then at the farmhouse, back to the barn, back to the farmhouse. Finally, he made a decision and took off running to Beacon Hollow, straight to Caleb Zook to tell him what he had just discovered.

Appalled but without seeming entirely surprised, Caleb acted fast. He pulled the shipment of Lapp wheat from the granary—effectively causing Billy's father to lose the year's crop. Next came the part that Billy hadn't anticipated. Under church discipline, Caleb and the other ministers paid a visit to the Lapp Farm to put Billy's father under the Bann. For six weeks, his father had to eat at a different table than other church members—family members included—and couldn't conduct business with them or accept gifts. At the end of that time, he would confess before the church and be restored to full fellowship.

Billy braced himself for backlash. He expected his father to be openly furious, his brothers to be stealthily vindictive. This time, there was a marked change. This time, there was nothing.

George cleared his throat, patiently waiting for Billy's answer: *Have you had a chance to see your father?*

Billy started rifling through the lost rose book, irritated. "No. And I'm not going to." Absolutely not. And what business was that of George's? A wave of regret washed over him—why had he revealed his underbelly to this hobo?

George picked up a pair of clippers. "May I?" He touched a few dead leaves on a rosebush with the tips of the clippers and waited for a nod from Billy before he began to snip them off. "Time is fleeting, Billy," he said softly. *Snip, snip.* Two dead leaves fell to the ground, one at Billy's feet.

Billy wanted not to understand his meaning. Was George suggesting that he take the first step toward reconciliation? Billy wasn't the one who had done anything wrong. He had no intention of according his father a morsel of sympathy or understanding. "Time passes on both sides."

If George was surprised by the sharp shift in Billy's tone, he didn't show it. He was preoccupied with the rows of potted plants. "This is where you first learned how to graft roses?"

"Yeah." He bent over to study a print, then his head snapped up. "How'd you know that? I don't remember ever mentioning grafting roses." But maybe he did. It was late and he was tired.

"I think you mentioned something about it last night. Plus I saw a lot of your grafting work back in the greenhouse at College Station." George bent over to sniff a rose blossom, an Old Blush China. "Grafting is fascinating work, isn't it? The tissues of one plant fused with another."

Billy nodded cautiously, head bent toward the book, but aware of George from the corner of his eyes.

"There are countless illustrations in the natural world that point to another reality."

Billy lifted his head, confused. "Say again?"

"Let's take the concept of grafting. Divining one green thing from another. You could liken it to how an individual becomes part of the family of God. You, for example. You're on your own, cut off from your family." He spun around to face Billy. "But you could choose to graft yourself to new rootstock. The living root. The source."

"*What* are you talking about, man?"

George's eyes swept over the plants in the greenhouse. "You can't love the stream without knowing the source."

Billy closed the book and placed the palms of his hands on the workbench. "George, this is probably just the reason you haven't been able to get regular work. Were you ever in the military? I've heard stories of what it was like in Vietnam. Hard stuff. Left good men with lingering problems. You're not alone. We can get help for you."

"No. No, I've never been in the military."

Really? Billy bit his lip. "Then . . . did you used to do drugs?"

"Drugs?"

"LSD, heroin, marijuana. I've heard they can scramble your head."

A look of surprise lit George's eyes, then a laugh burst out. First one, then another, and soon he had doubled over, guffawing. "Nope. Clean as a whistle." He wiped tears from his eyes, still laughing. "But I thank you for your concern." He walked over to the potted rose. "So this is the found?"

"Yup. I think I'm narrowing it down. I feel pretty confident it's got a German rootstock—it's either related to or precedes the Perle von Weissenstein. It could be the oldest known rose of German rootstock. In the entire world."

"How old?"

"At least four hundred years."

George crouched down to look at it more closely. "I guess from a human perspective, that's pretty old."

Billy cocked his head. "What other perspective would there be?"

Rising, George went to the other side of the bench to peer at the rose. "What else do you need to identify it?"

He pointed to the rose. "That bud needs to open."

"Can't force it. Gut Ding will Weile haben." *Good things take time.*

Billy's eyes went wide. "You speak Penn Dutch?"

George shrugged that off. "I pick up things here and there. Languages have always been a curiosity to me."

Billy eyed him carefully. George was an odd duck. It was sad to think a sharp guy like him had no ambition in life.

Carefully, George fingered a leaf. "Think of all this old rose has weathered in life to get to this point now. All the people who protected it, kept it alive. Four hundred years of care. Makes you think, doesn't it?"

"About what?"

"The purpose of this rose. That there's a reason it's survived so long."

"Not just survived. It's thrived. Look at that bud. Imagine that. An extinct rose blooming in December."

George chuckled. "Imagine that. Maybe even for Christmas. 'The heavens declare the glory of God; and the firmament sheweth his handywork.' I believe that's in the book of Psalms."

Billy cocked his head and squinted his eyes in disbelief. "Don't tell me you know the Bible."

"Shouldn't everyone?"

"I guess I didn't think of hobos as religious types." Though, he had never really thought all that much about hobos before meeting this one.

George wrapped his hands around the base of the plant. "Funny how the rose was here, all the time. Right under your nose."

"I haven't worked at Rose Hill Farm in quite a while."

"Well, it's timely that you're here now, isn't it? You wouldn't want to have missed this chance a second time, would you?"

Billy frowned. There always seemed to be two layers to George's words. The obvious one and the less obvious one. He wasn't sure which to pay attention to and which to dismiss.

George straightened and zipped up his coat—Billy's old coat. "Well, I'd better shove off."

"George, you obviously have an appreciation for this work. Maybe I could find some work for you, at least through the Christmas season. There's a little money in the budget to hire a seasonal assistant." There wasn't, actually, but Billy was a saver by nature, had few needs, and there was just something about this guy. He needed Billy. And, in a way, maybe Billy needed him. If he was going to have to head to Rose Hill Farm until this mystery rose bloomed, at least he could have George cover some of his workload in the greenhouse.

"Is that right?" George stroked his chin. "If you really need some help, well, why not? I suppose I could help."

Billy nodded. "It would be a big help." Not really, but he

wanted to straighten this guy out. "I could leave a list and you could come in during the evening. But . . . I'd rather keep this just between us. My supervisor might not be copacetic with our arrangement."

"Not a problem. You leave me a list and I'll make sure the work gets done."

"Who knows, George? If you do good work, I might be able to recommend you to get hired on after the holidays."

"Hmm . . . I'd better check that first with upper management." He grinned and wiggled his eyebrows.

Upper management? For hobos? It crossed Billy's mind that George might be delusional; he hoped not. He liked the guy, even if he did seem to be allergic to regular employment. "Are you heading back to College Station? If you don't mind waiting, I'll go back with you."

"Actually, I'm not headed back that way just yet. I've got an errand or two to do around here." George grinned at the puzzled look on Billy's face. "Don't ask. You'd be surprised. Even drifters have things to do."

"Okay. I guess I'll see you back at College Station."

As George walked down the length of the greenhouse, he stopped to bend over a blooming deep pink Gertrude Jekyll and breathed in deeply. He turned his chin toward Billy. "A rose always gets the last word in, doesn't it?"

"How so?"

George smiled in that amused way he had. "Lingering fragrance."

Billy went back to his books and notebooks, but thoughts of George kept distracting him. He was such a quirky guy, but there was something calming about him. Whenever Billy was in his presence, he felt his whole self settle. It had been a long, long time since he had felt that kind of calm in his gut. It reminded him of when he was little, those rare moments when his father and brothers were out of the house and it was just him and his mother. Peaceful.

He thumbed through pages in the book of lost roses, but his thoughts drifted again to the way George cupped the base of the pot, as if it held the answer to the rose's identity. He was eager to examine the root ball, to see why it was so heavy and what the tangled roots might reveal, though he had promised Jonah and Bess that he wouldn't disturb the rose in any way until the bud opened. He shouldn't change a thing. Not a thing.

Billy frowned. He wished Bertha Riehl were here to ask. He *knew* she had the answer to this rose.

He glanced up at the farmhouse. If he could just slip the pot off, get a quick look at the base of the plant, slip the pot right back on—it shouldn't disturb the rose.

On the other hand, if he were to disturb the rose's root system, it might cause the bloom to wilt, to be stressed. It might never open at all. And that could mean jeopardizing the biggest rose found of the decade.

On the other hand, the rose had survived this long. It must be hardy.

On the other hand, the rose still struck him as somewhat fragile, as if it were just coming back now after a long period of dormancy.

What to do, what to do, what to do?

Gut Ding will Weile haben. *Good things take time.*

Bertha used that phrase whenever she noticed Billy get itchy and impatient. Like now.

Gut Ding will Weile haben. *Good things take time.*

Bess squared her shoulders before she put her hand on the greenhouse door. Billy spun around at the sound of the squeaky door with an odd look on his face as she walked inside.

"I thought you were George. I thought he'd changed his mind and was going to stay."

She glanced back at the door. "Who?"

"George. A hobo, a drifter." He peered past her toward the open door. "He was just here. You couldn't have missed him. He's a black man, dark as midnight, with these cool-looking eyes."

"No. I didn't see anyone."

He pointed to the door. "But you must have . . ."

Bess saw the scar on his wrist and something tripped in her mind. One glimpse of his face and she realized something was very wrong. One hand came from behind her back and covered her lips. "Oh . . . ," she breathed, the truth at last registering.

He turned fiery red, jammed his hands in his pockets, and refused to look up. "It was a hard time," he stammered at last.

"Billy, I had no idea. Really, I didn't." She bit back the urge to say more, surprised he'd even acknowledged what she had plainly seen on his wrist. They stood between rows of clay pots holding shoulder-high Compassion canes, a climber tea hybrid, being propagated for winter blooming. Bess leaned forward just enough to grasp Billy's arm. He neither pulled away nor returned the pressure, but stood with his head turned away. *Oh Billy, Billy, who hurt you so badly? And what would it take to make you forget it?*

"It doesn't matter."

"Yes, it does. You do. You matter."

At her words, she looked up, he looked down. Billy was gazing at her in that soft way he once had. She felt the pull again, strong, undeniable, elemental. "Billy," she whispered. "I'm so glad you've come back."

His glance rested steady on her. Something good happened between them. Something warm and rich and radiant. Slow, matching grins grew on their lips.

A few strands of hair had come loose from Bess's prayer cap and he reached out to tuck it behind her ear, letting the back of his hand gently graze her jawline. There was no mistaking the touch for anything but what it was—a lingering caress.

O, Lord, to go back and regain what was lost . . .

Abruptly, Billy dropped his hand and stepped back, as if suddenly realizing his folly. His face went stern and stiff again, all traces of tenderness and vulnerability had disappeared as if they dropped through a trapdoor.

The door squeaked wide open. "There you are, Bess! Are you ready?" It was Amos, interrupting the harmonious moment.

Bess swallowed. Billy spun around to face the door.

Amos's face, alit with joy only seconds ago, suddenly lost its smile. He turned a quizzical expression to Bess. Speechless, he shot a questioning glance at Billy before returning to her.

Amos was the first to recover. He forced a welcoming smile and came forward with hand extended. "Billy! Billy Lapp. It's good to see you, man!"

"Hello, Amos. Long time no see."

Dear friends all their lives, the two clasped hands and pounded each other's shoulders the way men do, but the hearty clasp of their hands did little to lighten the strained atmosphere.

Bess's throat constricted and she turned away. Her mouth went dry, her palms went damp. She should have told Amos about Billy's return. She had a chance last night, when he stopped by to show her the paint sample he chose for the apartment. But how do you tell a man such a thing?

And then another thought pushed that one away. *How long had Amos been standing at the door?*

Amos had come to Rose Hill Farm this morning for a special tradition—the baking of the wedding cake. In his church, as in most Plain churches, a bride and groom did the task together, sifting and stirring and measuring. A metaphor, it was thought, of an upcoming marriage. He didn't know his way around a kitchen, but he had been eagerly looking forward to this particular task.

Until now. As Bess preceded Amos out the greenhouse door, he watched the stiff way she held herself. Tight-lipped, he stayed a half step behind her.

Of course he was glad to see his cousin, whole and healthy. A succession of uninvited pictures flashed through his head, of Billy's well-being the last time Amos had seen him. Of the close relationship Bess and Billy had, years ago. Of the guilty looks on their faces as he found them in the greenhouse, standing close together.

As Amos and Bess walked toward the house, four-year-old Christy ran from the barn toward them. She spotted the brown paper bag and tugged his sleeve. "Hey, Amos, what you got in there?"

Amos reluctantly pulled his attention from Bess and went down on one knee to talk to the little girl on her level. "Well, what do you think?"

Christy shrugged, her eyes fixed on the sack.

"Maybe you better look inside and see."

Her hazel eyes gleamed with excitement as she peeked into the bag, reached in, and withdrew two candy bars. "Candy," she breathed, awed.

"Chocolate." Amos crossed his elbows on his knees, smiling. "One for you, one for your little sister."

"Chocolate," she repeated, then to Bess, "Look it! Amos brung us chocolate!"

"Mind your manners and tell him thank you," Bess said. "And go ask your mother before you eat them."

"We'd better start baking our wedding cake," Amos said. "Christy, listen to Bess. Go on up to the house and show the chocolate to your mother. We'll be there in a moment."

Christy took a few steps, then whirled around. With the intuitive accuracy of a child, she shot a question that hit two marks with one stone. "Why didn't you want to tell Billy Lapp that you were going to marry Amos?"

"Go, Christy," Bess said.

"But during breakfast, when Maggie came around—"

"Go!"

Hurt by the sharp tone in Bess's voice, Christy turned and ran to the house.

Amos's and Bess's eyes met, then she dropped her gaze.

"There was no need to speak so harshly, Bess," he said gently. He watched the red creep up Bess's cheeks while he wondered again what had been going on at Rose Hill Farm today.

He searched his mind for something to say, something to ease the new discomfort between them, but as they stood there, it became more and more palpable. He glanced over at the greenhouse and quietly said, "It was quite a shock to see Billy." Billy Lapp. His favorite cousin. His rival for Bess's hand.

"Last week, I happened upon a rose that we couldn't identify. Dad called Penn State and asked them to send out someone to identify it. They sent Billy. Apparently, he's been working up there."

"So is he back to stay?"

"No, he says not. Just to identify the rose."

First relief, then guilt bubbled up inside Amos. He wanted Billy to return to the flock. And yet he didn't.

"Has he been to see his father? Does he know?"

She cocked a wrist and touched her fingertips to her heart. "No."

Amos gazed at Bess's downcast eyes. With a face like Bess's, it was easy to see how fellows were knocked off their pins. He certainly had been. Sometimes, he found it almost painful to look at her directly. Her pale skin was nearly translucent, her eyes a bright, demanding shade of blue. In every weather, her blonde hair shimmered as if reflecting summer sun. Gazing upon something so inarguably lovely was lulling. Whenever he looked at her, Amos wanted to keep looking, and then he found himself tongue-tied and confused, awkward even in the simplest conversations.

Amos had won Bess mainly through persistency. He just didn't give up; he steadfastly pursued her until she couldn't help but love him back. He had always known there was something between Bess and Billy. He respected it as any man would, but when Billy left town and had no plans to return, Amos was free to court Bess. And yet there was always a light cloak of guilt Amos felt on his shoulders. Billy's leaving had cleared the way for him, yet he was sickened by that knowledge.

Amos knew he wasn't Bess's first choice, but she was his now. He loved her more than she loved him, he was aware, but he figured that was typical of most marriages. One who loved more, and in this one, it was Amos. He didn't have a problem with it because he knew that the man who'd once claimed Bess's heart was no longer here. Until now.

Suddenly, she looked up at him. "Amos, do you like roses? You've never said . . ."

"Sure, of course. Why not? Everybody likes roses."

She couldn't hide her disappointment with his answer. What had he done wrong? "Bess . . . are you . . . I mean, is everything all right—" He tilted his head and studied her face until she looked away.

The silence stretched long, until at last, when the whippoorwill had called for the hundredth time, Bess reached for Amos's hand. She cupped it between her two hands. "Oh, Amos, nothing has changed . . . nothing."

He smiled, though his chest tightened with a sharp sadness that felt like the crisp snap of a twig. He wanted to believe her, but he had an odd feeling that the floor had just dropped from under his feet.

SEVEN

As the sun was starting to set, Bess crossed the yard from the barn to the house and heard the clip-clop of a horse down on the road. She stopped and saw the buggy turn into the long driveway of Rose Hill Farm and for a moment, she thought it was Amos, returning for the scarf he'd forgotten earlier today. She was surprised by the pit of dread that rose in her stomach—so unlike how she normally felt about his visits. But after spending the afternoon baking their wedding cake, and a quick visit to Windmill Farm, both of them working hard to try to pretend everything was fine between them, just fine, Bess felt exhausted. Miserable and confused.

Amos's mother had wanted her to admire the fresh coat of paint he'd given the Grossdawdi Haus where she and Amos would live after the wedding. Mary Katherine Lapp, her soon-to-be mother-in-law, had been so pleased to show the apartment to Bess, pointing out its assets as if she were trying to sell it to her.

For a brief second, Bess wondered how Billy's father would treat a future daughter-in-law. Indifferent if not downright cold, she supposed. Amos's mother, on the other hand, was kind and gentle, just like Amos. Bess felt completely safe at Windmill Farm. Wanted and cherished. Wasn't that love? And wasn't that the kind of love that would last longer than silly romantic feelings? Of course it was.

The buggy rose to the crest of the hill and Bess slumped with relief when she saw Maggie Zook holding the horse's reins. The buggy pulled to a stop and Maggie tumbled out, smiling as brightly as a full moon. "Bess! I got it! I got the job at the Sweet Tooth Bakery! Just through the Christmas season, but that's all the time I'll need!"

Bess couldn't hold back a grin as Maggie came running, her face lit up. "Look at my hands!" Maggie splayed out her hands, red and peeling. "I don't know how I have any energy left after the day I've put in for Dottie Stroot."

When did Maggie Zook ever run out of energy?

"For now, I'm just a dishwasher, but Dottie Stroot promised she'd teach me how to make her cinnamon rolls soon."

Bess stifled an eye roll. The owner of the Sweet Tooth Bakery was known for her big promises, all empty, but she did make a fine cinnamon roll. "Just don't tell her you're my friend, Maggie, or she'll never reveal her secret recipe." Lainey had worked at the Sweet Tooth Bakery until she started out on her own to make baked goods from home, which made a dent in the Sweet Tooth Bakery profits, and the owner had never forgiven her.

"I think I'm going to learn how to become a fine baker and move someplace far, far away from Stoney Ridge. Someplace exciting, like Indiana." A laugh burst out of Maggie, and Bess couldn't help but laugh right along with her. Maggie's laughter was like that. Infectious.

Bess covered her friend's chapped hands with her own. "You can't move. I would miss you too much."

"Well, if I were marrying someone like Amos Lapp, I wouldn't move either. But you took the only eligible bachelor."

"He's not the *only* eligible bachelor. What about Tommy Glick?"

"Bad kisser. Cement lips."

"Timothy Fisher?"

"Edith Stoltzfus has marked him off as her territory. She's already got their future sons named: Paul first, then Jimmy, and so on. Not planning to have girls, she said. Too much trouble. She told the rest of us to stay away from Timothy or else."

"Or else what?"

"Everyone's too frightened of Edith to bother asking. Even timid Timothy." She crossed her arms and rubbed her shoulders as a gust of brisk wind blew through the yard. "No, you plucked the only ripe apple from the tree."

Bess smiled. Maggie had never been shy about her opinions, though she wasn't shy about anything. So often, Bess wished she had more of Maggie in her. Maggie was often criticized for poking her nose in everybody's business, and while that was true, she always meant well. And her love of life was contagious. "There are other ripe apples, Maggie. You're just being fussy."

"Maybe, but I hear the boys in Indiana are much more handsome and manly than the boys in Pennsylvania."

"Any chance Edith Stoltzfus told all of you that?"

"Why, in fact, it *was* Edith!" Maggie scowled and squeezed her fists. "I was nearly duped."

"I don't know what I'd do if you moved away."

A smile returned to her face. "Not to worry. I don't think Dottie Stroot is planning to have me do much else besides wash dishes for a long while. She says I talk too much." She glanced in the direction of the house, then lowered her voice. "But that's only part of my news. Here's the other part: Billy Lapp's father is running out of days."

"Where'd you hear that?" Billy's father had been ill with something—no one knew exactly what—for over a year now and was rarely seen at church. Rarely seen at all, now that Bess thought about it.

"I overheard my dad tell Jorie."

Then it probably was true. Maggie was a skillful eavesdropper on her father's conversations, and while Bess should have frowned on hearing news that the bishop didn't intend anyone to hear, his daughter was a source of fascinating information. "You didn't tell your father that Billy was here, did you?"

"Why does everyone have such little faith in me?" Maggie shook her head vehemently. "I didn't say a word."

That was a relief. If Caleb Zook knew Billy was here, he would probably try to talk to him, to reason with him, to draw him out. To convince him to return. And with the tetchy mood Billy seemed to be in, that would send him scurrying off to his hiding hole, rose or no rose.

Another gust of bitter wind swirled around them, lifting dried leaves, and Maggie stamped her feet to stay warm.

"Do you want to come inside and warm up?"

"Can't. I just wanted to let you know about Billy's father. I hoped you might be able to convince him to go visit his father."

"I have no influence on Billy."

"You're kidding, right?" Maggie looked at her curiously, tilting her head. "He's still hung up on you, Bess."

Bess felt her face heat up. "That's not true."

"He couldn't keep his eyes off you during breakfast this morning."

"He was famished. Have you noticed how thin he is? If he was watching me, it was to hurry up and bring him a hot meal."

"No, Bess. Not like that at all. " Maggie's voice had none of her usual swagger. It was all seriousness now, and Bess glanced up at her. "He was watching you like a man who can't watch enough."

Bess dipped her head to study her shoes. She didn't want to hear that about Billy. But she did. "You shouldn't say such a thing. I'm to marry Amos soon. Very soon."

"Well, that doesn't mean Billy can shut off his feelings like that." Maggie snapped her fingers in the air to prove her point. "Bess, you're not having second thoughts about marrying Amos, are you?" She took a step closer to Bess. "Billy Lapp might be my second cousin, but he's hardly the right horse to bet on."

Bess rubbed her shoulders with her arms and glanced up at the farmhouse. "I need to get inside to help Lainey with dinner."

"Bess . . ." Maggie's voice had a warning note. "Amos is a wonderful catch. One of a kind. You would be crazy to have doubts about him."

"I don't have any doubts about how wonderful Amos is." And that was no lie. "I'll talk to you tomorrow."

Bess hurried to the house and up the porch steps, then turned to wave. Maggie stood where she was, watching Bess with a worried look on her face.

Later that night, in her room on the second floor, Bess prepared for bed with an odd feeling, like she'd swallowed a goose egg. The lamp in her hand flickered, hissed, and spat, low on oil. She blew it out and climbed into bed to consider her unsettled thoughts.

Amos, she thought. What a simple, dear man.

Billy. She frowned. Anything but simple and certainly not dear.

If only their personalities could in some way be stuffed into a paper bag and shaken up—Amos could use some of Billy's gall and Billy some of Amos's quiet self-control. After Amos's courtly manner, she found Billy abrupt, gruff, easily offended. How long could a man go without smiling? Without laughing?

Billy was so extremely aggravating.

And so handsome it hurt.

Had she only imagined that moment of connection between them in the greenhouse, right before Amos arrived? No, she hadn't. Billy had been aware of it too; she wasn't making it up. For one brief, revealing flash, she had seen it clearly in his eyes. Something had sizzled between them while they'd stared at each other.

It was awful. It was awesome.

She shook her head to rid it of longing. Had she not spent the last few years trying to unbind herself from yearning for a man who didn't truly love her?

The next instant she thought of Amos's wonderful eyes, the warmth of his devotion to her, the comfort of his faith. Amos was a man who knew how to love a woman. One woman. He was ready to be committed to her.

Why wasn't that enough for her? Why did she yearn for a man who didn't know the first thing about love?

Should she tell Billy all she knew about this rose? *Tell him. Don't tell him.* She needed to find the key that would bring Billy back to Stoney Ridge. This rose, she thought, might be it. But maybe nothing would make him stay.

Sighing, she rolled over and tried to find sleep, but when it came it was fitful and strange, filled with crimson roses and empty greenhouses.

As Billy rode the bus back to College Station, his mind rolled through the day past, the day to come, the years behind, the years ahead. He cringed, thinking of that unguarded moment he'd had with Bess in the greenhouse at Rose Hill Farm. Even now, hours later, he could feel the heat climb his neck. How ridiculous he must have looked to her, allowing his attraction to show. It was up to him to hold her at arm's length.

Then . . . in walked Amos Lapp, of all people. His cousin, his friend, a man to whom he owed a great deal.

His very life.

He rubbed the scar on his left wrist and thought back to that awful, horrible Christmas when he felt so hopeless, so lost. He hadn't been able to sleep for over a week, didn't have enough money for more than one meal a day, and felt unbearably lonely. On Christmas afternoon, his lowest moment, he picked up his pocketknife, fingered it for a long time, felt the edge of the blade, and impulsively drew it against his wrist. Watching the blood spill from his vein, he suddenly felt a panic, a desperate feeling. *What have I done? Oh, God, help me!*

He lunged for the door of his small rented room in a boardinghouse to shout for help and, miraculously, there stood Amos

Lapp, his arms full of gifts and groceries. Quickly and wordlessly, Amos assessed the situation, made a tourniquet for Billy's wrist, bundled him off to the emergency room, stayed with him until he was stitched up—turned out, he hadn't hit a vein at all—went with him to the psychiatric facility where he was admitted for a twenty-four-hour observation. Amos sat upright in a chair throughout the night and read aloud from the book of Psalms. Soothed by his cousin's deep voice, by the strong meds given to him by the nurse, Billy fell into a deep and healing sleep. When he finally woke up, two days later, Amos was gone. He had left a note for Billy with his phone number on it and two words: *Come home.*

But Billy couldn't. He planned to never go home again.

The psychiatrist at the hospital discovered that Billy knew a great deal about flora and fauna. He thought Billy needed a fresh start, a new beginning, and was able to secure a job for him in the greenhouses at Penn State. Billy worked hard at his new job, and knew more about roses than any other employee. After identifying a string of rare roses, he became known as a rose rustler. Then, as *the* rose rustler. Billy might not have been happy, but he wasn't unhappy.

And Amos never told a soul about what Billy had done in that small, dingy rented room and he knew he never would. That's the kind of man Amos was—a good man.

Billy had to make himself look away when Amos and Bess left the greenhouse. He felt jealousy billow when he noted the possessive way Amos had hold of Bess's arm, as if branding her as his. He'd best get used to it, he scolded himself. Once they wedded, were living and loving in their own home at Windmill Farm . . .

He shook his head. It was a punishing thought.

He took off his hat and rested it on his lap. It was the only possession that mattered to him. He circled the brim of his hat with his finger, remembering his grandfather, his mother's father, to whom the hat had once belonged. Billy had adored his grandfather Zook. He shadowed him around his farm as a child. He leaned his head against the bus seat and closed his eyes, traveling back in his mind to another winter. Against his will, an ugly memory surfaced.

May 1963. Billy was nine years old. He had found his brothers behind the barn, laughing and guffawing, circled around a metal bucket. Inside was a caught woodchuck. The brothers were taking turns stabbing it with their pocketknives. Billy was sickened by their cruelty and ran to his grandfather's farm. He found him out in the fields and flung himself into his arms, sobbing, accidentally knocking his hat to the ground—that very hat. His grandfather returned with him to the farm and told their mother what Billy's brothers had done. When their father heard about it, he whipped them. His brothers were seething, but silently so. In the middle of that night, they woke Billy and locked him in the woodshed with the dead woodchuck, hanging from a noose in the rafters, threatening far worse if he ever told on them again. Ever since, Billy had suffered from claustrophobia in small, dark places.

All three older brothers vied to be the first, the best, in their father's eyes—and their father was a hard man, a tough guy, who wanted to make men out of his boys. The little interest he showed in his sons was to bait them to compete with each other. Billy was the caboose of the family, much younger than the other boys, his mother's favorite, and most like a Zook in looks and personality. Whenever Billy tried to gain his father's approval—waking early to milk the cows for him, mastering a new skill—his father would only shrug as if he had expected it all along or point out how it could have been done better. Billy's resolve would only strengthen: *Next time,* it whispered. *Next time he will notice.*

His mother tried to explain away his father's indifference. She said he had a difficult childhood and had faced a string of disappointments in his life. After she died, his father grew even more distant and cold, as if the only warmth in his life had been snuffed out by her death. Billy had thrown himself into working alongside his father, trying to rekindle his interest in the farm, in life. Being obedient, he thought, unlike his attention-seeking, unruly brothers, would be the way to connect to his father.

For a few years in a row, his father had divided up the farm into sections for each son rather than have the boys work together. It was his way of pitting them against each other. His brothers preferred the no-till farming method, popular at the time and less work for them. Rather than plow the fields, they used chemicals to reduce weeds and fortify the soil. Billy farmed his section the old-fashioned way—tilling the soil, adding natural fertilizer deep into the earth, rotating crops, letting sections go fallow to renew their minerals.

Late in August of 1973, the summer before Billy left, he harvested a wheat field, sent the wheat through the separator, and discovered that his mule-plowed field had ended up with twice the amount of grain as his brothers did. Twice! "I knew it," he said. "I knew no-till was the wrong way to go." He turned to his father, pleased at the profitability his methods could provide to the struggling farm. Then he stilled, shocked by the cold, hard expression on his father's face.

His finger was in Billy's face now. "You think you're better than me, boy? You think you're somebody special?"

That became an illuminating moment for Billy. He realized that one person, even a son, couldn't make up for the string of disappointments a man faced in his lifetime.

Billy inhaled deeply, as if he could still smell the earthy, humus dirt from that buried memory. Loneliness was a thing he usually accepted with stoicism, but lately it weighed him down, causing a heavy ache in his heart that he couldn't control.

Eight

Amos Lapp had spent the afternoon searching for the perfect Christmas gift for Bess. He'd walked up and down Main Street, in and out of stores, hoping the right gift would jump out at him. He spent over an hour in a bookstore before it occurred to him that Bess didn't read much. He was the one who liked to read.

It bothered him that buying a gift for Bess was such a challenge for him. He didn't know why—he just could never seem to decide on the right gift. She wasn't hard to please; he knew she would be grateful for any gift he gave her. But he wanted to give her one she would always remember. After all, this would be their first Christmas together.

He walked past the Sweet Tooth Bakery and peered in the windows, wondering if he should get something to tide him over until dinner. The trays in the glass counter were almost empty. A chocolate-frosted yuletide cake stood on the top shelf next to a row of Christmas cookies shaped like trees and decorated with bright green icing. On the bottom shelf sat a lone strawberry-pink birthday cake. Dottie Stroot, hands floury, came out from the back and spotted him. She pointed to the pink birthday cake and mouthed, "Half off! My new girl can't spell," but he had no interest in toting around a pink birthday cake. He shook his head and hurried down the street to the hardware store to buy a new wrench.

As he turned the corner from Main Street, he collided with Maggie Zook and nearly knocked her over. She scowled at him and stamped her foot.

"Honest to Pete! Why don't you look where you're going, Amos Lapp?"

"But I didn't see—"

"That's the problem with the world today! Everybody is in such a hurry!"

That remark struck Amos as rather amusing because Maggie Zook had always reminded him of a hummingbird that darted about, never staying in one place too long. "Sheesh, it was just an accident, Maggie."

Before his eyes, Maggie's eyes widened and her face grew red. Her eyes filled with tears and all he could think to say was, "Oh no. No, no. Please don't cry. I'm sorry. It was entirely my fault. My mind is in a muddle. You're right. I should've looked."

Amos didn't have experience with crying women; his mother wasn't the crying type and he had no sisters. He rummaged through his pockets for a handkerchief and handed it to Maggie, hoping she would pull herself together and he could get back to his shopping. But as she took the handkerchief, she let out a big sob and he knew his plans had just been sidelined. *Oh, boy.* He looked up and down the street, hoping no one he knew was around to witness Maggie's meltdown. He led her to a bench and sat down beside her, wondering how long this would take.

Her scarf had fallen back and lay in soft folds about her collar. She looked up at him, all eyes, wide and pleading, very pathetic. "I'm sorry, Amos. It's not your fault. I started a job at the Sweet Tooth Bakery just yesterday. Everything was going so well . . . at least, I thought it was.

"Then, this morning"—she carried on with her story as if he had asked about it—"Dottie Stroot complained that I was spending too much time talking to customers and not enough time actually working."

"Was it true?"

Her brown eyes flashed at him. "I was only making people feel wanted and welcomed. You know Dottie Stroot! She barks at customers if they take too long to make a decision. She scares people away."

"So you didn't heed her advice."

"I pointed out to her that being nice to people was part of the job, if that's what you mean by taking her advice." She rolled her eyes. "I know that I have a tendency to speak before I think, Amos, but I truly believe Dottie Stroot has a bias against the Amish."

"But you didn't get to work?"

"Customers *are* the work!" She frowned. "That Dottie Stroot is very full of herself. Very hard to please."

Now things were making sense to Amos. "Any chance you misspelled a name on a birthday cake?" It wasn't a question.

Maggie nodded miserably. "I was supposed to write Happy Six and by accident I wrote Happy . . ." She took in a deep breath, as if to fortify herself, and her cheeks turned a half-dozen shades of red. "I wrote . . . Happy . . . Sex."

She cast a cautious glance at him as if she expected him to scold her, but he was struck dumb by the faux pas.

"I know it was embarrassing, Amos, but these things happen!" She wiped her nose with the handkerchief. "I didn't realize the mistake until the lady—the six-year-old's mother—came to pick it up. The mother was outraged . . . which made Dottie Stroot hit the ceiling. I ask you! I mean . . . I could have just changed one tiny little letter, but the mother stormed out . . . and then . . . and then . . ." Her shoulders started to shake and she took in great gulps of air before another round of weeping overwhelmed her. "Dottie Stroot fired me! She said I was ribald. Me! Ribald! Imagine, firing me . . . all because of a silly misspelled word . . . and I don't really count that as my fault." More weeping.

Do something, Lapp! But what? She'd already drenched his handkerchief. He looked down at her small head, heaving into her hands as if she had just been given news that the world was coming to an end. That was the curious thing about Maggie Zook. She felt things so deeply.

He gazed at her with amusement as she sobbed into his soaked handkerchief. It was hard not to be fond of Maggie Zook. Everyone was. For each moment of bafflement, like this one, there were far more moments of endearment. He reached over and patted her on the back, hoping she might stop weeping soon. Amos was amazed at the quantity of water that ran down Maggie's cheeks. Wasn't there a point when tears would shut off, like a faucet?

Finally, her sobs slowed and her lips parted, exuding small, panting breaths. He'd never noticed how nicely formed her lips were, full and rosy red . . . and . . . he had no business thinking that now. He shook off that thought and gave his coat collar a tug. "Maggie, what's the big deal? So you were fired."

"Now I have to tell my dad I got fired!"

"Your dad is an understanding man."

"Not about this. He didn't want me to work there in the

first place. Right after Christmas, Teacher Mary is quitting because of her sciatica, and he is under the mistaken assumption that I would make a good schoolteacher. Very worrying." Her eyes went wide. "You won't say anything, will you Amos?"

"Of course not." Besides, he didn't care.

She frowned. "I absolutely refuse to be a schoolteacher. I would feel like a bird with its wings clipped. Trapped in a cage. Held in captivity. And don't even get me started about the big boys in the back of the room." She shuddered. "Overgrown oafs with cowlike stares." She shook her head furiously. "Personally, I've never seen any earthly reason for school."

That was reason enough for school, right there. Amos heard her out, but he was not deeply moved. Maggie always did think she was smarter than anyone else and it was largely true. Amos was older than Maggie by five years, but they had overlapped in school and he well remembered her. Everybody did.

When Maggie first started school as a six-year-old, she had missed her mother so much that the teacher had her sit up at her desk, hoping to help her settle in. Eyes wide, glassy with tears, Maggie's nose just cleared the top of the desk. But as she sat on the throne and took everything in, she started to assume she actually was the teacher's assistant. It wasn't long before she even started acting like the teacher—wagging her fingers at the big boys when they cut up, shaking her head in a woeful way when Amos misspelled a word in a spelling bee. A princess at heart, all that was missing was a crown on her head and a pointer in her hand.

After a few days, even the teacher had enough of getting bossed around by her little assistant. She told her it was time to sit with her peers, and Maggie marched to an empty seat next to eleven-year-old Amos. She assumed she belonged with the sixth grade. Amos was mortified.

The teacher pointed to an empty desk near the other first-graders, appalling Maggie. She rose to her feet and calmly told the teacher she had learned all she needed to know and was going to quit school. Out the door and down the road she stomped, bonnet strings trailing in the wind. The entire classroom stared at her through the window, amazed and astounded. She was an instant hero among the big boys.

Sadly, her resolve was quickly overruled. The next morning, her father escorted her to school and sat calmly at the back of the room for most of the morning, pinning Maggie in place at her desk with his steady gaze.

"I suppose I should go tell my father," she said shakily, holding the drippy wet handkerchief out to Amos.

His hands shot up in the air. "You keep it."

"What are you doing in town?"

"I was looking for a Christmas gift for Bess." He glanced at the clock tower above the *Stoney Ridge Times* newspaper office. "But I couldn't find anything and now the stores are closing."

Maggie's face lit up. "For gosh sakes, why didn't you say something?" She slapped the palms of her hands down onto the bench as if that was that. "I've got just the thing!" She jumped up and grabbed Amos's coat sleeve. "Follow me."

They crossed the street to Pearl's Gift Shop and Maggie went right to the glass case in the window. "There." She pointed to a delicate sterling silver thimble. At its base was a band of painted tiny pink roses.

"You're sure? She doesn't like to sew. She didn't grow up with a mother teaching her, you know."

"She might like to sew if she had such a lovely thimble. I would definitely sew straighter lines if I had a thimble like that." She looked up at Amos. "I think it's perfect. Just perfect. And you know how Bess loves roses."

Bess did like roses. He knew that for sure.

But it still didn't feel like the right gift. He didn't want to hurt Maggie's feelings, so he went ahead and purchased it. There was still time before Christmas, he thought, to shop.

When he dropped Maggie off at her house, she talked him into coming inside to warm up, which led to an invitation for dinner. It didn't take much persuasion. First, he was hungry and cold. Second, he wanted to talk to Caleb Zook about a new idea for crop irrigation that he'd read about in a farming journal. It was after nine by the time he left. He drove by Rose Hill Farm and turned into the driveway, but just as he was about to stop the horse, he saw the light blow out in Bess's room on the second floor.

A week ago, he would have tossed a snowball up at her window and she would have thrown on her coat to come sit in the buggy with him. But that was a week ago. That was before . . .

Tonight, he turned the buggy around in the dark and left as quietly as he could.

As busy as Bess was with wedding preparations, she found time to dart out to the greenhouse and check on the rosebud two to three times a day, looking for changes, hoping there might be an excuse to leave a message at Billy's office. The rose capsule remained stubbornly intact, as if it wasn't going to budge until it was good and ready.

Riehl relatives streamed in and out of Rose Hill Farm,

cooking and baking and moving furniture, readying the farm-house for the wedding tomorrow.

Tomorrow.

In less than twenty-four hours, Bess was going to become Mrs. Amos Lapp. Earlier today, before the relatives started arriving, Lainey had come into Bess's bedroom with a newly sewn blue wedding dress and white apron draped over her arm and shut the door. "Bess, let's have a talk about what to expect."

At first, Bess didn't know what she meant and opened her mouth to ask when Lainey cut her off. "Sex. We need to talk about sex."

Oh. Bess's mouth clamped shut. Easily embarrassed, she felt her cheeks flame. She knew bits and pieces about what happened between a husband and wife, informed by Maggie, who claimed to be an expert in such matters. But Lainey was far more thorough than Maggie, more descriptive, and probably more accurate, seeing as how she was married and Maggie was not.

Nor was Lainey at all embarrassed by the topic. She gave Bess a very clear idea of what went on behind closed doors between a man and wife. "All the modesty, all the careful covering up that's been a part of your life—it's all set aside when it comes to your marriage bed. God intended for you to enjoy your moments."

Enjoy your moments. A beautiful comment; permission to savor the gift of intimacy between a man and a woman. Why, then, did Bess feel her heart grow heavy? Why did she feel so sad?

Amos was a hard worker and genuine and kind, fine looking, and she knew he would make a good husband. Bess didn't want to be alone in life. But she had seen the way Lainey and her father would fall into each other's arms if they thought no one was looking, as if they were hungry for each other. She didn't have those kinds of feelings for Amos.

"Any questions?"

So many. But how could Bess even begin to reveal the questions and doubts that were flooding through her?

Lainey gave her a thoughtful look. "Bess, if you—"

A shriek split the air, then silence . . . followed by a mournful wail. Either Lizzie or Christy had taken a tumble, and Lainey flew out the bedroom door to see which one was hurt and how badly.

Through the open door, Bess heard Lainey comfort her daughter and the sobs subside. Slowly, she closed her bedroom door and went to curl up on the window seat. Soon, she would be needed downstairs to help cook chicken and chop celery for tomorrow's wedding meal. She saw a buggy arrive, then another and another. She heard an uncle's voice call out a jovial greeting to her father. "Jonah, why don't we have any boys in this Riehl family? With five daughters, all I ever do is cook wedding meals."

She saw her father walk over to greet his uncle, laughing. Everyone was laughing, happy and cheerful. Everybody loved a wedding. She dropped her forehead to her knees and sighed.

Bess turned away from the window and noticed her blue wedding dress on the bed where Lainey had set it. Wrinkled, it needed a good ironing, and now, Bess decided, was just the time, plus the iron and ironing board were set up in her room, away from the gathering crowd in the kitchen. And it gave her an excuse to delay going downstairs. She took extra care with the white apron, starching it crisply, because the organza fabric always bunched up on her. Once a crease was ironed in, it was a bear to get out. Bess had to keep sprinkling water on the fabric, then starch. She spread out the new blue wedding dress on the ironing board, and suddenly, as she thought about the wedding, about standing in front of everyone, she felt as if her hands couldn't stop shaking as they pressed the heavy iron on the blue material. Her palms started to sweat and her heart felt like it might club its way out of her body.

Down the hall, Lainey was the first to notice the acrid odor of burnt fabric. "Bess! The iron!" She rushed into Bess's bedroom.

Bess lifted the iron and found a dark burned triangle right on the front of her dress. "No! Oh no!"

Lainey held the fabric up against the light and waved it to cool. "I think it'll lighten up as it cools off. Sometimes that happens." It didn't. The triangle shape of an iron remained—not even a dark blue. It was nearly black.

Bess's eyes filled with tears. "What have I done?"

"I wish there was some leftover fabric to redo that panel, but we used it all up." Lainey tried to make light of it. "Not to worry. Your apron will cover it up. No one will ever notice."

But Bess would know. A bride should look her best on her wedding day. She shouldn't have to worry about covering up a burned iron mark on her dress.

And then she caught sight of Billy walking up the long driveway and heading straight to the greenhouse. Lainey noticed that she noticed.

"Bess . . ." Lainey's voice held a note of warning.

Bess avoided Lainey's eyes and set the iron upright on the ironing board to cool. She put her dress on a hanger and the starched prayer cap on top of her dresser, where it sat like a plump hen. She could feel Lainey's eyes on her and felt a wave of relief when she heard someone down in the kitchen call up to her. As soon as Lainey left, Bess looked in the mirror, smoothed her hair, pinched her cheeks, bit her lips to put a little color in them, and crept down the stairs and out the side door to hurry to the greenhouse.

Billy seemed to be expecting her. He turned and glanced briefly at her as she slid in the door and walked down the aisle to meet him.

He was so much more of a man than she remembered. So tall and filled out. She lifted her chin toward the rose still tucked in the corner. "No real change yet."

"Slightly measureable. I didn't expect much of a change with the weather so cold. I only stopped by because I was sent to check out another lost rose in Gap."

"That's the only reason?"

"Yes," he said firmly.

"Was it? A lost rose?"

"No. It was an Albertine, a climber. Old, but not so rare." He turned and his elbow bumped the pot of a blooming yellow rose. He dipped his head to breathe in its scent and for a moment his face softened. "Magician. Known for its array of colors."

"Yes. One of my favorites."

"Magician," he said, rolling the word around on his tongue. "My father always said—" Suddenly his lips clamped, his head came down with a snap, and he shot her a cautious sideward glance. Enjoyment fled his face. "I better finish this up and be on my way," he mumbled, turning his attention to the mystery rose.

She stood next to him. "What did your father used to say?"

He crouched down and reached forward to drag the pot out. "Man! I don't know why this pot is so heavy."

"And your father always said . . ."

"He always said roses were nothing but fool's gold," he said softly, so quietly she barely heard him.

Without thinking, she knelt beside him. She could see his hands were trembling a little. Sensing how hard it had been for him to admit such a thing, she wanted to reach out and touch his hand, hold it to her heart, but she didn't dare. "Billy, you know that not all men are like your father and brothers. You know that."

He kept his eyes fixed on the rose. "What I know is that what my father thinks doesn't matter anymore. And that's why I want to spend my time doing what I love best—hunting down rare roses. Speaking of that, I'd better get back to work." With a grunt, he hoisted the pot up onto the workbench.

Slowly, she straightened, watching him. Though Billy tried to act nonchalant, something in his eyes—a glassy look—told Bess he was struggling with finding a way to overcome his prideful nature, a way to turn from the wrongs he'd been dealt and still maintain his self-respect as a man. "Did you know that Simon passed?"

"Bertha's brother?" He lifted his eyes momentarily and met hers self-consciously. "The one you gave your bone marrow to help cure?"

"Yes, but he didn't die of Hodgkin's Disease. He had a heart attack, just like Mammi."

"How long ago?"

"Over a year ago. Very sudden." She picked up a gardening glove and ran her finger along the leather edge. "I was always sorry I hadn't told him some important things before he passed. Things like . . . I had grown to care about him, as salty and blustery as he was. It was true. I even grew to love him, in a way. I meant to tell him. Seems like that's something that should be told to a person, but . . . there was never a good time. I thought there was plenty of time for that conversation. But then . . . time ran out. It does, you know."

His eyes flicked to hers, then immediately away. "Are you telling me this because of my father? Because if you are, you can save your breath."

That sharp edge had returned to him. She wondered what to make of Billy Lapp, so disagreeable and cranky at times, so vulnerable and vague at others. She stood beside him as he studied the flower bud and scribbled down measurements, resisting the urge to seize his hand and press it to her cheek, to make him look at her, really look.

He glanced out the window when he heard a buggy roll up the driveway to stop beside three parked buggies, then another and another. A swarm of black-bonneted women spilled out of the buggies and made a beeline to the kitchen. "I'll be on my way in a few minutes. Looks like you've got a quilting bee going on."

"No. Not a quilting bee." She swallowed, her breath shallow and quick. "They're here to help with the wedding."

The pencil in Billy's hand stilled for one brief second, then he carried on.

"Tomorrow. I'm to marry Amos tomorrow."

"Well, congratulations to you both."

Their eyes met, spoke silently. *You don't mean that,* Bess thought. *You just can't let down your defenses.*

"Tell me one thing. How long after I left did Amos start to court you?"

"What? Why should that matter?"

His voice was throaty. "How long?"

"We started courting two years ago."

"So at least he waited . . ." He shook his head, looked away.

She tugged at his elbow to make him look at her. What exactly did he mean by that? "Waited? For what?"

"To make sure I wasn't coming back."

"But you did come back."

He spun toward her and pointed at her with his pencil. "No. No I didn't. I've told you that. I'm here to identify this rose. That's all."

"That's all? No other reason?" Her eyes were wide and serious. "Is there, Billy? Any reason I shouldn't marry Amos?" she asked at last. She meant for her voice to ring out, but it emerged as a whisper. She held her breath. Everything hung on this moment—her future, Amos's, Billy's.

His brows furrowed in stern reproof as he stared at her from beneath the brim of his black felt hat. When he spoke, his voice was flat and crisp, cracking at the edges. "None. None at all."

She saw how fast he was breathing. She saw him fight with himself. She felt threatened by tears, and she swallowed fiercely to drive them back. Her cheeks burned, and her throat felt parched. Everything in her rushed toward him in a silent plea: *You stubborn, stupid, prideful man! Can't you tell what's in my heart?*

His eyes darted around the greenhouse as if seeking an escape, swept back to hers, then abruptly, he turned his attention to the workbench. To the rose. The light coming through the greenhouse ceiling played on and off the leaves of the rose like sun upon waves.

"Thank you for telling me, Billy," she offered softly, then, discomposed, swung away toward the door of the greenhouse.

NINE

Billy didn't need to turn around to know Bess had left, just as he knew when she had entered the greenhouse. His body seemed to have developed sensors that went on alert whenever she approached. In the silence that followed, the sensation withered, dulled, leaving him sitting on the wooden stool with a pencil gripped tightly in his hand, motionless. He turned his head, stared out across his right shoulder through the frosted window as Bess crossed the yard toward the house, head tucked down against the wind. Only when she had disappeared into the house did he release a rush of breath; his shoulders sagged, his eyes closed.

He'd known it would come down to this, but he hadn't expected it to hurt quite this much. He knew his words had hurt her. It was a lie that hurt him as badly as it hurt her. He saw the shock of rejection riffle across her face and steeled himself against rushing to her with an apology, taking her face between his hands and kissing her. But that wasn't fair to her or to him. Or to Amos.

He collected himself, exhaled deeply a number of times.

It's over. It's got to be, because she doesn't belong in my world any more than I belong in hers.

He heaved an enormous sigh, dropped his hands, lifted his head, and got back to work. He finished measuring the rosebud, put his tools into his backpack, replaced the heavy rose back in its corner, walked out of the greenhouse and down the driveway without looking back.

For the rest of the day he felt out of sorts, crotchety and malcontent. That evening, back at College Station, he accepted Jill's invitation to go out for a quick burger, but afterward, she looked vexed when he told her he needed to get back to work. "I thought you said this Stoney Ridge rose was no big deal."

"I never said, one way or the other." He fished for a response. He didn't want to lie, but he also didn't want to let on that this rose could be a found. Hedging was his best bet. "As soon as the rose opens, I'll be able to make a clear identification."

"I don't believe you. Something happened."

"What do you mean?"

"You've changed."

"In what way?"

"You seem distant. Preoccupied. Moody." She scrutinized Billy's face. "Did you meet someone?"

Billy felt his jaw drop and snapped it shut. "No. Nothing like that."

"People have hardly seen you around the greenhouses this week. Everyone's noticed."

The idea that his co-workers had noticed his absences bothered him. "Jill, you're the one who sent me to Gap to check out that rose. Do you have any complaints about my work?"

Slowly, she shook her head. "No, no. Your work is getting done, but I don't see you doing it."

Billy's stomach tightened like a fist. Had she seen George hanging around the greenhouse? He knew Jill would blow the whistle on the arrangement he'd made with the hobo. But from the look on her face, she didn't seem to suspect anything. If she didn't ask, Billy wasn't saying, and he wasn't staying. He rose to his feet. "I've been working late. In fact, I'm going there now. Need to check on those drought-resistant wheat seedlings. They're at a delicate stage." She didn't buy that, and he didn't really care. He just wanted to be back in the greenhouse, alone, where he could find peace.

The moment he walked into the warm, woodsy-scented greenhouse, he heaved an enormous sigh, tossed his backpack on the ground, and leaned his palms against a shelf. Suddenly Billy's life stretched out before him like a bleak, lonely purgatory. He hadn't felt this low, this full of despair, since that hard time. That awful Christmas.

He thought he had come so far from that day. He had diverted his pain into a kind of moat, buffering himself from despair. Rose rustling gave him a sense of purpose, a reason to get up each morning. His life held some meaning . . . and then *this* rose interrupted all that, reminding him of the life he'd lost. He felt like he'd climbed up a steep hill, only to slip near the summit and tumble back down again.

He heard the click of the greenhouse door and barely stifled a groan when he saw George amble in.

"What do you think?"

"Of what?"

George lifted an arm in a semicircle. "The pots. All rotated. And I swept the shelves clean."

Billy's eyes took in the changes. He hadn't even noticed the plants had been rotated from back to front, to allow for more sunlight, just as he had wanted them to be—though he didn't remember leaving a note for George to do so. And the wooden slats that held the flats of seedlings were swept clean of dirt and leaves and debris. "It looks . . . great. Wow." It was heavy, time-consuming work that must have taken him all day. "Really, really great."

George walked in and sat on the lone metal stool near the shelf that served as Billy's desk, then reached for a book tucked against the edge. "I noticed this while I was cleaning up." It was Billy's Bible, one that Amos had left with him at the hospital. He made a show of brushing off dust from the top of the weathered Bible, hacking and coughing and choking.

A smile tugged at the corner of Billy's mouth. "I guess I haven't read it much lately."

"Guess not," George said, leafing through it. "But this is how to know God. As you read it, your heart burns within you. As Jesus said, 'The Scriptures . . . testify of me.' John, I believe."

Billy stared at him. That was the second time George quoted Scripture to him. "How well do you know the Bible?"

"Not as well as some, better than others. Where I come from . . . well, it'd be like riding in a hot air balloon and reading a travel book with my head down instead of looking around."

Billy took off his coat and tossed it on the metal stool, trying to puzzle out George's words. There was surely no knowing or understanding him. "Where in the world *do* you come from?"

George's face took on a look of longing. "Quite a distance, Billy Lapp."

"Oh. You mean, like, Texas?"

George grinned. "Even farther away. Someday, I will take you there and show you around. Introduce you to my friends. They'd get a kick out of you."

Fat chance of that happening. Billy could just imagine the kind of place George came from. An empty railroad car, a highway underpass, a grimy soup kitchen.

George's eyes were on him, as if reading his thoughts. "So . . . since you seem to be back in Stoney Ridge pretty often, don't you think it's time to mend the rift with your family?"

"Rift?" More like a yawning crevice.

"No?" George scratched his head. "Isn't there a rift?"

"Do you realize you always answer a question with a question?"

"Do I?" He seemed astounded by that. "So, isn't there a rift?"

Billy's back stiffened, his shoulders tensed. Then, resigned, he felt the tension drain from him and he let out a puff of air. "Yeah. There is."

"What's it going to take to get you back home?"

Billy coughed a laugh. "Not gonna happen in this life-time."

"Ah," George voiced knowingly, "pride." He leaned back so his elbows rested against the shelves. "So you're just going to keep on living this solitary life, cut off from everyone you love. From your family. From your church. From Bess."

Billy's mouth dropped. George was getting onto ground, in more ways than one, where he did not want to be. "Whoa right there," he said testily. "I know for a fact that I never mentioned anything about Bess to you."

"You don't have to. You turn into a bundle of raw nerves whenever you've been near Rose Hill Farm." The greenhouse was warm and George unbuttoned his coat. "So are you ever going to let Bess off the hook?"

"Let her off the hook?" Billy was getting steamed. "Bess overheard my brother say I was seen with my old girlfriend and she jumped to the conclusion that I was cheating on her."

"And you weren't trying to be the big hero to your old girlfriend?"

Billy fit the edges of his teeth together and said nothing. He was incensed. Incensed and guilty. He *had* enjoyed the feeling of saving the day for Betsy Mast. She was desperate and needed cash, and it made him feel wonderful that she had sought him out for help. But it didn't mean he was two-timing Bess. He wasn't.

George the hobo was getting downright annoying. Billy turned back to the makeshift desk. As calmly as a frustrated man could, he pointed out to George that there was work to be done in the greenhouse. "You work for *me*, remember? You forgot to move those orchids on the lower shelf. I want them moved up a row. They're not getting enough light." He put on his work gloves and busied himself with an ailing potted rhododendron.

"Bess is only human, Billy. Everybody makes mistakes." But when Billy didn't respond, George moved quietly to the far end of the cylinder greenhouse, shifting delicate orchids from the lower shelf to the high one.

Blast it all! Billy tried to ignore George's comments, but they kept intruding in his thoughts. That old hobo had a way of rubbing salt in a wound. And yet he couldn't deny that George's insights were spot-on. About living a solitary life. About missing his family, his church. About Bess.

Tomorrow she was going to marry Amos. Knowing it was about to happen and he couldn't, *shouldn't* do anything about it—it upset him to the core.

He thought about whether he should have told her that he still cared for her, but what would that prove? She didn't love him. If she had, she wouldn't have let him down when he needed her the most. His life had lost value in the moment when Bess looked at him with doubt in her eyes. When would he learn?

Why? Why? What did he lack? What more must he prove?

Grow up, Lapp. When are you gonna realize that you're alone in this world? Nobody fought for you then, nobody'll fight for you now, so give it up.

George must have come up the aisle when Billy wasn't paying attention, because suddenly he was on the stool, sipping coffee, reading aloud from Billy's dusty Bible: "'Then they cry unto the LORD in their trouble, and he bringeth them out of their distresses.'"

Slowly, Billy straightened up and watched George—irritated at first, then calmer as he listened to the words, and, finally, a conviction from the words read aloud. It had been so long since Billy had dared have faith, and even then what good had come of it?

"'He maketh the storm a calm, so that the waves thereof are still.'"

Dare he trust it?

"'Then are they glad because they be quiet; so he bringeth them unto their desired haven.'"

What was Billy's desired haven? Where was it? This greenhouse. Any greenhouse. It was his safe haven. But was that enough?

What about someone to love? A family to care about, to be cared for? Why was such a haven denied to him?

George read the last few lines of the psalm, closed the book and then his eyes, reverently.

Billy turned away from George, feeling hard again.

"Billy, do you know much about the Pharisees?"

"A little. They were around in Jesus's time."

"They knew their Scripture. They knew their laws."

Billy looked up at George. "Maybe they were just trying to do what was right."

"Perhaps. They were certainly trying to please God. But they ended up smothering the Word of God with all their unbiblical traditions."

Billy wasn't sure where George's peculiar line of thinking was wandering to in this conversation. "Half the time I don't know what you're getting at."

George smiled. "The Pharisees tried to obey the law. They thought they were pleasing God, but in their efforts, they forgot the most important thing."

"Which was . . . ?"

"Loving God, loving others." George folded his arms across his chest. He stared at Billy a moment in that intense way of his, with his hand still on his Bible. In a quiet but firm voice, he added, "Billy, has it occurred to you that you've forgotten how to love your father?"

Billy stilled, deeply indignant though he tried not to show it. "Me? I didn't do anything wrong."

George reached into a box of crackers that Billy had left on the shelf. "Mind if I have one?"

"Help yourself."

"You might not have done anything wrong, but you didn't really do anything right, either." George chewed a few crackers with a thoughtful look on his face. "These need more salt. Speaking of salt . . . how are you going to be salt to your family when you're hiding away in a greenhouse in College Station? By staying away like you've done, you've only made things worse for your father. He has no one to pull him up. You might be standing on principle, but you're all alone."

"I'm not hiding away," Billy growled. "You're forgetting that my father didn't care whether I stayed or left."

"I'm not forgetting. But things aren't always what they seem. Your father needs you, Billy. He needs God even more. Be the son he needs you to be."

Billy's heart was pounding so hard, he clapped a hand to his chest to try to calm it. "So you think I'm a Pharisee? *Me?* All rules and no love?"

"When those rules didn't work for you, you tossed everything out the window, along with the most important things in life. About faith in God, about love, about forgiveness."

Furious now, Billy practically spat out the words. "You have no idea what it was like to be a child in that home. With *him* for a father."

Unruffled, George said, "You're not a child anymore."

Billy's throat went dry, resentment twisted his gut. The effort of revealing himself was mighty, and he felt a wave of fatigue. His gaze jumped to George, who stared back in earnest. When he spoke, his voice had a raspy, sharp edge. "It's been a long day. I think I want to be alone."

"Understood." George glanced at the clock on Billy's shelf. "It's that late already? I'm not good with time. It always seems to be running out." Slowly, he rose to his feet. "Thankfully, it's never too late to find your way back to God. He is faithful even when you are not. 'Then they cry unto the LORD in their trouble, and he bringeth them out of their distresses.'" He walked to the end of the greenhouse and put his hand on the door. "Go see your father, Billy. Don't wait. There's a lot at stake here."

As the door closed behind Billy, he mulled over George's final words. What did that mean—a lot at stake? What was he trying to say? He jerked his jacket from the chair and shrugged it on, then hurried to catch up with George. But when he got outside, the hobo had disappeared into the dark night.

Later, Billy sat on the edge of the bed with his head in his hands, his shoulders hunched, heavy with loss. He felt haunted by George's accusation, yet unable to act on it.

He flopped back, eyes closed, arms outflung. As he lay flat on his back staring at the ceiling, he pictured Bess in her blue wedding dress, next to Amos, dressed in his new black Mutza coat, standing together in front of the bishop. The thought made him miserable. All at once, he fiercely missed the life he could've—should've—had. He ended up rolling to his stomach, punching down his pillow, wishing for sleep to clear his mind of forbidden wishes.

TEN

In less than fifteen minutes, Bess was going to become Mrs. Amos Lapp. A bead of sweat rolled down her neck and continued down between her shoulder blades, making her squirm. She had twisted the ends of her freshly starched apron so much that the edges were curled. She glanced across the room to Amos and wondered what was running through his mind. His chin rested on his chest; he looked like he was praying. Then he must have sensed she was looking at him, because he lifted his head and caught her eye, giving her a reassuring smile. She tried to smile in return but felt it came out all wrong. He was such a fine man. A wonderful man. It was good she was marrying him. Everyone said so.

And then the bishop called her name. Bess took a deep breath, rose to her feet, wondered if her shaky knees might go out right under her, and walked up to join Amos. She kept her eyes on the steps in front of her, trying to keep one foot in front of the other. She didn't dare look up at Amos. If she did, she thought she might faint.

She had been doing fine, just fine, well, somewhat fine, until she and Amos had been taken into a room with the ministers while the guests were singing hymns. The ministers asked if Bess and Amos were ready to take this important step of marriage. Amos readily answered yes and looked at Bess with such hope and happiness on his face. She whispered yes. Then one of the ministers—she didn't even remember which one—started to describe some details about the marriage bed. He explained a woman's monthly cycle to Amos, instructed them both to abstain from the marital act for three days after today's wedding, according to the book of Tobias, so that their marriage would be blessed. Amos, whose face was beet red, kept his eyes on the tips of his shoes.

No wonder the bride and the groom always emerged from this ministers' conversation looking like singed cats. It was a birds-and-bees lecture given by graybeards, condensed into ten minutes. And it was mortifying!

As they returned to the crowded living room, the awful reality hit Bess full force. She felt pinned in place, queasy under the gaze of so many observers. She pressed her fist to her lips after getting an awful feeling that her breakfast might reappear. The burn mark in her dress felt like it was searing her. Her prayer cap tilting. Her head splitting.

She had imagined herself making a life with Amos, imagined sitting together at the table each evening to talk over the day and plan the next day. She could imagine catching his eye during the preaching and sharing a smile. She could imagine working the fields beside him at Windmill Farm, and picking apples or peaches on drooping branches in those orchards his grandfather had planted long ago. Picnics at Blue Lake Pond on summer days, holidays celebrated with the Lapps' large, extended family.

But when she tried to imagine going into the bedroom with him and undressing for him, to "enjoy her moments" as Lainey had said—though she had no direct knowledge of such couplings—the man's face with whom she imagined enjoying her moments belonged to Billy Lapp.

She had to take a deep breath to ease the pressure growing in her chest. At that moment a pain grabbed her gut, but she wished it away, telling herself it was only nerves.

She wished the bishop would stop talking. *Stop him somehow! Stop him!* But she didn't know how.

And now because she had made a promise to Amos, she was going to go through with the marriage. For the rest of her earthly life.

The bishop began to speak, stressing the importance of these vows. "They are not only vows between the two of you, but before God."

For a moment Bess closed her eyes, gulping, unable to swallow the lump of fear that suddenly congealed in her throat. Her knees were a pair of jellies. It was all happening so fast!

And that was when Bess felt a loud whooshing sound in her head, so loud she barely heard the rest of Caleb Zook's words. She saw Amos's mouth move, answering Caleb's questions, then she saw both Caleb and Amos look at her, a question on their face. Waiting, waiting, waiting . . .

The tension built and Bess felt like the rope in a tug-of-war. She felt light-headed and nauseated and removed from herself.

"Bess?" Caleb repeated. "Do you take this man to be your lawfully wedded husband?"

The pain in her gut wrenched her again, higher up this time, and she winced. She looked at Amos—dear, kind Amos, and then at Caleb—fine, noble Caleb. And then she pulled the apron up over her head and said, "I can't! I just can't!" She turned and fled to her room.

Bess sat on the edge of her bed, crying softly. For the longest time, there was only silence down below, but now she heard the voice of Caleb Zook begin to quietly read Scripture. She wished everyone would go home and let her be alone, but she knew that no one would leave until it was clear there wasn't going to be a wedding today. And there wasn't. Not today, anyway. She needed time to think.

And then she groaned. Everyone loved the wedding feast. She knew no one would leave, wedding or not, without being fed. It wasn't the Plain way to let food go to waste, whether the bride was upstairs crying into her pillow or not.

A gentle knock came at the door.

"Yes?" she answered weakly, thinking Lainey had been sent up to talk to her and find out what in the world had happened to her.

What in the world *had* happened?

Amos poked his head in—thoughtful, considerate Amos. "Are you all right?"

She had no explanation for him, no soothing response. "Not exactly." She wanted to be left alone. But she was terrified of being left alone. Her legs felt like they were shackled. Standing up was an enormous effort. "Is everyone waiting for me?"

"Yes. Can I do anything for you?"

"I'm afraid the offal I had for breakfast already did it."

"So then . . . you're sick?"

Bess's heart seemed to drop to the pit of her stomach. Her eyes met his directly as she wondered exactly what it was he was asking. But seeing the intensity there, the determination, she dropped her gaze to his chest, and she didn't know how to answer. She drew a deep lungful of air. "I don't feel at all well" and that was the truth. Bess watched as Amos grasped the back of his neck with one hand and dropped his chin onto his chest.

Their gazes met momentarily. They searched for something to say, something to do, but there was only one thing to do.

His voice was low and sure, easing her. "I'm going down to tell people that you're not feeling well. Will you be okay?"

Okay? she thought.

The silence between them was unbearable to her. She looked at him, and he looked back without turning away, his eyes clear and sad. She searched them for something: reprieve, forgiveness, love? She wasn't sure.

Amos took a step toward the open door, halted, drew a deep breath, then spun and clasped her against his chest so hard, the breath swooshed from her lungs. Then he released her and went down the stairs to tell the guests the wedding had to be postponed.

As she heard his footsteps descend down the stairs, Caleb's voice stilled. She knew what was transpiring, as sure as if she were observing it. Every face—each one dear and loved, was turned to Amos for an explanation. Then she heard his baritone voice explain that Bess had become ill—something she had eaten—and needed rest. The tears she had been trying to hold back became a deluge. Without warning, she was overcome and dropped her face into both palms while sobs jerked her shoulders.

The day had left her tired and miserable.

Amos took a big breath of air before he reached the bottom step. As he walked into the living room, he sensed people leaning back in their chairs as if to give him a respectful distance, watching as he made his way toward the center of the room. He did his best to wave off concerns about him and Bess, assuring people that the reason she didn't go through with the wedding was that she hadn't been feeling well.

He even sat down to eat the wedding lunch, a meal he normally found so palatable, now turned tasteless. When Edith Stoltzfus refilled his glass of water and said in a loud voice, "Better now than tomorrow," Amos reeled to his feet, suddenly in a hurry to get away and sort out his thoughts. He made up a lame excuse about needing to check on a horse, fooling no one, and hurried to the pasture where the buggy horses stood in the cold. They lifted their heads as he neared them, but he walked straight past them, behind the barn, then broke into a run and took off through the fields. He heard the crunch of frozen snow in spots beneath his feet, saw the startled look on a pair of grazing deer as he ran past them, scattered a flock of wild turkeys.

On any other day, he would have stopped and carefully observed signs of wildlife. This wasn't any other day and he just kept running and running. Near the top of a small hill, he plopped down and sat on a rock, drawing deep breaths, as if recovering from having the wind knocked out of him.

But then, he did have the wind knocked out of him. By this time today, he thought he would be married, sharing the wedding meal with his beloved bride, his Bess. Instead, he didn't know where their relationship stood. Was it over? Was it on hold?

He vehemently disagreed with Edith's words: "Better now than tomorrow." She made it sound as if there would be no tomorrow for him and Bess, and he refused to believe that could be true. He loved Bess and he believed she loved him.

But had she ever said as much? Whenever he told her he loved her, she responded with a kiss or a squeeze of his hand. He took such an act as love.

They had planned their wedding together—deciding which friends would act as attendants, where each would sit for the wedding meal. She had seemed pleased with the pale blue paint color for the apartment over the garage at Windmill Farm—their future home as newlyweds. Everything was going as planned . . . until Billy Lapp returned.

Billy Lapp.

Down through Amos's memory drifted his own voice, when he had first told Bess he loved her and wanted to marry her. "We could live in the apartment over the garage at Windmill Farm. You could grow your roses in the gardens."

And Bess, hesitating. "Amos . . . I'm very fond of you . . . but—"

"What if he never comes back?" Billy, he meant.

Then Bess again, choosing as she always chose. "I want to give him a little more time. Please try and understand."

And Amos, wishing that Bess would long for him the way she longed for Billy.

Was history repeating itself? Was it happening all over again? He felt a wary stiffness about his shoulders, as if he'd already guessed.

Oh Lord, why did Billy Lapp have to come back? Why now? Then . . . *What am I saying? What am I thinking?* He was a friend he loved. A cousin. Nearly a brother.

He felt tired, and in many ways, he felt defeated, but he was still himself, Amos Lapp, so he went back to Rose Hill Farm to face his friends and neighbors. With a hope that Bess might come downstairs to seek him out.

ELEVEN

The next day, Friday, midmorning, Billy stormed up the driveway of Rose Hill Farm and marched into the barn where Frieda stood in the cross ties as Bess brushed her down. "Tell me you didn't do it. Tell me you didn't leave Amos standing at the altar!"

Bess blinked and looked again and it was still him. "Who told you?"

"Maggie." He frowned, hands on his hips. Maggie had actually called the Extension office and left a message for Billy: *Billy Lapp! Bess left Amos at the altar. Come quick!* "Is it true?"

She didn't stop brushing the horse's long neck. "Maggie always tells the truth, even though no one ever believes her."

Billy dropped his head. "Why would you do such a thing?" He kicked a bucket so hard that Frieda skittered. The old horse's ears sharpened to a point.

Bess paused and dipped her head. "I . . . don't know. Everyone thought I was sick, even Dad and Lainey. But the truth is that I just . . . panicked. I couldn't go through with it."

"Amos is as good a man as ever lived and better than most. The best."

"I know he is."

"You'll never do any better than him."

Their gazes met momentarily. Her eyes were so sincere and her mouth trembled as she stood a heartbeat away. Once again he was assaulted by a sense of things missed, a yearning, a desire to reach out and touch her, to hold her close to him. When her gaze dropped to his lips, his pulse beat thudded out a warning.

He took a careful step back and pointed at her. "No. No way. Don't even start thinking that you can bat your big blue eyes at me and I'll buckle. It's too late for us, Bess."

Her chin snapped up at the tenor in his voice. "What did I do?" she demanded angrily. "What did I do to ruin our friendship?"

His jaw bulged. He glared straight ahead. Finally he bit out, "Nothing. You didn't do a thing. Not a thing. Not a blessed thing."

Bess unhooked Frieda from the cross ties and led her into the stall, then swung the door shut behind the horse and latched the hook. She walked up to Billy. Her breath came in quick, driving beats. "Billy, why do you fight it?"

His throat seemed to close. "I don't know." *Yes you do, Lapp,* he thought. Everything hung too heavy and silent between them. He slipped his hands into his coat pockets and did his best to look platonic.

"Is it so hard to admit that you care about someone?" she questioned softly. "Would that be so terrible?"

"It's not going to happen, Bess. You and I . . . it's never going to happen." His voice was husky, gruff, as if the effort of expressing deep emotion snagged his words like barbs on wire.

She reached for his left hand and turned it over, caressing it softly, drawing her finger lightly over his scar.

For a moment he found it impossible to move. He closed his eyes to gain control, then jerked back and pulled his hand out of her grasp. "Bess, don't." He stepped away from her. "Go back to Amos. Make things right between you. He deserves that much."

She let out a puff of air. "He does. That's true." She looked away.

He gave her a hard, thoughtful stare, then grabbed her shoulders to make her face him. "Don't throw away your future."

Bess shrugged his hands off her shoulders and took a step backward. "I think that I just had a hope for a different future."

She turned to head out of the barn, and the door slammed abruptly, leaving an absence so profound it seemed to swallow Billy.

Halfway to the farmhouse, Bess stopped and tipped her chin to the sky. Gusting winds had swept away gray clouds, leaving a wide swath of brilliant blue that was almost piercing. Her cheeks tingled, and then her eyes, and she knew tears weren't far behind.

It was partially, if not entirely, her fault that Billy left Stoney Ridge the way he did. When his brothers had insinuated that something was stirring between him and Betsy Mast, he had looked to Bess and saw that she doubted him, his honesty and integrity. It had lasted only a matter of seconds, but that's all it had taken to turn Billy icy. She had seen and felt his withdrawal like a cold slap in the face. That look on her face was the final straw for him. Billy left Stoney Ridge without a glance back.

She had known before he had reached the road that she had made one of the gravest mistakes in her life. She and Amos set out to find him, but every hunch, every lead, was a dead end. It was easier to find Betsy Mast living in Lebanon with her new boyfriend than it was Billy, and Betsy had no clue about Billy's whereabouts. It was as if Billy didn't want to be found.

She could well imagine what he must have suffered after he left; loneliness and desperation sharper than physical pain. A vision of that scar on his wrist brought on a wave of nausea. She had only herself to blame.

She would be expected inside soon, but first she needed to calm herself with sensible thoughts. She could hear her grandmother's husky voice, "Mer muss es nemme wie's gemehnt is." *Take things as they are meant to be.* But how was this situation meant to be? A sudden wind made her shiver, so she took in a deep breath, then dipped her head and hurried across the yard to the kitchen door.

Silence fell in the kitchen as Bess walked inside and hung her coat and mittens on the wall peg. She knew that Lainey and her dad, seated at the kitchen table, had been talking about her. About the wedding. About the non-wedding.

Yesterday, they had been gracious to her, giving her plenty of space and time alone. Now and then, Lainey checked on Bess, brought her a plate of food that remained untouched on her dresser, but never questioned why she acted like a silly fool and ran away in the middle of the wedding ceremony.

But that was yesterday. Today, they wanted answers. Her father sat at the kitchen table, a half-empty mug of coffee in his hands and an open newspaper fanning across the table. He looked up when she came inside. Lainey was washing breakfast dishes at the sink, the little girls played with tin measuring cups at her feet. Bess could feel their eyes on her as she crossed the kitchen to fill a mug with hot water from the teapot on the stove and add a tea bag. She'd just as soon get this conversation over with.

Tea bag infused, she turned to face her dad.

"You're feeling better today?" he asked.

The sight of her dad's dark eyes, brows knitted with concern, nearly overwhelmed her. Against her will, tears sprang up again. "Much better." She went to the table to sit down, and blew on her tea, then swallowed, buying time until she felt her emotions were under control. "Dad, I'm sorry. For all the work you and Lainey did to prepare Rose Hill Farm for the wedding. For all the cooking done by the relatives. For the benches that were brought in." They were still all over the living room. "I am . . . so sorry."

He reached a hand out to cover hers, warmed from his coffee mug. "You don't need to apologize for anything."

"All those people watching me . . . I . . . panicked."

Her father nodded, understanding. "I just wondered if . . ." His voice drizzled off and he exchanged a look with Lainey.

"You wondered what?"

"Was your panic really because of nerves?"

She bit her lip. "I think so." *I hope so.* "Amos and I, we'll set another date soon. I'll make it through the next wedding."

Lainey came to the table and sat down. "Bess, maybe you should hold off on setting a date. Take a little time to think it over. Be absolutely sure you and Amos are meant for each other."

Bess gave her a shaky smile. "There's nothing more to think about. I just felt overwhelmed. You know how I can be. Next time I'll know what to expect." Her fingers were curling the edge of her apron. "At least I'll be able to fix that iron mark on the dress. I'll have to buy more fabric." She let out a half moan and clapped her hands on her cheeks. "Everyone must have seen that burn mark when I pulled my apron over my head."

"No one noticed," Lainey said. "Or if they did, no one commented."

"Just Edith Stoltzfus," Jonah said with a grin. "She noticed *and* commented."

And with that, Lizzie bonked Christy on the head with a tin measuring cup. Christy screamed and pulled Lizzie's hair, Lainey jumped up to quiet the ruckus, Jonah finished the last swallow of his coffee and left the chaos of the kitchen to flee to the barn, as men do. Bess let out a sigh of relief. Everything was back to normal.

Everything except for her and Amos.

For the next few days, Amos stayed close to home, expecting Bess would come seek him out, explain what had happened during their wedding to cause her to panic, and set a new date. Hoping, hoping, hoping she would. But she didn't.

So he worked. And worked and worked. Sunup to sundown, he never stopped.

The one who did come seek him out was Maggie Zook, fresh as a daisy from her nonworking days spent avoiding her father. She was worried about Amos, the way his mother was worried about him—but his mother understood what he was going through. Similar to him in temperament, she let him work out his conflicted feelings in peace. He knew Maggie wanted him to talk it out and share his feelings, but he'd never been good at that kind of thing.

Maggie Zook, she was something else again. Forever babbling, bubbling. She sure didn't know how to put a button on her lip. Spending time around her made him feel like he was bouncing from season to season: she was bright, bubbling spring, and he was deep winter.

On Wednesday, Maggie stopped by Windmill Farm yet again and trailed along behind him as he did his barn chores. She was named well, he decided. A chattering magpie.

He was cleaning the frog of a horse's hoof in the middle of the barn, half listening, as Maggie stood nearby with her hands on her hips, loose strands of her curly brown hair tucked behind her ears, her glasses slipping to the end of her nose. "Do you think these glasses are too big for my face?"

The question caught Amos by surprise and tipped up the corners of his lips. "They seem fine," he answered quietly. He couldn't imagine Maggie without her glasses.

She had first starting wearing glasses when she was in second grade; Amos was in seventh grade. Amos remembered the morning when Maggie walked into school with her new glasses, passing them around for other girls to try on. All the girls went home that day squinting like newborn owls, insisting they couldn't see well and needed spectacles. Suddenly, the Stoney Ridge optometrist had eight new customers—though, as it turned out, all the girls had perfect eyesight. What was it about Maggie that made everyone want to imitate her?

"Amos, we need to do something to get your mind off your troubles."

We. He made note of her word choice but merely said with a hint of stubbornness in his tone, "My mind is on my work." He hadn't asked her opinion, but she was, with her usual exuberance, giving it to him anyway.

"Well, didn't you say you were out of liniment? Let's get out of this stuffy barn and go down to the Hay & Grain. You need a change of scenery. I need some fresh air."

The horse did need liniment before he wrapped up her ankles. Why not? He threw the brush in the bucket. "Let's go."

Ten minutes later, they were in the buggy heading into town. It was a sunny winter day, the air crisp and sharp. Maggie pointed out the winter birds in the trees—a red cardinal male, a pine siskin. "Look up there. Is that an American sparrow?"

"Close. It's a white-throated sparrow."

"Have you ever had a pine siskin eat out of your hands? I have. Twice." Her eyes scrutinized each passing tree as the buggy rumbled down the road.

A smile lifted the corner of his mouth at her delight in each bird sighting. Maggie's face radiated more than the reflection of sun through the buggy windshield. She loved birds like he loved birds.

With a slight movement of his hands, he steered the horse onto Main Street. As the buggy passed the Sweet Tooth Bakery, Maggie suddenly dove down, headfirst, just in case Dottie Stroot was gazing out the window. Amos laughed out loud at that. "Do you really think she cares, Maggie? She hires and fires girls on a regular basis."

But Maggie was still smarting from getting fired so unceremoniously and, he had just discovered this morning, the reason she was spending so much time at Windmill Farm was because she hadn't gotten around to telling her father she'd been fired.

"Soon," she had promised Amos after she finally confessed the truth. "I'll tell my dad about getting fired soon. As soon as he hires a teacher. Then, I'll tell him."

Amused by Maggie's situation, he realized he hadn't felt that sharp ache about Bess in his heart for at least ten minutes. But after he bought the liniment at the Hay & Grain, he drove the buggy back down Main Street and saw Bess and Lainey and the two little girls head into the fabric store. He inhaled sharply, and Maggie gave his arm a reassuring squeeze, as if sensing how the sight of Bess shook him.

He stopped his buggy next to the fabric store with a sinking heart. He had kept alive a small hope that Bess really was sick—that was why she ran upstairs during the service, that was why she hadn't come to see him. As Bess scooped up the toddler in her arms to cross the street, she didn't seem like someone who'd been recently ailing.

He let out a puff of air. Should he go in and try to talk to her? He had questions to ask her and was getting tired of waiting. But he wasn't good at talking deeply in the best of circumstances, and a fabric store filled with women seemed like the worst of circumstances.

"Give her time," said Maggie, who could evidently read minds. "She needs to sort a few things out."

For a moment neither of them moved. He felt rooted by

surprise and curiosity about Maggie, as if he were seeing her in a new light.

"Amos, come skating with me at Blue Lake Pond. Just for an hour or so. We don't have to talk about Bess or Billy or the wedding. It would be good for you to take a break from too much serious thinking." She swept a glance in the direction of the fabric store. "Your troubles will be here when you get back."

Slowly, he shook his head. "Not today."

"Tomorrow, then?"

He flexed his gloved hands, picked up the reins, and shook them to get the horse moving again. "Maybe tomorrow."

Her dark eyes shone with delight. "Excellent. Tomorrow, then." She hummed all the way home. One thing everyone knew about Maggie Zook: if she wasn't talking, she was humming.

TWELVE

Billy waited a few days to return to Rose Hill Farm to check on the rosebud. He knew the rose wasn't ready to open yet, and he wanted to speak to a few rosarians to learn more about old German roses. From one elderly man in Pittsburgh, he learned that of the eighteen hundred cultivars bred between the end of the nineteenth century and World War II, many were extinct. The rosarian hoped Billy might have stumbled onto one of those German roses, but Billy was confident the mystery rose dated earlier than the nineteenth century. He didn't tell the rosarian that. Not yet.

Mostly, though, the reason he stayed away from Rose Hill Farm was that he needed some emotional distance from Bess. As hard as he tried, she was rarely absent from his thoughts. He kept envisioning those blue eyes with those long blonde lashes, eyes that were incapable of concealing the truth.

His curiosity about the rosebud finally won out and he was on the bus back to Stoney Ridge. Get in, check on the rose, get out; that was the plan. That girl had better stay away from the greenhouse.

Bess did exactly that when he first arrived, but within the

hour, she made an appearance. He was sitting on the wooden stool, studying the veining in the rose's leaves and comparing them to some information he'd gathered from the database. He finished and sat back to study it, then felt eyes on him. He looked over his shoulder and there she stood, still as a statue by the door, hands clasped behind her back.

His heart did a double take. His spine slowly straightened as he turned to face her.

She remained motionless, hands still clasped behind her. "Am I interrupting you?" she asked meekly. Automatically, without thinking, she reached a hand out to snap off a fading white Popcorn bloom, a miniature rose that had just been developed a few years ago.

Billy studied her awhile, a pencil in one hand and a book in the other. "Yes," he replied and went back to work, poring over a chart of rose genealogies.

She moved closer to him with careful, measured footsteps until she reached the workbench, where she stood in a pose of penitence. "Billy?" she said very quietly.

"What?"

"Won't you at least talk to me?"

Slowly he raised his eyes to look at her. The Popcorn rose bloom trembled in her hands. Tears shimmered on her lower eyelids.

Of all the things he'd expected, this was the last. Did the woman not know what effect she had upon him? The sight of her made his heart quake and his belly tense. He swallowed twice; the lump of emotion felt like a wad of cotton batting going down.

"I think I figured out why you're so angry with me," she said softly. "It finally dawned on me what you meant when you said I had done nothing to ruin our friendship. You meant *nothing*, didn't you? You meant that because I didn't say anything—at that moment—I ruined our friendship."

Billy just looked at her as she spoke, listening less to what she was saying than to how she was saying it.

"Please forgive me."

He could have insisted there was nothing to forgive, but they both knew she had hurt him.

For several inescapable seconds, while their hearts thundered, they stared at each other, hurting, fearful. Then she swallowed and dropped her hand. "It didn't take me two minutes after you left to realize you would have told me if Betsy Mast was back in your life. You would never have kept that hidden from me. Not you." The appeal in her voice was lost on him. He stubbornly continued his work. "Billy?"

But the hurt within him was still too engulfing. So he returned in a cold, bitter voice, "Yeah, well, you were two minutes too late, Bess." He tossed his pencil down and rose to his feet. "Do you know what it did to me when you looked at me that way, like I was some—some crummy two-timer?'

"Why didn't you tell me about Betsy asking you for money? Why didn't you tell me what your brothers had been up to? If you had, it wouldn't have come as such a shock to me that day. Everything happened so fast—you got a new buggy, your father and brothers arrived at Rose Hill Farm and found the box of collectibles in your buggy, and everyone was upset because one was missing . . . then . . . your brother said you had loaned money to Betsy Mast . . . and rather than explain anything, you just got on your high horse and left. You walked away. From everyone. Including me."

Abruptly, Billy swung around and confronted her with

fists balled and veins standing out sharply on his neck. "I shouldn't have had to tell you I wasn't guilty. You should have known what kind of man I was. But I saw it in your eyes, Bess. I saw that flicker of doubt, so don't deny it."

"I won't," she whispered, sounding ashamed. Then, a little bolder, she said, "But you should consider what it felt like on my end. I didn't have any idea where you had gone. I kept thinking you'd come back, sooner or later, or would try to get in touch with me. Amos and I spent weeks, months, trying to locate you. Right around Christmas, someone told Amos where you were living east of Lancaster. He went to talk to you, to bring you home, but when he returned, he said you just wanted to be left alone. He said that if you wanted to come home, you would, but no one could force you to do something you didn't want to do."

"That's about right." Billy swallowed and stared at the glass wall, feeling a clot of emotion fill his throat.

"After that, I realized it was time to abandon hope of seeing you again. There was no mistaking the meaning of your silence."

"It doesn't matter anymore. It doesn't change anything. It's all ancient history."

"You don't mean that, Billy."

"Don't I?" he shot back, telling himself to disregard the tears that made her wide blue eyes shimmer. He stood like a ramrod, too stubborn to take the one step necessary to end this standoff. "I'll leave you to wonder, just like I felt after I left."

For the moment neither of them moved. He tried to tear his eyes from her, but it didn't quite work. He realized one of them had to be sensible, and was the first to look away.

"Well," she said in a small, remorseful voice, "I am sorry, Billy." She took a step closer. "I've wondered about one thing."

He kept his eyes on the graphs spread out on the workbench.

"What do you think ever happened to the Santa Claus bank? To that collectible?"

Most likely, his brothers sold it and wasted the money on liquor and ladies. Did it even matter anymore? "Like I said, it's ancient history. The only question I want answered is about the identity of this rose. Are you absolutely sure you don't remember anything about this rose? Anything your grandmother might have said about it?" He studied her face carefully, increasingly convinced by the way she avoided his eyes that there was something she wasn't telling him. He pointed a finger at her. "Bess, I want the truth. I've asked you before and you act slippery. Cagey, just like your grandmother. What do you know about this rose?"

She looked down at her hands, then drew a breath as if to say something more, but didn't.

"Bess. If there's something you know about this rose, you need to tell me."

"I vaguely remember something about a special old rose, but I can't know for sure if it was *this* rose. Mammi had so many special roses."

"I heard all that before. Tell me what you do know."

"It's a long story."

"I want to hear this." He patted the wooden stool. "Sit. And talk."

"It goes back to that autumn after my grandfather passed and I was staying with my grandmother for an extra week to help her adjust. A week turned into a month, and there was still no discussion of me returning to Ohio . . ."

Late October 1969, an overcast, dismal day. Bess and her grandmother were crossing Main Street in downtown Stoney Ridge just as a pickup truck rounded the corner. Mammi jammed her fists on her deluxe-sized hips and planted herself in the middle of the road. The driver had to veer wildly to avoid hitting her and ended up swerving his truck far to the right, then jerking to the left to miss a telephone pole, before he ran his truck off the road and came to a stop.

The driver climbed out of the truck, beside himself in outrage.

You'd never seen a more surprised look on Mammi. "Well, skin me for a polecat," she said, thunderstruck. "If it isn't Charlie Oakley."

He threw his cap on the ground. "Look what you've done now, Bertha Riehl!"

"Me? You're the one who nearly ran over a poor, defenseless little child." Mammi pulled Bess in front of her to prove the point. "You never did know how to drive a straight line."

Charlie Oakley was the bane of Mammi's existence. He seemed like a harmless old man, with bib overalls over a graying T-shirt. But Mammi had warned Bess not to be fooled by Charlie's stature. He called himself a grower and Mammi called him "a fellow who didn't know the difference between thine and mine." He had a reputation for sneaking into people's yards to dig up valuable perennials from their gardens and selling them to unsuspecting nurseries. He had made a serious mistake when he slipped onto Rose Hill Farm under the dark of night and made off with Mammi's Most

Special Rose. Yesterday, she had discovered the disappearance of her rose and it lit a fire under her.

Charlie unlatched the tailgate of his pickup truck and climbed up. He uprighted a few boxes, then finally shook his head, furious with Mammi. "I'm supposed to get these over to a fellow in Lancaster by five p.m. or I don't get paid. I gotta call him."

Mammi had her nose in the back of the truck. She hitched a leg up on the tailgate of the truck. "Give me a boost, Bess."

It was slow going. Bess huffed and puffed and pushed until Mammi heaved herself up onto the bed of the truck.

All the while, an agitated Charlie sputtered and complained, pointing a long finger at her. "You stay out of my merchandise, Bertha Riehl."

For her part, Mammi didn't seem to be paying any attention to Charlie Oakley's travails as she peered into boxes. "You got something to hide?"

Charlie's face grew red. "You just leave my merchandise alone. I've a mind to sue you for jaywalking."

She reached down and picked up a box thrown on its side, then opened it up to look closely inside. "Now, Charlie, even you wouldn't be mean enough to sue a poor little widder lady."

Charlie started to sputter again and Mammi told him to simmer down, that she'd find a way to get his truck out of the ditch for him. "Bess, go run to the Sweet Tooth Bakery and ask Dottie Stroot to call Caleb Zook. You remember him—he's the one who buried my Samuel. He won't mind helping and he doesn't live too far. New ministers love jobs like this. Tell him to bring a good horse or two, and rope.

Lots of rope. Take this reckless driver down to the bakery with you. He can use the phone there."

"Reckless? Reckless!" Charlie's jaw started flapping.

"You run along, Bess," Mammi said, ignoring him. Charlie eased himself off the back of the truck and followed behind Bess.

Dottie Stroot was extremely annoyed that Bess didn't intend to buy anything from the bakery. When she heard Bertha Riehl had sent Bess to make a phone call, the news practically sent her through the roof. "That woman!" She pursed her lips like a dried berry and finally relented after Charlie exclaimed his very livelihood was in jeopardy if he didn't get to Lancaster by five o'clock. Plus he bought a bag of day-old pastries.

By the time Bess and Charlie Oakley returned to the crime scene, Mammi was resting on a sidewalk bench. She supervised from afar as Charlie and Bess set to work to get the boxes turned right side up in the bed of the truck. They were nearly done by the time they heard a familiar clopping of hooves and jangles of harness, and there was Caleb Zook in a wagon behind two enormous horses with hooves the size of dinner plates.

Caleb Zook laughed as Bess studied the horses' big heads. "They're called Percherons. My wife Jorie breeds them. They're stronger than a tow truck."

Bess and Bertha stood out of the way as Caleb tied ropes to the truck's back bumper and attached the ropes to the horses' harnesses. "Pull," Caleb called to the horses. Bess was fascinated to see the way their nostrils flared as they strained to pull, pull, pull. Little by little, the truck was pulled out of the ditch.

Satisfied that there wasn't any damage to his truck, Charlie thanked Caleb, scowled at Mammi, and hopped into his truck to speed off to Lancaster.

"Well, Bertha," Caleb said, "that's that. Do you need a ride home?"

"We'll take you up on that," Mammi said. "I'm so worn out from helping Charlie Oakley that I want to fold up like an empty feed sack."

Bess scrambled into the back of the wagon as Caleb heaved and hoisted Mammi into the passenger seat. Slow going for him too, Bess noticed. As he led the horses down Stoney Leaf Drive, he asked Bess how long she planned to stay in Stoney Ridge.

"Just a little longer," Mammi answered for her.

"Where's Jonah?" Caleb asked.

"He went home after the funeral. Had to work. Plus, too many memories for Jonah in Stoney Ridge. Bess is staying on to help me in my time of sorrow."

Caleb glanced over at Bertha. Bess wondered if he was thinking the same thing she was: Mammi didn't seem to be a woman who needed much coddling, newly widowed or not.

Later that night, Mammi could hardly get through her chores for her haste. She had two pans in the kitchen sink, one of suds, one to rinse. She washed, Bess dried, and she was hurrying her along.

"Mammi, where are we going?"

"Got an errand. Bundle up. It's a brisk night."

By then Bess knew she was in for something.

Mammi hurried into the barn and reappeared a moment later, pulling the reins of Frieda, the buggy horse. In the blink of an eye, she hooked Frieda's traces to the buggy shafts and away they went down Stoney Leaf Drive, heading toward town a few miles away, on a moonless autumn night. When they reached the ditch where the truck had swerved, Mammi pointed with a flashlight to something large under a tree. "There it is."

"A box?" Bess said, confused. "Did Charlie Oakley forget a box?" Understanding dawned on her. "You knew! You put it there! While I was making the phone call to Caleb Zook at the Sweet Tooth Bakery . . . you hid this box!"

"Nonsense. Charlie Oakley forgot it. He was in such a blamed hurry to get to Lancaster by five o'clock to collect his money. No wonder he practically ran us down." She pointed the beam of the flashlight at the box. "Go on."

"Me?" Bess's voice came out in a squeak. *Of course, me.* She carefully made her way down the ditch toward the tree on the other side. She picked up the box and climbed back to where her grandmother sat in the buggy.

"Mammi, isn't it stealing?" Bess said as she set the box on the floor of the buggy.

Mammi was dumbfounded. "Charlie Oakley's done the stealing. We're putting things back where they belong."

They'd barely gotten back home and Frieda in her stall when Mammi pulled out her flower books and started to hunt for rare roses. "What kind of rose is it?" Bess asked.

"It looks like the rose my great-great-great-great-great-great-great-grandmother brought over from the Old Country, her most treasured possession, and planted in the side yard—until it went missing. I trimmed it a few weeks ago. I was so busy tending Samuel that I didn't notice until yesterday."

"Was it a special rose?"

"Very." She fingered her chins thoughtfully. "The most special one of all."

Bess yawned. "I've got the wearies." Mammi was muttering away about the rose—so absorbed that she hardly noticed Bess was heading to bed. At the bottom of the stairwell, she turned to say good night, smiling at the details about the rose that Mammi was listing aloud—almost like ingredients to bake a cake. "Good night."

Mammi waved her away. "Don't interrupt my strain of thought."

"Train," Bess corrected, but Mammi wasn't listening. While it might have been true that her grandmother didn't need much coddling in her new widowhood, it was the first time she had seen a bounce in her step since her grandfather's funeral.

As Bess told Billy the story, he listened, amazed. He rubbed his jaw, looking at the rose. "Do you think this could be the rose she was talking about? The most special rose of all?"

"I don't know for sure. I really don't."

"Don't you remember what she called it? What class it might belong to? Or anything about the bloom? Single or double petals? Any clue to help identify the rose. Any clue at all."

Bess shook her head. "Billy, I was only twelve and I didn't love roses yet. That didn't happen until the summer I was fifteen."

He remembered. "What about the color of the bloom?"

She bit her lip and he had trouble keeping his eyes from wandering there. "I'm pretty sure the rose wasn't in bloom. It looked pretty sickly."

"Okay, okay—that actually helps." He pressed his fingertips together. "Let's see—this was late October. That means it probably wouldn't have been a repeat blooming bush, which means it isn't a modern rose. So that definitely rules out the China roses." He loved this. Loved it. Rose rustling was like detective work—tracking clues, narrowing down the field, creating a hypothesis, drawing a conclusion. "Didn't Bertha keep any records?"

"No." Bess tapped her head. "She kept her rose knowledge up here."

Billy bit on his bottom lip. "But she did like to talk about roses. Bess—she *must* have talked about it. Think, Bess, think. Try to remember anything she might have said."

Bess squeezed her eyes shut and didn't say a word for a long moment. "Deep pink. Bold fragrance. Medium, full, small clusters, button-eye, cupped bloom form." She bit her lip, concentrating deeply. "And light green foliage." Her eyes popped open in surprise. "I remember! Mammi was at the kitchen table, the rosebush was next to her, and she listed aloud its characteristics as she went through her book, repeating them over and over to herself. I thought she was sun touched."

He grabbed a pen and piece of paper and scribbled down Bess's list. "Now we're getting somewhere." A grin lifted the corners of his lips. "I haven't thought about Charlie Oakley in years. I can just picture a standoff between Bertha and Charlie Oakley. I'll bet my last dollar your grandmother had it all planned out to force his truck into the ditch. She was something else, that Bertha Riehl."

"She was . . . one of a kind."

Billy lifted his head and their eyes met. His were bemused,

hers relieved. A smile began tugging at one corner of his mouth, a smile as slow as molasses. He chuckled. Inside him the laughter built until it erupted, and Bess started to giggle, then she joined him. They stood in the greenhouse laughing together for the first time. When it ended, a subtle change had transpired.

He wanted to reach out and touch her cheek, to see if her skin was as soft as it looked, velvety as a rose petal and warmed from the sun shining through the greenhouse. Bess had asked him if it would be so terrible to admit he still cared for her. Would it? He studied her, finding it so hard to let loose.

He wondered if her insides were stirring like his. He might not have known had she not at that very moment dropped her gaze and fussily checked the hair at the back of her neck. He leaned closer to her, his senses swirling with her nearness.

Just then a horse and buggy appeared at the top of the driveway and came to a stop at the rise.

"Well," she said at last, the single word coming out on a soft gust of breath.

"I'd better get back to work," he said, ending the moment of closeness.

From the greenhouse window, they saw someone step out of the buggy and Bess gasped.

Amos Lapp had arrived.

THIRTEEN

Bess flew out of the greenhouse and ran to the buggy, hoping Amos wouldn't have noticed which direction she came from, but he had. Even before she reached him, her heart hurt. He stood by the buggy, his sad face turning pink as he self-consciously shuffled his feet. His eyes looked a little to the side, not right at hers.

Bess could almost reach out and touch the gulf between them. She willed herself to stay calm, clear the sticky cloud of confusion out of her voice. "Amos, I wasn't expecting you today. But . . . I'm glad you came." She realized she was still holding the fading Popcorn rose bloom and handed it to him. "It's a new cultivar. Bred in 1973. A miniature." He took it in his hands and looked at it thoughtfully.

Silence fell again, strained, before she thought to offer, "Lainey made some fresh gingerbread if you'd like to come inside."

"No, thank you. I just needed to see you. To talk to you for a moment." Their eyes met and she was surprised at finding them so different from Billy's. Amos's brown eyes were mild, calm, Billy's stormy blue, so like their temperaments.

Despite the knife-cold wind, a trickle of perspiration coursed down her spine, reminding her of the importance of this conversation. Amos only stared at Bess, not moving a muscle. When he finally spoke, his voice was guttural with emotion. "Bess, we made a promise to each other, you and I. Promises are meant to be kept."

"I know, Amos," she reassured him. "I know that." She saw his Adam's apple move in his throat.

Their eyes met briefly. "I'm worried that I'm losing you."

A thorn seemed to pierce her heart. "I just need a little more time," she said.

"That's all?"

"That's all," she repeated. She reached out for his hand. He grasped it like a lifeline and squeezed so hard, her knuckles cracked softly.

A poignant silence fell. She felt herself on the verge of tears and her gaze dropped to his chest. He lifted her chin with a finger.

"Aw, Bess, honey . . ." He wrapped her close and rocked her.

He released her and leaned back, holding her elbows with his hands. "Maggie wants us to meet her at Blue Lake Pond to go ice skating this afternoon. I was hoping you'd say yes and come along with us."

"Oh, I'd like to, but—" Her eyes darted automatically to the greenhouse and instantly she regretted it. A sense of impending ache, gone for a brief moment, returned to settle between them.

He swallowed and stared at the greenhouse. "Why did he have to come back?" Amos said thickly, reaching out to hold Bess so tightly it seemed he would squeeze the breath from her.

"Amos, what are you saying?" she cried, struggling out of his arms. "He's . . . he was a friend you loved. Your cousin. Are you saying you wish he were lost to us?"

"I didn't mean I wanted him lost, Bess . . . not lost." With a horrified expression, Amos leaned against the buggy and dropped his face into his hands. "What am I saying?" he groaned miserably, shaking his head.

Studying him, Bess, too, suffered. She understood the conflict of emotions that battled inside of Amos. She felt the same conflicts. She cared for them both, each in a different way and for different reasons, yet enough to want to hurt neither.

"The rose will open soon, Amos. Then everything will go back the way it was."

He reached out and cupped her cheek in his hand. "Of course. Of course it will." His voice still hinted of skepticism. A small bird darted past them and his gaze followed it up to a tree. "An evening grosbeak." He turned back to Bess with a quizzical look on his face. "Do you like birds? I've never asked."

"I like them well enough, I suppose. I like them best when they eat aphids off the roses. I like them least when they take their job too seriously and peck right through the buds."

He tilted his head as if he were considering her answer. Then, without another word, he climbed back in the buggy. After he drove off, she noticed he had dropped the white Popcorn bloom she had given to him on the driveway.

And she thought of how differently he viewed the roses than Billy had.

Slowly, Bess turned and walked to the farmhouse. Lainey stood by the kitchen sink, grating carrots for coleslaw. Bess slumped down at the kitchen table and put her head on her arms; the tears she'd held at bay since morning came gushing with a vengeance. A moment later, Lainey's consoling arms were wrapped around her.

"Why, Bess, is this about the wedding? I saw Amos come and go so quickly. Did he say something to upset you?"

"Oh, Lainey," she wailed.

"Shh . . . shh . . . it can't be as bad as all that."

"It is." Bess reached for a paper napkin from the pile in the center of the table. "It's j-just awful."

Lainey drew back to see Bess's face. "What could be so awful? I can't help you if you won't tell me."

"I . . . l-love him."

Lainey barely bit back a smile. "What's so awful about that? I would think Amos would be happy to know that."

"Not Amos." Bess shook her head, tears splattering. "B-B-Billy."

"Ah. I see." Lainey blew out a puff of air. "I was afraid of that." A new rash of weeping wilted Bess. Lainey rubbed her shuddering back. "Does Amos know?"

Bess nodded wretchedly. "I think so."

"Poor Amos."

"He still wants to set a new date. He said that promises are meant to be kept."

"That's true, but you haven't actually made a promise yet. Have you spoken to Billy about your feelings?"

"Yes. Sort of. I tried to, anyway."

"Well, that took some courage. What did he say?"

"He said no. Absolutely not. 'Never going to happen' were his exact words. And he wouldn't tell me why."

Lainey frowned. "That boy is just as stubborn as his father."

"Don't tell him that. He wants nothing to do with his family. Or with the Amish. Or with me."

"Poor Billy. Poor Bess. Poor Amos." Lainey handed another paper napkin to Bess. A pile of scrunched-up napkins sat on the table. "So what do you want to do?"

"I want to keep everyone from getting hurt," Bess said miserably.

"I don't think that's possible, little one."

Lainey's eyes lifted to the window and Bess followed her gaze. Billy was striding past the barn from the greenhouse and paused for a moment, looking up at the farmhouse as if he considered coming in. He wavered, right on the brink. Then he dropped his head, tucked his hands in his coat pockets, and hurried down the hill.

The bleak gray sky seemed the perfect accompaniment for Amos's morose mood. He guided the horse over to Blue Lake Pond, not because he really wanted to go ice skating, but because Maggie had said she would wait for him. She was still sneaking around during the day, postponing the inevitable: telling her father she'd been fired from the Sweet Tooth Bakery until after he had hired another teacher. Amos spent an extraordinary amount of time trying to think up a solution to Maggie's problem, until it occurred to him that it wasn't *his* problem.

He steered the horse down a road he seldom used, a familiar shortcut to get to the pond. Far off in the distance, he spied the rooftop of Billy's childhood home.

Billy Lapp seemed to be everywhere.

The days turned back and Amos was a boy again, a time

when Billy's mother was still alive, and Amos had felt comfortable slamming in and out of their house at Billy's heels. He was fishing with Billy, presenting his mother with a fresh catch, staying for supper when she'd cooked it. Playing tricks on Billy's brothers to quietly get back at them for bullying Billy: greasing horse reins with Vaseline, adding weights inside of hay bales, putting mice in their tack boxes, loosening screws on their bedroom door handles so they would get locked in.

How many times had he and Billy run along this road to swim in the pond on a hot summer day? He pictured the two of them as they'd been then, but immediately Bess's face alone emblazoned itself upon his memory. He moved onto the turnoff for Blue Lake Pond, wondering what Bess was doing at this very moment.

"Amos! Amos Lapp!"

He snapped out of his funk to see Maggie Zook waving to him near a row of buggies. She had saved a prime parking spot for his horse and buggy, and the sight of her frantically waving to him made him grin, then chuckle. He pulled the horse to a stop, grabbed his skates from the seat of the buggy, tied the horse's reins to a tree, and joined Maggie to walk down to the pond. In the cold her cheeks were bright red, her eyes snapping brown. She pointed to a bird preening on an icy branch. "Is that a white-winged crossbill?" she asked in a reverent voice.

"I think it is." They stilled for a moment, until it flew off.

Her arm brushed against his as they walked along the narrow path. Face warming at this familiarity, he stole a look at Maggie. Lately he felt a bit odd alone with her, as if their old camaraderie was slipping away and turning them in a new direction.

They sat down on a big log to put on their skates. She finished first and stood on wobbly legs, carefully picking her way down the shore to join other skaters as they skimmed across the ice. Leaning back on the log after lacing up his skates, Amos took off his hat and ran a hand through his unkempt hair. He sighed, wishing Bess had agreed to come skating, wondering if she was going to spend the afternoon in the greenhouse with Billy. He knew this outing was intended to get his mind away from his troubles, but his troubles kept finding him.

Maggie whirled around in her usual fashion, reminding Amos again of the erratic flight of a hummingbird—darting this way and that with such abrupt turns that it seemed she wasn't done with one turn before heading for the next. He watched her in amazement.

Unexpectedly, Amos felt his spirits rise as he skated after Maggie, hands behind his back. She began to skate away from him, circling and doing a little twirl. He sailed past her, then turned to face her, skating backward.

She slid to a stop and clapped with happiness. "Teach me how to do that!" she called, her breath curling in the icy air.

Clasping her mittened hands, he tugged her toward the center of the pond where the ice was smoother.

"Push with your calf muscles," he instructed her. "Let your legs take you backwards."

The lake's surface was slick in places and she nearly fell, but Amos was always near, steadying her, until she got a sense of the movement required to skate backward. They skated until their feet grew numb with cold.

He pointed to the bonfire on the shore, where skaters were warming themselves. "Let's go."

They drank hot chocolate from a thermos Maggie had brought along and ate a few Christmas cookies she had baked. The gray cloud cover from earlier in the day had broken up and moved on, swept away by a brisk wind from the north. Maggie's gaze was on the wispy white clouds.

"Mares' tails, my dad calls them, as they gallop across a delft-blue sky." She looked at him square in the eyes. "Do you ever wish you could jump on a cloud and skim across the sky, the way we skated on the pond?"

He actually had such a thought now and then, but would never have dreamed of saying so for fear of sounding silly. "Maybe," he admitted, ill at ease with her sitting so close.

Maggie pointed out clouds that resembled, in her vivid imagination, people in their church—one with a big watermelon belly like the new minister, another with a pointy chin like Sylvia Glick, three soft puffy ones who reminded her of her ancient great-aunts, who considered themselves first-rate matchmakers. He laughed out loud at that. Bachelors were known to slip out windows and hide under beds when Maggie's old aunties arrived at the door, bearing a long list of eligible girls.

Time seemed to stand still, easing the soreness he felt over Bess just a bit.

FOURTEEN

With not a minute to spare, Billy had caught the last bus out of Lancaster to College Station for the day. After he left Rose Hill Farm, he felt himself drawn toward his old home, almost as if he couldn't help himself. He wanted to be alone, he didn't want anyone to know that he might stop in—he wasn't even sure if he was *going* to stop in—but he couldn't seem to keep his legs from taking him down that familiar road. The air was searing cold, but he stood for a long time at the base of the driveway and stared up at the farmhouse. It looked strangely empty. If it weren't for a thin tendril of gray smoke curling out of the central chimney, he might have thought it deserted.

The fields, he had noticed, weren't just silent in winter's rest. The dirt was gray, no longer brown. Years of no-till farming, with cash crops like tobacco and wheat and corn that depleted the soil, had taken a toll. The ground looked spent, exhausted. He left the road and approached through the woods, standing hidden in the trees, studying the place. It was a mess: piles of rusting tools and busted implements littered the barnyard, at least two corners of the front stoop needed jacking up and looked about to drop off the house, peeling paint from outbuildings, missing roof shingles, a sagging clothesline, a gate to the yard off its hinges. What had his brothers been doing all these years?

The Lapp farm had never looked pristine and cared for like other Amish homes, but *this* . . . this was pathetic. Worse than anything he remembered.

He stood there a moment, feeling lonesome, even shaky, as his mind reviewed the last week he had lived in his father's home. First came the wheat harvest, then came the discovery that his brothers were adding sawdust to their wheat sacks, which, it turned out, was his father's mastermind. Finally, the Bann for his father. And then Billy felt surrounded by an invisible, impenetrable fog. His brothers avoided him, his father didn't look him in the eye. Tension was mounting at home, silent but palpable. Something was coming.

September 1973. A few days after Caleb Zook had placed his father under the Bann, a truck blew a tire as it rounded a sharp hairpin turn not far from the Lapp farm. Billy was in the phone shanty down by the road, listening to messages, when he heard the burst of the blowout and the flap-flap-flap of rubber shards hitting the road. He ran outside to see if he could help. The driver was already out of his cab and in the back of his truck, checking on cargo, worried the blowout had caused the contents to jostle. Inside the truck was antique furniture covered in thick pads and boxes of collectibles destined for auction in New York City. Billy's brothers drifted over to see if they could help. The driver had a spare tire and a jack, but no wrench to loosen bolts, so Billy was sent to the barn to get tools. Soon, the tire was changed and the driver was gratefully on his way.

Billy went back to the phone shanty to finish listening to messages. He had ordered a courting buggy months ago from the local buggy maker. It was time to court Bess properly and he planned to use the money saved up from his Rose Hill Farm job to purchase it. His father, unlike other Amish fathers, didn't see any reason to buy courting buggies for his sons. There was a message on the answering machine that the buggy was ready for pickup. Later, Billy realized the timing could not have been worse.

That afternoon, he'd gone to town to withdraw his savings to pay for the buggy. As he walked out of the bank, he happened to see his old girlfriend, Betsy Mast. She had just come from a visit with her parents and was quite upset. She needed money and they refused to help her. She asked, with those big round eyes of hers, if she could borrow a little to tide her over. How could he refuse? He spared what he could, and Betsy threw her arms around him in gratitude. That was all there was to it—Billy had to hurry to get to the buggy maker before supper. Back at the farm, he hid the buggy behind the barn and covered it with old blankets. He was afraid his brothers would take it out on a joyride and he wanted to surprise Bess with it tomorrow.

When he walked into the farmhouse, he found his father and brothers at the kitchen table, waiting for him.

"What's happened?" Billy said, a feeling of dread rolling over him.

Ten seconds passed in cold silence.

"Sit down," his father said.

Billy took his place at the table and tried to read his brothers' faces, but they were the very picture of innocence.

"The truck driver with the flat tire came back to the house this afternoon," his father said. "He said a box was missing from his truck. Most of the items in the box weren't extremely valuable, but there was a rare cast-iron Santa Claus bank made before the turn of the century that he said was worth thousands of dollars. He claimed he would lose his job if that collectible wasn't returned."

"So he thinks one of us took it?" Billy said, incredulous. "We were trying to help him."

Billy's father raised his chin at him directly. "Your brothers said you slipped up to the barn while they were changing the tire."

So. This was it. This was how his brothers would exact revenge. Instead of feeling cowed, Billy felt a surge of power. He raised his own chin, aware of how similar his profile was to his father's. "I did not steal a box from that truck." But he was pretty sure he knew who did.

His father opened his mouth as if he were going to say more, but instead, he rose stiffly and left the room.

In the middle of the night, Billy slipped out to the barn with a flashlight and searched through his brothers' hiding places in the hayloft, where his father never went. It didn't take much effort to locate the box. Obviously, Mose's handiwork. Mose was a liar and cheat, but he wasn't clever like Sam and Ben. Billy opened the box and there, on the top, cradled in old newspaper, was the rusty old cast-iron Santa Claus bank. Billy took it out and looked it over. It was rusty, dented, with peeling paint, and surprisingly heavy for a child's toy. Amazing to think it was worth thousands of dollars; to Billy it looked like junk. Carefully, he tucked it back in the newspaper nest and stashed the box in the back of his new buggy. Tomorrow, after work, he would head to town and ship the box to the truck driver. But this time, he would handle it quietly. He wasn't about to go to Caleb Zook about Mose's pilfering.

The next afternoon, Billy had just finished cutting spent canes in a rose field at Rose Hill Farm and was on his way to the greenhouse to put away some tools when he saw his father and brothers standing beside his new buggy. All the tension in their grim expressions seemed focused on Billy as he approached them.

For a moment no one spoke, then his father leaned forward, knitting his fingers together. "Son, you lied to me." He looked more sad than angry.

"What are you talking about?" Billy asked.

"The box from that truck. Your brothers found it in your buggy."

"I know. I found it in the barn." Billy looked at Mose first, then Sam and Ben, each one, though they kept their eyes fixed on their father. "I was going to send it to the truck driver this afternoon."

"What about that iron Santa Claus bank?"

"What are you talking about?" Billy went to the back of the buggy and saw the box was open. He rooted around in the newspaper, but the Santa Claus bank was gone. "Where is it?"

"That's what we want to know," Sam said. "What have you done with it?"

"It was there this morning and now it's gone." Billy saw his brothers exchange a look. They were trying to frame him.

But his father . . . did he believe Billy had taken it? "Do you honestly think I would have stolen it?"

"Out of the blue," Ben said, "you've bought yourself a new buggy."

"Out of the blue? I ordered it months ago! I worked hard for that buggy. I earned it from my work here at Rose Hill Farm!"

Sam turned to Billy with thinly veiled hostility. "Kind of curious timing, wouldn't you say?"

Billy wasn't interested in what Sam thought. He looked his father straight in the eye. Dry-throated, expressionless, he asked him flatly, "And you think I did it?"

His father frowned. "Even a saint is tempted by an open door."

Billy looked at him in disbelief. Then his eyes skimmed over his conspiratorial brothers. "You're kidding, right? Pulling my leg?"

"It's hardly a laughing matter," his father said. "The facts are the facts. That collectible's gone missing and you're suddenly tossing money around town."

"Tossing money around town? What?"

"Sam said he saw you handing cash to your old girlfriend Betsy Mast," Ben said.

"Betsy Mast was clinging to you for dear life," Sam said, a bit too loudly.

She was grateful, that's all, Billy was about to say, when it occurred to him that Sam was projecting his voice for a reason. He whirled around and there was Bess, standing not ten feet away from them, overhearing the entire conversation. Eyes rounded in dismay, her face was a mixture of shock and disappointment.

"Oh Billy . . . ," she admonished breathily. "Not Betsy Mast. Not again."

"You've been caught red-handed, Billy boy," Sam taunted, a malicious smile curling his lips. "Don't bother denying it."

"Don't even bother denying it," Mose echoed.

Billy's face felt hot enough to ignite. He took his time answering, the words came out low and reluctant, though his insides felt hot and shaky. "I'm not denying that Betsy saw me in town and asked me for a loan. I gave her some money. But that was all there was to it." His eyes met Bess's, silently pleading with her to believe in him, but her gaze broke from his and she looked away.

Oh Bess, Bess, not you, too. They could all think whatever they wanted, but she was his girl, his friend. She thought him capable of such a thing?

At that moment, Maggie Zook came out of the greenhouse, brushing dirt off her hands. She stood next to Bess and looked at Billy and his family, standing off to each other. "Hi there! What am I missing? What's going on?"

Billy looked at Maggie, at Bess, then turned back to look at his father. This was unbelievable! Were they all going to believe something based on his brothers' hearsay?

He thought about fighting them—but for what? He was tired of fighting. It seemed he'd been fighting his whole life. And a single questioning stare from his father, one from Bess, had undone him. "Nothing, Maggie," Billy said, disgusted. "You haven't missed a thing."

He'd had it. Everything he thought was important changed in that moment. Family, friends, church, and faith. He threw his clippers and gloves on the ground and walked down the driveway. He left it all behind in Stoney Ridge.

Billy found a job working at a commercial nursery over in east Lancaster, one of the nurseries that ordered Bertha's roses for special requests by customers. The owner had offered a job invitation to Billy once, and now he took him up on it. He rented a room out of a lady's house, and he waited. He waited for the collectible to turn up, for his father to see through his brothers' flimsy story and find him, to ask him to return home. He waited for Bess to come to him and apologize for not trusting him.

Give them time, he told himself. They'd all come around to see the truth.

Days went by, weeks, months. Time crept like a snail. The days limped by. November, then December. By the time Christmas arrived, Billy sat alone in his rented room in an old lady's dingy house and faced the truth. No one was going to come. Not his father, not Bess.

Billy had been forgotten.

A pair of black crows jabbered above him, squawking at him, snapping Billy back from the past to the present. He took in a deep breath, and that was the end of the remembering for a while.

Part of him longed to go knock on the door and tell his father he was home. But what good would that do? Nothing would have changed; he'd slip right back in the same role—Der Ruschde. *The runt.*

As he stood watching the farmhouse, he felt a wave of loneliness. It was a familiar feeling to him, like a sad old friend. A cold wind cut right through his jacket and he suddenly realized how late it was getting. Evening was drawing on, darkness was climbing the trees. When he looked up at the sky, it seemed impossible that his father and his brothers saw the same sun and stars he did. He felt too far away to share the same heavens.

He spun on the heels of his boots and walked back down the road.

The wind came up in the night and the old farmhouse creaked and groaned like an arthritic old man. Bess knew the chill would take its toll on her father's fragile back and the thought worried her. She wondered if the day was coming when he would need to move to a warmer climate, like Pinecraft, Florida. Summer all year long.

But what would that mean for Rose Hill Farm? Who would tend Mammi's roses?

She writhed in bed for a long time. It had been an emotional day. Every part of her life felt like it was hanging on a precipice—just a slight push and things could go one way or the other.

Late in the afternoon, Amos and Maggie dropped by after ice skating, and again he hinted to Bess, in his gentle roundabout way, about setting a new wedding date. Again, she hedged—told him to wait until after the holidays, pretended everything was fine. But they both knew: there was no pretending. Billy was there between them every hour of the night and day.

She felt guilty, ashamed. She didn't want to hurt Amos or betray him with her constant thoughts of Billy.

Billy. Today she sensed a slight loosening of that stiff distance he maintained so carefully. They had a moment of closeness in the greenhouse when time melted away and it was just the two of them again, sharing a love of Mammi's roses, finding a way back to each other. And then Billy closed up, a clam in a shell. Another precipice.

Watching his face tighten into that calloused mask nearly broke her heart. What would it take for Billy to trust again?

She had nearly told him how much she had missed him, how not a day had passed when she didn't think of him and wonder about him, but she was afraid to say it, afraid of being rebuffed again. Her precipice.

Somewhere between thinking of a move to Florida for her father's back and remembering the summer she had come to live at Rose Hill Farm, she dropped off to a troubled sleep. She was tending roses with her grandmother in the greenhouse and saw Mammi fussing over a potted rose. Bess didn't recognize the rose, so she turned to her grandmother, while at the same time thinking, *Mammi has passed on*, and asked, "What's the name of that rose?"

"That rose?" Mammi said. "That's the Charming Nancy. My most precious rose of all. My great-great-great-great-great-great-great-grandmother brought it over on the ship from Rotterdam. But I'm worried about it. The leaves are yellowing. That no-good Charlie Oakley nearly killed it when he dug it up. Billy says it needs more iron."

Bess startled awake. Her eyes snapped open. *Charming Nancy!*

FIFTEEN

The grandfather clock in the living room chimed softly. Bess stirred, blinked a few times, then sat bolt upright in bed. Pearl-gray morning light filled her bedroom—that shivery extra-early hour. What time could she reasonably expect Billy to be in the greenhouse at College Station? Seven o'clock? Eight o'clock? She had to tell him about the rose. About the Charming Nancy. She took a measured breath.

If this rose was Mammi's Charming Nancy rose, then Billy would be able to identify it. And he would leave. Then what?

She didn't know. She just didn't know.

A memory rekindled in her head, a forgotten scene, a wispy remembrance about Billy and a rose. Something cried out in her mind: This rose! It was this very rose.

July 1972, a hot and humid summer morning. So hot, Mammi said, that chickens laid hard-boiled eggs. Her sleeves were rolled back on her big arms and she was in a state over a potted rose she had placed on newspaper on the kitchen table. "Breaks my heart," Mammi muttered. "My Charming

Nancy is ailing again." Her jaw clenched in a familiar way. "Charlie Oakley," she said, like that explained it. "Nothing but a horse potato."

"Patootie." Bess had grown accustomed to her grandmother's peculiar mangling of the English language. "What's wrong?"

"It was finally coming back after Charlie Oakley dramatized it—"

"Traumatized."

"—and nearly snuffed out its life by yanking it out of the ground like a bird digging for a worm. For three years I have babied it and nursed it back to life, and now it's suffering all over again."

Bess joined her at the table to peer at the rose. "Why do you call it the Charming Nancy?"

Mammi clutched her chest. "Hasn't your father taught you anything about our people?" She shook her head. "It's a dire worry to me."

Bess didn't think Mammi worried about much of anything. She wasn't a thinker. She was a doer.

"It's a story of how our people came over the ocean from the old country. They'd been tortured and beaten and burned alive and they had to escape Europe. So they set off in a little ship called the *Charming Nancy* and sailed to America. Hearty folk."

"I think you mean hardy," Bess said.

"That's what I said."

"Sounds nice, the *Charming Nancy*."

"It wasn't. It was a stinking floating bucket of filth."

"And they brought roses over on the boat?"

"The ship. A boat fits on a ship."

Of course. Mammi was suddenly an expert on the sea.

"And just one rose. My great-great-great-great-great-great-great-grandmother tried to bring more. There's a long story attached to it—I'll tell you one day. She loved roses."

"Like you," Bess said in a thoughtful voice.

"And you." Mammi peered at her over her spectacles. "It's part of being a Riehl. You can't help it. Roses are in your blood."

It was true. She was fifteen now and had grown to love roses.

Billy was crossing the yard to the barn with a sack of rose blooms slung over his shoulder. Mammi dried them in the barn and used them to make soaps and jam. Mammi shouted out the kitchen window at him. "Billy Lapp, why would a rose leaf turn yellow?"

Billy stopped and looked up at the house. "Could be a lot of reasons. Is the vein dark?"

"Yes," Mammi barked.

Billy set the sack on the ground and shielded his eyes from the sun. "It might be your soil needs some amendments. When the veins stay dark green but the interveinal areas turn light green to yellow, that usually means it needs something. My guess is iron."

"It's never happened before."

"It's not unusual," he intoned, folding his arms on his chest in what Bess came to recognize as his schoolmaster mode, "especially since soil around here"—he swept his arm in a half-circle—"doesn't have much clay in it. You see, iron aids chlorophyll formation, and forms sugar-burning enzymes that activate nitrogen fixation. Iron is required for healthy, vigorous plants with dark green leaves. An iron deficiency usually affects younger plant leaves first with a general lightening of the leaf color."

Mammi's lips puckered in disgust. "Can't you speak plain English?"

Billy grinned. "It means you need to find a way to add iron into the soil."

"How?"

"You buy soil amendments."

Big mistake. Mammi didn't like to part with her money. She could squeeze the eagle on a quarter until it begged for mercy. "What else?" she shouted. She meant business.

"Well," Billy said in a droll tone, "you could bury a cast-iron fireplace poker along with it and wait a few centuries."

Mammi slammed the windowsill shut on that suggestion and turned to face her ailing rose. She patted her hair in a satisfied way, the faintest ghost of a smile flickering across her face.

Thinking back on that interaction, Bess laughed out loud. Could it really be *this* rose? It was followed by another thought that left her feeling sad and sorrowful. Mammi died before she had a chance to tell the story of the rose on the *Charming Nancy*. It seemed as if the last few weeks had been filled with reminders of lost opportunities, past regrets. She sighed, then shook off her remorse. If nothing else, these reminders served as a lesson to not allow more moments to pass by without saying what needed to be said.

After leaving a message at the Penn State Extension office for Billy, Bess spent the rest of the morning helping Lainey and Christy make Christmas cookies and candy. She kept one eye on the road, waiting for the sight of Billy's long stride.

It was past lunch when she spotted that familiar black hat bobbing up the driveway. She threw on her coat and mittens, told Lainey she'd be back soon, and practically flew down the driveway to meet him.

"I got your message to come right away," Billy said. "Why? Has the bud opened?"

"Not yet."

Billy frowned, so Bess quickly added, "I remember! I think I remember what it was called. Or at least what Mammi called it and where it came from, originally."

"So," Billy said, growing impatient. "Tell me."

She smiled. "Not here. Let's go to the rose."

Together, they went to the greenhouse and Billy made a beeline to the rose, dragged it from its corner, and hoisted it up on the workbench.

"Mammi said that her great-great-something grandmother—I've lost count of how many greats—came over from Europe on the *Charming Nancy*, and smuggled a rose with her."

"What?" Billy whispered, incredulous, turning his face to Bess. "On the *Charming Nancy*? The Amish *Mayflower*? Are you kidding me?" He drew in a breath and spoke with urgency. "Was it a rootball? A cane? A slip? A rosehip?"

"I don't know. Mammi was mostly annoyed that I'd never heard of the *Charming Nancy*."

"So this rose might have come over on the *Charming Nancy* ship." There was a hushed reverence in his voice. "I think the ship came over in 1737. This lone rose could be centuries old. Older than the Perle von Weissenstein. It could be the oldest known rose of German rootstock. An extinct rose."

"You really think *this* is that rose? I mean, I hope it is, but how could you know for sure? It's just a story Mammi told me—and you know how she embroidered the truth."

"Oh, we'll know all right. As soon as that rose opens up." The sepals were off, the rosebud was swelling, partially opened. And the fragrance! Its perfume was starting to lift and float through the greenhouse, its scent strongest near the workbench. For now. He grinned, then smiled broadly. "Just another day or two."

His smile, when he turned it on full force, was numbing. It turned her bones to butter and made her heart dance.

Maggie Zook was still spending her days studiously away from Beacon Hollow during her father's search for a new teacher. This morning, she stopped for coffee at Windmill Farm, said she was making her way, slowly, to Rose Hill Farm, and Amos jumped to offer to drive her there. He was eager for any excuse to see Bess, hoping more interaction might repair the strain between them. Last night, after he and Maggie dropped by Rose Hill Farm after ice skating, he felt even more uncomfortable and distant with Bess. He left her home wondering if it would ever be the same between them again. Whether Billy stayed in Stoney Ridge or not, he was never far from Bess's thoughts. Obviously, she still had feelings for him.

As the horse trotted down Stone Leaf Drive, Amos told Maggie that she couldn't keep up this facade of working at the Sweet Tooth Bakery much longer. "You're going to be found out. And what then?"

"I know, I know," she said in a glum tone. Then her face

brightened. "But I think today will be the last day. I heard Dad tell Jorie that he was going to ask Tillie about taking the teacher's job."

"Tillie Miller?" Amos shuddered.

Maggie nodded vigorously.

The poor scholars. Tillie was peculiar even for a school-teacher. She was a beady-eyed, sour spinster with a reedy, chirping voice like a rusty hinge and she made school a misery. Her only pleasure in life was to use large unnecessary words, as if she'd swallowed a dictionary. "Isn't she a little . . . old?"

"Gross is die Lehr." *There is nothing like knowing how.*

"Es is en langi Lehn as ken End hot." *It's a long lane that has no turning.* Long and dull.

Tillie Miller used to teach when he was a scholar. Once, in the prime of spring, Amos and Billy concocted a brilliant plan: they coughed and gagged like they were coming down with tuberculosis. Teacher Tillie pinched up her face like a prune, sent them home to bed, and off they went, sneezing and gasping for air, until they reached the bend in the road and took off in a gallop toward Blue Lake Pond. They spent the entire week fishing and swimming and lying in the sun. Somehow, their parents were never the wiser for it. Until the report cards came out. Billy and Amos were given big red Fs in every subject, with a note that they would need to double back for seventh grade.

"Yes, Tillie Miller. And stop making a face like that."

"Like what?"

"Like you just bit down on a popcorn kernel and broke a tooth." Maggie's spine went all stiff and starchy, reminding him of a schoolmarm. "Children learn best when they're given clear expectations. Tillie will bring order to the classroom. You have to give her that."

"Order, sure. With a ruler, she'll bring order. Wham! Those poor little children will have bloody knuckles by the end of the first day."

"Sore knuckles will cure a wandering mind."

Amos found it interesting that Maggie was such an expert on what was required to educate children, considering she wanted nothing to do with teaching. "Tillie will scare them into submission."

Maggie bit her lip. "She's the only choice left. Everyone else said no. Dad's asked six others. He's scraping the bottom of the barrel. Getting desperate." She started chewing on her thumbnail, a cue to Amos that she was getting nervous.

He eyed Maggie a little longer, wondering if she might be weakening her position toward the notion of teaching, then settled back again, staring at the road ahead. From far away came a faint sound like the rusty hinges of a swinging gate. It amplified into the rusty squawk of Canada Geese heading toward the Atlantic flyway. He and Maggie watched them grow from distant dots to a distinct flock. "Oh, pull over, Amos. Let's watch!"

She didn't even need to tell him. Amos was already turning the horse to the side of the road. Maggie leaned near him to peer out his window, so close he could smell the clean scent of starch from her prayer covering.

The wedge of geese came on, necks pointing the way south, wings moving with a grace that filled the buggy with silent reverence. They watched and listened, thrilling to a sight that stirred their blood.

Maggie suddenly looked up at Amos as if she knew his

thoughts. Their eyes met briefly before returning to the sky. As if unaware of its action, her hand moved gently to fit in his. He looked down at her hand, so small and soft, then closed his hand around hers. The cacophony of geese became a clatter that filled the air over the fields, passed over them, then drifted off, dimmer, dimmer until the graceful birds disappeared and the only sound remaining was the rustle of the wind in the treetops.

Seconds later, when she took back her hand to clap with delight, his hand felt remarkably empty and cold. The touch of her small hand still lingered, as though it had left its memory.

Billy had been in such a hurry to get to Rose Hill Farm after he received the message from Bess that he'd left without his backpack; it was filled with charts and notes and an important book he'd found on old German roses. He had hoped the rosebud had fully opened by now, but this news from Bess about remembering the Charming Nancy was almost as good. Maybe even better.

Bess had gone up to the house to help Lainey finish baking for Christmas—only a few days away, she reminded him, and invited him to come for Christmas dinner. He declined, of course, because he knew that meant there would be a large gathering of relatives. And that would mean his father would know he was in Stoney Ridge. He would know and he would ignore him, and Billy would be right back where he started. Forgotten.

An odd feeling came over Billy as he settled into the greenhouse, and he realized he wasn't alone. He turned around and discovered a little girl, the oldest one, standing about halfway up the brick path. She had padded into the greenhouse as soft as a cat. What was the girl's name again . . . Carrie? Kayla? No . . . Christy! that was it—she stared at him with her mouth plump and her eyes unblinking, watching.

"Hi there."

Christy stared at him with big violet eyes, so like her mother's. She lifted one hand, palm up. Billy strode down the path to see what she had and found a Christmas cookie, a star with cinnamon heart decorations, lying flat in her hand. Two of the arms of the star were crooked, and the cinnamon hearts were jammed into an extraordinary amount of icing that oozed up and over them.

"It's for you," she whispered with a lisp. "I made it all by myself. It's the Christmas star. It was in the sky over baby Jesus."

"For me?" His chest tightened and a lump formed in his throat. He wasn't accustomed to children and their gentle ways. "You made it for me?"

Christy nodded and handed it to him. "It's a Christmas present for you. Bess said you'll be all alone. So's it's to wish you a Merry Christmas."

Billy held the star in his hands, then something quite unexpected happened. Christy lifted her arms for a hug. He leaned down and she clasped her plump little hands around his neck without restraint. It was so unexpected, so sincere. Then, just as quickly, it was over. Christy wiggled away and skipped down the brick path.

"Hey! Where are you going?"

She whirled around. "Mama's making me take a nap." She made a distasteful face. And then she slipped out the door.

Billy went back to the workbench and sat on the stool, staring at the cookie star in his hand. It was an odd feeling for a man to whom gift-giving was strange. He'd never had a child give him a gift before, had never guessed how it got to your insides and warmed you through and through. He felt wanted. Cared about. He thought he might never eat this little cookie.

He set the cookie on the workbench and started to refocus his mind on some parentage charts of German rootstocks that he'd brought with him. The door to the greenhouse squeaked open and a man's heavy footsteps echoed down the brick path. He could tell the footsteps didn't belong to Jonah and hoped they weren't Caleb Zook's. Slowly, he turned his head, curious about who had come to see him.

George the hobo.

"Look. Look what I brought!" He held up Billy's backpack.

Billy took the backpack, amazed, and unzipped it. Inside was the book and files he'd just been wishing he'd brought with him. "Thank you, man. You saved the day!" He stacked the books on the workbench and opened one, started skimming through it, then realized he was neglecting George. "I really appreciate it." He reached into the pocket of his backpack. "I forgot to pay you for the work you've been doing for me." He handed George a bundle of twenty-dollar bills.

George shook his head. "It's too much."

"No, I calculated it all out. You've been a big help to me up in College Station these last two weeks, and then there's bus fare you've had to shell out to get to Stoney Ridge. Twice now." He pulled a book out of the backpack and set it on the table. "There's a little extra for you. A Christmas bonus."

George smiled and put the bundle of twenties in his coat pocket. "Well, thank you."

"I'm the one who's thankful. You've been a big help, filling in for me while I've been in Stoney Ridge. My supervisor has hardly even realized I've been away." He didn't want to say more, but since he was *this* close to identifying the rose, he wouldn't need George's help any longer. The realization made him a little sad, despite knowing that George didn't want or expect to be tied down. He liked this hobo.

George was poking around the greenhouse and stopped to examine a blooming white rose. "Christmas Snow? Rambler, right? Timely blooms for this special holiday, wouldn't you say?"

Billy nodded. "You sure do know your flowers."

"Well, I told you my father's a dedicated gardener."

"So you did. Just where does your father live?"

"He's all over the place. Everywhere."

"So that's where you get your drifting nature."

George stilled, then burst into laughter. "I'm not quite like him in that regard."

Billy was only half listening, rifling through the index of a book, completely absorbed. The greenhouse door squeaked open again and he looked up, grimacing, because he realized he'd forgotten all about George again and that he might have just left. His pen paused above the book of lost roses he was studying, and the corners of his mouth drooped.

Amos Lapp.

Billy straightened and, for a brief moment, he assessed his friend. Amos was a farmer through and through, always had been, and his grown body was strong and fit. He walked up the brick path and stopped a few feet from the workbench, his feet planted wide in a new way to which Billy was not accustomed. It seemed suddenly intimidating, this farmer's stance, so solid, so self-confident.

Billy extended his hand, and for a moment thought Amos would refuse him. But at last Amos's hand clasped Billy's and their touch couldn't help but bring back memories of years of friendship. There was an ache to restore that friendship, as well as the realization that it would never again be what it once was. Not with Bess between them.

"Hello, Billy."

"Amos."

They dropped their hands. George coughed politely and Billy turned to him. "Amos, this is George. He's doing some work for me."

Amos looked at George curiously. "Have we met?"

"Hmmm, have we?"

"Yes. I'm sure of it. I can't quite place it, but I've seen you somewhere."

"Well, they say that context is 90 percent of recognition." George clapped his hands together. "I've got some things to take care of this afternoon. Better keep moving." He lifted a hand in a wave and walked around Amos, down the brick path of the greenhouse, and out the door.

Amos watched him go. "I know I've met him."

"He's been in and out of Stoney Ridge this last week. Maybe you've seen him around town. He's a drifter, a hobo. He's been doing some work for me."

Amos's gaze drifted to the top of the workbench. "So that's the rose Bess told me about?"

An enormous void fell, a void four years wide. It used to be so easy to talk to each other. "Yes."

"Doesn't seem like much."

"Not yet. Wait until it blooms. It might be an extinct rose." He pointed to the open book of botanical drawings on the workbench. "If so, it's an important discovery."

As Amos leafed through a few pages, Billy watched his hands, remembering them, thinking of the hundreds of times they'd threaded bait for each other at Blue Lake Pond, or sledded down Dead Man's Hill on a winter day. Amos had hard, calloused hands, tanned to leather by the sun, hands of a farmer who'd worked the land.

And those hands had caressed Bess.

A conflict between old loyalty and new rivalry created a turmoil of emotion within Billy.

"That's why you're hanging around Rose Hill Farm?"

Billy replied without looking up. "That's why I stop in every few days." He leaned a hip against the workbench. The unsaid hovered between them. "But that's not really what you're asking, are you? You want to know if I'm going to stick around."

Amos lifted his head, a challenge in his eyes. "I'm not giving her up, Billy."

They confronted each other silently for a moment. "I don't blame you. You may not believe me, but I'm not trying to come between you."

"And yet you are."

"Amos, as soon as this rose blooms and I can identify it, I'll be gone."

Amos dropped his eyes. "That's not what I want, either."

"So what is it you want?"

"I want you to stay with our people. I truly do. But I want Bess to choose me."

"Well, I can't do anything about Bess, but I can tell you that I'm not staying. I have no reason to."

"Aren't you going to see your father?"

"No."

"Billy, he's not well. He hasn't been at church in months. And your brothers took off long ago."

"They . . . what?" Billy's gaze snapped to Amos. "Where did they go?"

"Sam left first. I think I heard something about Montana. Ben and Mose got into trouble with the law over poaching without a hunting license. I'm not sure where they are now, but my guess is they're staying out of the county. Far away from the game commissioner."

"They left my father all alone?"

"Well, the church tries to look after your father. As much as he'll let anybody. He's . . ."

"Stubborn as a mule."

Amos nodded. "My dad used to say your father was as crotchety as a mule eating bumblebees."

They were second cousins, their dads, but never close. No one was close to Billy's father. "How sick is he?"

"Not sure. Like I said, I haven't seen him in a few months. Maggie knows more. She's up in the farmhouse now, visiting with Bess." He walked toward Billy and put out his hand. "I hope you'll consider coming back. But I meant what I said about Bess. I'm not giving her up."

Billy shook his hand. "You'd be a fool to give her up, and I know you're not a fool."

Amos opened the greenhouse door. Half out, he turned back, a startled look on his face. "Now I remember where I saw that George fellow. It was Christmas Eve, four years ago, when you—" His eyes went to Billy's wrist. "George stopped me on the road and said I should go visit my cousin, Billy Lapp, for Christmas. That everybody needed to be reminded of Christ's coming. That it was meant for each person." He shook his head. "It was a strange encounter . . . but not in a bad way. He even told me where you lived. That's why I showed up at your boardinghouse when I did on Christmas Day. Odd." He tilted his head. "Really odd. Never saw that man before that day. Never saw him after. Until now."

As the door closed behind Amos, Billy's heart started to pound and he had to sit down.

So. George wasn't a drifter.

Sixteen

Bess waved goodbye to Amos as his buggy drove down the long driveway of Rose Hill Farm. He had stopped by the kitchen to sample Christmas cookies after speaking to Billy in the greenhouse and she would have liked to be a fly on the wall for *that* conversation. No, she didn't. She didn't want to know what Amos might have said, or how Billy might have answered.

Yes, she did.

No, she didn't.

Conscience-torn, she watched Amos's buggy turn onto the road, wishing her thoughts were as easy to steer down the straight and narrow path. He asked her again if she was ready to set a wedding date and she told him she still needed a little more time. The disappointment on his face pierced her heart.

Maggie came outside to stand beside her and slipped a shawl around her shoulders.

"Maggie, are people starting to talk about me? Do they think I'm crazy? Everyone must wonder if I was truly sick at the wedding. Otherwise, we'd have set a new date by now."

"Everyone wants only the best for you," she said loyally, which was good of her. "Including Amos. When you're ready to set the date, then you'll set it. He'll wait patiently. Amos is nothing if not patient."

Bess gave a slight nod. "Let's go inside and get warm. Lainey made cinnamon rolls that beat Dottie Stroot's."

Maggie grinned and the two went up to the house, arm in arm. On the way, Maggie told her about what a fine ice skater Amos was and she was sorry again that Bess didn't join them, because she would have been so impressed. "Amos can skate like he was born on ice. Did you know that? He can zig and zag and do figure eights and I don't think he ever fell down. Not once."

She's falling in love, Bess thought, watching Maggie's eyes flash and her hands dance in the air as she went on and on about Amos's ability to skate backward. *I think she's falling in love with Amos Lapp.*

Oh my, oh my. This, Bess thought, *this is a conundrum.*

Not much later, Jonah came in from the barn, stomping the snow off his boots by the threshold. He removed his black felt hat and hung it on a wall peg beside the door in a smooth, accustomed movement.

Bess filled up a mug with steaming hot coffee and handed it to her dad as he sat in his chair at the kitchen table. Christy scrambled up on her father's lap while Lainey cut a generous cinnamon roll out of the pan and set it on a plate.

"Has Billy left?" Maggie said. "I needed to talk to him for a minute. His dad's not doing well."

"He's still in the greenhouse," Jonah said. He took a bite of the roll. "It's hard to believe the problem between Billy and his father all stems back to that missing collectible."

"There'd been problems brewing for a long time," Bess said. "That collectible was what tipped everything over."

Lainey picked up Lizzie from her high chair and held her on her hip. "I agree with Bess. It wasn't just the missing collectible. It's never just one thing."

"What collectible are you talking about?" Maggie asked.

Jonah cut the cinnamon roll with his fork. "A truck had a flat tire near the Lapp farm. The Lapp brothers helped the truck driver change the tire to a spare. In the truck was a load of antiques and collectibles, about to go to auction in New York. Apparently, one box went missing while the tire was being changed. It was found in Billy's buggy—the box—but something valuable in the box was gone. Never has shown up." Jonah took another bite of cinnamon roll, thoughtfully chewing. "It still rankles me that it seemed to have disappeared at Rose Hill Farm. You'd think it would turn up, sooner or later."

"Unless Billy's brothers were the ones who took it and sold it," Bess said. "And they've vanished."

Maggie looked like a bazooka had just been fired three inches from her ear. "Um, do you happen to remember what that valuable collectible was?" Her voice was weirdly quiet.

Jonah squinted his eyes. "What was it? Bess, do you remember?"

"I never actually saw it, but one of the brothers said it was an old cast-iron bank."

Maggie's face suddenly blanched, and for a moment she was too stunned to speak. Bug-eyed, breathless, she stammered, "An iron Santa Claus? Like, a piggy bank?"

In the middle of a sip of coffee, Bess's hand froze. "Why?"

"Oh, boy. Oh, boy." Maggie dropped to a chair at the

kitchen table and covered her face with her hands, muttering, "Oh double dinged donged d—oh! I'm sorry, Lainey. I'm working on my cussing."

Bess pressed a hand to her hammering heart. "Maggie, just what do you know about that bank?"

Maggie jumped to her feet and paced the room. She stopped and waved her hands. "The thing is . . . I didn't know it was worth anything. It looked like a piece of junk. Wrapped up in old newspapers. I figured Billy was tossing stuff out."

"Slow down, take a breath," Jonah said. "What are you talking about?"

Maggie was nearly hyperventilating. "It goes back to that last summer before Bertha passed. One of her special roses needed iron and she didn't want to spend the money on buying iron supplement, so she gave me the job of finding an old cast-iron tool or frying pan or something that had iron in it. The rustier the better, she said. So I looked and looked and brought her back one thing after the other—but she complained about anything I found—too big or too small. I mean . . . you knew what Bertha was like. Fussy as could be about her roses."

Jonah whirled his finger to hustle the story along.

"And then, suddenly, Bertha passes to her glory, right there in her rose field. I completely forgot to keep looking for an iron tool. I forgot about the ailing rose. I forgot for nearly a year! Until I stopped by to see Bess one day and noticed Billy's brand-new buggy. No one was around, so I climbed in and looked it over. You know how good a new buggy smells. Then I saw the big box and got a little curious and it was easy to open—"

Jonah gave her a look.

"It was, Jonah! The masking tape was all undone. Why doesn't anyone believe me? I always tell the truth. It *was* easy to open and inside was a bunch of junk. I figured Billy had cleaned out a closet or was selling scrap metal or something like that—I mean, you know what a dump the Lapp farm is. Then I noticed the Santa Claus bank and remembered Bertha's rose. That bank was just the right size and shape to fit in the pot. It was something I could do for her—the last thing." She bit her lip. "So . . . I pulled up the rose and stuck the bank in the bottom of the pot and jammed the rose back in and put it in the back of the greenhouse and by the time I came outside . . . there was that big broohaha going on between Billy and his father and brothers . . . and I just forgot all about it." She clasped a fist against her mouth. "I really thought it was a worthless piece of junk."

"A pot in the greenhouse?"

"Yes. One of Bertha's. That rose plant she babied so much."

The kitchen went silent; all that could be heard was the drip, drip, drip of the sink faucet. Three, two, one . . . Bess and Jonah rocketed out of their chairs and raced to the greenhouse, Maggie trailing behind, offering up excuses, which they ignored.

As they burst into the greenhouse, they startled Billy and crowded him around the workbench. All talking at once, they filled him in on the story. He was shocked at first, then everything slid into focus for him. He put his hands around the base of the rose pot, gently and purposefully, and turned it on its side. He ran a pocketknife around the edges, then carefully, oh-so-carefully, he tugged on the stem of the rose until it finally started to loosen and shift out of the clay pot. There, tucked inside a thick swarm of impacted roots, was the cast-iron Santa Claus bank collectible. For nearly a full minute they all stood utterly still, staring at the root ball of the rose, until Billy said, "So *that's* why the pot was so heavy."

Maggie swallowed. "Jonah, how much did you say that Santa Claus bank is worth?"

"Thousands and thousands of dollars, Maggie."

"Oh, double dinged donged d—." She stopped herself. She pointed to the rose and her face brightened. "But look at how healthy it is now. That's all because of me."

Billy looked at her as if she'd suggested the moon was falling. "Why in the world did you tuck it away in the corner to be forgotten?"

Maggie shrugged. "Bertha said you told her the iron needed time to work its wonders. She told me it needed plenty of time."

Gently, Jonah inspected the root ball of the rose. "Should we try to extract the Santa Claus bank?"

"No," Billy said. "Not necessary. It's been paid for, courtesy of my new buggy."

Bess winced at that comment, but when she glanced at Billy, instead of the tight expression that he wore so consistently, his face seemed relaxed, released. Free.

"I don't want to change anything with this rose," he said. "Whatever's keeping it alive and making it thrive is working."

In the quiet, Bess said, "Billy, you need to tell your father about the collectible."

Maggie's face, alit with joy only seconds ago, suddenly lost its smile. "Oh no!" Her hands flew to cover her mouth. "I completely forgot! That's why I came over here in the first place. Billy—this morning I was listening to my father and Jorie—"

"Eavesdropping, you mean."

She ignored him. "You need to get over to see your father. Today. Right now."

"You mean go over there?" The animation left his face and his voice quieted. "I don't think I can do that."

Maggie exchanged a look with Bess. "Billy—I'm sorry to be the one to tell you, but you need to know. Your father is dying."

As Billy stood in front of the dilapidated Lapp farm, his heart ticked faster. The shadows lent a velvet richness to the dusky clearing, disguising its rusted junk and dung and weeds. Even still, he couldn't forget how sorry it had looked by daylight. And what a wreck the house was.

Maggie had filled him in on when and why his brothers had left home, one by one, over the last few years. Sam got a girl in the family way and didn't want to marry her, so he fled to Montana. Ben and Mose were laying low in another county. His father had been alone for over a year. Maggie said she thought he had some kind of cancer and refused to see a doctor about it, despite Caleb Zook's persistence. He didn't want anybody's help, he told Caleb, and he meant it.

If Billy took a guess, his father had lung cancer. He smoked like a chimney all his life and had been warned to cut down, if not give it up entirely. His father would only scoff at the warning and dismiss it as government propaganda. He grew tobacco, you see.

Billy eyed the yard, imagining it clean. He eyed the chick-

---

ens, imagining them penned. He eyed the woodpile, imagining it chopped, ranked, and filed. He turned in a half circle and gazed out at the fields, imagining the soil to be dark brown, resplendent with minerals.

He walked up to the house, knocked on the door, waited, knocked again. His pulse was a drum in his ears, and his nose was running from the cold. He felt terrified but strong, as if he were swimming for his life.

The door swung open and Caleb Zook stood there. His eyes opened wide in surprise. So Maggie had finally learned to keep a secret. Good for her.

"Billy. Billy Lapp. How did you know? How did you hear about . . . ? Never mind, it's good you've come." He opened the door wide to let Billy in.

The sour odor of sickness in the house nearly undid him.

"Your father's in the other room. He's not . . . well."

"I know."

"He's dying, Billy."

"Dying," Billy repeated inanely. He had never expected this. Not now. Not yet. He thought he had plenty of time before he would face this day. Plenty of time to repair the damage. He thought of Bess's comment about Simon—thinking she had time to tell him he meant something to her. And she didn't.

"He doesn't want anyone here, but I was planning to stay until . . ."

Billy looked around the dismal room. "Caleb—I'll stay. You go home and be with your family. Tomorrow is Christmas Eve."

Caleb took a long time answering. "It won't be long, I suspect."

Billy nodded. "I want to spend whatever time I can with him. Alone."

Caleb spun his hat in his hands, hesitating, until Billy reassured him this was what he wanted to do.

At the door, Caleb grabbed Billy's hand in both of his. "It's good you've come home, Billy." He walked down a few steps, then turned. "I'll stop by in the morning. You can call if you need anything. I left the number on the kitchen counter. I'll check the phone shanty every few hours."

Billy closed the kitchen door and took a deep breath. It was curious how calm he felt at this moment, despite four years of anticipating and dreading it.

He found his father lying on the La-Z-Boy recliner in the living room and was shocked by the changes in his appearance. Painfully thin, a gray pallor to his skin, less of his thinning swoop of gray hair on his head than ever. His eyes were closed and for a second, Billy thought he might have already passed.

"What do you want?" His father's voice sounded flat, wary, deeper and gruffer than usual.

"It's me." He moved no closer, but stayed where he was at the edge of the kitchen door. "It's me, Dad. It's Billy."

His father's eyes flew open and Billy was shocked to see the whites of his eyes were yellow-tinged.

His father squinted for a closer look. "Take off your hat so's I can see you."

Once the hat was off, Billy stood fidgeting, letting his father get a look at his face. "So, boy. Where you been?"

He curled a hand around his hat brim. "Here and there." He lifted his chin defiantly. "Working with roses."

His father gave up a short snort. "Figured."

Billy moved closer to the recliner and studied his father's form. "I heard that Sam and Ben and Mose are gone."

A spasm of coughing gripped his father and Billy felt a spike of concern. The room was so cold, the air so dank. He moved to add some chunks of kindling to the fire Caleb had started in the wood-burning stove, and filled up a teakettle with water to set on top of it.

He sensed his father's eyes following him as he moved about the dimly lit room. He washed a mug and found a tea bag in the cupboard, then brought a cup of soothing chamomile tea to his father. When he reached for it, he shifted into a sitting position and Billy put some pillows behind his back to support him.

"Sit down. You're making me dizzy."

Billy scraped a chair up to sit next to his father and stared into his familiar eyes. The lines on his face had deepened. He looked old, tired, and beaten, and an unexpected urge to protect him rose within Billy. "Maggie Zook tells me you're dying."

His father waved his palm. "You know how Maggie tells tales. I'm just a little under the weather." But they both knew that wasn't true.

Billy looked up and met his father's eyes squarely. "We have some things to settle between us."

As Billy's father studied his face, he saw a weariness in his eyes that went bone deep. "Yeah, I know."

The room grew still. Outside, a soft snow had begun, but inside the fire glowed gold and pink. In the firelit room all was silent, waiting for the words that hovered between them to be spoken. "Dad, I never stole that cast-iron bank."

For a moment, his father's eyes were tormented. "I know.

Your brothers did." His voice fell to a murmur. "I suspected it all along."

"You knew? You never thought to come find me? To tell me that?"

"I was . . ." He gulped to a stop and Billy saw his body tremble. His father's eyes pinched tightly closed. "I was angry about the Bann. Too stubborn."

Billy sighed and slumped his shoulders in relief. "Must be a family trait. I was too angry and stubborn to come home. Until now."

His father silenced him with a movement of his hand. "I thought you were getting high and mighty. Thought you needed to be taken down a peg."

"You were right. I was. And I did." It was Billy who needed to take the first step, his heart thumping hard. "Can you forgive me?"

"You? I'm the one . . ." His voice grew even more raspy as he went on. "I'm the one who needs . . ."

Self-consciousness suddenly bloomed between them, for the words needed not be said to be felt. His father held out his hand, and Billy took it. His grip was claw-like. Surprising strength for a weary man. "You're home now," his father said, his voice gravelly with emotion. "That's what matters."

Hearing his father's words brought a great, crushing feeling of relief to Billy. His father's eyes drifted shut and he slept, his chest lifting painfully, a hissing sound whistling between each breath that escaped his dry lips.

The death rattle had set in, Maggie had said. Pneumonia.

Billy sat on a chair, slumped over, watching his father's labored breathing. He felt a quiet, a deep calm that he didn't want to leave or disturb. He stayed very still, and his mind and heart grew still as well.

Suddenly, he realized he wasn't alone.

George had come and was leaning against the doorjamb of the kitchen, arms crossed, one ankle looped over the other.

Billy leapt to his feet. "Oh wow." His heart went wild. The room seemed to spin around crazily while he stared at George, struggling to comprehend the incredible. At last he stammered again in a choked voice, "Wow. Wow. Wow. You're not a hobo, are you?"

George smiled. "I never said I was. You called me that."

Now Billy understood why George's presence always brought him a measure of ease. His tranquility somehow seeped into him and calmed him. "You're a death angel, aren't you? An avenging angel."

George's eyebrows lifted in amusement. "What's that?"

"You kill people. Like in the Old Testament, during Passover." Billy made a sweeping paintbrush movement, like he was marking a house. "Don't tell me you weren't there."

"Actually, I wasn't there. Not me. There's rather a lot of us." He crossed the room to warm his hands by the wood-burning stove. "Lots of misconceptions about angels out there. But I do get a kick out of some of them. Hollywood. Crazy stuff." He rolled his eyes. "My biggest pet peeve is when Hollywood makes it seem like angels wish they could be on Earth, like they're missing something. We come from a place that is without sin. Hard for you folks to understand, but there's a whiter white than what your eyes can see. Bluer blues. Greener greens. Once you get a taste of Heaven, you never long for Earth. 'For a day in thy courts is better than a thousand.' I believe that's in Psalms." He sat down in a chair across from Billy, pulled an apple and pocketknife out of his jacket, and sliced the apple. He stabbed it with the tip of the knife and picked it up. "You want it?"

Billy shook his head and eased back in his seat. *Man, this angel eats constantly.*

"I'm always hungry when I'm down here. Never feel satisfied."

"It kind of freaks me out when you read my mind."

George chuckled. "Another misconception. Angels aren't omniscient. Not even the Dark One." He ducked his chin and peered at Billy as if to say, *And we all know who that is.* "We don't need to be mind readers. You people give yourselves away. Just to straighten things out, only the Father is omniscient." He chewed a slice of apple. "I'll grant you one thing—we angels do seem to scare people a lot."

Billy was lost. "Wait a minute. If you're a death angel, you're here for my father, right?" His eyes went wide. "Or are you here for me? That's what you meant by a lot at stake, isn't it? Am I the one who's dying?" His heart started pounding again.

"Interesting question. Everyone and everything is in a state of decline. You know it as the Second Law of Thermodynamics. We call it the fallen world. As for the moment of *your* death—no, that's not happening right now. There will be a day when your time on earth comes to its end. But that won't be a minute before your life is complete." He went into the kitchen to find a mug, helped himself to a tea bag, then poured the mug full of hot water from the teapot on top of the wood-burning stove.

George sat back down again and stretched out his legs, steeping the tea bag in the mug with a steady beat, up and down, up and down. "Earlier today, a fellow had a heart attack and the ambulance was driving him to the hospital. His heart had stopped. But then the ambulance hit a pothole and jump-started his heart. He's good as new." He made a seesawing motion with his hand. "Sort of. He was a little shaken up. But he's back on track now." He took a sip of the tea. "Nothing like a little jolt of mortality to get a man interested in knowing his Maker."

"George . . . did you put that pothole in the street?" Billy held out his wrist. "Did you send Amos to find me that Christmas afternoon?"

George grinned, revealing a row of even white teeth. "Tell you what. We'll have a lot of time in the future to talk about curious coincidences. For now, let's talk about why I'm here."

"Why are you here?"

"What do you think?"

Exasperated, Billy's hands flew up in the air. This angel couldn't give a straight answer. "If I could figure that out, why would I think you're here to kill me?"

"That's another pet peeve—that people think angels are sent to kill. Only God determines when a person's life on earth is complete."

"I never thought I'd hear an angel say he had a pet peeve." Though Billy never thought he'd be having a conversation with an angel, either.

"Well, sure." George sliced off another piece of apple and chewed it. "We do have personalities. Michael, for example, he's always in a hurry. Eager to carry out his business and get home again. Me, I like to take my time. Get to know my business."

Billy coughed a laugh. "So . . . I'm your business?"

George smiled. "Since August 3, 1962."

"What happened then?"

"You don't remember?" George chuckled. "You were seven and saw a rainbow. You looked up at the sky and said, 'Thank you, God.' *That* was your moment."

"My moment for what?"

"Of first knowing God. Thanking him. Giving praise. That was when your spiritual journey truly began. That was when you were pointed out to me. 'Keep an eye on that one,' Mario told me." He squinted and looked at the ceiling. "I think it was Mario. Might have been Monroe."

When had Billy last looked at a rainbow and thanked God for it? He felt so far from God right now. And now, when he needed God the most, he had no right to ask for help. "Let me get this straight. If you're not a death angel, then you're a guardian angel?"

George smiled. "One of many. 'For he shall give his angels charge over thee, to keep thee in all thy ways.' Another Psalm. You folks down here . . . you need a lot of help." He leaned back in the chair. "I'm not saying it's easy. There's a lot of troublemakers around here. You'd be amazed. They're all over, just looking for ways to drag a soul down." He glanced at Billy's sleeping father.

"It doesn't seem to take much."

George laughed. "No. No, it doesn't. Takes a lot to keep your eyes on the prize." He lifted his eyes upward. "Oh, but what a prize awaits, Billy. Have no fear. 'But as it is written, Eye hath not seen, nor ear heard, neither have entered into the heart of man, the things which God hath prepared for them that love him.'" He dropped his head. "Paul penned that in a letter to the Corinthians, I believe."

"Then, the Bible is relevant to you, in Heaven? I would think it would be kind of . . . old news."

"'For ever, O Lord, thy word is settled in heaven.' Another Psalm. I love those Psalms." George was watching him, with eyes as exacting as calipers. "You still don't get it, do you? 'If we believe not, *yet* he abideth faithful: he cannot deny himself.' A letter to Timothy, I believe." He sighed, growing exasperated with Billy's denseness. "Seriously, man! Do you not *ever* read the Good Book?"

Billy chose not to answer. It just hadn't occurred to him to look to the *Bible* for answers.

"It means that God is faithful, even if you are not." George closed his eyes and shook his head, as if to say, *What a wasted opportunity.* "You know, a lot of problems in life would be solved if you people would just read the Word of God. It's all there. Everything you need to know." George reached out to adjust the quilt that lay over Billy's father. "All you need to do is to accept God's help. Just ask, Billy." He leaned back. "You did it before." He glanced down at Billy's wrist.

Billy's turned his wrist over and thought of how differently he would have handled his family had he known how much he mattered to God, if he'd known he hadn't been forgotten, if he'd realized he was being looked after. He had felt so hopeless, so all alone. And yet he had never been alone, not even during that hard time.

For a long time, they sat without speaking, sipping on their tea, honoring the deep quiet. It was past midnight. Billy felt unnaturally alert, aware of the preciousness of each passing hour. Once or twice, his father's eyes flickered open, then closed again.

Then George stirred, as if he was preparing to leave.

"Don't go, George." Billy cleared his throat. "Please don't go." He wanted George with him this long night.

George smiled. "I won't go until you're ready for me to go."

His father's head bobbed slightly, then fell back down. His chest seemed to strain for each bit of air.

Billy closed his eyes—*Lord, don't let George leave, not yet*—and knew that the gift of faith was being offered to him. From somewhere inside him a yes rose up, and an unfamiliar peace replaced the restlessness in his soul.

When he opened his eyes, George was gone. On the chair, neatly folded, was the blue winter coat Billy had given to him on the day he had first met him, and the handful of twenties he had paid him for working in the greenhouse.

SEVENTEEN

Amos and Maggie had spent the morning wandering in and out of shops in Stoney Ridge, looking for a gift for Bess for Christmas.

"I don't know why the thimble with roses won't do," Maggie said. "It's beautiful. It's stunning. It's exquisite."

"It just doesn't seem quite right."

Maggie stopped in front of a bench and flopped down. Amos sat down beside her, looking up the street to see what other options there might be: the fabric store, the Hay & Grain, the Acme grocery store.

"Doesn't it tell you something, Amos, that you don't even know what to get Bess?"

Amos's lips compressed and a muscle ticked in his jaw, but he stared squarely at Maggie. "What are you getting at?"

Softly, Maggie said, "Amos, it might be that you have an idea of who Bess is, who you *want* her to be, without really knowing her."

"No," Amos said, peeved. Maggie thought she knew everything. "You're wrong about that. I know her. I've known her for years. I know her very well. Very, very well."

Maggie sighed. "I've tried to be kind, but I can't hold back any longer. Amos, Bess just doesn't feel the same way about you that you feel about her."

He snapped a glance at her, then turned away again.

She seemed to be waiting for something. "You've got a strange way of not saying things, Amos. How's a friend supposed to help when you keep closed up so?"

He heard something confrontational in Maggie's voice. He didn't want to fight. He didn't want to feel. He didn't want to think. He didn't want to know. "Bess made a promise to me," he said in a raspy voice. "We made a promise to each other."

"She can't help her feelings for Billy any more than you can help your feelings for her."

Amos stared at her, not moving a muscle.

Maggie pushed her glasses up the bridge of her nose. "Sometimes you can't stop yourself from loving someone." She lifted troubled eyes to him, then looked away. "As much as you try, you just can't help yourself."

A poignant silence fell.

"After Christmas, she said we could set a date. She hasn't told me she wants to call off our wedding. Just postpone it."

"You have to be the one to let her go, Amos. She won't break things off with you, but not setting a date is her way of telling you. That's just the way Bess is." She took his hands and squeezed them, in a grip that surprised him. "I'm not saying this to hurt you. I wouldn't be a good friend to you if I didn't tell you the truth and I always tell the truth. Marriage is hard enough without being married to someone who would rather be with someone else."

Hearing in her voice what he already knew brought a great, crushing feeling to Amos's heart. For a moment they both concentrated on their joined hands. "Thank you, Maggie," came his gruff words. "And I want to be just as good a friend to you." He leaned toward her. "Stop lying to your father and take that teaching job."

Her eyes went wide and her mouth opened to a silent O.

During the night, snow had started to fall. Bess woke early, wide awake, and decided to do the barn chores for her father. A Christmas Eve gift for him. She fed Frieda and the chickens in the henhouse, then went into the greenhouse to check on the mystery rose, half hoping it would be open, half dreading it would be open. When it did, Billy would identify the rose and then he would leave.

Two minutes later, she left a message on the answering machine at the shanty of Billy's father's farm. "The rose has bloomed!" And then she waited for him.

All during the morning hours, snow continued to fall. The snow lay on the land nearly six inches deep, with little sign of abating, though it was a gentle storm: no wind, fat downy snowflakes. After lunch, Bess waited for Billy in the greenhouse, wondering if she should go over to his farm. But then again, if his father was passing, it would seem terribly awkward to walk in and happily tell him that a flower had bloomed. She heard the door click open and eagerly spun around to face the door, smiling brightly. "It's here! It's bloomed!"

There stood Amos. Her eyes widened in surprise. He couldn't have missed the droop of disappointment on her face as she realized he wasn't whom she expected.

"Mind if I come in? It's cold out here."

"Oh, of course!"

Halfway down the brick path, he stopped. "Has there been a death message yet about Billy's father?"

"Nothing yet."

"I haven't given your Christmas present to you yet, Bess," he said, his voice soft. "Maggie helped me pick it out." He fished in his coat pocket and pulled something out, then strode closer to her and opened his hand. On his palm lay a small silver thimble with a band of pink roses painted around the base.

She picked it up. "It's beautiful."

"It is that. But . . . it isn't the gift you really need from me." He swallowed. "Christmas being a time of giving, I thought it might be appropriate to . . . give you what I know you want most from me, Bess. Your freedom." He sounded not bitter, but resigned.

Bess was speechless. "Amos—"

He lifted a palm to cut her short. "Don't say a word. Maggie was the one who set me straight. Why would anyone want to be married to someone who would rather be married to someone else? Marriage is hard enough, she said." He gave a half laugh. "Not that she would know. But I do think she's right." He took her hands in his. "I'll always hold a soft spot for you in my heart, but I know I need to release you from your promise." He lifted her hands to his mouth and kissed them, but didn't release them. "Would you tell me one thing? Did you ever love me at all? Even a little?"

His dark brown eyes, filled with unspoken misery, locked with hers. The tears splashed over her lashes and ran in silver streaks down her cheeks. "Oh yes, Amos. I did. I do. I just . . ."

"You just love him more." His eyes were soft with understanding. He squeezed her hands one more time and released them.

There were no more words. Bess felt a lump gathering in her throat. She swallowed, but the emotion couldn't be gulped away.

Amos glanced at the door. "Well . . ." The word hung in the cold air like the ting of a bell in a winter woods.

"Yes, well . . ." She spread her palms nervously, then clutched them together.

"I'm not exactly sure what one says at a time like this."

"Neither am I," Bess admitted.

Amos looked down into her eyes. "I've always wanted only your happiness."

It struck Bess that Amos was one of the kindest persons she'd ever known. He was a gentleman all the way through, was Amos. She took his hand and placed the thimble in its palm, then curled his fingers over it. "It's actually a little small on my finger. But I think it might fit Maggie's perfectly."

He fell silent for several long, long seconds. "I'd better go. The Zooks invited my mother and me for Christmas Eve supper." His eyes found hers at last, and for a moment she thought he meant to kiss her. But in the end he only nodded formally and reached out for the door handle. "See you around, Bess."

When the door closed behind him, Bess sighed and sank back against it, closing her eyes, savoring the sweetness of the moment between them. In an instant, the door that led to a life with Amos had closed, and though she had never been entirely convinced that she wanted to pass through it, she felt a final spark of doubt. Had she been mistaken in not marrying Amos? But she knew the answer.

She kept an eye on the driveway all afternoon, waiting for Billy, but he never came. By day's end, she went back down to the greenhouse one last time to put the rose back in its corner for the night. The air was knife-cold; the hazy winter sun hung low in the sky. The strong, sweet fragrance of the blooming rose filled the greenhouse. For a long moment, she stood in front of the rose, thinking how delighted her grandmother would be to know this rose had survived another generation. She heard a squeaky noise, spun around. And there he was.

"He's passed," Billy said, standing in the open doorway. "My father died a little while ago. I waited until Caleb Zook came over. He's there now, calling the undertaker."

"I'm so sorry."

He closed the door behind him and walked down the brick path toward Bess, stopping a few feet in front of her. "We made our peace, he and I." His voice had a quiet sincerity she hadn't heard in years. "All night long, he slipped in and out of consciousness. But when he was alert, we talked. We actually talked a lot. He told me . . ." His voice cracked and his eyes grew glassy. "My father told me he was proud of me." With the back of his hand, he wiped away tears. "It's strange. My father is dead and I don't feel the way I thought I always would on this day—sad and empty. I feel . . . grateful. I was with him when he died and it was . . ." Billy swallowed, trying to keep his emotions tamped down. "It was something I'll never forget, as long as I live. He let go of his bitterness and disappointment and his face grew so . . . peaceful. It's hard to describe, but I don't think I'll ever be afraid of dying after today." He put his hands in his pockets. "Someone told me there's a verse in the Bible that says 'Precious in the sight of the Lord is the death of his saints.' I never thought of my father as a saint, but I suppose from God's point of view, he was. We all are. And death, strangely enough, is a precious thing."

Bess didn't know what to say so she didn't say anything. The deaths she had experienced—her grandmother's, Simon's—they didn't feel precious to her. They felt awful.

He took off his hat and spun it around in a circle. "He told me to find my brothers and bring them back to the fold."

"Ohhhhhhhh." Bess drew out the word for emphasis. That was a huge and complicated deathbed request.

"He also told me I was a fool to let you go."

Bess swallowed. "He was right."

Billy crossed the distance between them in four long strides. Then his hands were on her shoulders and his eyes became suddenly fierce and she felt her pulse leap. "Are you going to marry Amos?"

She shook her head. "No . . . no, I'm not. We spoke about it this very afternoon. We called off the engagement."

His eyes searched hers. "Was Amos all right about that?"

"More than all right. He was the one who told me the wedding was off. I think he knew . . ."

"Knew what?"

Bess took in a sharp breath. "I think he knew that as hard as I tried, I couldn't stop loving you."

Suddenly he scooped her into his arms, kissing her with passion, stirring to life every feeling she had and a few she never knew existed. Too soon, he lifted his head, holding her face in his hands, searching her eyes with a harrowed look. "I love you," he said hoarsely. He pulled her against him, enfolding her so tightly in his arms it seemed he'd never let her go.

She wanted to laugh and cry at the same time. How was it possible to feel such happiness? They kissed again, less hurried now.

"So you got my message."

He kissed her eyes, her forehead, her cheeks. "What message?"

"The rose! It's bloomed."

Abruptly, Billy released her; in a few short strides, he was in front of the workbench, standing in awe at the open rose bloom. Bess followed behind him, pressing close to him. He examined the rose closely—sniffing it, peering into it, counting its petals and stamens. He looked in an old botanical print book and compared the drawings to the rose in front of him.

"Well? Is it the rose?" Everything inside her was on tiptoes.

"It'll have to be verified . . . but it has all the characteristics of a German rootstock dating prior to the Perle von Weissenstein." He closed his eyes reverently. "Imagine that. The oldest known rose of German rootstock. Right in front of us."

"Think of the stories it could tell. The long trip over the ocean on the *Charming Nancy*. All those rose lovers who kept it alive over three centuries."

His hand found hers and curled around it as they soaked up the rose's revelation. "So George was right. It's a wonderful Christmas."

"Who's George?"

Billy put his arm around Bess's shoulder and pulled her close to him. "It's a long, long story. I'll tell you later. For now, Merry Christmas, Bess."

"And to you, Billy." They stood a moment, arm in arm, admiring the bloom. "What should we call the rose?"

"It will be given an official Latin name that no one can pronounce or ever remember. Part of me would like to call it the Bertha Riehl. It has the same kind of impact on others that Bertha used to have—tricky and stubborn, spikey with thorns, interrupts your life, turns it upside down."

"And thank heaven for that, Billy Lapp," Bess said, in a brash tone that surprised even her. He was right. She was getting more and more like her grandmother.

"Another reason we should call it Bertha Riehl. Just like her—*exactly* like her—this rose has to get the last word in."

"How so?"

Billy grinned. "It leaves a lingering fragrance."

That it did. Its sweet scent had infiltrated the greenhouse. "But she wouldn't want a rose named after her. Too prideful, she would say."

"Then we should call it what she called it. The Charming Nancy. After all, it's our turn to take care of the rose."

The rose. This elusive, mysterious rose. With a practiced eye, Bess gathered every detail about the rose, confident that the same thoughts were being catalogued in Billy's mind: class of Gallicas; a large, dramatic bloom of pink-mauve color, packed with petals; deeply fragrant. What couldn't be described was why it was the most important rose in the world. This rose had brought Billy Lapp home.

She felt his gaze and lifted her eyes to him. *Our* turn, he had said. It was their turn in the long line of rose lovers who had protected and nurtured this rose. To ensure the rose's ongoing survival for *their* children, to pass its tending on to their children's children, was what he meant.

Bess had not known a heart could smile.

CONVERSATION GUIDE

This conversation guide is intended to enrich the reading experience, as well as encourage you to explore topics together—because books, like life, are meant for sharing.

1. "God is faithful even when we are not" is a central theme in *Christmas at Rose Hill Farm*. Which characters needed reminding of that theme? Discuss the ways in which the characters come to peace with this biblical truth.

2. The rosebud seemed to have a personality of its own: stubborn, slow, resilient, enduring. It was more than a legacy. What do you think the mystery rose symbolized in Billy's and Bess's life? Is there a beloved treasure in your life that might have a similar meaning to you?

3. Some parts of an Amish wedding might seem strange to you—the bride and groom's meeting with the ministers before the ceremony, for example. Let's flip the picture. Do you think there might be aspects of a typical American wedding that seem strange to the Amish?

Which ones? Doesn't that awareness give you an appreciation for how our culture shapes and molds us?

4. Let's consider Amos Lapp and the broken engagement. At one point, Maggie Zook questions Amos about why he can't seem to settle on the right Christmas gift for Bess. "It might be that you have an idea of who Bess is, who you want her to be, without really knowing her." Do you think Amos truly loved Bess? Or was Maggie on to something? By the way, if you'd like to find out how Amos Lapp's love life unfolds, you might enjoy reading the Stoney Ridge Seasons series.

5. Billy's home life was less than ideal: brothers who bullied, a father who encouraged competition between his sons. Finally, Billy had enough and left home. George pointed out to him that he had acted like a Pharisee: all rules and no love. "How are you going to be salt to your family when you're hiding away in a greenhouse in College Station? By staying away like you've done, you've only made things worse for your father. He has no one to pull him up. You might be standing on principle, but you're all alone."

   What were your thoughts about George's bold remarks to Billy? Was he asking too much of him? Billy certainly thought so. George was trying to show God's perspective on his role in his family. What difference would that make to someone in a difficult relationship?

6. What were your thoughts about the character of George the hobo? You might find it interesting to know that the story about the ambulance and the pothole is a true one. Granted, there's no way of knowing if an angel was

involved, but it does give one food for thought. Have you ever had a curious coincidence occur that became strangely pivotal in your life?

7. Toward the end of the story, Billy reflects on some of the truths George has taught him. "Billy turned his wrist over and thought of how differently he would have handled things had he known how much he mattered to God, if he'd known he wasn't forgotten, if he'd known he was being looked after. He had felt so hopeless, so all alone. And yet he had never been alone, not even during that hard time." That insight isn't just for Billy. It's a biblical truth meant for me and for you. How does such knowledge affect you?

8. It would be nice, wouldn't it, to have an angel like George appear at critical junctions in our life: times of uncertainty, times of needed healing, times of crisis. George didn't stay, even though Billy wanted him to. Why? Had he stayed, what might have been Billy's temptation? The folded coat on the chair, the money on top—they were signs that George's work with Billy was complete. What final message did George deliver to Billy? To you and to me?

Emmanuel, God is with us.

Scriptures Used by George

(I didn't think angels would have need of the chapters and numbers given to Bible verses so mere mortals could locate Scripture. The Amish actually use the German Luther Bible, but for obvious reasons, I used the King James Version.)

"Search the scriptures; for in them ye think ye have eternal life: and they are they which testify of me." (John 5:39)

"The heavens declare the glory of God; and the firmament sheweth his handywork." (Psalm 19:1)

"Then they cried unto the LORD in their trouble, and he bringeth them out of their distresses." (Psalm 107:13)

"He maketh the storm a calm, so that the waves thereof are still." (Psalm 107:29)

"Then are they glad because they be quiet; so he bringeth them unto their desired haven." (Psalm 107:30)

"For a day in thy courts is better than a thousand." (Psalm 84:10)

"For he shall give his angels charge over thee, to keep thee in all thy ways." (Psalm 91:11)

"But as it is written, Eye hath not seen, nor ear heard, neither have entered into the heart of man, the things which God hath prepared for them that love him." (1 Corinthians 2:9)

"For ever, O LORD, thy word is settled in heaven." (Psalm 118:89)

"If we believe not, yet he abideth faithful: he cannot deny himself." (2 Timothy 2:13)

Note to Reader

Did you know the rose is America's favorite flower? Four states claim it as their state flower (New York, Iowa, Georgia, South Dakota) and, over thirty years ago, June was dubbed National Rose Month. Today, there are over one hundred species of roses in the world, the majority of which are native to Asia.

Traditionally, the rose is known as the flower of love. In Greek and Roman mythology, the rose was used as a symbol of Venus and Aphrodite, the goddesses of love. In Christian iconography, the rose is associated with Christian martyrs. Its five petals are said to represent the five wounds of Christ. It was Shakespeare who penned the famous words, "A rose by any other name would still smell as sweet." Never mind the killjoy who altered the adage: "A rose by any other name would still get black spot."

The history of growing roses goes back a long, long time—over five thousand years. In the eighteenth century, Europeans began experimenting with different varieties of roses and created several hundred new versions. And that's where this story begins . . . with roses from the 1700s that have "gone missing" over the centuries.

Lost roses have a fascinating backstory. It's believed to be highly possible that extinct roses are in people's backyards, brought over from Europe by someone's great-great grandmother. Old roses, prior to the first China tea hybrid in 1867, are durable, cold-hardy, and remarkably sturdy. Old cemeteries remain the best places to find old roses.

So . . . have you gone wandering around an old cemetery lately?

P.S. If you're interested in reading more about Bess and Billy, get hold of a copy of *The Search*, winner of the 2012 Carol Award for Long Contemporary. *The Search* takes place in 1972, a few years prior to this story set in 1977. And if you want to follow up with Amos Lapp (hint: Maggie Zook has a significant role in his future), read the Stoney Ridge Seasons series, starting with *The Keeper, The Haven*, and wrapping up in *The Lesson*. Though, the stories of Stoney Ridge never really end. Life goes on and on . . .

Acknowledgments

It probably never occurs to anyone how much help goes into the making of a book. This story started in the living room of my dear friend Nyna Dolby, who is something of a flora genius. She was the one who gave me the idea of waiting for that stubborn rosebud to open, before it would reveal its identity.

As I wrote about George, I wanted to make his character as biblically accurate as possible while allowing imagination to stretch and fill in the blanks. I treaded carefully around this special messenger and asked quite a few respected students of the Bible about areas that seemed uncertain. For example, do angels read the Bible? Lots of interesting responses to that question. Some believe the Bible won't be relevant in Heaven, others feel strongly that it is. Overall, I believe that the chief purpose of angels who visit Earth is to turn our eyes toward the Almighty. I hope you'll see that purpose throughout George's visits.

As if all this help wasn't enough, other people contributed too. My trusty first draft readers, Lindsey Ciraulo, Wendy

How, and Nyna Dolby, spent hours reading the early version and offering ideas and support, helping to fix details that were too often lost on me.

To Andrea, Barb, Michele, Twila, Cheryl, Robin, Lanette, and all the other excellent people at Revell, many thanks for making this Christmas story possible and getting it into readers' hands. Just in time.

Emmanuel, Christ is with us!

Rose Hill Farm's Baked Oatmeal

Ingredients:

3 cups	rolled oats
1 cup	packed brown sugar
2 teaspoons	baking powder
1 teaspoon	salt
2 teaspoons	ground cinnamon
2 teaspoons	vanilla extract
2	eggs
1 cup	milk
½ cup	butter, melted

Optional add-ins: ¾ cup dried cranberries, dried cherries or raisins, diced apple, sliced almonds, chopped walnuts
Additional milk

Directions

Preheat oven to 350°. In a large bowl, combine oats, brown sugar, baking powder, salt, and cinnamon. In another bowl, whisk eggs, milk, vanilla extract, and butter. Stir into oat mixture until blended. Add optional ingredients like fruit or nuts, and stir.

Spoon into a greased 9" × 13" baking pan. Bake 40–45 minutes or until set. Serve warm with milk. Yield: 9 servings.

Suzanne Woods Fisher is the bestselling author of *The Letters*, *The Calling*, the Lancaster County Secrets series, and the Stoney Ridge Seasons series, as well as nonfiction books about the Amish, including *Amish Peace*. She is also the coauthor of an Amish children's series, *The Adventures of Lily Lapp*. Suzanne is a Carol Award winner for *The Search*, a Carol Award finalist for *The Choice*, and a Christy Award finalist for *The Waiting*. She is also a columnist for *Christian Post* and *Cooking & Such* magazines. She lives in California. Learn more at www.suzannewoodsfisher.com and connect with Suzanne on Twitter @suzannewfisher.

CPSIA information can be obtained
at www.ICGtesting.com
Printed in the USA
LVHW031156230419
615216LV00001B/167